AGENTS AND ADEPTS

ALSO BY KATHRYN SULLIVAN

The Crystal Throne

AGENTS AND ADEPTS

BY

KATHRYN SULLIVAN

To Doug and Helen,
May all the aliens you meet
be friendly

AMBER QUILL PRESS, LLC
http://www.amberquill.com

AGENTS AND ADEPTS
AN AMBER QUILL PRESS BOOK

This book is a work of fiction. All names, characters, locations, and incidents are products of the author's imagination, or have been used fictitiously. Any resemblance to actual persons living or dead, locales, or events is entirely coincidental.

Amber Quill Press, LLC
http://www.amberquill.com

ISBN 1-59279-917-5

Rating: PG-13

Layout and Formatting provided by: ElementalAlchemy.com

PUBLISHED IN THE UNITED STATES OF AMERICA

With thanks to
Mary Jean Holmes, Jean Danielsen,
and Regina Gottesman
for giving me a chance at the beginning of
my writing career and even asking for more stories.
Thanks also to Deb Walsh
for feedback and support and pushing me to
"do something" with the Mead stories.
And a special thanks to Gary Russell
for uttering the fatal words,
"I'd like to commission you to write a short story..."

Thanks also to my sister, Rose Marie Sullivan Shusis
for the wonderful map she created for The Crystal Throne,
and to computer wizard extraordinare *John Stafford*
who helped me modify the map
for pre-curse days.

Thanks to Trace Edward Zaber
for saying "sure" (twice!) to a query about a short story collection
and for inspirational artwork (and a beautiful cover).

Thanks to Karin Story
for her editing and thoughtful comments.

Thank you also to Winona State University
for a sabbatical that gave me time to
work on this collection.

Lytleaf Forest
Village of the Open Door
The Watcher
The Fens
Healic Ranges
Dewin Heights
The Great Woods
Lake
Eage
Wandering River
Glen of Ancient Voices
Mirror of Truth
The Ea
Highlands
N
Gimstan Mt.
Dune's March
Windgard
The Wasted Land
Hills
Rocktooth Pass
Gray
Silent Forest
Mts. of Illusion
The Mist Lands
Shadow Lands
Dreamer
Silver Haired
Mt. Ircis

Table Of Contents

THE DEMONS' STOREROOM

Brambel sighed unhappily at the short wand in his hand. Its moonglow spell never wore off unless he needed it. He rummaged through the chaotic clutter of his shelves. No spare wands. And he had so wanted to gather dragonwort under tonight's full moon!

He tugged thoughtfully at his sparse gray beard, then scratched his bald pate. Much as he disliked it, he would have to obtain a few more of the moonglow wands. And that meant paying another visit to the demons' storeroom. He shivered at the thought. He was only a minor wizard. Not for him the dangerous and frightening adventures of dragonslaying and spell-gathering. He much rather preferred tending his small garden. But if he wanted dragonwort he would need another moonglow wand.

Sighing, he gathered the materials needed to travel to the demon world. Incense mixed with sulfur, his bottomless satchel, the blessed candles to protect his cottage against any returning evil, and lastly, the pentagram portal drawn on the floor with colored sand.

The glowing brazier filled the room with clouds of incense. Brambel stepped inside the portal with his satchel and lit the candles at the points of the pentagram with his last magic flint. He double-checked the pentagram lines to make sure that all were intact, then uttered the magic words of transference.

Instantly he stood within the demons' storeroom. The room was dark, but the lines of the pentagram glowed faintly on the floor about him, marking the portal.

He scurried hastily out of the pentagram. He had little time; no telling when a demon might enter, and he had no desire to meet one after his last near encounter with one of their watchguards.

Brambel hurried up and down the aisles, searching by touch and memory for the wands, not risking the light of his magic flint. The demons were sensitive to fire. Finally he found the wands three shelves down from where he last remembered them. He stuffed a generous supply of them into the satchel, adding several handfuls of the short spell containers.

He closed the satchel and listened for any approaching demon. He might have time to gather a few more needs. The demons kept a few plants in this storeroom, but they were prickly things, and he wanted no evil growth in his garden. Perhaps just a few more of the magic flints. Carefully he retraced his steps to the pentagram. The flints were kept near there, behind a long table.

Hurriedly he gathered the flints, surprised anew at their various sizes. He rummaged about the table, hunting for more. He sensed the light trap the second his foot broke it. Clever demons! Bells clanged outside the storeroom, and he heard a far off moaning. He scrambled around the table, bumping into things in his haste, and dove into the safety of the portal, quickly saying the words of return.

The cottage reappeared about him, and he swiftly erased the pentagram. Safe! Safe! Brambel mopped his forehead and patted his bulging satchel.

* * *

Officer Finseth shook his head in disgust as he returned to his partner. "Same as last time," he said. "The manager says that all that's missing are a few flashlights, batteries, and a lot of lighters."

"Same sulfur smell, too," his partner commented.

"I don't get it. The guy breaks into the mall with no visible signs of entry, hits the same drug store every time, and only takes a few flashlights?"

"You know what I think—" his partner started.

"Yeah, yeah. But what would the Devil want with a lighter?"

"The Demons' Storeroom" previously appeared in Another Realm, *December 1999*
Reprinted from Fury, *April 1993.*

GOODBYE, JENNIE!

Dear Jennie,

Burn this after you've read it.

Within a short time you will be hearing that your beloved sister is dead. An accident, they'll say, with flames consuming car and occupant. I won't be dead, Jen, but you must pretend that this is so. Never let anyone know the contents of this letter, and I mean *anyone*—not friends, not even Grandfather and Grandmother. Let this just be our little secret, and twin, this is an important one! There are quite a number of people around who would not take very kindly to what I am about to tell you (that is, if they believed you to begin with).

I suppose I should have just let you believe, along with everyone else, the news of my death—it certainly would be safer for you if I did—but knowing how we both felt when Mom and Dad died, I couldn't do that to you. Believe me, if there was any other way to disguise my going, I would have used it. I know the real truth won't make you any happier, but knowing my twin sister as well as I do, I had to make sure that you wouldn't simply set out to disprove my "death." Please, just let the story stand unchallenged. A good deal depends on that story holding up.

Now don't get worried at all this secrecy. I'll explain as I go along. All that really matters is that I am well, and happier than in my wildest dreams. The reason? I'm finally going into space! No, I haven't joined the space program. I doubt NASA would want a skinny redhead who can't remember her math. I found another way.

I suppose I'd better start at the beginning. Remember that meteor shower last week and how I drove up to our old summer place in Wisconsin especially to see it? (Yes, I know my vacation ends this week, but Dr. Larson will have to find a new lab technician.) Anyhow, I reached the cabin without any trouble. The forest seems smaller than it once looked from a ten-year-old's eyes, but the meadow below it is as spacious and wide as ever. I watched the meteors from there, madly clutching a flashlight for company. I say madly because that night was so dark and so quiet that for the first time in my life I was lonely. I don't mean no-other-person-around lonely; I mean the-last-living-creature-on-Earth lonely! Then the meteors came.

Jen, mere words cannot describe that meteor shower. It wasn't just a collection of wandering space rocks burning up in the outer reaches of our atmosphere. There was something more about it, something so strange and wonderful that, just watching it, I felt somehow different. A warm feeling of kinship with the rest of the universe rose in me as I watched those falling rocks, along with a frightened, yet wondering awe at the cold glory of the watching stars. It was *so* beautiful.

The last meteor gone, I was still wrapped in that awe when I had a creepy feeling of someone watching me. You know me, I don't have sense enough to be afraid; so, instead of leaving quietly and quickly like any normal person, I turned on the flashlight and looked around the meadow. I didn't see anyone, but then I suddenly realized that I didn't *hear* anything, either. No crickets, no owls from the woods, not even a mosquito buzzing around my ear. It was a little frightening, but I kept looking. I knew that there was someone around watching me, and you know me and my stubbornness. Finally my light caught an answering glint from the grass in one corner of the meadow.

Investigating further, I found a small globe of what appeared to be glass nestled in the long grass. It looked like someone's paperweight, but if it was, it was an awfully odd one. The globe filled the palm of my hand but felt so light for glass and too glassy for plastic that I didn't know what to make of it. And when I turned my flashlight full on it, it seemed to be filled with swirling mists of green and white.

Right at my ear, a voice suddenly remarked, "You'll do."

To say I jumped is putting it mildly. I was so startled I dropped the flashlight and almost dropped the sphere. But that was only a light shock compared to the next one. Jennie, the meadow was empty! The only thing that voice could have come from was the sphere!

"Wh-what did you say?" I stammered. The globe was glowing now; I could see the swirling green and white mists quite clearly.

The sphere…chuckled. Sounded just like Grandfather. "I said, 'You'll do.' And you proved my point nicely."

I will never know why I didn't throw that globe away and run screaming to the cabin at that point. This thing didn't feel like a machine or a new kind of walkie-talkie. It felt…unearthly. Still, I didn't run and I didn't scream. I guess I'm just too curious for my own good.

"Who, or what, are you?" I asked.

The sphere chuckled again. "You might call me a friend. One who has come a long way to meet you."

At that moment, the stars seemed to close in on me. "What…do you want?" I ventured.

"Open your mind," the little alien said.

I really don't know what happened next. I stood gazing into that sphere for what seemed to be an eternity, with that calm voice droning on inside my head. I don't remember anything that he said, but after he stopped I looked up at the stars and *knew*. I knew what this little visitor was, what he wanted of me, and why. Best of all, I could look up into that brilliant night sky and see not just faint and faraway suns, but the universe! Jen, the galaxy was opened before me! I saw the planets as Apson, the little being inside the globe, saw them. And I saw the stars as I had never dreamed I could. The universe is filled with life, and in so many varieties and forms it could take several lifetimes to know them all. And I'm going out to meet them!

By now you probably think that your sister has gone crazy, or worse. I know how you feel because I thought I had, too. Even now after several days of thinking and organizing (Apson's handling my "death"—my poor, beautiful car will be totaled) I keep feeling that I must be dreaming, that this can't be happening to me. Then I see that little blob of alien life sitting on Dad's desk and know that my dream is reality. (Yes, I stayed on at the cabin, although I'll be gone by the time you receive this).

Why me? Why, out of several billion people on this planet, did Apson pick me to go back into space with him? That's a question I can't answer. All I know is that somewhere among the stars is a race of beings whose entire purpose in life is to help others along the path to maturity. They pick natives of the more advanced planets, train them, and appoint them to watch over and, whenever necessary, nudge their home planet and others onto the right road. And I know your next question. How can I be sure that Apson isn't lying and that your gullible sister is not going to be kidnapped by alien mist-monsters? He opened his mind to me, Jennie. I could see his every thought, and I know for a fact that he is telling me the truth and would never hurt me. I have a friend in the truest sense of the word, Jen—one from the stars, no less!

But, even for me, the decision to go was a tough one. Sure, I could see the stars as I've always wanted to, but that kind of travel has quite a few disadvantages. I'm going to be on my own, more so than when Mom and Dad died because you won't be there to pull me out of trouble and give me a good talking-to when the responsibility becomes too much. You probably won't see me again, not unless something earth-shaking happens in Evanston, and even then you won't recognize me. I'll have to remain dead as far as my friends are concerned, since the role or roles I might have to play could raise some very embarrassing questions if someone recognized me. That's why you'll soon be hearing of my "death." There's truly no other way to mask my going without raising questions.

But, looking at it another way, I had to agree. I might have a chance to stop some of the blind cruelties of today's world. Plus I'll be working with Apson. That part was irresistible. You'd like him, Jen. He's a sweet little guy, even if he is older than Grandfather and can sometimes act more dignified than that cat of yours.

Get that envious glint out of your green eyes, Jennie. You're the homebody half of us. I've always been the adventurous one, never content to sit still. This new life will be fun, but it will be dangerous, too. I'm looking forward to it just the same.

Still, I know I'm going to miss you terribly, Jen. Think kindly of your nutty twin when you see the stars at night. Goodbye, Jennie.

Your wandering half,

Janice.

"Goodbye, Jennie!" previously appeared in Shadowstar *#3, October 1981.*

LONELY

"Of course, with these summer cottages you have full access to the lake," the tall young man was saying.

Marian stood in the dusty gravel road and listened to the advantages of renting one of his cottages with a slight trace of boredom. What had she expected? When she'd felt that faint probe at her mind last night, she'd instantly thought of another esper, one unknown to her. But after a morning of searching in the direction from which the probe had stemmed and finding nothing but mind-blind people, she was ready to give up.

The young man smiled at her, and Marian returned it, feeling anything but pleasant toward this dull individual. She watched him carefully, frowning behind her mask. She'd pinpointed the probe to this area, but, exasperating enough, nothing showed on her mental sweep of the neighborhood. It was beginning to look more and more as if she were the only young, sane esper in this part of the country. All the others she knew of were either old, dying people who were vaguely disturbed by their strange new abilities, or insane individuals who couldn't handle the full powers of their minds. Marian had thought she was going insane herself when her abilities had suddenly appeared.

She sighed. It was lonely without someone who also talked mind-to-mind; she was still of an age to wish for a friend, one who was as different as she. She had friends among the normal people—those without ESP—but how many of those would remain so if they knew she could read their minds? She hated being on her guard at all times, watching what she said and did so no one would suspect she was different. Wasn't there someone with whom she could relax and be herself?

"And that comes to only $800 a month," the young man finished.

Marian was about to thank him and go on her way when a small chipmunk darted under her car, followed by a large gray cat. Raw fear touched her mind. She peered under the car. Large yellow eyes glared warily at her as their owner cradled the chipmunk between its forepaws. The cat was toying with its captive, letting it escape only to close savage jaws on it and drag it back to its paws again and again.

The shared terror hurt. Marian picked up a stone and slung it at the cat. With a yowl of pain, it leaped to its feet, releasing its prey. Marian could feel its mind whirl with pain and anger as the chipmunk dashed out from under the car. Fury at the loss of its captive overwhelmed the pain, and the cat raced after the chipmunk.

The tiny animal was trapped between Marian and the cat. Marian moved back to give it room to escape, but, much to her surprise, the chipmunk sprang into the air and landed on her shoulder. She was startled, but rose quickly, her hand reaching up to protect it as the cat circled her feet. She gently pushed the cat away with her foot, but it lashed at her angrily.

Ignoring the open-mouthed man beside her, Marian calmly hit the cat with a mental blow of terror. Yowling with fear, it vanished behind the cottage.

"Careful, miss," the man stammered. "Animals don't act like that unless they have rabies."

Marian ignored him. Animals couldn't harm her as long as she could control them. She suppressed any thought of biting in the small creature's mind and tried to get the chipmunk off her shoulder. Slowly she released its claws' frenzied grip on her blouse and gently deposited the chipmunk on the ground. Instead of fleeing from her, however, it sat at her feet and looked up into her face. Then it flipped its tail as if in farewell and scampered away.

Marian stared after it. No wild animal had ever acted like that, not even when she controlled its mind. Probably had been tame once, she decided. She dismissed the incident and thanked the boring young man for his time. As she got into the car, she saw a chipmunk—was it the same one?—watching her from the branch of a tree. "Forget it," she told herself firmly and drove to the next town.

She finally returned to her apartment late that night. Tired, she gave only slight attention to an unfamiliar car in the parking lot. If someone was having company, she wasn't interested in checking out a stranger at this late hour.

Marian approached the building entrance, fumbling for her key. A dark figure detached itself from the building's shadow, and she froze, directing all of her senses towards it.

"Good evening," a familiar voice said.

It was that boring young man from the cottages. Marian started to relax, then realized that something was wrong. His mind seemed asleep, almost as if he were not controlling his actions. She peered deeper into his thoughts. "Hmm, someone learns fast," she muttered softly.

She reached out with her mind and snapped the strands of thought controlling the man. He sagged weakly, like a puppet with cut strings, and caught himself with a hand against the building.

"Are you okay?" she asked as he blinked at her. "Do you know where you are?"

"Where?" he repeated slowly. "How—how did I get here?"

"Don't you remember? You brought me some brochures about the resort." She pointed. "Isn't that your car in the lot?" Marian sensed upset from another's mind as well as his. Better to end this conversation quickly.

"Yeah, that's my car. Funny, I don't remember driving here." The man shrugged. "I'd best be getting back."

"Thanks again." Marian watched as the man hurried to his car and drove away.

She waited a bit longer, making sure that the nosier neighbors had left their windows.

I'm sorry I overlooked you this morning, she said silently. She unlocked the entrance to the building and waited, holding the door open.

She sensed forgiveness and approval in another's mind.

The chipmunk darted out of the shadows and stopped before her. It sat and watched her.

Now that I've passed your test, Marian said silently, *you and I have a lot to discuss.*

"Lonely" reworked from the version in Shadowstar *#4, December 1981.*

TRANSFER STUDENT

"Well, it's a typical first night back at the dorm," Cheryl said. "Did you see all the suitcases in the lobby?"

Tina grinned and leaned against the elevator wall. "More people at the bars tonight, too." The doors opened, and she winced at the loud blare of stereos. "Study floor, hah! Why do they always have to put freshmen in with us juniors and seniors?"

Cheryl laughed. "You expect it to be quiet on the first night? Wait until after classes start, grump."

"Humph. Remember last summer session? When you had to sleep on the floor in our room because your neighbors on both sides had midnight-until-two-A.M. parties? Hope we have a better RA this summer."

She followed Cheryl through the maze of boxes and plants outside one door. "Did you hear Kara going on and on about her new major? Sounded as if she expected us to rush right out and change our majors, too."

"Well, e-t studies is interesting, and there are more jobs in it."

"Not more than nursing." Tina eyed her roommate. "You going to change majors again? You'd have two years before graduating rather than a year and a half, but I always said you were wrong to change from sociology. How many isolated tribes are left to study firsthand? What good is cultural anthropology?"

Cheryl shook her head. "Look, Kara may have been your roommate last quarter and e-t studies may be a great new field according to her, but I—"

"Only said at the end of last quarter that you were bored stiff with anthro, so don't try to tell me differently."

"What I'm trying to tell you is that there's something strange about this new major. When did you ever hear of new courses being offered during the summer instead of the fall? And did you know that this is the only university on Earth to have a major in e-t studies? This tiny little university?"

"Kara's only been telling me that all night. Anyway, we've only met one alien race. Why 'extraterrestrial studies?' Why isn't it called 'Parrot studies' or 'Parrot culture' or something?"

"You think those are the only aliens in the universe? Anyhow, the correct name isn't 'Parrot.' That's just what the media call them."

"Who can pronounce the real name? Much less spell something that has to be whistled." Tina attempted a few notes.

Cheryl rubbed her ear. "If I have a choice, I'd rather listen to the whistler in the shower." She glanced down the hallway. "It's awfully quiet on this end of the floor. Wonder why?"

Tina stopped outside their door and rummaged for her key. "I wonder why I always have to unlock the door. What's wrong with a little quiet? Probably everybody's still out at the bars. We'd still be there if we both didn't have classes at seven-thirty tomorrow morning."

"There're lights on under most of the doors."

"So people are still unpacking."

"Who do you know that can unpack quietly?"

Tina sighed and opened the door. "You going to conduct a behavioral study of college students at eleven o'clock at night? Again?"

"Hmm. Let me brush my teeth first." She grinned at Tina's exasperated expression.

The splash of water in the sink competed with the whirring hum of the blowdryers across the bathroom. Cheryl glanced down the row of sinks to see who was using the dryers, and froze, the toothbrush halfway to her mouth.

The alien's blue and green fur was still damp from the shower. Eyes closed, and trilling softly, it stood under the directed flow of three wall blowdryers, the brush in one clawed hand fluffing its blue head fur out in the hot air. Cheryl numbly wondered how the being planned to dry its tail.

At first glance the extraterrestrial resembled either a furry dinosaur or a human-sized parrot with arms rather than wings. The strong hooked beak strengthened the parrot resemblance, as did the featherlike fur, dark blue on the head and short tail and damp green down to its bare pink feet with two black-clawed toes pointing forward and two back. The furred hand holding the spiky brush had three clawed fingers and a clawless thumb. A circle of bare, chalk-white skin surrounded each eye, giving it a masked appearance.

The blowdryers abruptly shut off, and with a whistle that was almost a sigh, the e-t opened its eyes and reached for the dryer's controls. The large dark brown eyes fastened on Cheryl, and the brush hesitated in midstroke. "Hello," the alien said.

Tina walked through the door behind Cheryl and stopped. "Oh no," she moaned, closing her eyes. "Don't tell me I'm going to have to give up beer."

"You're not seeing things," Cheryl whispered swiftly. "I just found out why they put that crazy toilet in this bathroom."

She carefully put her toothbrush down and walked over to the e-t, not wishing to shout across the room at it. *No*, she corrected herself, *that "it" has to be a "she" to be in here.*

"Hello. I'm Cheryl and that's my roommate Tina."

The e-t placed the claws of one hand against her furry chest and bobbed her head. "Cheryl. Tina. May your nests be filled with glad music. I am"—she whistled a long, sweet trill—"but the humans on the ship shortened that to Sstwel."

"Sstwel." Cheryl hesitated, then copied the e-t's bob. "May your nest be filled with glad music."

Sstwel seemed delighted, bobbing her head vigorously while chortling deep in her throat. Tina giggled. "You've got a nice laugh, Sstwel."

The e-t bobbed to her. "I had feared that I had committed some"—she whistled a sour note—"to offend you humans. Silence among my people is used to correct hatchlings."

Cheryl and Tina exchanged glances. "Freshmen," Tina said disgustedly. "Who's the idiot RA on this floor?"

"What can she do?" Cheryl said cynically. "She's only the resident advisor." She turned back to the puzzled e-t. "Sstwel," she began, "the young of our species are...fearful of strangers."

Rims of orange cornea appeared as the brown of Sstwel's eyes shrank, then dilated. She clicked her beak. "Our young are much alike. *Tweeel*, the fears I had when I was to become adult! The home nest seemed so safe and the outside world so big and unknown. This university has young-who-would-become-adult, as well as adults?"

Cheryl firmly pushed her desire to hear more into a back corner and tried to think of a way to help the e-t. "Uh, yes. Sstwel, you must be cold in your damp fur. I have a hand-held blowdryer that will do a better job than those wall units. Come, you can use it in my room."

Puzzled, Tina watched as Cheryl all but pushed Sstwel out the door. Cheryl mouthed one word behind the e-t's back and jerked her thumb towards the opposite hallway door. Tina smothered a laugh and dashed out, counting rapidly on her fingers. "Renae and Jil are on this floor, and Donna might be back by now. Wonder if Kara would be willing to come over from her dorm at this hour?"

* * *

There was a limit as to how many people could fit in a dorm room, especially when one of them had a tail. Neighbors came out to see what was causing all the noise, and more than a few of them stayed. The popcorn party spilled out into the hallway and spread to other rooms, but the largest group of people stayed around the main attraction.

"What's it like to travel in hyperspace? Does it feel any different from normal space?"

"Don't interrupt, Kara. Sstwel was telling us about the singing insects."

Sstwel bobbed, nibbling delicately on a piece of popcorn. The e-t was delighted with the treat and ecstatic over the music recordings, trilling along with each selection unless distracted by a question. Tina muttered that the e-t seemed to be getting drunk on either the music or the attention.

Cheryl grinned at her roommate. "Both, I'll bet. She's probably never met this many strangers all at once."

"There're as many Parrots as humans."

"Only because they colonized another planet. Don't you remember that big uproar a few years back? When the very people who once said space exploration was useless threatened to sue the space agency because it hadn't found a planet for us to colonize?"

"I don't have the time to read newspapers.You wouldn't either if you didn't have that job at the library."

"Never mind. You remember that 'nest' Sstwel spoke of? It's a big inter-related family. The young don't come into contact with anyone outside the nest until they reach adulthood, when each one becomes apprenticed to an older family member's trade. Sstwel won't begin her apprenticeship until after she finishes here, so she isn't even accustomed to social contact among adults of her world."

Tina blinked. "Cheryl, if you don't stop speaking anthropologese, I won't be able to understand you all summer." She shook her head. "That explains why you looked so disgusted with us when we came in. You certainly learned a lot from her in a few minutes."

"I only hope she learned enough from me about humans to psych us out before any misunderstandings develop."

"Will you stop being the anthropologist studying the aborigines for once and relax?" Tina indicated the knot of people about the e-t. "Look at her. Everybody likes her. Why should she get into any trouble? Never mind; don't answer that."

She glanced into their crowded room and sighed. "Well, you started this. Now think of a way to get this mob to leave before they camp here all night."

* * *

Due to lack of sleep, Cheryl gave up trying to concentrate on her seven-thirty class halfway through the lecture. She stared unseeingly at the clock and wondered how Sstwel would be received by the campus.

By the time her nine o'clock class started, she knew.

"Hey, everybody!" an excited sophomore yelled as he burst through the door. "There was a big green chicken walking around Memorial Hall!"

The bearded graduate assistant permitted himself a skeptical chuckle. "A green chicken?"

"Parrot," a junior corrected scornfully. He noticed the assistant's confusion and added, "One of those aliens. I saw it at breakfast. Somebody said there are five of them on campus."

"A real alien?" The grad assistant nervously fumbled his papers. "What is an alien doing here?"

"They probably plan to colonize this planet, too." The junior scowled. "Lousy aliens think they're so superior."

"I wouldn't say they're superior," the sophomore said, calming. "We found them, after all."

"Look, kid—" the junior started.

"But what are they doing here?" the grad assistant repeated.

"There is only one e-t," Cheryl said, deciding she had listened long enough. "And she's a student, just like us."

"She? It's a she?"

"Well, I think it's very brave of her to come among us *lousy aliens*," the sophomore said, enjoying the junior's discomfiture.

"A green chicken," the grad assistant said uneasily.

Cheryl heard similar comments on her way back to the dorm. She frowned as she noticed someone demonstrating Sstwel's stooped, pigeon-toed walk to a disbelieving audience.

That the powers-that-be had seen fit to throw a young, naive e-t into university life without any preparation on either side was to be expected. Ditto the fact that the University's newly hired expert in e-t psychology wasn't due to arrive until fall quarter. At least Sstwel's first day hadn't sounded *too* bad.

The cafeteria buzzed at lunch. Cheryl stared curiously at the high table adjoining theirs, then carefully placed her tray down with enough force to rattle the flatware.

"I saw you coming," Tina said, not lifting her eyes from her textbook. "You didn't need to announce yourself."

"Just wanted to make sure you hadn't fallen into your usual trance." She slid into the chair opposite Tina's. "What's been happening? I heard two instructors fainted."

"Hmm? No, just one. You remember Dr. Hager? Seventy if he's a day and still believes the world is flat."

"He's also so nearsighted that he can't find his own office without help. How did he get close enough to Sstwel to even guess she's an e-t?"

Tina laughed and closed her book. "Her feet are too big for stairs unless she goes up them sideways. Fortunately, all her classes are in buildings with elevators."

"What does that have to do with Dr. Hager? Oh."

"'Oh' is right. From what I heard, Dr. Hager stepped into an elevator and told the student there to press the button for the second floor. The rest you can guess."

"Hi, fellow humans! Sstwel will be down for lunch in a minute." Donna slid the small stack of books away from Tina and settled herself into the vacated spot. "You should have seen Sstwel at breakfast!"

"We had earlier classes. What did we miss?"

Donna laughed. "She wears make-up!"

Tina stared. "Where?"

"You know those big white circles around her eyes? Brightly decorated with the most brilliant orange paint I've ever seen. She also had a wide belt of the same bright orange." Donna shook her head. "The cafeteria was so quiet I could hear her claws click on the floor."

"And?" Cheryl prodded.

Donna shrugged. "And nothing. Who's awake at breakfast? A few people did look at her as if she were a new kind of pink elephant, but that was about it. Plus, part of my floor and some of yours ate with her." She gestured vaguely at the high table. "I'm not used to people standing while they eat, but her people don't sit. They do talk and eat at the same time, though. She seemed really excited, twittering and nodding her head all the time."

Tina smiled. "It's the kid's first day of school. Say, Cheryl, how can Sstwel be starting as a junior if there're no universities on her planet?"

Cheryl reached for her glass. "I think the University's considering her a transfer student. After all, she has had her people's equivalent of general education at college level."

Donna nodded. "So all she needs here is her major. Know what it is?"

Cheryl shook her head and Donna grinned at them. "Marketing. She plans to go into advertising."

"Marketing?" her audience chorused.

Donna's grin broadened. "And I found out who the RA on your floor is."

Tina groaned. "From that nasty look on your face she must be that Lynn Whats-her-name we had last summer. How did you find out? We didn't see any sign of her last night."

"She introduced herself to Sstwel at breakfast."

"How did she explain last night's silent treatment?" Tina growled.

"According to Lynn, most people aren't used to blue and green fur."

"She hasn't changed," Tina muttered. "Still sticking her foot in her mouth."

"Yep. Renae and Kwang immediately asked if she was implying that there was something wrong with Sstwel's color. Then, while Lynn was standing there with her mouth hanging open, Sstwel started twittering that the red-and-oranges may be more numerous, but the blue-greens outnumber the red-greens or the grays." She laughed. "Good thing for Lynn that we had to leave for class at that point. Sstwel still had a few more colors to go."

Cheryl smiled and wondered if Donna knew that the fur colors of Sstwel's people, unlike human hair colors, included all the shades of the spectrum and that the possible combinations were endless. Sstwel had been telling Lynn the colors of her nest.

Tina looked up and waved. "Kara! How's e-t studies coming?"

"Don't ask." The petite blonde dumped her books atop the growing stack and rummaged through a folder. "They canceled one class on the"—she whistled the eight note name—"since the instructor now won't be here until fall. All that's offered is the introductory class, and the reading list is nothing but science fiction."

Cheryl glanced at the reading list held out to her. "All the classic first contact stories."

"But we've known the Parrots for four years now and have found several planets without intelligent life!" Kara replaced her folder. "What's wrong with a little facts in with the theory?"

"Seems odd, doesn't it?"

"Don't get Cheryl started," Tina groaned. "It's just the introductory class, Kara. Freshman level, right? So it's as basic as possible. The higher level classes will get into the probes."

"How are the guys on your floor reacting to the idea of an e-t?" Cheryl interrupted.

Kara shrugged. "The same as the girls. Mixed reactions, with some grumblings and some curiosity. Everybody is waiting to see what everybody else will do."

Donna grimaced. "Five weeks for this session, a week off, then five weeks for second summer session. It's going to be a long summer for Sstwel if everybody just waits."

"It certainly will be an interesting one," Cheryl said absently. Sstwel had entered the cafeteria, and Cheryl began counting how many people actually drew away from the e-t versus smiled or greeted the furry being. She nodded in satisfaction, noticing a larger group of curious watchers. "Yes, it will be interesting."

Donna scrambled to her feet. "There's Sstwel. Hurry, so we can go through the lunch line with her."

"Why? I already have my lunch." Tina warily prodded her sandwich.

"If you go through the lunch line with Sstwel, you can get whatever's left of *her* type of food. It's pretty good."

Tina pushed her sandwich away. "That's what you said about the meat loaf last night. Is it safe for humans?"

Donna shrugged. "She can eat some types of our food. C'mon, it's much better than the normal food served around here."

* * *

"It's *blue*!" Tina drew away from the plate held out to her.

"The lizard eggs this morning were bright red, but still good." Donna deftly snagged the plate.

Kara gulped. "Don't tell us what we're eating, Sstwel. Please."

Sstwel's large eyes studied Kara. Her head tilted as the claws of one hand combed the fur about her beak. She shook her head and whistled in confusion. "It is only heated grain, like your popcorn."

"Blue popcorn, yet," Donna said happily.

Tina sidled up to Cheryl on their way back to the tables. "If Donna asks to try that brown thing with the legs, I'll scream. Blue popcorn I can take, but roasted bugs?"

Cheryl chuckled. "Think of it as a brown lobster with twelve legs. Anyhow, nobody's asking you to try it. The servers didn't give any to us, only to Sstwel."

"Yeah, but with my luck, it's probably better than last night's meat loaf."

Cheryl did not feel like laughing later that afternoon. Kara was waiting for her in the dorm lobby when Cheryl returned from her job.

"Renae called," Kara said quickly, falling into step with her, "and asked me to come over and warn you when you got back from the library. There's trouble on your floor. It seems Sstwel's neighbors don't want to be her neighbors."

Cheryl checked her watch. "Sstwel won't be back from class for another half hour. Did Renae say anything else? Such as what the RA is doing to settle this?"

"Just her usual imitation of an RA. First she agrees with the neighbors, then she agrees with Sstwel's friends from last night's party."

Cheryl pressed the elevator call button. "She never should have been given Sstwel's floor. This is all the result of stupid planning on the University's part! As usual." She pushed the button again.

Kara's eyebrows raised. "Why blame the University?"

"I have the feeling that Sstwel was supposed to be part of an experiment. All the others of her kind here on Earth are full adults, professionals of one type or another. Ambassadors, musicians, businesspeople. As professionals, they'd be on their very best behavior all the time, so we humans wouldn't form any bad impression of them. We also get a rather biased view of them. Same thing happens with our people on their worlds."

"So?"

"So when our two cultures finally do mix, when travel to their planets becomes as commonplace as a flight anywhere on this world, Sstwel's people will be in for a shock! Of course, Sstwel's people may not all be as polite as she is, too. Our two cultures have to learn to not always expect the best behavior from each other. There're examples all through our history of cultures contacted by polite, educated people only to have near-wars start up when full contact is achieved and the tourists arrive."

"I think I see what you're getting at, Cheryl. Sstwel was sent here to show us what an average Parrot is like. And she's doing that. So where's the problem?"

The elevator doors opened, and Cheryl stepped in and jabbed her floor button. "The problem is that something has obviously gone wrong with the experiment. Your e-t classes, I'll bet, were supposed to help us humans understand her culture a bit, but none of the qualified instructors appeared. There was supposed to be an e-t advisor here to help Sstwel understand us, a bit. Instead, Sstwel's been thrown into this entirely on her own."

The elevator doors opened on an extremely noisy study floor and Kara grinned. "Oh, I wouldn't say she's entirely alone, Cheryl. She has quite a few friends here."

The shouting match was centered in front of Sstwel's room. Renae and a shrill-voiced brunette were at full volume, while between them, Lynn tried vainly to make herself heard.

"I don't want to live next to some bird!" the brunette shrilled. "It started whistling at seven this morning!"

"And you heard her whistles all the way down in the cafeteria?" Cheryl said as the brunette paused for breath. "While you were having breakfast?"

"Oh, so she was in the cafeteria, huh?" Renae crossed her arms and glared at her opponent. "You must have extremely sensitive hearing."

"That thing is either chirping or whistling all the time!"

"And some people talk all the time!" Renae retorted. "I certainly wouldn't want to be *your* neighbor! Sstwel sounds better!"

"That's right," murmured the group behind her.

"Girls, please!" Lynn said, and seemed surprised when she had their attention. "The, uh, best solution would be to, uh, simply change rooms."

"Fine by me," the brunette agreed. She studied Renae. I'm sure you wouldn't mind being the thing's neighbor."

"Fine by me," Renae mimicked.

"No, Renae," one of her friends said. "I'd like to be Sstwel's neighbor."

"No, no! I will!"

"I think you're missing the problem," Cheryl interrupted. "The problem isn't who's going to be Sstwel's neighbor."

The entire group stared at her in silence. "It isn't?" Lynn finally asked.

"Of course not. There are several people right here willing to be Sstwel's neighbor. The problem is, who wants to be *her* neighbor?" Cheryl asked, indicating the brunette.

"That's right! Renae, you can't move! I don't want to live next to her!"

"Me neither."

"Now wait a minute," the brunette started, flushing.

Renae grinned. "A show of hands! Who wants—I mean, who can tolerate her as a neighbor?"

The brunette glared at her former supporters.

"I don't live on this floor," one of them said..

Another, timid under the laughter of Sstwel's friends, half raised her hand.

Cheryl nodded. "You're one of my neighbors, right? Juanita, you're on the other side of my room. What do you say?"

The young woman shrugged. "All right. But she'd better be a very quiet neighbor."

* * *

"What," Tina asked in the reasonable voice reserved for humoring the insane, "do you think you're doing?"

Cheryl picked up an armload of clothes and stopped as Tina blocked the doorway. "We're moving."

"That's what it looks like, all right. Why?"

"One of Sstwel's neighbors didn't want to be her neighbor."

A loud squawk came from outside the door, followed by mournful squeaks.

Cheryl dropped the clothes. "Tina, couldn't you have told me that Sstwel was outside?"

The e-t was crouched in a furry huddle, beak tucked tightly against chest, in the center of the hallway. Tina clapped her hands over her ears. "Sstwel, will you stop that squeaking?"

Cheryl squatted beside the e-t. "Sstwel, open your eyes and look at me."

A brown eye peeked out at her from the blue and green huddle. Struggling not to laugh at the comical sight, Cheryl tried to inject a sad note in her voice. "Sstwel, don't you want to be our neighbor? Tina and

I are moving next door to you."

The squeaks stopped, but Sstwel still remained in her huddle. "Banging on wall not sign of friendship?"

Cheryl shook her head. "No."

The brown eye closed and the squeaks resumed briefly. The huddle shuddered as Sstwel took a deep breath. "I will help you move," she said, unwinding.

Cheryl glanced among the curious crowd that had gathered in the hallway and noticed that Sstwel's former neighbor had the decency to look ashamed of herself. Cheryl patted the e-t's arm, briefly marveling at the silkiness of the fur. "Don't worry, Sstwel. The first day of school is always the worst."

* * *

The days passed slowly but not uneventfully enough for Sstwel's friends. A hasty turn by Sstwel in the library stacks cleared several shelves of their books and trapped her tail in the debris. Cheryl watched worriedly from main desk as librarians hurried toward the source of the racket, but Sstwel's rescuers only asked the e-t to watch her U-turns in the future.

Cheryl managed to control a fit of the giggles when Sstwel crouched in the apologetic posture and knocked down a few more shelves with her stubby tail. But a conspiratorial wink from the head librarian destroyed her composure as Sstwel was gently steered to a less dangerous aisle.

A few rainy days the second week resulted in Sstwel's first trip downtown after one instructor gently but firmly informed her that students in his class did not shake themselves dry inside the classroom. After the first few stores, Cheryl decided that salespeople were too accustomed to the odd shapes of human customers to be shocked by a mere extraterrestrial. Sstwel in her new raincape and hood soon became a familiar, if comical, sight on campus.

"Strangers smile and wave now," Sstwel twittered happily. "Does the coat make me look more like a human?"

On the floor, Cheryl held her brush away from the exercise she was copying in Sstwel's language and struggled to swallow her laughter. "No," she choked. She sat back on her heels to look up at the e-t and wondered why the being still wore fluorescent green eye paint and matching belt. Make-up was usually only for classes. "No, I think people are friendly now because they no longer see you as a stranger."

Sstwel chirped disbelief and hit a computer key with her claw. "But, friend Cheryl, packaging makes all the difference."

"Don't start quoting your textbooks at me. You're not a product; you're a person."

"Sstwel, do you have the blowdryer again?" Tina, a large towel wrapped about her hair, appeared in the open doorway. She looked about the room and shook her head. "Never will get used to how much space a dorm room has without the beds and dressers," she muttered.

Cheryl followed her gaze. The only furniture Sstwel needed was the high table serving as a desk and the nestlike pile of cushions in one corner. A photo of Sstwel's closest nestmates stood on one end of the bookshelf and one of the Forever Tree on the other, while gigantic posters of the Grand Tetons and the Swiss Alps covered opposing walls.

Sstwel rummaged through the clutter atop her desk. "Still, Cheryl, if I had worn my cape the day you and Donna taught me to throw Frisbees, more strangers would have stayed and become friends."

Tina glanced curiously at the e-t. "How many friends do you want? Half the dorm was playing and the other half hanging out the windows watching."

"There weren't that many, Tina," Cheryl disagreed.

"Well, no, not after Sstwel caught that Frisbee in her beak and bit the thing in half."

Sstwel crouched low. "I did not mean to damage it."

Cheryl frowned at her roommate. "Oh, Sstwel, get up. Tina knew that. So did the guy who owned the Frisbee. He wouldn't have asked us to play again this Saturday if you had broken it deliberately."

Sstwel squawked sharply in dismay. "No blowdryer, friend Tina."

"Cheryl, are you hiding it again? I can't find it in the room."

"But I always leave it on the—" The worried expression on Tina's face urged her to her feet. "I'll be back, Sstwel."

Tina hurried her into their room and closed the door.

"The blowdryer's right here, Tina."

"I know." Tina pulled the towel off her head and tried to pat her dry hair into order. "I couldn't think of any other excuse." She gestured Cheryl away from the wall by Sstwel's room and waited, listening. Soon Sstwel, never long silent, began trilling softly to herself.

"Tina, what's all the mystery about?"

"There's a strange character going around campus asking questions about Sstwel."

"There're always strange characters on campus. What kind of

questions?"

Tina shook her head. "I don't know. Jil overheard him in the union and followed him around campus all afternoon."

Cheryl frowned. "Then I'd better talk to Jil. Where—"

"She's waiting for you down in Donna's room. So're Renae and Donna."

Cheryl smiled and shook her head. "And Kara's probably on her way over, right? Sounds as if you're calling a war council."

"Well, Jil said he didn't act like a student."

"He didn't act like a teacher, either," Jil said a short time later. "He asked a lot of questions and noticed everything. From Sstwel's table in the library to her beak marks on some of the trees."

Cheryl smiled faintly at that. Sstwel did enjoy climbing things. The University had received more than a few complaints about Sstwel monopolizing the town park's jungle gym.

"He even knew about the Committee to Ban Claws!" Jil finished.

"Those three guys in the men's dorm? Donna grinned mischievously. "I thought they gave up after that rumor went around that they were against long fingernails on women, too."

"I wish Whats-her-name, Sstwel's ex-neighbor, would give up so easily," Tina muttered. "That girl's becoming a real nuisance. And Lynn's no help at all."

"You expect her to be?" Donna asked in amazement. "What's Whats-her-name up to now?"

"One problem at a time," Cheryl interrupted. "Jil, what kind of questions did this man ask? The what-has-Sstwel-been-doing type?"

The junior nodded. "He always asked that first with each person he talked to. And then he'd ask how they felt about her being here."

"And?"

"That was it."

"That's all?" Cheryl saw that the others did not share her puzzlement. "He just asked for opinions? He didn't try to stir up any bad feelings?" Jil shook her head. "Did he have any recording devices?"

Jil shook her head again. "I thought at first that he might be a reporter, but he didn't take any notes that I could see."

Kara glanced out the window. "If he's not a reporter or another troublemaker, what could he be up to? Most of the grumbling stopped after Sstwel got a 'C' and a 'D' on her midterm exams." She snapped her fingers. "Maybe he's a spy for the anti-alien groups!"

"With enough anti-alien students here on campus to do all the spying needed?" Cheryl shook her head. "The groups don't need to bring in any outsiders. They're already winning."

"Winning what?" Tina asked. "Cheryl, you haven't made any sense the past two weeks. So a few kids started a petition. They only got twenty signatures."

"Jil, where is the man now?"

"Somewhere in Altgeld Hall. I lost him in the administrative wing. There're too many interconnecting offices. Ben was out there trying to straighten out some problem with his records—"

"Ben's that guy from one of Sstwel's classes who's been tutoring her on marketing," Renae explained to Kara.

"—so he will try to see if he can spot that man leaving."

Renae whistled sharply. "There are at least ten exits from Altgeld."

"And six of us," Cheryl replied. "Let's go give Ben a hand. I'd like to see this curious stranger."

Donna flung open the door, almost overbalancing the sunburned individual who stood outside it, one hand ready to knock. "Is Jil—Jil! Why didn't you tell anyone where you were going? Took me the last half hour to track you down!"

"Ben!" Jil squeaked. "What are you doing here? Did the man leave? Did you lose him?"

Ben shook his head. "He's here! Upstairs, talking to Sstwel."

"What?" six voices chorused. Ben barely got out of the way of the stampede in time.

"Wait, wait." Tina stopped, blocking the stairwell door. "We can't all go rushing up there at once."

"Why not?"

"Cheryl, tell your roommate to get out of the way."

Tina shook her head. "What if he *is* a reporter? We need someone to check out the situation, while the rest of us sneak into my room and listen at the wall." She beamed at her roommate. "And I know just who would be best at the job; after all, she started this business of being friendly with aliens."

Jil chuckled. "You did say you wanted to see this stranger, Cheryl."

"I know, I know." She eyed Tina. "I suppose it helps that I've left my notes over at Sstwel's?"

"You always did think of the best excuses," Tina agreed as she opened the door for her.

Cheryl paused outside Sstwel's door and frowned thoughtfully at the swift whistle-speech she could hear inside. She felt eyes watching from the distant stairwell as she knocked. Claws clicked across the floor and the door flew open.

"Cheryl! You have returned." Sstwel's claws plucked at her sleeve. "In, in."

Leaning comfortably against the far wall was a man with flecks of gray at his temples and laugh lines about his eyes. Sstwel twittered excitedly. "Cheryl, this is my dearest adopted-nest-elder, Commander Lohrey."

Cheryl suddenly realized that she was gaping at him and shut her mouth. "C-commander Lohrey? Not as in Dr. Lohrey, the e-t psychologist?"

"The same," he said, shaking her limp hand. "And you are Cheryl. I've heard a good deal about you. I had thought you might be that sandy-haired young woman who shadowed me all over campus, but—"

"That's Jil." Cheryl shook her head dazedly, and from the hallway came the distant rumble of six people sneaking quietly into the next room. "Uh, you weren't supposed to be here until fall quarter."

Dr. Lohrey chuckled. "I was supposed to be here *this* quarter. However, a minor emergency on Sstwel's planet delayed me. I was just explaining to this troublesome young"—he whistled a series of descending notes—"that I had left word for her to delay her departure until I could accompany her."

Sstwel's head lowered, but her claws busily groomed her neck fur. "I have made many good friends," the e-t said proudly, her head fur fluffing out so that she seemed taller.

"Luckily for you," the psychologist growled. "Or else a certain young colonist would have had her branch on the nestworld's Forever Tree given to a more obedient nestling."

This time Sstwel crouched correctly in apology, her head fur sleeked against her skull. But the brown eye nearest Cheryl closed in a hard-learned wink, and Cheryl knew the e-t was not greatly intimidated by the threat.

"I'm sorry about your experiment, Dr. Lohrey," Cheryl interrupted. "We tried to help, but—"

"My experiment?" The psychologist's wondering innocence was polished perfection, and Cheryl decided that he was probably a diplomat as well. He smiled pleasantly, and Cheryl could not restrain her answering grin. The man was truly an expert in his field.

He leaned back against the wall. "Tell me about this 'experiment.'"

"Well, it's just a theory of mine. But suppose someone wanted to show that humans and some alien lifeform—"

"Like the Parrots, perhaps," Dr. Lohrey suggested with a grin.

"—could get along if they were gradually accustomed to the idea. You—I mean the experimenter—might start off by having alien students attend human universities, and humans attend the alien universities, or their equivalent."

"You might," Dr. Lohrey mused thoughtfully. "But why universities?"

"Because the people who work and study there are educated enough to be open-minded, to be able to tolerate ideas and people that are a little out of the ordinary." Cheryl sighed. "But it didn't work. They aren't open-minded. I'm sorry, Dr. Lohrey, but the experiment didn't work."

The psychologist gave her a quizzical look. "When I was last here to start preparations for Sstwel's arrival, opinion on e-ts was sharply divided between the science fiction people and the don't-cares. Ninety percent of the people I spoke with thought the Parrots had to be dangerous simply because they had claws! As if a tree dweller should only have suction pads or a great deal of rope."

Sstwel hissed indignantly. "Suction pads! I am no singing leaper or herd bug!"

Muffled clapping came through the wall. "That's telling them, Sstwel!"

Dr. Lohrey's eyebrows raised.

"We thought you were one of the enemy," Cheryl said with a grin. "The rest of the troops are listening next door." She shrugged. "I suppose the general feeling towards e-ts has worsened now."

"No, quite the contrary," he said mildly. "About seventy-five percent now think e-ts are just like humans. A trifle clumsy, perhaps, but—"

"Too narrow!" Sstwel squawked. "Everything—rooms, buildings—too narrow! I must always stand straight. No place to stoop in comfort indoors without bumping my head or catching my tail in something!" She snapped her beak angrily.

In the silence that followed, Tina's voice could be heard quite clearly. "How should I know why they're both picking on Sstwel? I suppose we'd better go over and rescue her, though."

As Sstwel, chuckling, went to answer the door, Dr. Lohrey said casually, "There will be about ten more of Sstwel's people starting here fall quarter. Do you know of any people who might like jobs as RAs in the dorms or as mentors?"

"Oh, I might know a few." Cheryl grinned. Sstwel bobbed like some mad toy as her friends entered.

"Good." The psychologist thoughtfully rubbed his jaw. "I think I'll need help with this new group—would you be willing to be my assistant? But only for a year," he added as Cheryl opened her mouth. "After that…hmm. Have you ever considered finishing your education abroad?"

"Transfer Student" previously appeared in Twilight Times, *January 2000. Reworked from the version in* Shadowstar *#2, June 1981.*

AND SOFTLY FOLLOW

The wizard watched as the young Free Trader removed a heavy golden ring from his finger and placed it on the table between them.

One narrow eyebrow lifted as she looked from the ring into his face. "It seems you came prepared to counter any objections I might have," she said. The wizard's eyes lost their focus for a moment, then she smiled. "Very well, Glen Cliffson. I will grant your request and send you to your friend." She stepped away from the table, then turned back to him. "She might not welcome you."

The young man grimaced, glancing at the ring on the tabletop. "I don't expect her to. We didn't exactly part on the best of terms."

"Then why must you go to warn her? As I have said, I cannot help her, but I can easily send her your message."

Stung at the suggestion, although that had been his original intention, Glen straightened and looked full into the wizard's knowing gaze. "Amber and I have been sword-brother and sister since we came of the age to handle daggers. If she is in danger, I must go."

The wizard nodded slightly. "There is a life-debt, and your dreams always come to pass? Two human visitors after years of silence," she mused, "and both with Talent. The Lands are changing." She thoughtfully reached out and touched the gold ring. "I will place-shift you close to where Amber Snowdaughter now rests."

Glen adjusted his pack and gripped the hilt of his sword. "I am ready."

The wizard tossed empty air at him—and abruptly he was elsewhere.

* * *

Glen blinked, his eyes quickly adjusting to the darkness after the candlelit shadows of the wizard's cottage. Tall trees surrounded him, and the cricking of night insects was all that he could hear. Then a light breeze ruffled his curly hair and brought him a faint whiff of woodsmoke. Smiling, he followed the scent.

His nose led him to a small fire burning on a cleared patch of ground. There was a pot filled with liquid beside it, but no sign of whoever had placed it there.

"You are quiet, stranger, but not quiet enough," a cold voice came from behind him.

Glen carefully kept his hand away from his sword. Turning slowly, he saw a slim blonde in travel garb similar to his own. The arrow in her drawn bow pointed directly at him. "I didn't expect this kind of welcome, Amber."

Her blue eyes widened, and she lowered her bow. "Glen Cliffson! What are you doing here?" Puzzlement was in her eyes, along with a wariness Glen was disturbed to see directed at him. "You're a long way from Clearwater Ford—and the rich lordling's daughter."

"Amber, I—"

"But don't worry. I shan't ask about her, or the courtship."

Glen smiled sadly. "I know you won't. You're the only one who hasn't warned me against her."

She studied him with a frown. "What are you doing here?"

"I've been looking for you. Snow said you plan to become a wizard."

Amber Snowdaughter lifted her chin defiantly. "That's right. An all-wise 'friend' told me that the Guild is no place for someone who can..." The pot beside the fire suddenly rose into the air and settled carefully into the flames. Challenge was in the look she turned upon him, and Glen wondered uneasily what else he had said that drunken night long ago.

"Snow said you were no longer hiding what you can do," he said slowly.

Amber's face set in a scowl. "Useless to hide it any longer after you babbled it to everyone. And now that I'm training to become a wizard..." She let the sentence trail off. "I'm on a quest right now."

"That's what your wizard said. Why a quest?"

"You talked with Calada, too? As well as my mother? You *have* been trying to find me. Why?"

"What kind of quest, Amber? You don't have to fight a sorcerer, do you?"

"Me? Against a sorcerer? Glen, the only magic I know is what I've had all my life. I'm not Calada's apprentice. Not yet. Not until I succeed at this quest."

"What is the quest?"

Amber moved back to the fire and set her bow and quiver down. "I thought you had talked with Calada." She looked at him, then shrugged. "I have to find something. Something lost so long ago that it had been forgotten back when Calada was young—whenever that was, since wizards never age." She pushed her long braid back over her shoulder. "Care for some serwasn?"

"You still drink that stuff?" He grimaced. "Boiled leaves in water isn't my idea of a drink."

Amber retrieved her pack and pulled out a mug. "I forgot, you have more expensive tastes now," she said coldly. "I'm afraid I didn't bring any brandywine."

Glen winced. Foolish of him to have brought that up. This was not going at all well. Perhaps he should have had Calada send a message. He looked at the cold-eyed stranger his childhood friend had become, and sighed. "I guess I deserve that. But you said you wouldn't mention Pegeen."

"I didn't. I was thinking more about her brother." She poured some of the serwasn into her mug and scowled at the drink. "And besides, I don't drink the leaves." She studied him as she drank, her blue eyes icy.

"Amber, I told you I was sorry about that night. How many times must I—"

"You don't even remember half of what you said."

"If that half was as bad as the half I do remember, I don't want to remember. Amber, I'm sorry, especially about betraying your secret. Sword-sister, can't you forgive me?"

"*Forgive*!" She gestured so violently with her mug that serwasn splashed onto the fire. "You came so close to getting yourself killed that night! Walking—no, staggering!—through the streets drunk as…as—and then picking a fight with those kingsmen!" She stopped and sipped at her drink. "You would have been killed," she repeated.

"If you hadn't come to my rescue," Glen said softly. The one clear memory he had of that night was of her dropping softly out of the darkness to land on the street between him and the kingsmen. Her sword had glittered like ice in the moonlight.

Amber's eyes flashed angrily as she glared at him. "Yes. One of the most foolish things I've done in my life. I had to dodge your sword as well as theirs, and even then you managed to stab my sword arm."

"You said it was only a scratch," he said weakly.

"And the thanks I got once I dragged you back to the inn. To have heard you curse, one would have thought I had taken away your chief delight. Crossing swords with kingsmen! I should have left you with them!"

"I had never had brandywine before," he said in a small voice.

"So I noticed. Pegeen's brother is a shrewd judge of people's weaknesses." She took another sip and stared thoughtfully into the flames. "I still haven't decided if he was only hoping to disgust Pegeen or if he had indeed planned for the kingsmen to attack you."

Glen nodded. He had begun to wonder the same about the sly lordling. "Then why did you abandon me?"

She choked on her drink. "Abandon you? In an inn full of our friends? And after what you said?"

"But I don't remember what I said! Amber—"

"And don't you dare tell me that it was the drink talking. You've been drunk before, but never, *never* did you say—" She broke off and turned away. "I can neither forgive nor forget, Glen."

Glen was taken aback. "You can't mean that, Amber! What did I say?"

She settled herself comfortably beside the fire and refilled her mug. "I know you, Glen. You haven't come a long way to find me just to apologize. Why *did* you come?"

Glen swallowed his protests. Amber could be as stubborn as an elf when she chose to be. At least she was willing to listen. He sat down across the fire from her. "I had a dream."

Amber glanced sharply at him, then took a sip of her serwasn. "Describe it."

"It's only snatches so far. I saw you, in a yellow robe, like the one Calada wears. Only I didn't know what the robe meant until I saw Calada. Calada's apprentice…" He stared into the fire, unsure as to why that image disturbed him now.

"Go on," Amber prodded. "You see me in a yellow robe."

"Surrounded by flames. Gray flames." He shook his head. "That doesn't make sense either."

"No, not now. But it will, Glen. What else?"

"A shadowy figure with gray light in one hand. And a huge wolf running down an alley." He looked up to meet her intent gaze. "That's all. The same dream almost every night for several months now."

"So you came to warn me." Amber studied her serwasn. "I see. I thank you for the warning, Glen. Will you be leaving for Clearwater Ford in the morning?"

"Leaving? Amber, I didn't come just to warn you! I came because I thought you were in trouble! Or will be."

Amber looked puzzled. "But, Glen, surely you realize that if I am wearing Calada's colors in this dream of yours, what you see won't take place for quite some time."

"And I will be near until then," Glen insisted stubbornly. "I owe you a life."

"I don't want you around!" She bit her lip. "Glen, we've exchanged life-debts so often that who owes whom no longer matters. You owe me nothing."

"I'm staying."

Amber looked thoughtfully at him. For a moment her expression softened. Then she frowned and shook her head. "No. You have gone your way, and I am going mine. I neither need nor want your help."

"You're getting it whether you want it or not. I'm coming with you."

Amber scowled at him. "I wouldn't suggest trying."

"There's little you can do to stop me. If you won't let me come along, I'll simply follow you."

* * *

Glen awoke early the next morning. He looked about for Amber and smiled ruefully when he didn't see her. Somehow he had expected her to be gone when he awoke.

His dagger was stuck in the ground beside him. Scratched in the soft dirt beyond it was the Guild's code ciphers for "Don't follow." Glen pulled his dagger out and shook his head in amusement. He had expected Amber to leave a warning message like that. Not that he intended to obey it.

He smiled and stretched, then suddenly frowned and stared at his feet. He hadn't expected her to take his boots.

He sat up and glanced towards where he had left his pack. The pack and his sword were also gone. Only the empty scabbard remained.

"*Amber*!"

When he caught up the scabbard, he found another message scratched in the ground beside it: "Check the trees."

Since Amber had also swept the ground clear of any tracks, it took Glen most of the morning to find his pack and one boot. He counted himself fortunate that Amber had picked easy-to-climb trees. With her ability to move things without touching them, she could very easily have lifted his boots into the most prickly trees in the forest. Her anger had cooled since last winter in Clearwater Ford.

Last winter in Clearwater Ford. What had he said to make her so angry? And hurt. He knew he had hurt her somehow. What had he said?

It couldn't have simply been that he had betrayed her secret, although that was bad enough. His ability to dream true was much easier to hide than her magic. If they had been among only traders that night, his slip would not have been so serious. Those of the Guild were accustomed to magic. But to the city dwellers—the kingdom humans—magic could only be evil. He had placed her in great danger by babbling her secret to an innful of strangers. But he had never known her to run from danger before. What else had he done?

Glen sighed wearily and leaned against a tree. Amber had outsmarted him this time, but not by as much as she may have thought. He had not told her all of his dream. Whatever danger faced her this time, he knew, would come soon, within a city or town. The nearest such that he knew of from his travels was the walled city of Bluefield. Once he found his sword and remaining boot, he would head directly there, without wasting time trying to pick up her trail.

He stared up into the branches overhead, hoping to catch a gleam of metal, then moved on to the next tree.

*   *   *

Five days later, Glen stretched out comfortably upon his cloak and stared absently up into the star-studded sky. He had reached the hills above Bluefield just as the city gates were closing for the night. Although he had seen no sign of Amber's trail on his way here, he knew she could only be a day or so ahead of him. Once the gates opened in the morning, he would soon find her in Bluefield.

On that confident thought, he closed his eyes and fell instantly into a dream.

He stood in gray fog, silent and still. Suddenly, he heard a voice filled with despair. Amber's voice. "Help me, Calada! I can't handle this alone!"

A patch of fog before him dissolved into gray flames, curling and leaping about a column of yellow light. The light solidified into Amber, her long hair—as yellow as the robe she wore—unbound and flowing down her back. Amber turned away from him, looking at something behind her, and the gray flames rose up, engulfing her—and vanished.

Amber was gone. Empty darkness surrounded him. Then a spark of gray light appeared in the direction Amber had faced before her disappearance. Slowly the spark drew closer, until Glen could almost distinguish the outline of the figure which bore the light.

The light grew brighter, illuminating the furnishings of a small room, but somehow leaving the strange figure in shadow. The room abruptly came alive. Chairs and small objects flew through the air as if tossed by unseen hands. A cloak wrapped itself about the figure's head.

"Calada! Help me!"

Glen snapped awake. His breathing slowed as he listened to the night insects and felt a light breeze dry the sweat on his brow. "It's close," he said, his voice shaking. "Soon, now."

* * *

Glen looked about the small room in dismay. The tumbled chairs and broken pitcher and bowl rested exactly where he had seen them in his dream. Amber's cloak lay in shreds in the center of the room.

He sat down cautiously on the edge of the bed, regretting the time it had taken him to check the three previous inns. He stared dumbly at the wreckage.

He was too late. Amber had not won this fight. Her pack, bow, and sword were still in the room; she would not have willingly left them behind. What could have happened after her fight with the shadowed sorcerer? Where was Amber now?

He refused to believe her dead. If death had met her last night, his dreams would have warned him long before. No, Amber may have been captured or hurt or both last night, but she was alive. And in need of whatever help he could give, since Calada would not.

He heard the innkeeper's grumblings drawing nearer in the hall and quickly added Amber's possessions to his own. He looked over the room one last time and saw something yellow move outside the small window. Reaching the window in two quick steps, he was disappointed to find only a yellow cat seated on the window ledge.

"...and who's going to pay for all this damage, I ask you?" the innkeeper demanded, finishing his tirade in the doorway.

"Nothing broken but pottery, good sir," Glen disagreed, "and two coppers should more than cover the cost of replacing it."

"Four."

"Two," Glen said firmly.

"Two it is, then," the innkeeper sighed. "I should know better than to haggle with a Free Trader." His eyes glinted as Glen dropped the beads into his pudgy hand. "From a King's Trader, I'd have gotten four."

"Possibly." Glen shrugged. "Or nothing but the point of his sword." He suppressed a smile at the innkeeper's suddenly frightened expression and added, "Now, good sir, would you know in which direction the Guildhall lies?"

After leaving the inn, Glen spent some time studying the alley outside the window of Amber's room. The yellow cat watched with interest from the window ledge as Glen examined the ground beneath. He rose slowly to his feet. "She didn't leave through the door, and she didn't leave through the window," he mused aloud.

"Mrow?"

Glen looked up, but the cat was watching a tabby prowling the far side of the alley. He walked away from the window, studying the ground.

"But someone stood over here last night. Waiting for Amber? Must have been the sorcerer, since the footprints end right in the middle of the alley." Glen picked up a withered leaf from beside the last footprint. He sniffed at the leaf and broke into a paroxysm of coughing. Flinging it down, he scuffed dirt over it with his boot and staggered over to lean against the wall of the inn, still coughing weakly. "Shadows!" he cursed as he wiped his streaming eyes. "Amber's tangled with a tragleaf chewer!"

He stared thoughtfully at the wrinkled leaf half buried in the dirt. The trag plant grew only about the Shadows' ancient lairs, abandoned long before human or elf had entered the Lands. Trolls and ogres relished the plant, but even the leaves were pure poison to an elf. It was said that chewing tragleaf could enhance magical powers, but it was also said the price of such powers was high. Any user of tragleaf—according to legend—would gradually come under the Shadows' domination, and eventually be controlled completely by those wraithlike beings from their distant place of imprisonment.

With a shudder, he stood away from the wall and made a simple Green Blessing over the leaf. The loose dirt covering settled as the leaf dissolved into dust.

Glen shivered again, then glanced up at the overcast sky and pulled his cloak out of the pack. Shrugging it on, he looked once more about the alley, then started for the Guildhall.

He had not gone far before an ill-featured man in the livery of someone of rank stepped directly into his path and waited, callused fingers near the hilt of his sword. Noticing another swordsman flanking him on the right, Glen stopped and studied the badges on their sleeves. Servants of a demar, at the least, although from their looks alone, Glen would have thought them more hired mercenaries. He did not at first notice the richly dressed woman beside the second swordsman until she moved forward.

Wealth was reflected in the gems studding her long belt, arrogance in the tilt of the head with its coils of black hair, but Glen noticed a hint of surprise in her dark eyes. "How may I help you, Lady?" he asked with a slight bow.

"Bow lower to the tomarch," the fellow on his right growled, stepping forward.

Glen moved easily out of the guard's reach, at the same time swinging his cloak back over his shoulder to free his sword arm. The Guild owed allegiance to no king or lord.

"Enough, Rantig," the tomarch snapped. Her expression was thoughtful when she turned back to Glen. "I have seen that attire before."

"Possibly, Tomarch," Glen said patiently. "I am of the Guild of Free Traders; many of us who travel with the caravans wear these colors."

"Ah, a Free Trader." She straightened the folds of her embroidered sleeve. "Tell me, Trader, have you seen a yellow cat?"

Glen mentally sighed. The whims of petty lordlings! "There was one in the alley beside that small inn," he said, pointing.

"Thank you, Trader. Rantig!"

The guard obediently trotted down the street. The tomarch turned to her second guard. "Move aside and let the Trader pass."

"Thank you, Tomarch." Glen inclined his head to her as he left.

When he reached the next side street, he turned and looked back. Rantig was just emerging from the alley, shaking his head in negation. At his heels trotted a large wolf-dog.

Glen ducked into the side street as the tomarch and her guards turned in his direction. Questions chased each other through his mind. Was that dog the wolf he had seen in his dream? What did it mean?

His unanswered questions soon multiplied when he reached the Guildhall. None of the Guild residing at the Hall had seen Amber anywhere in Bluefield. Nor had any heard word of a user of magic in the city or vicinity. But, as he had hoped, a few of the Hall residents knew Amber by sight, and these promised what aid they could in finding her.

After stowing his and Amber's gear in one of the rooms set aside for traveling members of the Guild, Glen went out to search again. So far he had more questions than answers, and the most urgent of those was Amber's present whereabouts. That she was still in Bluefield he was certain, for his dreams had contained a city's streets and alleyways. But where was she? What had she sought here?

He had not gone far from the Guildhall before he sensed that he was being followed. His pursuer seemed to be an expert at the game of hunter and hunted, for Glen could neither lose nor catch sight of his follower. Only the faint sense of *presence* nagged him from behind.

Glen walked, hoping his pursuer would soon tire of his seemingly patternless stroll. Glen himself did not know exactly what he sought, but he knew his dream would guide him. If street-rumor did not already know Amber's location.

Rumor knew more about a murder only six days past. A wealthy man of learning had been found on the Street of Silence, dead of a broken spine. Toothmarks on the body had led some to believe that a wild animal had been responsible, but none knew of an animal so large it could seize a grown man in its jaws and at the same time be small enough to hide in the narrow streets of the city.

Glen asked about the black-haired tomarch and found that she had arrived in the city but a few days before the murder, as had also a strange hunch-backed man calling himself the Great Ganet, who juggled and did small tricks.

Intrigued, Glen tried to locate the juggler, only to discover that he had disappeared as mysteriously as had Amber.

Glen walked on. By late afternoon he abruptly came upon a wide alley and stopped as if he had been struck. Here was a place from his dream, exact in every detail. Several unsteady stacks of crates—taller than himself—leaned against the wall to his right. Down the wall on his left marched a line of empty barrels and kegs awaiting the brewer's wagon, and on the door in the left wall was a faded and chipped painting of an auroch.

"Mrrof?"

Glen turned away from the door at the sound, then relaxed as a cat emerged from behind a barrel. It looked up him with enormous blue eyes. “Mrrof?”

Glen smiled at the small bundle of yellow fur. “I didn’t see you in my dream.” He turned and studied the alley carefully, looking for other doors in the stretches of walls. “Now what could be so important about this alley?” He glanced over his shoulder, suddenly realizing that he no longer sensed his persistent follower.

The cat stretched lazily. It padded after him as he walked down the alley a short distance in each direction. Finally, Glen returned to the door, upended a keg, and sat down. The cat sat a short distance away and began cautiously licking a scratch along its side.

Glen frowned thoughtfully as he studied the alley. “Not a sign of her anywhere. Amber knew I wasn’t far behind her. If she was free, she would be trying to find me. She’s not a wizard yet, thank the Green; she wouldn’t be foolish enough to refuse aid freely given. She must have been captured. And I can’t find her!”

Glen looked up at the dark clouds and sighed. “Amber has to be somewhere in this city. I *will* find her. Even if she believes I came only for the life-debt!” He rose to his feet and went over to study the crates again. The cat scampered after him.

Glen heard the cat give a startled hiss, then begin a steady, threatening growl. Surprised, he glanced down and saw that the cat was staring at something behind him. At the same time he felt a familiar presence. Turning, he saw a large wolf-dog seated in the entrance to the alley.

He looked at the other end of the alley and saw two guards in a familiar livery advancing toward him, their swords drawn.

Reaching for his own sword, he turned back to the other entrance, prepared to dispatch the dog if it attacked, but froze before his sword left its scabbard. An archer stood behind the dog, an arrow drawn and ready. Beside the archer was another swordsman.

“What do you want?” Glen asked, letting his sword fall back into its sheath. The cat’s growls grew louder.

The dog began a steady, deliberate advance. The cat stood its ground at first, then, slowly, it gave way until it was backed up almost against Glen’s boots.

“What game is this?” Glen demanded as the guards advanced.

“No game at all, Trader.” The black-haired tomarch moved into the alley entrance to stand beside the archer. She walked slowly toward Glen. “No game at all.” She looked down at the cat at Glen’s feet. “You have my cat, Trader. Give her to me.”

Glen looked down at the growling cat and then back up at the tomarch. "If this is your cat, Tomarch, *you* pick it up."

Color flared high on the tomarch's cheekbones. "Rantig!" she said in a dangerous voice.

Rantig bent and reached for the cat. With a savage yowl, the cat lunged at him, claws extended. Rantig almost fell over as he backed away, his hands bloody.

The tomarch reached for the folds of her sleeve. The snarling cat sprang at her, sinking claws and teeth into that sleeve. Screaming shrilly, the tomarch shook it loose, and the cat landed to speed away down the alley, avoiding the two guards with ease. The archer shot an arrow after it, but almost hit one of the guards instead.

The tomarch searched her ripped sleeve frantically. "It's gone! She's taken it! Go after it, Darkling!" Her voice suddenly became cold and deadly. "And make certain you kill it this time."

The wolf-dog whined and dashed away.

The tomarch turned back to Glen. "And as for you," she said, her tone still deadly, "I don't know how you managed to break into my house, but I do wonder how you could believe that vandalism like that would go unpunished. I am not wholly dependent on my potions."

Glen stared at her. "Your house? I don't know what you're talking about, Tomarch."

The tomarch examined her clawed arm. "Don't play the fool with me, Trader. You arrived in this city but a day after another thief, who was also attired in the same garb as yourself."

"You can't go around 'punishing' people for the clothes they wear!" Glen protested. Inwardly he was wondering. Amber? Did she mean Amber?

The tomarch eyed him. "Yes, I think the same punishment would be suitable for you as well." She turned to her guards. "Teach him some manners and then bring him to me."

Glen glanced at the watchful archer and carefully eased back toward the crates.

"You will not enjoy our next meeting, Trader," the tomarch said with a vicious smile. She pulled a small wrinkled leaf from a pouch at her belt and placed it into her mouth. Glen watched in shock and horror as she disappeared like a shadow in bright sunlight.

"You two can start," Rantig said, walking over to lean against the far wall and study his scratches. "Scargat will watch in case that cat comes back this way."

"And aim at the cat this time, Scargat," one guard growled, "not at me."

The three guards turned as a cat's yowl of pain and fear echoed down the alley. "Darkling's getting careless," Rantig commented. "Killed seven men last month and now he's taken all day just to kill one cat."

"She's had him hunt too many small animals of late," one swordsman commented. "Vermin are too easy to kill; he's lost his speed."

"Just don't take too long with this one," Scargat said. He glanced uneasily at the entrance to the alley. "You know how she hates to wait."

"Then she won't like this," Glen said. He had unobtrusively drawn his dagger while the archer's attention had been distracted. Now, in one swift motion, he hurled it at Scargat, then whirled and pushed the crates beside him on top of the two nearest guards. His sword rasped from its scabbard.

Rantig's blood-slick hands fumbled on the hilt of his sword. He swung clumsily at the trader, and Glen leaped back to avoid the cut, then lunged. Rantig died without a sound.

With a glance at the two guards wading through the wreckage of the crates, Glen stepped quickly over to the fallen archer. His dagger had snapped the bowstring before burying itself in the man's chest. With a muttered, "Oh well, I don't like to use bows anyhow," Glen retrieved his dagger and turned to face the approaching guards.

These two were obviously accustomed to fighting. One's nose was bent as if it had been broken several times before, and the second had an old knife scar that had split one eyebrow in two.

Splitbrow charged with a two-handed chop at Glen's shoulder and Bentnose swung for the trader's head. Glen leaped out of Bentnose's way and swung low, drawing blood from a slash on Splitbrow's leg. Splitbrow stumbled back, and Glen parried Bentnose's next overhead swing. He lost sight of Splitbrow, but only had a moment to wonder where the second guard had gone.

Bentnose swung forward with a cut aimed at Glen's midsection and Glen began to step back. Abruptly he was shoved hard to the side, out of Bentnose's path, and into the alley wall.

The trader turned, looking to see who had pushed him, and instead saw Bentnose impaled on Splitbrow's sword. Bentnose's swing aimed at Glen had obviously connected with Splitbrow, for the smaller man was doubled over, grasping his midriff. Glen watched as he slowly collapsed.

Bentnose staggered, his eyes bewildered. "How…did you move so fast?"

"He pushed me," Glen said as Bentnose's eyes glazed and the man fell to the ground. "Didn't he?"

Glen rubbed his right arm thoughtfully as he stared at the fallen men. Who had shoved him out of danger? No one had been near besides the guards, and neither of them had any reason to save him. "Amber? Amber, are you here?"

Silence answered him. Keeping his sword unsheathed, he edged cautiously around the scattered crates and walked farther down the alley, glancing warily at shadows.

A short distance away, the alley narrowed and split into two branches. One branch led into a dead end. He was about to leave, when he saw a dark bundle along the base of one wall. He went closer, and his breath caught in his throat.

The wolf, shrunken in death, looked as though it had been slammed into the wall. Glen swallowed and started to back away.

To his knowledge, Amber had never before used her ability to kill. To kill with magic was a thing best left to full wizards. At the least, the backlash of energy would be painful indeed, but there were tales of those whose use of magic for death had left them open to attack by the Shadows.

Glen stared at the dead wolf. "Am—"

Abruptly a change came over the body, as if a dark shadow had flowed over it. Its outlines seemed to ripple and blur until the wolf was gone and a man's body lay huddled against the wall.

Glen stared at it in amazement, half expecting it to change again. He started to reach forward to touch the dark-clothed shoulder, then pulled back at a sudden thought. "By the Green! That cat! Amber!"

He ran out of the dead end, then stopped short as gray fire blazed up across the alley from him. Seated in the center of the flames was a yellow cat, one white foot resting securely on a short rod of gray.

The gray flames rose higher. The outline of the cat suddenly wavered and dissolved into a column of yellow light. Slowly, the light reformed into a familiar figure, robed and hooded in yellow. Then the gray fire vanished and Amber stood before him, clad in her normal travel garb.

Amber opened her eyes and glanced down at herself. "I…did it!" She swayed, catching herself with one hand against the alley wall. A gray rod fell from her other hand.

"Amber!" Glen ran towards her.

The blonde trader held her head a moment, then straightened. The gray rod flew to her waiting hand. "I'm sorry I put you in danger, Glen," she said, avoiding his gaze, "but it was the only way I could get the Graylod back from her."

Glen nodded. Amber was back to normal. He glanced at the branching alleyway, thinking to ask her about the wolf, then saw that she had paled at his movement. He left the question unasked. "You pushed me out of danger back there. Now I owe you two lives."

Amber glanced askance at him and gave a faint sigh. "Where's my gear?"

"At the Guildhall. Weren't you following me?"

"I had better things to do than follow you. One was to make certain that that tomarch shapechanges no one else for a time."

"*You* broke into her house!"

Amber nodded. "Smashed every last bottle and jar I could find. Also destroyed her store of tragleaf. All she has left is that in her pouch." She glanced at the deepening shadows. "And that much will probably be all she needs to destroy us. We'd best leave while we can; we can return for our belongings some other time."

"Amber, wait." Glen caught her free hand. "Amber, couldn't you have tried to tell me that you were the cat?"

Puzzlement was in the blue eyes as Amber searched his face. Then wariness took over, and she pulled free of his grasp. "This is *my* quest, Glen. I had to find the Graylod here" —she hefted the small rod— "and bring it back to Calada. Only I didn't know our Shadow-touched tomarch was looking for it as well."

She looked at the gray rod in the palm of her hand. "I'm only glad she used the Graylod to shapechange me. I might have had trouble breaking the spell if she had used her potions."

"How did she get the Graylod?" Glen asked, confused.

Amber glared at him. "Because I was stupid enough to put it down. She must have followed me when I retrieved it from its hiding place. I went back to the inn, set it down, walked away, and poof! She appeared, snatched up the Graylod and turned me into a cat. A fine wizard's apprentice I turned out to be!"

Glen suppressed a smile. "At least you got it back."

"Yes, but I won't have it long if we stay here. She's the impatient type; she might come looking for....Darkling and the Graylod." She began to tuck the short rod into her belt. "Come, the gates are this way—" She stopped, staring, as the Graylod began to glow. She looked down the alley and caught Glen's arm as he took a step. "Look."

Tendrils of dark smoke drifted lazily down the alley toward them. Glen sniffed and started coughing. "Tragleaf! We have to go back!"

"That's what she wants," Amber said grimly. She looked at the short rod in her hand. "I wish I knew how to use this." She stared into its glow.

"Amber!" Glen caught her arm.

"It answered me when Darkling had me trapped, Glen. I had only intended to push him aside. But I had the Graylod. It *answered* me, Glen. You saw how I broke the shapechange spell on myself."

"Yes, I saw." Glen coughed, saddened by the excitement in Amber's eyes.

Amber glanced at him. Coughing, she turned and led the way out of the smoke, tucking the Graylod into her belt.

Smoke filled the alley behind them as they returned the way they had come. "Try and stay out of sight," Amber whispered quickly. "I've angered her, but it's the Graylod she wants."

"She's not too happy with me, either." He glanced at Amber. "You don't intend to give her the Graylod, do you?" Amber looked sideways at him and Glen nodded. "Thought not. Well, stubborn one, what now?"

Amber scowled. "I have become very tired of all this sneaking about."

"So you plan to face her openly? Who once told me 'I do not fear death, but neither do I willingly seek it?'"

"As I recall, you thought we could take on ten kingsmen with only our daggers. This is different. We know more about the Green and the Shadows than did the city-dwellers she's hunted. Tragleaf dulls the mind. She doesn't know about my ability. The only time she saw me use it, she thought it was backlash from her use of the Graylod."

"How do you know that?"

"I told you that I had better things to do than follow you."

The tomarch waited at the entrance to the alley, her closed fist poised above a small fire burning in the tall brazier beside her. Glen could see the shock and surprise in her face as Amber stopped before the tumbled crates, not far from the fallen bodies of the tomarch's guards. He stepped beside his fellow trader and ignored Amber's frowning glance in his direction.

"You're very wasteful of your tragleaf," Amber commented. "The Shadows must not be too pleased with you."

"You." The tomarch's face grew suddenly ugly. "How did you break free?"

"I'm not as powerless as you think, pawn of Shadows. Did I not find the Graylod, for which you have searched these many years?

"Amber—" Glen whispered warningly.

The tomarch cast the contents of her fist into the fire. A dark, almost violet smoke began to rise. Glen felt a chill run up his spine. "Amber, she's invoking the Shadows against us!"

Amber watched the tomarch. "Not yet." A crate not far from her boot shifted slightly.

The tomarch held up her scratched hand. "I hold here earth, which contains a drop of blood. Your blood, Thief."

Amber tensed, and Glen suddenly remembered the long scratch he had seen on the cat's side.

"And a fragment of cloak which I found on my guard's sword." She smiled viciously. "I warned you, Trader, that you would not enjoy our next meeting." She moved her hand towards the fire.

Several things happened at once. A crate shot into the air and smashed into the tomarch. At the same time, the brazier rocked and began to topple over. The tomarch's hand opened as she fell backwards and a small bit of fabric flew away. A tiny clump of earth, however, fell directly into the cascading embers.

A thin dark bolt flashed out from the hanging smoke, touching Amber's side briefly before it vanished. Amber cried out and fell against Glen.

"Amber!" Glen caught her. He saw that the tomarch was hurriedly trying to right the brazier. The dark smoke above her had dissipated, while that behind him was beginning to thin out and fade. "Amber!"

Amber looked dazed, and her skin was icy to the touch. Glen drew a Green Blessing in the air above her, hoping that it would aid against a Shadow-inflicted wound. Much to his surprise, green light followed his finger as he drew. The symbol hung visible in the air when he finished.

Amber blinked, her eyes focusing on the fading green symbol. "By the Green!" she breathed in awe.

The tomarch had relit the brazier and now emptied her belt pouch into the flames. A thick cloud of dark smoke rose upwards. "Kill them!" she shrieked. "Consume them utterly!"

The dark cloud rolled towards them.

Glen hurriedly drew a Green Blessing in the air before them. As before, green light followed his finger, but it began to fade before he had even finished.

Amber fumbled at her belt, and a short rod appeared in her hand. Its glow filled the alley.

"Kill them!" the tomarch screeched.

Using the rod like a writing stick, Amber swiftly redrew the symbol in the air. Gray light and green formed one atop another and abruptly fused, becoming a bright wall across the alley. The dark cloud rolled into that wall and bounced back.

The violet smoke grew thicker, until Glen could no longer see into it. It filled the alley before the shining wall and again tried to break through. Failing, it grew darker. Violet bolts were spat out towards the wall. Where each bolt touched the barrier, however, a gray or green bolt flashed back into the cloud.

The cloud seemed to recoil. It rolled back, gathering speed as it retreated. The tomarch suddenly screamed, and then the smoke disappeared.

Glen and Amber glanced at each other as the bright wall faded. The alley was empty before them. The tomarch was gone. Even the guards' bodies had vanished without a trace. All that remained was a fallen brazier.

* * *

Glen and Amber stopped in the hills above Bluefield and watched as the city gates closed for the night. Amber adjusted her pack, and Glen was glad to notice that all signs of stiffness from her Shadow-inflicted wound had disappeared. She caught him watching her and frowned. "You didn't have to come just because *I* couldn't stand to be in that city longer than it took to collect our gear." She glanced up at the gathering stars. "I hate cities."

Glen smiled at the reminder of their eternal point of disagreement. To him, cities meant easy trading and wealth. Amber, however, was more content to plod the back ways of hill and dale, haggling endlessly with dwarf or elf. It was an old argument, worn by repetition into a comfortable habit. But somehow he could not say the familiar reply. He turned away with a shrug.

He looked back to see Amber studying him with a puzzled expression in her eyes. "Glen, are you all right?"

Glen straightened. "Me? I'm fine." He looked up as a light sprang into being higher up the slope.

"See how it flashes almost every color of the rainbow," Amber said. "Has to be a wizard's fire. And I'd wager my sword that it's Calada's."

A short time later the two reached the multi-colored fire. "Come, put down your packs, eat and drink," Calada greeted them. "We have much to say to each other, but our tidings can wait."

Seated a short distance from them, she ignored them as they ate, her attention seemingly caught up in the net of bright strands she was weaving. Glen studied her surreptitiously. This was what Amber would become. Separated from other humans by knowledge and time. He remembered Amber's comment about wizards and age and looked closer at the wizard, wondering how many years were hidden under the seeming of a young woman. He glanced at Amber, suddenly painfully aware of the gulf now between them.

As if sensing his gaze, Amber looked up and met his eyes. *Don't go*, he wanted to say—and could not.

Amber set down her mug and rose to her feet. She reached into her belt and drew out the Graylod.

Calada rose gracefully as the trader approached. Amber sighed and slowly put the Graylod into the wizard's waiting hand. "You were right, Calada."

"I am sorry to hear that." The wizard glanced at Glen, then back at her student. "But, even so, I allowed you to attempt a quest on which I would normally send only a full apprentice."

She raised a hand as Amber started to speak. "No, you did not fail me, child. I awarded you my colors when you resisted her first attack."

"But I killed, Calada. Using magic."

"And paid the price of that death." Calada gestured toward Amber's side. "The touch of the Shadows is painful to resist. You confirmed my belief in you. I would be proud to have you as my apprentice, Amber Snowdaughter."

Glen picked up his pack and stole quietly away.

He walked long into the night, his mind in too great a tumult to allow rest. Amber had been right; she had found her own way. How could he have expected that he could resume the same life he had had before Pegeen? That all it needed was a simple apology? He had thought at first that Amber had changed, but perhaps it was only his perception of her that was no longer the same.

His reflections would not allow him to rest even after he had broken his journey for the night. Glen rummaged in his pack and brought out the piece of carving he had been working on during his wanderings before the dreams had appeared. Concentration on the figure taking shape in his hands would be the best way to still his mind.

He had not been working long when a faint sound came to his ear. Listening, he frowned but kept to his carving. "You're quiet, stranger, but not quiet enough."

"You left rather abruptly," Amber said as she stepped out of the night.

Glen kept his attention on his hands. "I thought you'd be glad to see me go." He glanced sideways at her.

Amber shrugged. She leaned against a tree and stared up into the night sky. "Apprentices always go on a quest to find some magical object. Sometimes they're allowed to keep them." She looked at him. "Calada offered me the Graylod."

"I'm glad for you, Amber. You'll make an excellent wizard."

"I guess. Couldn't have succeeded without you, though."

"Ha. You would have managed fine without me. You were right; you didn't need my help."

"Ha, yourself. The debts balance now, Glen."

"Oh no. You saved me from those two—"

"And if you hadn't been around keeping her attention solely on you, I never would have been able to break into her home or get the Graylod back. She would have learned quickly enough of my ability if you hadn't been there to distract her. The debts are balanced and cleared. You no longer need walk halfway across the Free Lands to warn me again."

Glen stared into the fire. "If you say so."

"I do." She was silent a moment. "Glen, what happened to the ring the lordling's daughter gave you? The one you swore would never leave your hand?"

Glen turned his hand and glanced at the bare fingers. "I gave it to Calada in payment for a spell." He looked up and saw that she was frowning thoughtfully.

"A spell with that high a price would only be…" She studied him. "Then, when you appeared so suddenly—"

"Place-shift. It was the only way to reach you in time."

"Oh. Pegeen will be angry."

"Pegeen married the demar her father chose for her in early spring." He stood up and looked full into her eyes. "And save your sympathy, because I'm not sorry about it at all."

Amber looked at him, then nodded. "Where will you go now,

Glen?"

He put his carving away. "I don't know. I had had hopes that maybe you weren't serious about becoming a wizard, that maybe we could partner a few trips again, like before. I've missed those times, Amber."

She turned away. "I have, too."

"I thought at first that I came to warn you because of the life-debt. I was wrong, then...and before. But that's of no value, now that the Graylod is yours. I won't hurt you again, Amber."

He looked up at the sky and noticed the position of the Western Wheel. "The yearly caravan to the Guild festival will be forming soon. I'll probably join it."

"If you try to leave without me," Amber said slowly, a teasingly familiar echo to her words, "I'll simply follow you."

Glen looked at her.

"I gave the Graylod back to Calada, Glen, to hide for the next questing apprentice. She had told me when I first came to her that I didn't really want to become a wizard, and she was right."

Amber shook her head. "The partnership will be different this time." She stood away from the tree and walked closer to him, looking deep into his eyes. "I might look for a wagon at this festival, Glen. Or *was* it only the brandywine that made you say what you did?"

Glen blinked. He had always had to buy the wagons for their trips, since, in the Guild, if a woman purchased a wagon, she was proposing—

"You mean, that night, I told you I—" Glen felt a great weight fall away from his heart. "If you do that, Amber Snowdaughter, I will buy a team of weosun to pull it." He smiled as he added, "And I will make certain that neither of them are shapechanged."

"And Softly Follow" previously appeared in Dragonlore *#4, December 1983.*

THERE WAS A CROOKED STAFF

Mead Mistdaughter froze in the shadow of an oak when moonlight glinted off bared steel not far ahead of her. Trusting in her dark hair and garb to blend her into the night shadows, she cautiously edged forward until she could see without being seen.

Only two ogres this time, rather than the scattered bands of five or six she had skirted as she followed Acorn's trail through this strangely quiet forest. Only two, yet with but a single arrow remaining in her quiver, Mead did not relax her vigilance. Not for the first time did she wish she still possessed her quarterstaff. Foolish of her to have left it with Rand when he and his brother had replaced herself and Acorn Willowdaughter for their shift at tending the grazing herds slowly following the trade caravan. Yet who would have foreseen any attack on the well-defended caravan when even greedy kingsmen no longer tried?

Returning to the caravan from the herds, she and Acorn had reached the edge of the woods when the peaceful night sky had abruptly flared with a shower of blue skysparks. A clear warning to any trader, for Thoor would never needlessly waste valuable tradegoods. But even Mead's recurring secret ability to sense her mother's feelings had not confirmed any danger. Mist felt worried, true, but otherwise safe, calm and unhurt. What could have occurred? And what could gather ogres in such numbers, all better armed than the usual solitary ogre encountered in the mountains?

One ogre turned in her direction and Mead watched and waited, her thoughts seething. Her questions would be more quickly answered if she were free to seek out the caravan, rather than skulking about searching for a lack-witted, city-bred child!

Where was Acorn? None of the ogres so far had held a captive, and Acorn's pale hair betrayed the girl in the deepest shadows. Perhaps by some miracle she had blundered back out of the woods and returned to the herds. Perhaps, but Mead doubted such good fortune.

The watching ogre grunted, sniffing the air, and Mead smiled grimly, confident that it would scent only the loras leaves which she had carefully rubbed into her skin and clothing. If ogres could indeed scent anything above the reek of the ill-cured skins they usually wore, along with remnants of clothing taken from their victims.

The long nose twitched as the ogre sniffed again. The second ogre muttered irritably and the watcher abruptly whirled and cuffed its hairless head. The struck one snarled and was struck again, the blow knocking it into the bushes. The watcher returned to its survey of the woods, until its fellow sprang back at it.

Under cover of the fight, Mead eased through the shadows, thankful that her mother ignored the rulings of petty kings against trade with the Fair Folk. Only the First Born knew how to move without stirring a single leaf, and she now put her playmates' lessons to good use. The sounds of the melee would bring other ogres and, as much as she wished to run, she dared not draw any attention.

She kept moving, the same sense that told her she was heading away from the caravan also insisting that Acorn had gone *this* way. She could not abandon Acorn. Ogres considered human flesh a greater delicacy than that of their own kin. And the child had, in truth, only obeyed Mead's own orders, to run if the two of them were attacked. Mead had not expected to be obeyed so well, however. After all, they had only been attacked by one ogre.

A night bird called in the distance ahead. Mead tensed, recognizing the cry as well as the fact that mothbirds were only found in the eastern highlands. She mimicked the call, adding the "where?" note of the caravan.

Silence answered her. Mead frowned in indecision. Could Acorn know that bird call but not the whistle signals used by traders? A sudden explosion of ogre yells and hoots closer by decided her, and she hurried to see the cause of this battle.

She ducked under a low branch and paused, finding herself at the edge of a small clearing. Within the clearing, three jeering, hooting ogres were closing in on a smaller figure half-hidden by two ogres' backs. Moonlight flashed on the menacing swords, shone suddenly on pale hair.

Mead carefully aimed her last arrow. The ogres toyed with their captive, slowly drawing the ring of steel in about the girl. Her small dagger delayed their teasing grabs, but not for much longer.

Mead's ears caught a soft thud behind her as she released the arrow. She whirled, her dagger out, to find that the low branch had somehow fallen off the tree.

Across the clearing, the ogre nearest the captive had fallen with an arrow through its throat. The two remaining ogres bewilderedly peered into the night, giving their captive enough time to scoop up the sword beside the body.

"Run, Acorn! You don't know how to use a sword!" Slinging her bow onto her back, Mead caught up the long twisted branch and leapt into the clearing with her makeshift staff.

Bellowing, an ogre charged at her with its sword raised. She blocked the blow with the branch and stared in amazement as the ogre backed away, gibbering with fear, its pasty-gray skin turning grayer. She lowered the branch and saw that it had somehow suddenly lost its bark and leaves to become a staff of polished white wood.

Not stopping to question the change, she shifted her grip and drove one end of the staff into the pit of the ogre's stomach. As the creature doubled over, she changed her grip again and brought the thick end down upon its head with all her strength. The dying ogre crashed to the ground, and she ran to Acorn's aid.

The girl was doing surprisingly well, keeping the last ogre so busy that it never noticed Mead's approach until the staff smashed against the back of its bald head.

"Acorn, that was—" She stopped and stared in amazement at the figure wiping her bloody sword on the dead ogre's clothing. "But you're not Acorn," she said foolishly.

The elf pushed her long white blonde hair back out of her face and looked quizzically at Mead with large sea-green eyes. Her gray travel garb was stained and tattered, but something in her manner reminded Mead of those of the High Court.

Automatically, the trader inclined her head and switched to the Common Tongue of the Folk. "Pardon, my lady, but I thought—have you seen a young human girl with very pale hair?" The elf only stared at her, and Mead returned the stare with equal curiosity.

A blonde elf. All the elves Mead knew of—from the Great Woods to the Silvergreen Hills—were dark-haired. And tall, though not as tall as the ogres. This elf stood of a height with Mead herself, who was not uncommonly tall for a human.

Mead swallowed the questions born of her trader's instincts. Now was not the time to ask from where this elf had come. She glanced at the fallen ogres, spying more dead on this side of the clearing. "Are you hurt, my lady? Can you travel? More ogres will come."

She studied the elf again, her thoughts whirling in confusion when her suspicions were confirmed. What in the names of the Eight Human Kingdoms was a pregnant elf doing in an ogre-infested wood?

The elf's sharp-featured face betrayed equal bewilderment. "A human who speaks the Common Tongue!" she exclaimed in Middle Elven with an accent Mead could not place. "What trickery is this?"

The suspicion in her face startled Mead. It was true that some humans were fearful of the Fair Folk, but the mistrust had always before been on the human side alone. "No trickery, Lady," Mead said quickly. "I am friend to First Born," she added in her faltering High Elven.

The elf relaxed her defensive stance, then the distant crashings of heavy bodies through underbrush alerted them both. Mead pointed with the staff. "That way, quickly."

"That way" led among more dead, elf as well as ogre. Ignoring the pursuing danger, the elf knelt beside one still warrior and, after a brief moment, exchanged the ogre sword she carried for an elf blade.

Mead glanced at the pale hair of the dead elves. She must speak soon with this elf about trade rights. Turning to better watch their back trail, Mead wondered when the time would be right for questions. To have stumbled upon a new group of elves in such a manner— She saw the large eyes fasten on her swordless belt and hastily demurred as the elf reached for another sword.

"My thanks, but I prefer a staff to a sword, my lady." She hefted the crooked stave, wondering anew at its strangeness but thankful that its magic had not reacted adversely to her manner of usage.

"To leave them for the ogres..." The elf let the sentence trail off, but Mead felt as sick as if the dead had been her own kin. Had she not come this far to protect Acorn from a similar fate?

Mead peered into the shadows, then glanced back at the elf. "Can you not hide them in some way with your magic, Lady?"

The elf's eyes lit with hope, then faded. "There is no time."

"I will give you the time you need," Mead said firmly. She quickly collected what loose arrows she could. Their eyes met as she turned to leave. "Hurry, Lady. I will do what I can."

She paralleled their back trail for a few yards, looking for a likely spot in which to wait for any pursuers. Abruptly, she stopped, her tracking sense tingling. Acorn! Acorn had passed this way!

But not alone. Her fingertips lightly traced a clear imprint of a small boot among a jumble of ogre tracks. Yet the surrounding brush was not broken or bruised. It was as if the trail had magically closed up behind them. She glanced back to where she had left the elf. The bootprint was fresh; Acorn must have come back this way after going through that place of elfin dead. Perhaps she had been captured there, or soon after.

She marked the place in her memory. Once the Lady was finished with her spell, they would pick up the trail again here. Her hand clenched tightly around the staff. Acorn would not be a captive for long.

She craned for a glimpse of the elf. Mead had only a vague idea of how long such a spell might take; scowling at herself, she realized that she should have set up some form of signal. Yet they seemed to have lost their pursuers. The forest was unnaturally silent.

Mead waited and watched for a few moments more, then turned back towards the elf. The lone mothbird called not far away, and she quickened her pace. The caller might be friendly, but Mead had an uneasy feeling about this forest, and the Lady had faced enough dangers alone.

The clearing was darker than she remembered, filled with deep shadows that moved when she stared too long at them. "Lady?" She took a tighter grip on the staff. Could the ogres have attacked without her hearing? "Lady? The ogres seem to have left." Had the elf left as well?

The drifting shadows stilled. A figure with hair the color of moonlight emerged from the clinging darkness. "It...is done." Wearily she stretched, her elf blade glinting by her side. "The spell will hold. Whither now?"

Mead pointed with her staff. "I stumbled upon my friend's trail back—"

"No! Do not kill!"

Warned by the faint brush of air behind her, Mead had begun to throw herself aside at the elf's cry. Sharp pain struck at either side of her neck, and she was falling.

She suddenly seemed to be slammed into near-blinding white light.

She tried to raise her hand to shield her eyes and discovered that she could not. She did not seem to possess a body here. Yet she could see—if total whiteness was sight—and she could hear a soft whisper of chimes about her.

Mead snorted softly and was surprised to hear the sound. This was not her idea of death, but what, then, had happened?

"What's that? Who's there?" an old crotchety voice suddenly demanded. "Ah, you found a staff, did you? Hee hee, I knew those little toys would locate new wizardlings to train."

"Wizardlings!" Mead laughed. "No, I'm—"

"You are," the voice said testily, "else the staff would not have responded. Now, do go away. I'm rather busy at the moment. When you have learned enough to begin your training, you will find me."

"But—"

"Go away. Shoo. Shoo-shoo."

She was suddenly shoved backwards, out of the light. Darkness surrounded her, and Mead abruptly fell back into her own body, heard the sounds of the forest about her once again.

"Sir, it will not break!" a faraway voice exclaimed in Middle Elven. "Our swords bounce off it!"

"Set it aflame, then," came the reply near Mead's ear. "We must destroy it."

"A fire? With ogres about?" Mead recognized the Lady's voice. "Are you Shadow-touched, kinsman? First you attack one who has done me naught but good and now you wish to destroy her staff? Why?"

"Why? To free you from the enchantment."

The scene above her slowly swam into focus. Feeling queerly light-headed, Mead blinked at the fair-haired elf crouched beside her, his eyes on the Lady above him. Seeing them so, close together as they were, Mead was struck by the resemblance between them. The guard's hair was shorter and more golden than the Lady's, but their features were like enough to be brother and sister.

"To free me from—" the Lady repeated incredulously. "By the Green, what enchantment are *you* under?"

"Truth, Elder," a shadow-hidden elf agreed. "But a few moments past, we all saw a heavily cloaked figure, with a staff like unto that one, leading a group of ogres who held you captive."

"We followed the trail here," her kinsman continued. "Do you deny—"

"I do indeed!"

"Acorn," Mead said fuzzily. Both elves looked at her as she struggled to rise to a sitting position. Her shoulders and neck tingled strangely, and she rubbed the afflicted area, pretending to ignore the dagger in her attacker's hand as well as the watchful swords of the five elves behind him.

Five *blond* elves. She pushed the thoughts that raised, along with the questions of where she had been and what had happened, into a corner of her mind. First she had to concentrate on calming this unusually hostile group of elves.

"They must have seen Acorn. My friend, Lady. She has hair like yours, and at a distance—"

"They could have mistaken her for me as you did," the Lady finished for her with a relieved smile.

"A human who understands our language and speaks the Common Tongue," her guard said wonderingly. Mead was relieved to see him put his dagger away.

"That does not explain why she has this rod of power," another elf said suspiciously, holding up her unsinged staff.

The Lady smiled. "That is but a toy, compared to a true rod of power."

"That's what he called it," Mead said, before she could control her tongue.

The Lady turned to her. "With whom did you speak regarding this? I saw how you found it, saw it change in your hand and your surprise. Who else knows of it?"

Mead rubbed her neck, wishing she had remained silent. "I shall have to learn your manner of attack," she said to the Lady's kinsman. "When you struck me, I was sent somewhere else." She described what had occurred in the space of white light.

"He said 'toys,'" the Lady mused when Mead had finished.

"Humans and magic!" the elf with Mead's staff snorted. "A disastrous combination!"

Mead decided the best thing she could do would be to leave. She looked about for her bow and quiver. "Lady, now that you are safely with your people, I will go rescue my friend."

"But not alone, Lady of the Dark Eyes," her guard disagreed, moving her bow out of her reach. "My debt to you" —he looked toward his kinswoman, who had retrieved the crooked staff, then back at Mead with a winning smile— "is too great." He drew his dagger and offered it hilt first to her with a slight bow. "I am called Taeryelun, my lady."

Stunned at the honor he did her, Mead accepted the gift of dagger and name. "I am Mead, of the Traders' Guild. I thank you for your offer of aid, sir, but surely you do not mean to abandon the Lady?"

"Abandon? No." He settled back and watched the Lady. "If I know the Elder, it will not come to that." A faint smile tugged at a corner of his mouth, and Mead suddenly noticed that her bow and quiver were now within her reach.

The Lady thoughtfully studied the crooked stave in the faint moonlight. She lowered it and studied Mead with eyes that did not seem to see the trader. "Kinsman."

He rose and went to her side. Holding the staff horizontally in her two hands, she met his eyes. "How similar was the staff you saw to this?"

Taeryelun studied the staff without touching it. "The other was as straight as a sword, yet the wood seems like. I had no time to see the aura."

The Lady frowned. "If whom you saw has found another of the aged one's 'toys'…" She broke off and turned toward Mead.

The trader gathered her bow and quiver, very conscious of the eyes watching her, and rose to her feet as the two neared her. She was surprised when the Lady handed her the staff.

"Elder!" came the shocked protest from the watchers.

The Lady did not turn, but spoke directly to Mead. "It is Wild Magic—not of the Green, not against it. The staff is attuned to you, my friend. You will discover how to use it. One does not throw away arrows in enemy territory."

"In truth, Lady, you would be better served to trust my arrows than my wizardry," Mead said ruefully, glancing at the strange staff.

The sea-green eyes searched Mead's face. The Lady opened her lips to speak, perhaps to warn, then closed them with a smile and a shake of her head. "Lead, and we shall follow."

* * *

They moved swiftly through the night. The Lady kept up easily with the pace, despite the small burden she carried. Mead glanced back only once, to reassure herself of that, before concentrating completely on the trail she followed. She could not rid herself of a grim foreboding. It had nothing to do with the caravan, nor with the company she led. It seemed rather to emanate from the woods around her, growing stronger as she advanced. Yet the elves did not appear to sense what she did.

They heard the ogres long before they saw them. At Taeryelun's nod, two of the archers went up into the trees, to spy on their enemies from above. He held Mead back from advancing, instead sending a swordsman forward to scout. The trader, knowing that the elf could move far more silently than she, did not protest. Yet she wished to could see for herself what they faced.

Her hands trembled on the staff. Suddenly it was as if she *could* see! The intervening distance, trees, darkness—all this did not exist. She could see Acorn!

She ignored the feasting ogres, shut out of her mind what they ate under the trees, and instead focused on the girl. No ogres stood between Acorn and where Mead waited, only one hooded figure stood beside her, shaking a white staff menacingly at the cowering girl.

Her sight returned to normal, and Mead stared at her staff in wonder. *This*, a toy? Quickly she tightened her grasp on it and wished that Acorn now stood beside her.

Nothing happened. Mead shook her head at her folly. Truly only a toy, able perhaps to respond to small, simple wishes, but nothing else. She caught the Lady's eyes upon her, and quickly explained to her and to Taeryelun what she had seen. "Acorn is guarded only by that one," she finished. "We should be able to free her and make our escape before the rest realize we were ever there."

Taeryelun glanced upwards to see if the archers were in position. "The risk is great—"

"Not as I will do it," Mead interrupted, a plan forming swiftly. "I will separate Acorn from her guard. You and your people can wait close by, in case what I plan goes awry. I must be the one to do this," she added, looking at the Lady. "Acorn and her kin are unaccustomed to your people. She would flee from anyone else."

The Lady glanced at the staff Mead held. "Do you believe you have uncovered all of its secrets?"

Mead shook her head. "Only the little to aid me now. It will be enough."

"Unless we are mistaken as to the hooded one's source of power," the Lady disagreed. "If that one is instead a full wizard, his spells would be more than I could counter."

While his kinswoman spoke, Taeryelun listened to the returning scout's report. He nodded as the scout finished and signed that he should wait. "Elder, if that one be a wizard, then our only course of safety is to leave now, abandoning his captive. I will not do so. I will follow our trader. Do but signal us before you attack, Mead, and we will provide a distraction."

Mead nodded.

The scout slipped into the shadows, Mead and the remaining elves following. Mead tried once or twice to spot the sharp-eyed archers waiting above, but failed as she had expected to. She took a tighter grip on the staff. So much depended on one wish.

The elves stopped and settled into position. The hoots that were ogrish laughter were almost deafening, but the elves did not speak this near to their enemies. Taeryelun pantomimed smashing someone over the head with a club, then grinned. The Lady made the Green Blessing sign, green light following her fingertip and glowing briefly in the air after she had finished before it faded.

Mead went on alone, working her way cautiously towards where she had last seen Acorn. Her courage almost faltered at her first glimpse of the ogre horde. So many! She was no wizardling; how could she dare play so with magic! This was as ill-advised as sorting Thoor's firestuff by the light of an unshielded candle.

Mead told her fears to quiet. She was Mead, the same Mead who, when her father had been killed by bandits, had helped Mist track down the murderers for killing in their turn. She would endure.

She could hear the hooded one's shouting now, close as she was. The words were in the Common Tongue of the Folk; no wonder the uncomprehending Acorn looked so frightened! The sly child was clever enough to bluff, had she but understood. The hooded one was shouting, "Teach me! Tell me how to further use the staff, elf! You must know! Show me, or I'll feed you to them!"

That threat, accompanied as it was with a gesture towards the feeding ogres, Acorn seemed to partly understand. She shrank away from her captor, bursting into wild sobs when he caught her arm.

With an exclamation of disgust, he flung her away from him. Acorn tripped and fell sprawling on the ground. She stayed there, sobbing hysterically into the long grass. The hooded one leaned on his staff. "You *will* teach me, elf! I will be king!"

Mead seized the moment. Gripping her staff tightly, she concentrated on her wish, that Acorn alone would hear her faint whisper. "Acorn, tis Mead. I am near."

Acorn's sobs faltered and Mead could see the child lifting her head.

"Betray me not!" Mead whispered hurriedly. "Acorn, at my signal, turn to your left and run. Run as fast as you can and stop for nothing but my whistle. Do you understand? Stop when I whistle. I would rather not have to hunt all over the forest for you again. Take heart; you will be free soon."

Acorn's sobs continued, but Mead knew the girl had understood her. Now if she would but obey.

Holding on to the thick but springy branch she had found, Mead glanced once more at the hooded one. Because of his staff, her arrows might serve only to alert him and his ogres. Now, if he but— She froze as she felt the familiar brush of emotions not her own. Mist! Her uncontrollable sense deserted her as quickly as it had appeared, but not before Mead realized that the direction in which she had sensed her mother was not that of the caravan. Mead shut out any thought of worry. Mist was more than capable in any situation, and Mead would need her wits clear for Acorn's rescue.

Holding onto the branch and her staff with one hand, she waved at the waiting elves with the other. Instantly arrows flew deep into the ogre horde. Ogres lunged to their feet, bellowing with fear.

Before Mead could signal Acorn, a bright flash of blue flared on the opposite side of the horde, along with an earthshaking rumble and clouds of smoke. A tree slowly toppled over.

Mead stared. What were the elves doing? She suddenly realized that the hooded one had turned away from Acorn. "Now, Acorn!"

Acorn scrambled to her feet and ran. The hooded one, slow to realize what was taking place, started after her.

Mead let Acorn pass her hiding place, her eyes only on the girl's pursuer. He was almost beside Mead when she whistled sharply and released the branch.

Freed, the branch of the small tree sprang back to its original position—and knocked the hooded one off his feet. The hood fell back and Mead, staff in hand, found herself facing a human-sized ogre!

Surprise slowed her. The short ogre grinned nastily as its fingers ran over the staff on the ground beside it. The stave's outline blurred and the ogre was abruptly holding a long white sword pointed straight at her. The ogre's small eyes, almost hidden beside the big nose, narrowed as it glanced at the staff in Mead's hands. The sword point wavered only a little as the ogre pulled the hood back over its bald head.

Mead shifted her grip on her staff, battle instincts taking over. She nimbly evaded the ogre's thrusting lunge as it regained its feet, but her answering blow against the creature's ribs made her suspect that it wore mail under its cloak.

Raising its sword as it turned, the ogre swung downward. Mead raised the staff to block. The sword and staff crashed together—and the world exploded in a blaze of white light.

Mead felt earth beneath her hands. Her eyes were tearing but she could not see. Her mouth tasted of blood yet she could hear.

An old voice was wailing somewhere. "No, no! What have you done? My beautiful toys, all destroyed!"

"Oh gods!" Acorn moaned sickly.

Mead turned toward the voice. "Acorn?"

There was a small gasp. "Mead, your face!"

Mead carefully felt her face, finding it bloody from a small cut but her features intact. "Never mind my face." She fumbled about for the staff. "Where is the ogre?"

"It's d-dead. It's all burned." Acorn sounded sick again and Mead was suddenly glad that she could not see.

A small hand gripped her shoulder. "Someone's coming, but he doesn't *look* like an ogre."

Mead put her hand over Acorn's to hold the younger girl there. She could hear Taeryelun's voice as he shouted up at the archers. "The ogres' swords have changed into sticks? All? I will inform the Elder. There are humans with firestuff on the other side. Try not to strike them." His voice came closer. "Trader, are you hurt?"

Mead blinked slowly and painfully. She could dimly perceive blotches of light and dark and had decided that the mysterious distant flashes of light she saw must be thrown skysparks, not the result of serious injury to her eyes. "My eyes…the light dazzled them. Acorn says the ogre is dead." She switched to her own language to reassure Acorn.

Acorn needed reassuring. She could feel the girl's hand shaking under her own. Even the news that Mist and perhaps Acorn's own parents were coming did not quiet her. Mead felt the girl's hand jump. "Acorn, stay here! They will not hurt you!"

Delicate fingers touched Mead's face. "Lady?" she asked, forcing herself to remain still.

"I am here. Your people should reach us soon. The ogres scatter like dust before the wind." Her fingers moved lightly around Mead's eyes as she spoke, a soothing coolness spreading in their wake. Mead began to relax under the Lady's ministration.

"M-mead?" came a small voice from behind her.

"All will be well, Acorn. You should be thankful for the Lady. Had you not resembled her so much, the ogres might have killed you. They thought they had captured her when they caught you."

"They thought I looked like *her*?" Mead caught the delight in her voice and relaxed her grip on Acorn's hand.

The Lady laughed. "How pretty she is when she smiles! What did you say to her, Mead?"

"That the ogres thought she looks like you. Lady, why did the ogre die but I live?"

"The recoil of energy from the two staffs' meeting went back along the length of the staffs. You held yours horizontally, and above you. There are" —the Lady's hands went away for a few moments— "burned patches on the nearby trees. The ogre's staff was pointed over your head...and back towards itself."

"A deadly toy," Taeryelun commented.

Mead closed her eyes. White light flickered behind her eyelids and the faint echo of a chime rang softly within her mind. That wizard. Somehow she would have to find that old man.

"But not alone, Lady of the Dark Eyes," Taeryelun said softly.

Mead did not wonder how he knew her thoughts. "Tis my life he had touched with his toys, not yours."

She felt the touch of the Lady's cool hand upon her forehead. "And thus ours is the debt."

Mead sighed inwardly. Far easier to change the sun's course than to win an argument with an elf. And did she truly wish to win this one? Taeryelun's aid alone would be invaluable. And with the Lady's... Mead's careful planning faltered to a halt. With no magic of her own, just what did she expect to do when she finally did meet the old one face to face?

Mead slowly opened her eyes. Her sight was still unclear, but she noticed a slight improvement. "My eyes will heal," she said, not asking.

"Yes," the Lady agreed. "Your eyes are inflamed, but I sensed no lasting injury. Allow them time to rest. Once you are fully recovered, we will—"

"A human approaches," came the warning.

"Mist!" Acorn shouted happily.

Mead dimly saw her mother against the light of skysparks. She could easily picture Mist's quiet study of the unexpected scene. "Well, daughter," Mist finally said in the Common Tongue, a faint tremor in her voice, "did you find looking after Acorn to be as boring as you had expected?"

"There Was a Crooked Staff" previously appeared in Errantry *#1, May 1983.*

THERE WAS A BROKEN ARROW

The soft murmur of voices that had filled Mead Mistdaughter's dreams became clearer upon her awakening.

"Another caravan follows ours," Mist was explaining in the Common Tongue of the Folk. "We will not move on until the threat of further ogre attack is gone. When the light increases and we can better control the weosun, we will bring our herds through."

Taeryelun's voice groaned. "They *herd* weosun!" he muttered swiftly in Middle Elven. "You spoke truth, Elder. Humans lack knowledge of fear." He switched back to the Common Tongue, and Mead sleepily remembered his puzzlement upon learning that her mother did not understand the Elven tongues. "Why do your people tame the most dangerous grass-eaters about, Trader?"

Mist laughed softly. "Tame? No one tames the weosun, Leader. They pull our wagons, give us milk and wool, and of course their deep hatred of ogres and goblins can be most useful. But…"

Most useful indeed, Mead agreed, the voices blurring as she fell back into sleep. If the ogres had not attacked at night, the long-horned, shaggy-coated weosun would have made short work of the creatures, magical swords or no. But then she would never had met the Lady—the blonde elf Elder and her equally blond escort now speaking with Mist—nor would she have found that crooked staff and been forced to do battle with the hooded ogre, itself also the finder of a magical staff. Of course, she reminded herself, if Acorn Willowdaughter had stayed by her side, rather than wandering into the grasp of the hooded ogre, the deeds of the previous night would have been vastly different.

Mead wondered idly with what Mist had dosed her to make her so loath to wake. Slowly she opened her eyes to a whiteness almost as blinding as that which had filled her eyes when the two staffs had met and destroyed each other. Soft chimes rang now in her ears, and Mead suddenly realized that she was no longer within her body. "Wizard," she called. "I would speak with you."

"I will grant you another chance," the crotchety old voice she remembered remarked testily. " 'Ware your thoughtlessly destructive tendencies this time."

"But I have no desire to become a wizardling," Mead said patiently. One did not yell at a wizard, no matter how much one wished to. "Old one, you must find another way to locate students. Your toys are endangering many lives."

"You are what you are, wizardling. When you have learned enough to begin your training, you will find me."

"Listen to me, wizard! You must stop this—"

"I am very busy now. Go away. Shoo."

She abruptly fell back into her body and for a moment wondered if she had landed on her head. Why else did it ache so? Her face was wet, and her questing fingers found a soaked cloth over her eyes. Pulling that aside and opening her eyes, she quickly closed them at the sharp dazzle of sunlight. Mead reasoned with herself that it was yet early morning and the sunlight could not be unbearably bright, especially since she had fallen asleep under the wagon. Unheeding, the dull ache in her head intensified behind her closed eyelids.

"...season, our people come together for a ... tradegather," Mist was saying from somewhere nearby, substituting Trade words for what was otherwise untranslatable. "A time of bargaining and bonding and the telling of news from among the Kingdoms and Folk."

"And you are on your way to this...meet at present." Taeryelun, surprisingly, sounded interested. Mead wondered what had happened to the Taeryelun who had been so suspicious of humans. "And this meet is for only people like yourselves?"

"The Traders' Guild, yes. And guests of Traders, if you would care to come."

"As guests? You would permit— This meet is not for humans alone?"

Mead smiled faintly. Ah, there was the Taeryelun she had met. She slowly opened her eyes to the merest slit.

"Ah, judge us not by the kingdom dwellers," Mist said. "The

Traders' Guild is not wholly of humankind, much as the kings pretend us to be. There are also those elves and dwarves and others of the Folk who do not like to be tied to one place."

"Tied," Taeryelun repeated softly, and Mead wondered at what she heard in his voice. He added in a more normal tone, "As does this weosun calf dislike being on your tether, missing the opportunity to hunt with his mother."

The sunlight was not too bright when viewed from a slit. Mead cautiously opened her eyes farther, blinking painfully in an attempt to resolve the blurred shapes outside the dim shadows under the wagon Her eyes felt as if they were full of grit. Mindful of the wagon above, she levered herself up on one elbow and held the damp cloth against her eyes for a moment. Finding some measure of relief from that, she held the cloth against one eye at a time and absently tried to place its herbal scent. She stared at her hand and felt fear withdraw. She could see!

"Kinsman," the Lady teased softly in Middle Elven, "one could almost believe that you were the one leaving the Highlands, not I."

Mead peered at the dark blurs, waiting as they resolved into cloaks and boots—one pair in close company with the spindly legs of a young weosun.

"We share the same blood, Elder," Taeryelun said slowly. "The more I see of the lands Outside, the more I wish to see. Your decision to bear your child among his father's people has—by this journey—opened my eyes to the prison the Highlands have become for me."

The Lady's voice held an undercurrent of worry. "You should not speak thusly! What if you are overheard?"

"What remains of my command watches the great hunt of ogres by weosun. Only my second is within call. He did not wholly trust our safety amid these humans." And that, Mead thought indignantly, after she and Mist had moved their wagon far from the caravan! "Fear not for me, Elder. He will not betray me."

The Lady sighed. "Ah, kinsman. The Council believed—after our people's differences with his—that mine was a marriage of duty, and little realized that I had found my heart. If they had, I do not think they would have permitted me to leave for any space of time. And had I known the cost in lives… I would fain not lose you to the outlaw horn."

"Nay, Elder, I am no oathbreaker."

"What then do you plan?"

"I gave my word to deliver you safely to your consort. I shall abide by that. Afterwards...I have not thought as yet. Perhaps, fearful of your safety amid our distant brethren of the Great Woods—"

The Lady made a choked sound.

"—I could stay on, to protect you for a time. If you but permit. The Outside beckons me and I would see more ere I return. My second can lead the others home."

"If he could desert you in such danger," the Lady teased him. Her tone turned thoughtful. "He still has a time ere he can assume his command. This wizard—"

"Aye, the dark-eyed Lady has need of our aid. How does she—"

Mead heard a rustle of cloth, but before she could play-act ignorance there came a twinge of fear from her mother's mind, the demanding bawl of a weosun calf, and a half-smothered exclamation in Elven. A head of bright shaggy brown, not the silken blond strands of an elf, invaded her resting place, and the body attached to the head would have followed if the wagon had been but a fingerspan higher off the ground.

With the ease of long practice Mead evaded the weosun's large tongue and scratched the youngling's horn buds, hearing Mist's apologies drift closer. A moment later Mist herself peered under the wagon.

Mead blinked. A multicolored light had seemingly flashed before her eyes when Mist appeared, but now she could once again see the familiar features, the long hair—lighter than Mead's own—pulled into a single braid, and the dark-lashed hazel eyes—so small compared to the large eyes of an elf—which now watched her with worry in their depths.

"A timely rescue, Mother," Mead said softly in the Trade tongue, "as always."

Mist cocked her head. "The little one knew the moment you woke, and our guests so intent upon their conversation, why need I remind them that you understood what I could not? Your sight has cleared?"

"Somewhat." Fending the calf off with one hand, Mead shaded her eyes with the other and edged forward. She saw the Lady's boots beyond Mist and switched to the Common Tongue. "I can see, but the light still pains me."

Mist slipped off the weosun's leash and slapped his rump. "Guard, Toh." The calf met her gaze, then backed out from under the wagon and scampered away.

Mead opened her mouth to warn about the elf watching their camp, then closed it with the warning unsaid. A watchful weosun was what that suspicious one deserved. Mist nodded slightly and murmured in Trade, "There is one in the trees. We should hear Toh's challenge soon."

Mead stifled a smile and held still as Mist studied her eyes. "The day will have clouds," Mist said thoughtfully, slipping back into the Common Tongue, "but you should keep to the shadows." She turned back to the elves. "I would be honored for your opinion, Wise One." Hidden by her body, Mist's long fingers flashed in the signal for "talk later." Mead touched her sleeve lightly to indicate her understanding.

Mist backed away to allow the Lady access and Mead followed, determined that the Lady should not have to crawl under a wagon. She came close to regretting her decision as she emerged from under the wagon.

Green light filled her eyes, near blinding in intensity directly before her, but muted to a cooler greenness towards her left. She flung up one hand and closed her eyes.

"Mead!" Mist's strong grip on her other arm maintained her balance. "Sit, daughter."

"So bright." Mead obeyed and felt cool fingertips lightly touch her eyelids. She lowered her hand, feeling foolish.

"No, not foolish, my friend," the Lady said softly.

A loud triumphant bawl of a weosun calf—nowhere near the majestic tones it would reach as an adult—suddenly split the air, followed shortly after by the solid crack of a hard skull against wood.

"Toh found someone," Mist said unnecessarily. "I must go; he will not abandon his prey and it might only be one of the traders."

"I will come as well," Taeryelun agreed.

The bawl came again. "This way, then, Leader!"

Mead cautiously opened her eyes. The light was bearable, not painful at all. She smiled at the elf crouched before her. "My thanks, Lady."

"Look towards me."

Mead obeyed. She had not had many opportunities last night to see this elf so clearly and she had wondered what other differences this short, white-blonde elf possessed from the taller, dark-haired elves of the Great Woods. The light of day did not reveal any more, however. The Lady's large eyes, like those of any elf, dominated the rest of her face so greatly that her nose and mouth seemed very small in comparison. She stared into their sea-green depths for a moment, wondering just what the Lady beheld when she looked at the human opposite her. How had this group of elves become so wary of humans? And where were these Highlands of which she and her kinsman had spoken? Mead bit back the questions she wanted to ask. After what she had overheard, her hopes of trade with these elves seemed as probable of coming true as Toh toppling the tree the elf second was in. She swallowed a smile.

"Now look to the side. No, move only your eyes."

Mead saw that the Lady had changed her stained and tattered garb for fresher apparel. She had not seen any packs last night, but if the Lady was indeed moving to the Great Woods, she would have baggage. And with the ogres retreating, her escort could have easily found wherever their belongings had been dropped in the attack.

"Can you look into that patch of sunlight?"

Mead cautiously slid her gaze over to where the wagon wheel was bathed in light. She blinked. No pain. Greatly daring, she looked upwards to find the sun shining amid the treetops. "Again my thanks, Lady. Sunlight no longer pains me."

"Your eyes but needed rest and time to adjust," the Lady said slowly. Mead turned toward the elf and wondered at her thoughtful expression. The Lady extended her hand. "What color do you see?"

"Color, my lady? I see the pink of your hand and the gray of your sleeve." Mead was puzzled and troubled at the Lady's expression.

"Naught else?"

Mead looked again. "Naught. Why, my lady? What do you fear? My sight—"

"—is well. I but feared that mayhap sunlight was not the cause of your hurt." The Lady studied Mead's face, then sighed softly. "You are a mystery to me, my friend. From birth I have been told so many tales about humans and yet you and your mother are not like unto those people."

Mead smiled. "I will not ask 'how so,' my lady. I have heard too many tales of how kingdom dwellers see elves to know the fallacy of such." She shook her head. "But such tales are born when people come not into contact. Never had I heard of elves isolated as are kingdom dwellers. Your people would not then welcome trade?"

The Lady laughed. "And thus speaks the Trader. 'S'truth, I fear they would welcome you not, not even on my bidding. Doubly so when I shall not return thence for many a year."

"Ah." Mead felt relieved, and then guilty, that she was thus able to put away the trader in her. "Lady, I would not pry whither you go. But—" She paused, hearing a familiar step. Toh suddenly burst from the brush and scampered to her side. He nudged Mead, and she obediently scratched his horn buds.

"But," Mist continued, following the weosun more sedately, "their guide was among the first to perish in the ogre attack. Is that not so, Wise One?"

Mead raised an eyebrow at the older trader over the calf's shaggy back, thankful that she had told Mist about the wizard. Was there any misfortune that Mist could not turn to some benefit?

Toh switched his attention to the elf and the Lady indulgently patted the young weosun. "And what did this small one find?"

Mist's eyes twinkled. "Your pardon, Wise One. I had not realized when I set Toh to guard that one of your people had decided upon the same project. Toh happened upon him and attempted—"

"—to knock down the tree he was perched within," Taeryelun finished, close upon the trader's heels. "The little one was most insistent on that."

The Lady smiled. "And your second?"

"Shaken. I fear that he remains unconvinced, however."

"As to which is the better guard?" Mist inquired.

Mead smiled to see the elf and trader grinning at each other. Her mother was always so different around elves, as if their very presence brought back the Mist that had existed when Mead's father had been alive.

"Were you of a mind to offer your services as guide?" the Lady asked softly.

Mead turned back to the Lady. "I am, Lady. I am not yet rid of this wizard who would have my apprenticeship. I can feel him at times," she added, tapping her head. "And now it comes into my mind that I should leave my people until such time as I am free of this mage. Until then I would be a danger to them." She took a breath. "I may be a danger to you, as well."

The pale-haired elf smiled and stroked the quiet Toh. "The risk is small for the pleasure of your company. But, 'friend to the FirstBorn,' do you even know whither we go? Have your wanderings taken you to Drwseren?"

Mead smiled at pleasant memories. "Many times, Lady. When would you leave?"

*   *   *

They left at sunset. Mead walked unconcernedly among the returning weosun, but she noticed that a few of the Lady's escort gave the shaggy beings more than enough room in which to pass by.

Mead blinked slowly and steadily, resisting the urge to rub continually at her eyes. The light of the setting sun seemed in some manner to be reflected off the back of each new weosun she saw. Yet she could see nothing that could cause such upon a second glance. She took a tighter grip on her old, nonmagical staff, resolved not to say anything to the elves about this new development. The light flashes were not painful, but their appearance, added to the Lady's odd behavior earlier, produced puzzling speculations indeed. Were these lights some new game of the wizard? She concentrated on her staff hand and the carvings beneath her fingers, determined not to pursue that line of thought. Her attention was distracted by a conversation behind her.

"I tried talking with some while we watched the hunt, but they refused to speak to me."

Mead did not turn around, but she recognized the voice of Taeryelun's scout.

"Odd indeed for any animal to behave so to a FirstBorn," Taeryelun commented. "Still, we are Outside, the first of our people to travel this way in an age or more. Many of our beliefs have been challenged already; who knows what others will—"

One large weosun suddenly charged toward Mead with a loud bellow, and the trader heard a stifled exclamation behind her as she continued to advance calmly toward it. The weosun stopped short of her toes and nuzzled her affectionately. Mead patted the shaggy head. "I am sorry, Geoc," she said in Trade, "but Mist needs you now more than I. You would not want to miss the Tradegather, would you? Especially with Toh along."

Toh's mother snorted and pawed the ground, eyeing the elves behind Mead.

Recognizing the protective gleam in the large brown eye near her, Mead stayed where she was, effectively blocking the sweep of the long deadly horns. She reached over one horn and tugged at a large brown ear. "I shall be safe. If all goes well, I will join you at the Gather."

Geoc snorted again, then licked Mead's hand and trotted away.

"See, Leader," came a whisper behind her. "The weosun will listen to a human, but not to us!"

"I suspect," the Lady inserted, coming up to stand by Mead's side, "that what the weosun listens to is not the human but the language. Is that not so, Trader?"

Mead took one last look at Geoc's sturdy back disappearing among the tree trunks. "Yes. The friendship of weosun and traders goes back many years, almost to the founding of our Guild."

"Yet when we withdrew into our Highlands," Taeryelun's second said, "no one could approach the weosun with impunity. What spell did your people use on the beasts to tie them so to you?"

"Naught but friendship and mutual interest," Mead replied, hiding her excitement at what the elf had betrayed. Highlands again. They had to be from the eastern highlands, where none of the Folk or humankind had dared enter for untold years. And these elves had withdrawn into the Highlands, had closed themselves off from the rest of the Lands. Why? And why were they emerging now?

But, Mead reminded herself sternly, when dealing with the Folk, a trader never pried, lest trust be felt betrayed. A trader always waited for confidences, for information to be volunteered—unless life was threatened. For the first time that she could remember, Mead chafed under the training of a lifetime, valid as she knew the restriction to be. She longed to be able to come straight out and ask the elf why he mistrusted humans so. But therein laid danger, and one from which she was best removed.

Adjusting her bow and quiver, Mead turned toward the Lady and Taeryelun. "I will scout out our path and see how far the weosun has cleared it of ogres." Taeryelun began to say something, then glanced at the Lady. "If there is any danger," Mead continued, "and I cannot come back to warn you, I will give the warble of a plains gemwing." She hesitated. "Are you familiar with that bird cry?"

Taeryelun nodded. "A good choice for long distances. Do you plan to be far from us?"

"Of late I try to prepare for any possibility." She glanced at the sun nearing the horizon. "I will mark a safe trail, so you need not wait for me to return. We will continue this westerly heading for another day or so."

* * *

Mead walked slowly along the stream edge in the gathering dusk, studying the ground. She stopped finally, straightened, and rubbed the back of her neck. She had seen no sign of weosun or ogre since she had passed the last ogre body some distance ago. She had chosen this stream edge as her last place to check before heading back to the elves, and it had proved clear of ogre tracks as well.

She adjusted her bow, shifted her quarterstaff to her other hand, and set off in the proper direction to rejoin the elves. She had taken only two steps when she heard a sharp *crack* beneath her foot.

Mead looked down in surprise. She had seen nothing underfoot save grass. How came she to miss two arrows—one sticking straight up with point buried in the ground, and the other now broken under her boot?

She dropped to one knee to study the arrows closer. The color of the intact arrow repelled her gaze. She gathered up the broken pieces of the second and examined the two halves in the fading light. The arrowhead was of an odd blue-edged brown stone which almost exactly matched the coloring and pattern of the fletching. There appeared to be runes in a strange tongue inscribed lengthwise on the blue shaft, and the break had occurred in the exact center of a rune.

She looked for the intact arrow to see if it had the entire script and found that it had vanished. She smoothed the grass all around the spot where she remembered seeing the arrow but with no success.

Mead frowned thoughtfully. First she had missed seeing two arrows at her very feet, and now one of the two had vanished. What had been its color, that she had disliked to even look upon it? Had it not in fact been the same color as the one now in her hand?

She looked down at the pieces, then blinked in astonishment. There were no runes on the arrow shaft!

Mead rubbed her forehead wearily. She saw light flashes when nothing was there to cause them, arrows appeared and disappeared, and now runes as well. Could she trust her sight even as to the absence of ogre tracks?

She felt the familiar brush of emotions not her own and smiled at the pride in her mother's mind. Mist never seemed beset by doubts; she had unfailing faith in her own abilities and in those of her daughter. Mead ran her thumb along one of the blue-brown feathers, pondering the value of Mist's confidence in a matter such as this.

Suddenly Mead froze in shock. She could sense yet another besides Mist! The mind of this other seemed full of tightly controlled hatred capped with a fresh layer of resentment. Its owner seemed to be drawing closer to her and Mead turned to face the direction of its approach.

She looked thoughtfully at the pieces in her hand, then dropped the half with the pile into her quiver. After all, as the Lady had once said, one did not throw away arrows in enemy territory. She could always affix the point to another arrow. She studied the blue-edged brown feathers on the remaining half, mildly curious as to what bird had possessed such bright plumage, then shrugged and added it to her quiver. Perhaps she could make use of that half as well.

Mead rose to her feet and stepped into concealment beside the thick trunk of a willow. She had lost contact with the other's emotions, but whoever it was had to be very near.

The other was also silent of foot. Mead watched as a shadowy figure passed by the tree, then turned and faced her. "Trader?"

Mead stared at Taeryelun's second.

"The Elder grew concerned when you did not return," the elf continued, not noticing Mead's surprise.

Mead looked around the willow trunk, then turned back to the elf. "You did not see anything?"

"No. Why?"

"I thought I sensed—" Mead glanced at the elf and cut herself short. The obvious answer was not too hard to believe.

She gestured at the untrodden stream edge. "The ogres did not flee this way. You may tell the Lady that our path will be safe for a time."

The elf folded his arms. "The Leader bade me return with you."

Mead raised an eyebrow. That explained the resentment. But why hatred? And why had she sensed this elf when ere now she could only sense Mist? She adjusted her bow. "Lead, and I shall follow."

* * *

"You are so quiet, Trader," the Lady said much later as they walked through the night. "You never ask, yet I know your mind must brim with questions."

Glancing briefly up at the stars, Mead smiled faintly. "It is the way of my people not to be overly inquisitive among the Folk."

"Ah, that explains your hesitation earlier. But how, then, do your people learn the ways of others?"

Mead shifted her staff to her other hand. "Until we are trusted enough to be told those ways, we watch and observe."

"And do you learn much with your patient watching and observing?"

The trader smiled ruefully. "Only enough to raise still more questions, I fear."

The Lady studied her. "I am intrigued. Tell me what you have learned from watching us."

Mead hesitated, then decided to begin with the most innocuous.

"There are few women among your people. You originally traveled with a large escort—far larger than either honor or safety demanded. And twice now the Leader would have held me back from scouting. When a people is that protective of women, either women are held in low esteem, or they are few."

"They are few," the Lady agreed. "The number has steadily dwindled during the ages of our isolation." She looked up at the stars and sighed. "The humans were new to the Lands when my people disagreed with their brethren. The disagreement was so sharp that my people withdrew to their gateland and closed its borders against any intrusion."

She looked at Mead and smiled. "Ah, again you do not ask. Do you still feel mistrusted?"

Conscious of other eyes watching her, Mead phrased her reply with care. "I have been given no use-names, Lady," she pointed out. "You and the Leader may trust me, for what I have done, but I have not yet earned your escort's trust. I shall wait with my questions."

The Lady nodded. "When you feel trusted, ask, and I shall answer."

Mead fully expected to hear protest, but there came none. She inclined her head to the Lady and shifted through her meager vocabulary of High Elven. "You do me honor."

The Lady smiled and lightly touched Mead's head.

Mead blinked. For but a moment she had seen the merest shimmer of green about the Lady, shining brightly in the darkness.

The Lady looked ahead to where Taeryelun had stopped to confer with his second. "I know not much of humans, but I do know that, unlike us, they need sleep. How often will you require this?"

Mead resisted the urge to rub at her eyes. "I have traveled with your brethren before. I can sleep briefly during our rest stops."

The Lady looked down at herself. "Which may be frequent. My little one taxes my strength."

Mead kept her face impassive. She estimated that the Lady was only halfway through her pregnancy and thus more than capable of keeping to any pace her kinsman set for far longer than Mead herself. But she did not demur as the Lady sent one of her escort to request her kinsman to find a place of rest. Perhaps sleep might cure her eyes' strange lapses.

* * *

But sleep instead seemed to have intensified her light sensitivity. Mead hurriedly shut her eyes and waited, concentrating on the sounds around her, then slowly eased her eyelids open. She avoided looking at any of the elves, since the lights had seemed especially bright around them.

She had not slept long; the stars still glittered overhead. The elves did not seem inclined to immediately resume their journey, so Mead moved farther out of sight and tried to think.

The Lady had assured her that her eyes had suffered no lasting hurt. If these strange lights were some doing of the wizard, what was his intent? To bring madness upon her? What was the purpose of lights and things that appeared only to disappear? Recalling the arrows, she delved into her quiver and found the fletched half of the broken arrow. At least she had not imagined this.

Mead leaned back against a tree and closed her eyes, her thumb idly stroking the feathers. The wizard said he had given her another chance to become a wizardling. Were the flashes of light the result? What if they were not?

Her thumb stilled as she suddenly became aware of another's mind. This one was again not Mist's, but it held only friendship and concern.

"Dark-Eyed Lady?"

Steeling herself not to wince at any light flash, Mead opened her eyes. "'Mead' is my use-name as well as my true name, Leader." She looked up at Taeryelun and was relieved to see only his shadowy figure.

"Of what can you humans be thinking," he mused lightly, "to give power over yourselves so readily? What did your friends among my distant brethren call you?"

"Wilobe," Mead said, wondering if he would notice the pun.

"'Friendly Spirit,'" Taeryelun translated. "A play upon your true name, yes? It suits you"—he glanced over at his company—"but I prefer another. We shall be ready whenever you wish us to depart." Moonlight silvered his hair as he started away. "You have a pretty wristlet, Lady of the Dark Eyes."

Mead stared down at her hands in amazement. What wristlet? And when had the arrow half vanished? She did not remember dropping it, but it was gone. And around her right wrist was a solid ring of blue-edged brown feathers, so thick she could barely discern the wooden band within. Nor could she locate any break or seam to enable her to remove it from her wrist.

Mead sighed and reached for her staff. That wizard!

She glowered at the feathered wristlet as she rose to her feet. The arrow had been broken; its power should have been as well. What strange properties did this arrow possess? Remembering that the magical staff had responded to simple wishes, Mead wished that the wristlet was gone from her wrist. Nothing happened.

She searched through her quiver for the second half of the arrow. The elves had been unable to break the magical staff, but when it had been struck by the ogre's staff, both had been destroyed. Perhaps simple contact of one half against the other might break this one's hold on her wrist. Recalling the aftereffects of the two staffs' contact, Mead hoped that that was all it would do.

Hatred touched her mind, and she looked up to see Taeryelun's second approaching. "We are rested, Trader, and our scout reports our way ahead clear."

Mead tried to close out his hatred, but her normally intermittent ability persisted. She glanced at the feathered wristlet. "You might be wiser to continue onward without me."

Surprise dulled the hatred. "Trader?"

Mead adjusted her quiver and took a tighter grip upon her staff. "I must speak with the Lady."

The elf Elder stepped out of the shadows behind Taeryelun's second. "Is there trouble, my friend?"

Mead held out her arm with the wristlet. "But a few moments ago this was a broken half of an arrow."

The Lady studied it from afar. "The wizard?"

"I think so. I stepped upon an arrow while on scout and saved the pieces. Both pieces. Now this half has hold of my wrist, and the second half is gone from my quiver."

The Lady met her eyes. "What would you have us do?"

Mead hesitated, then decided her first impulse was correct. Wherever that wizard's toys appeared, the Lady should not be. "The risk of danger because of me is no longer a possibility. I shall give you directions to Drwseren."

Joy touched her thoughts from one mind, but the Lady frowned. "And thus you abandon us? I had thought more of your word, Trader. You promised to guide us to Drwseren. I shall hold you to that."

"But—" Mead faltered.

The Lady smiled. "Our fates are bound together for a time, Wilobe. Accept what you cannot change. Now come, we are eager to be off."

Mead smiled ruefully. Few could win an argument with an elf.

* * *

Despite the elves' overprotectiveness toward females, Mead soon managed to arrange the expedition to her liking over the days which followed. When she could not sleep during the Lady's rests, she went on ahead to scout, although often she found an elf following her back trail. But in this manner Mead found that she was not hated by all the elves. Eirin, a swordsman with hair almost as light as the Lady's, was the first to give Mead his use-name. Then was Coaeden, the long-haired archer who appeared to Mead to be the youngest of the group—as far as one could judge age among elves. Then Wybr, another archer, who was normally Taeryelun's first choice for scout, and Mordaeith of the strong swordarm, with hair as long as Coaeden, but clothing somehow finer than any of the other three. Only Taeryelun's second, whom Mead had begun in her own mind to call simply "Second," withheld his use-name. It appeared that although Second copied his leader in many ways—from the shortness of his hair to the way he held his sword—friendship with humans was not one.

Adjusting her perch upon the narrow tree limb, Mead idly smoothed the wristlet's feathers, conscious once again of the worrisome feeling of foreboding that had begun to haunt her every moment, waking or sleeping.

Mead toyed with a feather. Sleep was becoming difficult. She had never been one to have troubled dreams but now there were many and, more often that not, she would awaken with the sound of chimes in her ear. She sighed. What game was the wizard playing? And what was the wristlet's purpose? It had revealed no powers since sealing itself about her wrist, and she had never again found the second half of the arrow.

She frowned thoughtfully. Perhaps her diminished sleep was the cause of her now erratic ability. Whether it was also the reason she was now able to sense others besides Mist was less clear. She only had to be a certain distance from an elf in order to share his feelings. All except the Lady.

There came a soft sound from the ground. Mead looked down to see the blond head of an elf, and knew from its paleness that Eirin was her guardian today. He found her staff hidden at the base of the tree and looked up with a smile. "Ho, Wilobe! What see you from there?"

Mead mentally shook her head. For some reason these elves refused to call her simply "Mead" She swung down out of the tree and dropped lightly to the ground. "There is smoke several leagues distant to the east. Kingsmen, judging from the plume. Only they would announce their presence so blatantly."

He frowned as he handed her her staff. "Do you think they will come this way?"

Mead shook her head with a smile. "If they are kingsmen, such a thought would fill them with terror. Kingdom dwellers seldom venture outside their borders, and we have entered the fringes of the Great Woods, a place they consider magical, and thus forbidden."

"Forbidden? These dwellers in kingdoms fear magic?"

Mead nodded. "Most of them. They shun many of the Folk for the same reason."

"How strange," Eirin said thoughtfully.

* * *

A strange sound penetrated Mead's waking mind, but she remained still. Over the days of this journey, she had schooled herself to wake fully before opening her eyes, as she had painfully discovered that they were most sensitive when sleep-clouded or exhaustion-dulled. The sound was repeated, and she wondered what the elves were about. Then moistness touched her cheek, and Mead decided to risk the light flashes. She opened her eyes and found herself looking into the light blue eyes of a white wolf.

Mead remained perfectly still. A white wolf. Shier than either the friendly gray or black wolves, the white wolf was rumored to be the rarest of the four Great Wolves. Its fur was popular with kings, but any kingsman so rash as to attempt hunting them found himself pitted against a mind fully as keen as his own.

The white wolf had withdrawn his nose and backed a step when she had opened her eyes, but now he moved closer. Allowing no trace of fear to enter her mind, Mead slowly lifted her chin so that her throat was exposed and vulnerable and gave the soft whine used among the black wolves. Startlement touched her thoughts. The white wolf hesitated, then whined back and licked her face.

Mead slowly sat up. "It is an honor to be in your presence, White One."

The wolf's tail wagged slowly. He turned and padded past Second, who was leaning with arms folded against a nearby tree. The elf looked at her without a word. Mead let her gaze follow the wolf and saw the Lady seated cross-legged beside a second wolf. A third wolf lay on the ground before the elf Elder.

Mead rose to her feet and started after the first wolf. Her pace slowed as she drew level with Second, and she controlled her by now ingrained impulse to turn her eyes away from the lights that seemingly appeared before her.

Pale green light shimmered about the Lady, and the greenness seemed to Mead's eyes to have stretched out to enclose the fallen wolf as well. Paying no attention to Second, although she could feel his gaze upon her, Mead moved closer to the Lady.

On the fallen wolf's side was a long angry wound that seemed to have been made by a spear graze. That in itself would have been painful, but the look in the wolf's eyes was of tormenting agony. The Lady held her hands above the wound and green fire blazed downward. The wolf's eyes closed, and it seemed to relax.

Mead blinked her eyes. The light over the wolf's wound was varicolored—green below the Lady's hands and blue-violet where she had yet to heal. Mead moved to a position level with Taeryelun and Mordaeith, outside the green light. She did not doubt that she was witnessing a healing of some kind—although the wound remained open and bleeding—and she marveled that she was able to see it in such a manner.

Finally the Lady lowered her hands. "It is done. Have you the salve, kinsman?"

"No, wait," Mead interrupted. The lights still filled her vision, and barely visible at the end of the line of green on the wolf's side was a pinprick of blue-violet. "Up past the end of the wound. There is some poison buried under the skin."

She barely noticed the Lady and Taeryelun exchange glances. "What color?" Taeryelun asked softly.

"Blue-violet," Mead replied, her attention focused on the wolf. There was a murmur of sound behind her, but whatever was said was not clear. "Can you not see it?" The wolf's companion came to sit before her. An anxious whine sounded in its throat.

"I see naught," the Lady said slowly.

"But it is there, under the fur." Mead felt curiously drawn to enter the green shimmer about the Lady, but she stayed where she was.

The Lady lightly laid her hand on the wolf's fur where Mead had indicated and recoiled with a gasp.

"Lady?" Mead asked in concern.

The Lady looked up at her. "Our Trader is correct. There is a bit of trag embedded under the skin. The spear must have been coated with its juice."

"Goblins," Mead said angrily and the unharmed wolf growled in agreement. The boney creatures often smeared their spear points with that plant's poison. No wonder the wolf had been in agony.

The Lady turned back to the injured wolf. "Give me your knife, kinsman."

"But, Elder, that is the human weapon," a voice from behind protested.

The Lady nodded. "All the better. Their metals do not react with trag as ours do." Taeryelun laid his dagger in her waiting hand, and she dug out the offending particle, then returned the weapon to him. Taeryelun drew a Green Blessing in the air about the blade, and the bit of trag shivered into dust.

"Wilobe," the Lady asked softly, "do you see any other pieces?"

Mead looked closely at the wound. A soft whine came from the wolf before her. "No. All is green now."

Taeryelun moved aside to allow Second to give the vial of healing salve to the Lady. Mead watched as the Lady smeared a light layer of the clear salve over the wound. Bleeding stopped as the salve sealed the graze. A favored item of trade from the elves, the salve was effective against all but the most mortal injuries and even some poisons. Pain was dulled at its touch, and the healing process greatly accelerated.

Mead felt a hand on her shoulder and turned toward Taeryelun. "How long have you been able to see auras?" he asked.

Mead stared at him. "Auras?" She raised a hand to her head, but restrained the impulse to rub at her eyes. "I have seen flashes of light since the two staffs met, and those but seldom, but auras? 'Tis that what I have seen?" She sighed with relief. "I had thought my eyes were overly tired, or that the wizard played some new game."

Another of the injured wolf's companions tugged at Taeryelun's sleeve and, with a nod toward her, the elf allowed the wolf to pull him aside.

Mead leaned back against a tree. Auras. The wolf seated before her nudged her hand with her nose. Mead looked down and the wolf whined softly. "I am sorry, Honored One, but I do not understand your speech."

The wolf sniffed at the feathered wristlet, then looked up at Mead, her ears perked.

"I know not what it is, either," Mead said ruefully.

The wolf's attention shifted to her companion, and Mead watched as the Lady moved away from her patient. The white wolf swung her head back to Mead and gave a soft yap. Then she rose and trotted to her injured companion's side, leaving Mead alone.

Or almost alone. Mead felt a familiar prickle against her thoughts. "Why seek you to have our Elder outlawed?" Second asked.

"Outlawed?" Mead turned and found herself facing Second and Wybr. She looked from one elf to the other. "I seek no such thing! I wish no harm to befall any of you, especially the Lady! Of what am I accused? And why?"

"Because you are human," Second responded. "Humans always seek to learn the unknown."

"And elves do not?" Mead countered. "How does this affect the Lady?"

Coaeden suddenly appeared at her side. "You wrong her," he said to Second. "The Trader does not understand our fears. She has never asked why we differ from our kin."

Second folded his arms. "Tell her, then."

Mead straightened. At last!

Coaeden brushed back a lock of his long hair. "Our Elders tell us that we quarreled often with our kin Outside," he began nervously, "and for many reasons. But foremost among them was the question of the teaching of magic to humans. Our Outside kin favored the idea. My people did not. When those of the lowlands began to aid humans in their dabblings, we closed off our gateland to prevent any disaster caused by human magic-users from vitiating us. If the Council ever suspected that the Elder had—"

"Have I," Mead interrupted, her anger growing, "at any time, ever asked to be taught magic?" She turned to Second. "I have no desire to learn magic, though neither you nor that wizard will listen to me. My sole purpose for being here is to guide you to Drwseren. My problems with this wizard are mine alone. I have not asked the Lady's aid, nor will I do so. I shall not endeavor to involve any of you in this!" She paused for breath, and the elves stared wordlessly at her.

"I have promised to guide you to Drwseren," she repeated in a calmer tone. "The Lady holds me to that promise, else I would have freed you from the defilement of my presence long ago. We are now but three days from Drwseren. If you prefer, henceforth I scout ahead and mark a trail for you to follow. You decide." She met Second's eyes. For a moment the hatred she sensed seemed to falter, but the moment did not last.

She turned to Wybr and Coaeden. "I shall go, then, and await your decision."

She started to pass through the elves, intending to gather her weapons, but Second raised a hand to block her. Abruptly Mead felt a warm presence at her hip and heard a low growl. She looked down to see the female wolf staring at Second, teeth bared in threat.

The elf moved out of Mead's path, a curious look in his large eyes. She mentally brushed aside his hatred, concentrating instead on Coaeden's astonishment and Wybr's confusion. The wolf stayed with her as she slung her bow and quiver across her back and picked up her staff.

She looked down at the wolf. "Thank you for your aid. I know you would not leave your companion alone for long so I shall say my farewell here."

The wolf caught Mead's left sleeve in her teeth and looked up at her with bright blue eyes.

Mead smiled. "Very well. Your company is most welcome."

The wolf released her sleeve and trotted off in the direction of Drwseren. Mead followed without a backwards glance.

Mead's anger turned inward against herself as she walked. She had over-reacted to Second's accusation. She knew that, before now, had any kingsman accused her of magic-use, she would have laughed in his face. But now—aye, how would she respond now with this wizard's toy about her wrist? Mead grinned ruefully. Probably the same. Magic was not evil because it existed. It was but a tool.

She sighed. Clearly she had responded wrongly. Unthinking temper was not the way of a trader.

The white wolf trotted back to her side and looked up at her with an anxious whine.

Mead shook her head. "Naught is wrong. Save that I am a fool."

The wolf caught her sleeve in her teeth and tugged gently. Releasing the fabric, she bounded away and then stopped and looked back at Mead, invitation in her mien.

The trader smiled and adjusted her bow. "A run sounds like an excellent idea." The wolf turned and dashed away, and Mead sprinted after.

They covered a long distance in easy comradeship, and when Mead finally stopped to rest, the white wolf sat patiently beside her. The last thing Mead remembered before her eyes closed was a faint shimmer of blue-green shining about her defender.

No dreams or chimes disturbed Mead's slumber. She awoke refreshed and alert—and conscious of two familiar touches against her mind.

Mead slowly opened her eyes. The wolf was nowhere to be seen. Coaeden, however, was seated a short distance away, looking as though he expected to be scolded. She sat up and finally located Wybr seated against the base of a tree.

"Did the wolf leave?" she asked with a yawn.

Coaeden looked distinctly uncomfortable. Wybr glanced sharply at him. "The Pack Mother waited until we arrived ere departing. She warned us not to wake you, but Coaeden, here—"

"Did not wake me," Mead interrupted, surprise clearing her thoughts. Her companion had been the Pack Mother? That indeed must have annoyed Second.

Coaeden looked relieved. He nodded toward a small pouch by her feet. "You left without any food."

Mead smiled at him. "Thank you, Coaeden. I *am* hungry." She raised an eyebrow at the smallness of the pouch, but waited for the elves to speak.

Coaeden waited until she had eaten a few bites of journeybread. "The Leader has asked me to return with you. Wybr will continue your scout."

Mead took another bite and chewed slowly. "Does the Leader know what was said?"

Coaeden glanced uneasily at Wybr. "No."

Mead also watched Wybr. "What was decided?"

Wybr leaned forward. "We wish you to return."

Mead could sense what they had not said. "But not all," she replied, and felt it reflected against her mind. She brushed the last crumbs off her clothing and tied the pouch onto her belt. "I do not intrude where I am not welcome. I shall continue on."

"But the Leader—" Coaeden began.

"Remind the Leader that I am guide and know the path well. Several of the streams ahead are prone to flooding and I best know the ways safest for the Lady." She rose to her feet and the elves rose as well.

Wybr came forward and placed a hand on her shoulder. "Do not tire yourself. The Elder will need time to rest from the healing."

Mead nodded, concealing her surprise. What had the Pack Mother said to them?

Coaeden still looked bewildered. "But the Leader—" he tried again.

The trader did not let the young elf finish. "He will accept what I have said."

Wybr looked downward. "Do not judge his second-in-command too harshly, Wilobe. He feels his responsibilities perhaps too strongly, but—"

"I understand, Wybr." The elf looked at her, and Mead nodded. "I have faced his kind of mistrust many times ere now. I understand. Tell the Leader I shall await all of you outside Drwseren."

* * *

Kneeling on the edge of a clear stream, Mead raised her head to listen, water dripping from her cupped hands. Nothing greeted her ears but the small ordinary sounds of wind and birds, but she waited a moment longer before finishing her drink.

She knew half of her uneasiness was due to guilt. No guide would ever have strayed so far ahead of those for whom she was responsible. Yet they were following the trail she had left—her directional sense confirmed that as well as the knowledge that elves could spot the slightest disturbance in the world about them. But still she felt she was not fully keeping to her promise to the Lady.

She finished her drink. A half day's travel should find them in Drwseren, and she would be free of the burden of Second's suspicions. She wondered for a moment how the elves would view their distant kin, and grinned at what Second's reactions would undoubtedly be.

Rising, she fluffed out a few damp feathers of her wristlet. An easier place to cross this stream was but a short distance upstream. She assembled a small pile of pebbles, then hesitated at the touch of emotions not her own.

Mead mentally sighed. The approaching mind held concern and worry, which meant she was about to be protected again.

She finished constructing her marker, then turned in the direction of the approaching mind. Abruptly she corrected herself. Minds. Hidden by the intensity of the first touch was a familiar prickle of hatred. Second. She braced herself.

Taeryelun stepped into view and bowed toward her. "You have found a pleasant spot for the Elder's rest, Lady of the Dark Eyes."

Mead smiled. "The best crossing is upstream, Leader."

He walked along the stream edge and glanced in the direction she indicated. "Excellent. You are ever watchful of our needs. However, the Elder misses her guide and wonders when she may enjoy her company once again."

Second appeared, but Mead spared only a glance in his direction. "I would welcome a return to the Lady's presence, Leader, but we are nearing Drwseren. I must go on to inform them of your coming arrival so that they may prepare a proper welcome for the Lady."

"You have exerted yourself far too much on our behalf already. One of us will go on."

Mead shook her head. "Leader, I think you know not the nature of Drwseren's defenses. Drwseren is built of air. One could wander within touching distance of it and never know it was there. I must be the one to go."

Taeryelun frowned. "Surely there will be those detailed to watch the borders of Drwseren against intruders. They can direct the Elder's messenger within."

"Yes, but—"

"Then it is settled. You and I shall await the Elder here, and my second will go on."

Mead glanced at Second. The elf's face betrayed nothing, but she suddenly realized that this opportunity to act as the Lady's emissary would be an honor for him. She abandoned the argument and gave Second simple directions to the borders of Drwseren. "…and then, simply request to see the Council," she finished.

"Request?" Second glanced at Taeryelun, then back at her. "Without any identification?"

Mead stared at him in astonishment. The day when any visitor to Drwseren would be refused admittance to the Council was one she did not wish to see. "But the Lady is expected, is she not?" Mead looked toward Taeryelun for support.

The Leader shrugged. "We left as soon as the Elder gained permission. There was not time to send a message."

Mead turned back to Second. "But, surely, as an elf, you need not worry about—"

"Appearances can be deceiving," Second interrupted.

Mead looked from one elf to the other. Their land must be strange indeed. Second's behavior seemed somewhat easier to understand now. She pulled an arrow from her quiver and drew her dagger. "Give them this," she said, marking the shaft of the arrow with two triangles joined by a line. "They will know it as mine, and I have marked it with my father's symbol as further identification. This will give you entrance to the Council."

Second looked curiously at the arrow as she handed it to him. He glanced at Taeryelun.

The Leader nodded. "Know you now how to find Drwseren?"

Second glanced at the arrow. "Yes. Safe journey, Leader."

"We shall see you soon."

Second bowed. He gave Mead a peculiar look, then turned and started upstream. Soon Mead could see him running among the trees on the opposite bank.

Taeryelun settled himself on the ground and leaned back against a tree. "Have you any food left?"

Mead leaned against another tree. "Some."

The elf eyed her, then tossed her a leaf-wrapped slice of journeybread. "Some?" he repeated. "I know how much Coaeden brought you." He shook his head. "Rest. The Elder is not far behind. We have made good time."

"Since the Lady no longer needed such long rests while I was not present," Mead finished for him. "I shall not ask if that was your idea or the Lady's."

Taeryelun studied her with a smile. "We thought that would not mislead you." His smile faded. "But it seems our efforts were not enough. You have grown wan over the days, Dark-Eyed Lady. The wizard?"

Mead looked away, up at the leaves overhead. "I know not. I seem to sense some danger approaching." She smoothed the feathers of her wristlet. "Mayhap the old one seeks to frighten me into learning the meaning of this. He knows not how stubborn I can be." She looked at Taeryelun and was momentarily taken aback to see a greenish shimmer shining about him. She controlled her expression as the aura slowly faded from view.

The elf did not appear to notice her surprise. He studied the wristlet. "Perhaps my brethren at Drwseren can rid you of that."

Mead put more hope in the possibility of Drwseren knowing the old one. Many wizards frequented the nearby Glen of Ancient Voices on their wanderings. Finding the old one might be less difficult than imagined. She fluffed a damp feather. "Is this Wild Magic, as was the staff?"

Taeryelun peered at the wristlet, then nodded. "You can see from the aura. And see how the blue from your aura has crept into the white? That shows it has become attuned to you."

Mead looked down at the wristlet in surprise. She had never thought to look for its aura.

"Ho, Wilobe!" a voice called.

Mead looked up to see Eirin approaching from among the trees. He waved at her, then turned to wait for the Lady and Mordaeith. Coaeden and Wybr brought up the rear.

The trader studied the shadows beyond Coaeden, foreboding stirring once again within her.

The day passed swiftly and pleasantly as they walked, and Mead almost hated for the journey to end. But all too soon they were within sight of landmarks familiar to her.

Mead was talking with Mordaeith at the point when a tall, dark-haired elf dropped down out of a tree before them. "Greetings, Mead!" He bowed to Mordaeith. "Welcome, kin. We have had glad tidings of your company's arrival."

The Lady and the rest of her escort came into view behind Mordaeith, and the dark-haired elf bowed deeply. "Welcome, Elder. All of Drwseren rejoices at your coming. I am called Faenoree and I bid you all welcome."

The Lady smiled at him, and Faenoree continued. "I must apologize for the inadequacy of my greetings and for Drwseren being ill-prepared for your arrival. The Council awaits you within Drwseren. If you will but follow me, I shall lead you to the entrance." He smiled at Mead. "Not to slight your abilities, Friendly Spirit."

Mead smiled back. "The honor of Drwseren could find no better guide than Third of Council."

Faenoree bowed slightly in reply, then led them forward. "I have heard some of the hazards of your journey, Elder, and, as I told your messenger, the Green smiled upon you in sending Mead as your guide."

Mead could easily imagine how Second would react to that. She felt answering amusement and pride in several minds, but the Lady's, as always, was closed to her. The sea green eyes turned upon her, and the blonde Elder smiled as she lightly laid a hand on Mead's shoulder. "We were blessed indeed."

While they walked, Taeryelun scanned the trees. "I see no guards," he said finally. "Are we far from Drwseren?"

"No." Faenoree crossed a tiny clearing and stopped at its edge. "We are here. This is the entrance to Drwseren."

"But naught is there!" Coaeden protested.

Mead could feel suspicion spring to life around her and decided to intervene. "Drwseren is built of air," she said. Recalling the placement of the large double doors, she walked among the bushes and trees on one side of the entrance. "Unless one knows exactly where the entrance is located, Drwseren cannot be detected by any means." She walked behind where the doors stood and stopped before Faenoree. He nodded to her, and she continued. "But if you know where the doors are—" she stepped forward to stand beside Faenoree, then backed through the entrance into Drwseren.

She felt the faint tingle of passage and knew that she had vanished from the elves' view, although she could still see them clearly through the open doors. Bumping into someone, she turned to see Second.

He nodded to her. "A better explanation than the one I was given."

She shrugged. "They have lived so long with it, they have forgotten how strange it can seem." She smiled at him in sympathy, then stepped back through the doors to stand once again beside Faenoree.

"A wondrous place indeed," the Lady commented. She allowed Faenoree to escort her inside, and the rest of the elves followed.

Mead lagged behind. The closer they had come to Drwseren, the more she had felt that some danger drew near. Yet none of the elves had seemed to sense what she did. Now would be a good time to investigate. She glanced at the hidden entrance, then turned and strode away.

She walked quickly at first, so as to be lost from sight of any watching from the entrance. Then her pace slowed until she moved cautiously along their back trail. Even here, in a place she knew to be safe, foreboding haunted her. The sunlight was bright and warm, but the shadows under the trees seemed especially dark. She almost felt as if the very shadows had eyes.

Catching a flash of light out of the corner of her eye, she began to turn toward it, bringing her staff up to guard, when, with a crack of splintering wood, something smashed against her left shoulder.

Mead stumbled back and raised her quarterstaff. Her left shoulder felt numb, but she spared not a glance at it as she peered into the shadows from whence the attack had come. That blow had been meant for her head.

But nothing appeared in her sight. Turning slowly, she trod upon pieces of wood by her left foot and discovered that her bow had been shattered over her left shoulder. Moving swiftly, she unslung her bow from her back so it would not hinder her. The damage done shook her momentarily. The lower quarter was but fragments. Only something with strength greater than a ogre could do such to an elven-built bow. Where was her attacker?

She turned at the faintest whisper of sound. Lumbering slowly toward her out of the shadows was a being the like of which she had never seen. As tall as an ogre, but broader, the creature seemed a solid block of muscle. It wore no clothing or ornamentation, yet needed none with its natural covering of purple scales. Its eyes were yellow and slitted like a cat's, and its neck was so short as to be nonexistent. Mead's attention fastened on the mace it held. She was briefly thankful that the pear-shaped head was not spiked.

"Who are you?" she asked. "What are you?"

The being only chuckled, and Mead realized her folly. Did she actually expect it to give its name?

"Why are you here?" she tried.

"You," the scaled being said in a voice surprisingly light for one so large. "I have come for you. The Shadows tell me I have a rival for apprenticeship to my wizard."

"He is your wizard?" Mead asked in surprise. "But I am no rival. I have no desire to become a wizard."

"Nor do I. The Shadows see that this wizard is new to the Lands. He thinks to determine by these foolish tests the two sides of Power and which he will cleave to." The being stepped closer, hefting its short mace. "The Shadows want this fool. And you will not keep me from him."

Staying in the sunlight, Mead back a step, hoping to draw the creature farther out of the concealing shadows. In her eyes the light about the being was multilayered—a shifting, blurring blue-violet on the outside with an inner layer of reddish-violet. "You sound very sure of yourself, servant of Shadows."

"I have Power. You have naught but that pitiful stave." The being paused and turned its entire upper body from side to side in an attempt to look around. "And friends. I cannot sense them. Where are those elves you traveled with?"

"Elves?" Mead hesitated. Did the Shadows know of Drwseren? The elf stronghold was safely hidden, but to have the Shadows even suspect it was near meant trouble for the future. "They have gone." She rubbed her numb shoulder and instantly regretted that bit of playacting at a sharp twinge of pain. "They left me behind."

"All the better, little one." The creature chuckled. "This is between you and I." Raising its mace, it charged at Mead.

Mead brought up her staff to block as the mace came down. The jar of impact awakened her shoulder to fresh agony and she almost dropped one end of the staff. She pivoted, letting the creature's momentum carry it past her, and swung at its back. Her blow was ineffective. The scales proved better protection than mail.

The creature ponderously stopped and began to turn. Mead hurriedly cupped one hand about her mouth and gave the carrying warble of a gemwing. She doubted any of the elves would hear, but now might be her only chance to warn them. Her bow had blocked that first attack from ambush enough so that her shoulder was intact, but even so that blow must have bruised bone. She would not be able to use her staff for long. She could barely stand to lift her arm now. But meanwhile her staff's reach was still longer than the being's arms, and she could ill-afford to let the creature come too close with that mace, inexpert as the being appeared with it. She shifted her grip on the staff.

The creature charged again. Mead swung full strength at its head, and the creature stopped as the blow connected. Mead pulled back the staff and thrust it directly into the being's middle.

The scaled creature did not even stagger. It laughed suddenly and plucked the staff from Mead's grasp.

Mead swiftly drew her dagger and was momentarily surprised to see a faint glow coming from the blade. Then she recalled that Taeryelun had gifted it to her. Elven steel had strange properties.

The creature looked at her staff, then casually tossed it aside. It laughed, pointed at her dagger, then deliberately laid its mace down. It raised one hand, and Mead suddenly saw the gleam of claws. "The Shadows have loaned me their powers, but I need them not against such a frail being as you." It reached out to slash her.

Mead ducked under the swing and stabbed her dagger deep into the creature's side.

The creature shrieked and swung at her. Mead heard a ripping sound as she danced out of its reach, but spared no time to look, watching the creature instead. She held her knife ready, relieved that elven steel was stronger than purple scales.

But the creature did not attack. Instead, it seemed to melt into the shadows. The mace, lying in a patch of shade, suddenly seemed to ripple as if darkness flowed over it and slowly faded away.

Mead blinked. There had been something…familiar about that mace in the very moment in which it had vanished. She peered into the shadows. Where was the being? She could see ground and tree trunks in the shadow whence it had disappeared, but there was no sign of the creature. She slowly scanned the shadows about her, keeping within patches of sunlight. She knew not what powers the Shadows had granted her rival, but unpleasant suspicions were already coming to mind.

Her left arm suddenly seemed hot and, without taking her eyes from her search, Mead shifted her knife to that hand and reached up with her right hand to find her sleeve ripped. Her fingertips came away streaked with blood.

A chuckle came from her right and she whirled, shifting her knife back to her other hand. Nothing faced her save tree shade.

Mead resumed her slow scrutiny. The dagger edge was still aglow; the creature had to be nearby. For what was it waiting?

Suddenly, in a large patch of shade, she saw faint sparkles of red-violet. The creature's aura! But why was it so diffuse, rather than outlining the being? Taking a step toward it, she stumbled slightly and caught herself with an effort.

Mead swayed. Something was wrong. She felt queerly light-headed, and the fire in her left arm seemed to have spread down her side. A chill crept down her spine. Poison. The creature's claws had been envenomed.

She took another step forward and abruptly fell. Arrows spilled from her quiver as she caught herself on her hands and knees. A chuckle came from before her.

Mead raised her head to see the red-violet sparkles slowly moving forward. They seemed to hesitate as she looked directly at them, then resumed their steady approach. More sparkles appeared and began to form an outline of the creature. Her fingers took a tighter grip about her knife hilt.

Glancing downward as she cleared arrows out of her way, Mead paused in surprise. On the ground directly before her was the broken half of an arrow, its blue-edged brown head pointed away from her and towards the approaching creature.

Heavy footsteps caught her attention, and Mead looked up to see the outline rushing toward her. Darkness rippled about it, as if the creature were reforming out of the shadows.

Remembering how the ogre's staff had become a sword, Mead dropped her knife and caught up the broken half of the arrow, holding it point first at the running creature. She needed something much longer than a knife.

The arrow half shifted in her hand and abruptly expanded outward in the same moment in which the creature, mace raised, fully materialized before her. Mead barely had the presence of mind to brace the end of the arrow half/spear against the ground as the creature charged onto the spear point. Scales were not proof against this weapon, either.

"Shadows curse you, human!" The creature attempted to pull the spear from its chest, but Mead leaned against the spear with all of her remaining strength. The being struck against the blue shaft with its fist, then raised the mace.

"No!" Releasing the spear, Mead flung herself aside just as the creature brought its mace down upon the spear shaft.

Light beat against her closed eyelids, and a scream began, only to be cut short.

Mead slowly and carefully opened her eyes. She glanced toward the creature, then hurriedly averted her gaze from its remains. A large patch of seared ground was all she could see of where she had been but moments before.

She levered herself to her knees, but any attempt to rise to her feet was beyond her strength. Her vision was blurring, and recurring waves of fire and ice swept through her frame.

Suddenly her vision cleared and she saw an elf by the fallen creature. For a moment she thought he was Taeryelun, then she recognized Second.

He rose and came toward her. "What has occurred here? I saw you leave us; what have you done?"

Mead raised a shaking hand to her head. "I found the second half of the arrow," she said—and pitched forward.

As if from a great distance, she felt herself caught and lowered to the ground. She could still see Second; he was saying something to her, but she could not hear. She could sense him, however: his hesitation and the sudden knowledge that delay would rid him of her were all too clear. She wanted to say something, but the words abruptly escaped her. She fell headlong into darkness.

Whiteness suddenly blazed about her, and soft chimes whispered nearby. "Must you always break things?" a crotchety voice complained.

"I did not—" Mead began, then cut herself short. "So the creature's mace was the second arrow?"

"Would anything else have reacted that way? Why must you continually break things?"

"But why two arrows? And why two staffs?"

"You already know why. That creature explained the situation rather well, I think. I am new to this land and wished to discover the poles of Power."

"So I am but a pawn in your game. You have no need of an apprentice."

"Ah, but I do. I am not one who guards his secrets so zealously that they will die when I do. You have potential, wizardling. I shall look forward to teaching you."

"You shall wait a long time, old one," Mead said slowly, "now that I am dead."

"I never waste time explaining to the dead. They already know. Now shoo, apprentice. You will find me when you are ready."

"I am not dead?" Mead felt the beginnings of a familiar push but this time she clung to the whiteness. "Wait, wizard! What is the purpose of the wristlet?"

"To aid your own meager power for a time, of course. Empathy is not the strongest of Talents, but it will be useful for your wizardry."

"But I do not wish to become a wizard!" Whatever she was clinging to suddenly dissolved, and she fell back into her body. She could feel grass against her palms and a familiar yet different prickle against her mind. She slowly opened her eyes.

Blond hair was all she could see at first of the blur bending over her, then her vision cleared to reveal Second's face. "I am not dead?" she asked fuzzily.

Second smiled faintly. "While I hold the salve of healing? No, you yet live." Puzzlement and shame touched her from his mind. "You expected me to let you die. I thought that was but the poison clouding your mind, but when you spoke, saying you understood, I—" He cleared his throat.

Mead kept her silence and examined her slashed arm. The salve appeared to have eased her shoulder's stiffness as well.

Second glanced over at the fallen creature. "Do you know what you have killed?" he asked in awe.

Mead glanced instead at the seared patch of ground and located a gleam of elven steel at its very edge. "We did not exchange names."

"That appears to be a fatal omission."

Mead glanced up in surprise. Was Second actually teasing her?

"I shall not repeat that one's error." The elf bowed slightly. "I am called Drycin."

He smiled tentatively at her, and days of mistrust fell away. She grinned. "I am called Mead."

"There Was a Broken Arrow" previously appeared in Errantry *#2, May 1984.*

BOUND BY A BELT OF WEB

The pale-haired elf paused to stare at the trees shining silver in the moonlight before him. Awe widened his large eyes as something in the very core of his being whispered *home* He turned slowly, studying the tall shining trees surrounding him. These had stood here in the Beginning Time. And before. Ageless were the silver-gray trees of the Glen of Ancient Voices, and magical its breezes, springing from deep within its heart where once the First Door had opened. Silver leaves rustled a murmur of sound, and he waited a moment, half-hoping a Voice would speak to him.

Taeryelun shook his head at himself not really. The Voices spoke only on matters of grave importance. They would hardly greet everyone who entered their Glen. He glanced swiftly about for sentries and was somewhat disappointed to find none. Disappointed, but not surprised. He had swiftly learned that his forest kin were beyond any understanding. To leave a Gate unguarded would appear to be the height of folly. So many rings of spells protected the Highlands Gate that the wardings were almost visible. The best warriors vied for the honor of watching its steep and rocky path. But here in the Great Woods, the first and foremost of the Gates—the doorways through which his people had entered the Lands—was left accessible to any and all who chose to draw near. Even humans.

The blond elf frowned slightly at the course of his thoughts. Even though he had come to learn differently, the teachings of the Highlands still influenced his thinking. The few human wizards he had met thus far in Drwseren did not resemble at all the brutish, greedy creatures that his Highlands upbringing had lead him to expect. Neither did the human trader whom he had followed to this legendary location. Taeryelun smiled slightly, recalling the grace and courtesy with which she had responded in their near-fatal first meeting. A puzzle in herself, that one.

Moonlight shone upon pale hair farther within the Glen, and, recalling his errand, Taeryelun hastened to join his Elder. Soon he had reached where she strolled in discussion with the tall, dark-haired Elder of the Drwseren elves.

His second detached himself from the night shadows. "All is well, Leader. Shall I go to guard Wilobe?"

Taeryelun located his Elder's other guard as he answered his second. "No, Drycin. Stay with the Elder. I shall be but a moment. Coaeden watches until my return, although our trader is safe within Drwseren."

"Safe?" Drycin repeated skeptically, but Taeryelun had already started toward his Elder.

Her long gown whispered against the fragrant grass as she turned from her companion to acknowledge his presence. "Kinsman," she greeted him, signifying that he might use the informal manner of address. "You have news?"

Taeryelun could not bring himself to such familiarity before the woodland First of Council. He bowed deeply to both Elders. "I come from the Seer," he told his kinswoman. "The messenger birds have reached him. He is but three nights away."

To his Elder, there was only one "he". The joy which shone in his kinswoman's eyes lightened Taeryelun's heart with its radiance. She lightly touched the bulge that was her unborn son and drew a shuddery breath. Yet when she turned toward the dark-haired elf, she was an Elder of the Highlands again.

* * *

Pools of colored light dappled the floor, stretching from the wall of multihued crystal shards to the block of clear crystal before her. Mead Mistdaughter stared moodily into its depths, attempting without success to shut herself off from both the mild argument at the door and the emotions of its participants. Coaeden, she noticed with a faint stirring of interest, was losing.

"No, and no again," the Seer insisted fussily. "The Seeing will be difficult enough without your presence. Now wait outside."

"But I must guard—"

"Yes, and you can do a wonderful job of it outside. By the Green, child, against what will you protect her? Me? Do you see anyone else lurking about in my chambers?"

The question was so like unto Mead's own that her temper stirred against its bonds. How much longer would these Highlanders insist upon guarding her among her friends? Of course, the sudden appearance of a Shadows' servant directly outside Drwseren had startled both groups of elves. So much so that the Council did not even protest the Highlanders' idea of security. But why that security had expanded to include her as well as the Lady was beginning to become a matter of some irritation to Mead. Taeryelun, the leader of the Lady's escort, felt he owed Mead a debt for saving his kinswoman's life. She had thought that debt balanced when they had aided her in rescuing Acorn Willowdaughter, but such was not to be. And now Drycin, Taeryelun's second, felt *he* owed her a debt of honor for his behavior towards her, a debt that was not even balanced by his saving her life. Mead sighed.

She would have to leave for the Tradegather soon. *Before* the Second of Council returned to Drwseren to gather the Lady under his protection, else she might find the Lady's former escort hers.

The light click of the closing door did not gain her attention as much as did the sudden lessening of Coaeden's emotions behind the shielding webbing lowered before the wooden portal. She looked up as the crystal awoke to the touch of the Seer's hands. His large elf eyes, dark as summer leaves, studied her. "You asked for my aid, Wilobe. You have no desire, then, to see the future?"

Her fingertips brushed the feathered band about her wrist. "When magic is involved, the future is better unknown. No, I seek only to learn aught of a wizard who has entangled me in his games."

The Seer stroked the smooth line of his jaw. "I have heard mention of your search. The Guardian was not able to aid you?"

"Had I a description of this wizard, I am certain she could. However, I have not seen him, only heard his voice in my head."

"A Seeing will be difficult if the appearance is unknown."

Mead held out the wrist encircled by blue-edged brown feathers. "This band came from the old one. Will it avail the Seeing?"

He fluttered his fingers at her, and she obediently held the band above the crystal block. A ripple of blue seemed to crawl through the clouding depths. The Seer sighed and tucked his hands into his sleeves. "Too many factors impede the Sight. It was formed of a material alien to the Lands, and sensitized to respond to the one who first touched it. It speaks only of you."

Mead stared down at the feathered band. "Then naught can be done to aid me."

"Did I say thus?" The Seer shook his head at her, the gold band restraining his black hair winking in the light. "For a Trader I would say aye, as the narrow trail a Trader must tread closes potential in favor of safety. But for a scholar who has mastered High Elven…" One brow lifted. "How strong are your memories of this old one, Mist's daughter?"

Mead looked quizzically at him. "Strong."

"Good. Then we shall use them as a base from which to See. Look into the crystal."

Knowing better than to touch the crystal block, Mead placed her hands firmly behind her back and gazed into the clear depths.

"Deeper. Now, draw out the memories of this old one's voice, aught you saw while he spoke to you, aught that you sensed in any manner or more."

Mead obediently pictured the blinding whiteness she saw whenever she spoke with the wizard, the soft chimes that seemed to accompany his voice.

"Impress those images upon the crystal. Try to see them reflected within, using your mind's eye."

Mead tried. When that attempt failed, she tried again, summoning up the old one's voice, his odd manner of speech, the "toys" he had placed in her path, only to have each impression dissolve into nothingness as soon as she tried to picture it within the crystal. Patiently, she began again with another set of memories, focusing on the various notes of the chimes and the absence of feeling she had experienced within the whiteness. Again the images disappeared. Thrice more she tried and thrice more failed, and finally she had to admit defeat. She could see nothing within the crystal's depths.

She raised her eyes up to meet the Seer's, confused at the approval she sensed in him. "I cannot…"

"Look again," the elf directed. "See with your mind's eye."

Mead glanced down and saw a small bubble of white suspended within the clear depths. She studied the small sphere in surprise, wondering if she dared ask what was "the mind's eye."

The Seer placed his hands upon the crystal. Yellow light sprang into being at the contact, spreading up his arms to enclose his upper body in a shimmering glow. Mead watched silently, curiosity stirred by the extent of her ignorance. The ability to see auras did not bring with it the knowledge of what meant the colors she saw. Ere long she must find someone to ask.

The bubble within the block split, spilling whiteness, which spread like a bead of milk through water. The elf stared into the white-streaked depths of the crystal, where yellow sparkles blossomed and danced.

"I See a hill against the stars. A figure shining white stands atop it, and before the figure hangs Lunemysee's Necklace. I sense a great weariness... He has come far; I See whiteness—snow below three moons."

"*Three* moons?" Mead murmured. The old one must truly be a stranger to the Lands.

"Wild Magic is strong about the figure; it distorts the Seeing. The form seems to shift; I cannot catch the features."

"I do not wish his face," Mead interrupted swiftly, echoes of Drycin's *"appearances can be deceiving"* whispering in her memory, "only some measure of him. Is his mischief born of malice or ignorance? I need to know why—"

"He is not far distant...south and east of this place," the Seer continued unheeding.

Mead straightened with a sudden unease. "Seer, enough. I—"

"He turns now, raising his staff. I can See—"

Blinding white light blazed within the crystal and a wild clamor of chimes filled Mead's head. "Not that way shall you find me, apprentice!" a familiar old voice cried.

The Seer screamed.

* * *

Taeryelun pushed through the curious onlookers filling the passage and stopped short upon entering the Seer's chambers. Before him a milk-white block of crystal shone with the clear brilliance of the Moon.

"It was much brighter when I entered upon hearing the Seer's screams," Coaeden said at his elbow.

Taeruyelun wrenched his gaze away from the shimmering crystal to study his young subordinate. The long-haired archer's expression was a mixture of excitement and relief, but he appeared to be unharmed, and Taeryelun glanced quickly around the chambers he had left but a short time ago. On the floor behind the block a healer tended the stricken Seer. Another healer, of an age with Coaeden, stood in close company with the Third of Council and a dark-haired human dressed in elfin garb. Wilobe appeared unhurt, but the watchful expectancy with which the healer was regarding her did not bode well.

"Know you what occurred here?" Taeryelun asked, also watching the human as the tall Elder spoke to her. There was a slump to her shoulders that he did not recall seeing ere now.

"No, Leader," Coaeden admitted, shame in his voice. "The Seer would not permit me to remain."

The healer abruptly turned away from the silent trader, hurrying past Coaeden and Taeryelun to draw the light web of shielding over the open doorway. Taeryelun glanced at Coaeden as the small group in the passage began to disperse. The youngest of his command did not seem to realize the significance of the healer's action or the human's sudden paleness, but his leader was content to have it thus. The trader's privacy had been disturbed enough.

"If the Seer did not permit your presence, then you could do naught else but as you did." He glanced at the webbing, knowing that he had best send Coaeden beyond it, yet wishing to not injure the young archer with a further imagined shame. The answer came swiftly. "Seek out our Elder and tell her what has transpired here. Tell her also that I fear the wizard's tampering has gone beyond what she and I have discussed, and await her instructions."

Coaeden nodded. "At once, Leader."

Taeryelun watched as the young healer returned to Wilobe's side. The trader absently brushed the feathers on her wristlet and he nodded to himself. He could now put the reason for her odd and sudden tendency to avoid company while they were on the trail. A hot spark of anger at the old one and his games flared, and he quickly damped it, chiding himself for his careless lapse. But his kinswoman was not the only one who had grown fond of the young human.

Taeryelun stared thoughtfully at the crystal until its aura appeared. The white streak of Wild Magic running through the yellow somewhat explained the Seer's condition. But not Wilobe's. He glanced in her direction again.

She looked less alien out of the dark and somber garb she usually affected. The bright colors of the clothing his Woods kin had gifted her, suited her. And, with her dark hair, she seemed akin to the dark-haired Woods dwellers. She was not attractive; no human could be with those too-small eyes and large nose and mouth. Although Wilobe's nose and mouth were smaller than those of other humans he had encountered.

He shook himself out of his reverie and started towards the trader, thinking how childlike she looked among the tall lowlanders. Yet she stood but a fingers-breadth shorter than himself.

"But we *must* learn," Third said persuasively. "What type of power has he, that he can reach into Drwseren itself as if our protections did not exist?"

"I have done enough already," Wilobe said softly.

"Mead," the Third of Council said. Taeryelun stiffened at the careless use of the human's true name.

"You cannot doubt what is before you," the trader said with a nod to the shimmering crystal. "Ask your Seer what he Saw, if he recovers." She glanced at the young healer. "He will recover?"

"Mead, the safety of Drwseren is at risk," Third said.

Wilobe tossed her dark shoulder-length hair back to gaze up at the tall elf. "'The safety of Drwseren?' You can best preserve the safety of Drwseren, Faenoree, by not holding me here to conduct another Seeing. The wizard did not want to be Seen. *I* am the cause of this!" She gestured at the Seer and the crystal. "The safety of Drwseren is threatened only so long as I remain in it. The wizard was not attacking Drwseren; he was warning me. And I shall take that warning and depart."

Their gazes locked for a moment, then the tall Third of Council nodded. "If you must. I cannot hold you against your will. But rest first from this 'warning.'" He turned to the healer. "Conduct her to her room and be certain of her recovery."

Taeryelun made to follow when the Third's voice stopped him. "A moment please, Leader."

Torn between duty and courtesy, Taeryelun glanced uneasily at the doorway through which Wilobe and the young healer had gone and was relieved to see Drycin pass by in their wake. He turned back to the Third of Council. "Yes, Elder?"

The Woods elf smiled. "I am but Third of Council. Only First of Council here deserves the title 'Elder.' But I did not delay you to speak of our different customs." He glanced at the crystal. "I would but ask you and yours not to gainsay Wilobe in her decision. I know she has become dear to your Elder; she is dear to many of my people as well, both as the child we knew and the trader she has become. Even so, the only aid she requested of us was the Seeing." He glanced at the silent Seer. "Which, I fear, has done naught but increase the burden she carries."

Taeryelun looked steadily at the Seer until his aura appeared. The white streak was not as pronounced as it was about the once-transparent crystal, but it was present, nonetheless. "Will you be able to break the spell?"

"Given time, as I am certain the wizard is aware. Mead has the right of it; the wizard but warns. Perhaps he warns Mead; mayhap the warning is for us."

"Not to interfere?" Taeryelun held his emotions in check. "And will you, like Wilobe, heed his warning? This wizard could cause her death by his games."

The taller elf looked toward the empty doorway. "I think she well knows that possibility."

* * *

The healer closed the door and crossed the room to where Mead examined the carvings on a panel of silver wood. "Your guard still waits outside," she said softly.

"At least he is not inside. You did well, Tomaralee."

"Few will naysay a healer. Even if she be but an apprentice." She peered over Mead's shoulder. "You are determined, then, to leave us?"

"I must. I have brought enough trouble upon Drwseren." Finding the correct design, she laid her palms flat upon it, then slid her hands apart. The panel silently opened to reveal a narrow passageway. A sturdy elfin bow leaned against the wall just within, and Mead glanced swiftly at Tomaralee.

The elf's air of studied casualness would have done justice to a wizard. "Your mother will be upset enough that you leave without payment. The least we could do was replace the weapon broken on our behalf. Now go quickly, ere your guard decides to make certain I have not harmed you. You remember the Hidden Ways to the entrance?"

Mead ran appreciative fingers over the smooth finish of the bow and nodded, her throat suddenly tight from the thoughtfulness of her friends.

Tomaralee, as perceptive as ever, lightly laid a hand on her shoulder. "I thought you would. The days when we all played within those passages are not that far distant. Hurry, now. I will give you a fifty count, then leave and tell your guard that you rest and are not to be disturbed."

"And if he wishes to check on my presence?" Mead shook her head. "No. I will not cause ill feelings between his people and yours. You leave first and say that I sleep. I will block the door afterwards to further delay any pursuit."

Tomaralee hesitated and Mead could understand her indecision. Although Tomaralee was much other than herself, the reckoning of age differed between their peoples. She had been considered adult for many years and was accustomed to responsibility. Tomaralee, however, the oldest of her elfin playmates, had but recently come into adulthood.

The decision was abruptly taken from them by a knock at the door. Tomaralee and Mead exchanged glances, then Mead closed the panel and waved Tomaralee over to the door.

* * *

The blonde Elder settled herself comfortably in her chair as Coaeden closed the door. She looked up at Taeryelun. "No, Leader, I shall not dismiss my escort. Would you leave me unprotected in the midst of strangers?"

"I do not ask for all, Elder, merely—"

"I wish for the Second of Drwseren Council to thank and commend each of you personally. All must be here when he arrives."

Taeryelun curbed his frustration and settled upon a new tactic. "Wilobe as well? She is more deserving of his thanks."

There was laughter in the sea-green eyes that only he could see, and he knew that his ploy had not deceived her.

"I agree. But I shall not dictate to Wilobe her comings and goings. Our trader's obligation to us has ended. We cannot keep her from her livelihood."

"But her safety!" Coaeden burst out.

The Elder's eyebrows rose, and Taeryelun slowly turned to look at the young archer. Coaeden quickly lowered his eyes. "Your pardon, Elder. But Wilobe's safety—"

"—matters not as greatly to her as does the safety of her friends," the Elder completed for him. "We have all had ample demonstration of that."

"By that much we can follow her reasoning," Taeryelun said, releasing Coaeden from his gaze. "But in other ways she has changed. She has no skill in the ways of magic. Why does she not ask our aid in this?"

The Elder glanced at the closed doors. "I feel certain she would, if she was free to ask."

Taeryelun straightened. "You suspect something restrains her from the asking? The wizard, perhaps?"

Coaeden made a small sound, and Taeryelun turned toward him. "You know aught of this?"

Coaeden was pale. "I...I had forgotten. She told Drycin, Wybr and myself that she would not ask the Elder's aid, nor involve any of us in... I did not realize!"

Taeryelun glanced helplessly at the Elder.

"A trader's word, it appears, is her bond," the Elder said softly.

* * *

Mead closed the concealed door and straightened her dark-colored traveling garb. The portals of Drwseren stood unguarded before her. Drawing the hood of her cloak over her head, she hastened out into the forest. Her steps turned of old habit towards the Glen, and, after a moment's hesitation, she allowed them to continue. The Highlanders would not expect her to go there and by going there she could turn Drwseren's safeguards against detection to her advantage. Pathways greatly used were protected by spell to show no sign of passage. Finding one such pathway, she quickened her pace.

Soon the soft hush of the Glen enveloped her as she walked among the silver trees. She glanced about at the shining trunks, renewing old acquaintances. She had always loved to be here. Her father would sit under the trees for the greater part of a night, waiting for the Voices to speak. They never did, which had greatly disappointed him, though not Mist. Mead had always been amused at how Mist would study her father for signs of trance whenever he returned from the Glen. It had availed him naught to explain to Mist—fearful of geas—that the Glen only advised, never commanded.

The hush suddenly seemed deeper. Mead stopped, scanning the area. The trees appeared to shine brighter than before, but that could be due to the rising sun. Silver leaves rustled around her. Her scalp prickled.

"Bind the Snow Peak's Child."

Mead whirled. There was no one nearby, no one within range of her senses. The leaves rustled.

"Bind the Snow Peak's Child."

The voice was neither human nor elfin. She could not recall ever hearing its like. Mead stared at the leaves stirring in the absence of any breeze and paled. "No, not you, too," she breathed.

"Bind the Snow Peak's Child," the Voice repeated a third time. The leaves stilled.

* * *

"You summoned me, Leader?" Drycin asked.

Taeryelun surveyed his stiffly precise second-in-command.

"Wilobe?"

"Rests still. Wybr guards her door."

Taeryelun nodded in relief that there was no need for haste, then glanced at the closed doors of the Elder's chamber. He wondered how she would take what he was about to say. "I place you in command of the Elder's escort, Drycin. When she decides she no longer needs those services, you will lead our force back to the Highlands."

From Drycin's expression, his orders were not completely unexpected. "What shall I tell the Highlands Council?"

"That I owed a life-debt for the rescue of a blood-kin. If they wish to outlaw me for that, then so be it."

Drycin looked stricken. "But, Leader, what of you?"

"I know not. But the lands outside the Highlands are vast, and I—" He thought a moment, then smiled. "I have a great desire to see a Tradegather."

* * *

Although her pace was not what she would have preferred, it was well suited for serious thought. And Mead had much to think upon. Of late, far too many had decided to direct her life. First that wizard, with an apprenticeship she had never requested, then those overprotective Highlanders, and now the Glen of Ancient Voices. And who or what was the Snow Peak's Child? She would probably have to travel to the mountains to learn the answer to that riddle.

"Enough!" she suddenly said aloud, startling both herself and a bird in the tree above her. It darted away in a whirr of white, and Mead curbed her tongue, wishing to avoid further betrayal.

Enough, she repeated to herself. *No longer will I allow others to direct my life. I will continue on to the Tradegather and forget about children of snow peaks and wizards that come from lands with three moons.* She glanced down at the wristlet of blue-edged brown feathers. *And I will not touch anything strange that appears in my path, be it branch of rock or leaf. The wizard shall not ensnare me in his games again.*

Mead shook herself. She needed a run, both as a release and to make up for lost time. But first she had best muddy the trail for any pursuer. She glanced up at the trees and smiled.

* * *

Taeryelun studied the ground and cursed himself for a fool. He should have realized Wilobe would attempt to leave unseen, rather than believing she rested. If Coaeden had not attempted to free her from the vow she had given to Wybr, Drycin and himself, they might still have thought her safe within their protection. Instead, she had probably been gone the greater part of the day.

His bewilderment grew as he detected no sign of her passage. How had she managed to leave no tracks? He had gone to the very limits of Drwseren in the direction of their arrival and had seen no sign of the trader. His only hope would be to press on in the direction from which they had come to Drwseren and hope that she was indeed returning to her people.

Wings whirred above him, and he glanced up to meet an inquiring gaze. "Ho, my friend," Taeryelun chirped kindly. "Have you seen aught of a human female?"

* * *

Mead glanced at the sun peeking over the horizon as she shook twigs and leaves out of her cloak. Trees were not the most comfortable of sleeping places, but they were the safest.

Spotting a large pawprint, she crouched to examine it closer. It was wolf, and from its size, one of the Great Wolves. She could discern no other prints nearby, but it was an old spoor. She wondered if its owner was one of the pack of white wolves they had encountered on the way to Drwseren.

* * *

Taeryelun stopped to scan the ground again, but Wilobe's trail had once more vanished completely. Amid his concern was admiration for the trader's skill; she was almost as good as an elf.

He straightened to peer into the distance. He was certain that he had probably overshot her. If only he could be certain of her precise heading! He was already far west of the path they had taken to Drwseren. Rather than returning to where they had left the trade caravan, Wilobe was most likely heading directly for the Tradegather. Unfortunately he did not know where the meeting of traders would be.

* * *

Mead leaned back against the tree trunk and sleepily watched the stars through the leaves. Before her hung the Great Wheel, the sky's signpost for any trader wishing to travel to the Tradegather. The stars in their circular pattern glittered like the gems in the necklace after which the elves had named the grouping. Lunemysee's Necklace.

Mead's eyes snapped open. Lunemysee's Necklace, the Seer had said. South and east of Drwseren. How close was she to where the wizard had been at the time of the Seeing?

She shifted uneasily on the cradling branches, then firmly closed her eyes. She was *not* going to worry about the wizard. He and his games were no longer a part of her life.

* * *

Taeryelun smiled as he studied the base of the tree. He *had* passed over her path the previous day. She had spent the night in this tree and had moved on but a short time ago. He should be with her very soon.

* * *

Mead scowled at the feathered wristlet as she walked. Her dreams had been filled with chimes again. That did not bode well. Neither did the sensation of late that she was being followed. She took a tighter grip on her staff. So long as she was on guard for any of the wizard's tricks, all would be—

She hesitated in midstride as white flashed briefly on the ground before her. Wavering unsteadily, she studied the spot carefully from afar, not daring to go any closer. Nothing seemed wrong; there were no fallen branches, not even a stick. Only a thick cluster of spiderwebs in the grass before her. She backed one step and then another, trying to catch sight again of that flash of whiteness. Nothing appeared, but suspicion grew in her like a thundercloud. She stared at the suspect patch of ground and tried to control her feelings.

"What have we here?" a human voice asked to her left.

Mead berated herself. To have been so oblivious as to mistake another's emotions for her own! She turned carefully, her staff held defensively. Facing her was a large bearded man, one hand resting negligently on the hilt of his sword. The language he spoke was Aldaian, as was his leather scale armor. The black tassel dangling from his left shoulder proclaimed him one of the Aldaian king's guards. And he was not alone.

"Might have known it would be a trader," commented someone to her right. Mead turned to keep both kingsmen in her sight, deciding that bandits would have been more preferable. The second speaker had his sword out, but held it as if he considered her no threat. "Meddling, interfering—" He spat.

The first kingsman looked back into the brush. "Tell Mile we finally caught the sneak." There was an answering rustle, and he turned back to Mead. "Been following us, eh, Trader? Springing our traps and fouling our snares? Afraid of competition?"

Mead stared at him in bewilderment. "I have done none of those things."

"Oh?" The second kingsman glanced at the first. "Seen any white wolves, Trader?"

* * *

Taeryelun watched the scene worriedly. He had seen the trader from afar as she studied a patch of ground which glowed with the aura of the wizard's magic, but had been unable to reach her before the other humans had appeared. Since he did not understand their language, he thought it prudent to wait before making his presence known. Wilobe's behavior indicated that the humans were not friends, but so far she did not appear to be in any real danger. He turned his attention to the other watchers, who had also decided to notice him.

The white wolf glided silently toward him, her blue eyes bright. **Two-legged-walker-with-magic.**

Mother-of-brave-warriors-and-wise-hunters, we meet again.

We meet again. Magic-walker, stay safe with me. Do not attempt to interfere with our hunt.

A chill brushed Taeryelun. Wilobe in the midst of a hunt? **Wise-mother, the she before us is not your enemy. Help me to save her.**

The wolf's jaws opened. **They hunt us. We hunt *them*!**

But not *her*! Remember her?

The wolf's head lifted, sniffing the air. Her ears perked. **Remember her. Small-she-with-magic-scent-and-clear-gaze. Remember her. Clear-gaze in danger?**

Yes. Taeryelun looked carefully about, locating others of the pack. **Clear-gaze in great danger.**

Will tell Hunt-leader. Her bright eyes studied him. **Stay safe.**

Taeryelun turned his attention back to Wilobe as the Pack Mother vanished. The glow of white on the ground near her boot was another source of worry. If Wilobe did refuse the wizard's newest toy, as indeed she seemed to be intending, then none of those humans could be allowed near it, else the wizard would gain a new apprentice. He quietly drew his sword, wishing for Wilobe's bow.

* * *

Mead forced herself to calm, difficult as it was with others' emotions invading her thoughts. She needed a clear head to safely win out of this trap, for if these kingsmen were indeed hunting white wolves, she was in danger from both hunters and hunted. She had no time to sort through the incessant barrage of sensations, but she dared not act without knowing to what she was reacting. *I should have let the*

Shadows have you, wizard.

She met the first kingsman's gaze. "I have been traveling and only now arrived here. I don't know what you're talking about." Her feet itched to turn and run. She could easily outdistance these armored kingsmen, but those wishing to keep a whole skin never turned their backs on kingsmen, who grew bolder whenever signs of weakness or fear were detected. In addition, if the wizard's latest toy was indeed hidden here, she dared not leave it for these creatures to find and use.

"She lies," the second man protested. "Norbet, she must. The only person in all the days here. She lies!"

Mead kept silent as three men appeared from the brush. The apparent leader, his bare arms heavily scarred and an untidy stubble on his chin, flicked a disdainful glance over Mead. "Well done, men," he growled. "So this is our trouble-maker?"

"She says she just arrived here, Mile," the second man said hurriedly. "She says—"

"She was looking at the ground when I found her," Norbet inserted thoughtfully, glancing at the spot by her boot. He lifted his gaze to her face. "She might have planted a trap herself."

"Is that true, Trader?" Mile started toward her, and she shifted her staff warningly. "Why didn't you disarm her?" he muttered to Norbet.

"A *trader*, sir?"

"I was looking for tracks," Mead said swiftly. "Someone I know may have passed this way." She glanced at the group, gauging their strength. "Have any of you seen an old wizard recently?" She knew that would give them pause, with the Aldaian king's fear of magic.

"A wizard," said someone. "Maybe he's the one."

"Someone is going to pay for all our trouble," Mile said. He glanced at Mead, then looked at his men. "Take her."

I could lose them in the forest, Mead thought as they started toward her, *then double back and keep watch over the wizard's toy.* In the back of her mind was the thought that things would be simpler if she claimed it herself, but she ignored that as she readied herself to fight. The leather scale armor protecting their chests would lessen the impact of blows there, but their heads, arms, and legs were unprotected. She struggled to clear her mind of them.

The ragged advance toward her suddenly stopped. Eyes widened as a wash of fear hit her, and two of the kingsmen actually retreated. Mead decided to risk a look behind her.

Taeryelun had emerged from behind a nearby tree and was walking swiftly toward her, his sword drawn. "Go quickly," he said in the Common Tongue. "I will guard your back."

Mead glanced hurriedly at the kingsmen to see if they understood. "I can fight—" she began in the same language.

"And have you yet sensed another's pain or shared a death?"

"What are you fools doing?" Mile cursed. "Kill them!"

Mead glanced at the kingsmen—and suddenly saw a gliding blur of white behind them. She felt chilled and was absurdly grateful for the warm brush of Taeryelun's concern. "No."

"Go, then." The elf pushed her behind him. "Use your bow once you are out of range of their minds and I will join you."

Mead glanced again at the kingsmen. Norbet and his skinny friend had regained their courage, but the other two were backing from Mile into danger. She shook her head to clear it with no success. She did not know how Taeryelun had guessed her difficulty, but it was apparent he understood more of its implications than she had.

"Go," he repeated gently.

"She's getting away!" Norbet yelled.

One of the retreating kingsmen suddenly turned to confront the waiting jaws of a white wolf. His fear stabbed her thoughts anew.

Mead turned and stumbled away. She had not gone far when a white wolf rose up to meet her. She froze, but slowly through the welter in her mind came the welcome the wolf radiated. "Pack Mother?" she asked hesitantly.

The wolf suddenly growled and leaped past her. Mead turned—and an abrupt stillness filled her mind.

Taeryelun was on the ground, atop the very spot she had thought to protect. Norbet stood with raised sword above him—and stabbed downward.

"NO!" An arrow was nocked and aimed before she realized she had moved, but a blur of white struck down her target. Man and wolf rolled and suddenly were apart. On his knees, the man stared into the snarling face of the wolf. Leather from his throat to his left collarbone had been ripped away, and his sword had fallen behind him. "Help me!" he called to Mead. "You're a human!"

The Pack Mother glanced expectantly at her as his hand closed about the hilt of his sword. The arrow took him in the throat.

Mead slowly lowered her bow. The Pack Mother turned away from the dead man to nose the still body of another kingsman. She didn't see any of the others; they and the wolves they had hunted had vanished.

She looked at Taeryelun and numbness stilled her thoughts.

Slowly she started toward him, afraid of what she would find. The Pack Mother returned to Taeryelun's side and sat, watching Mead.

Kneeling beside the fallen elf, she felt grief give way to hope. There was no blood on his back, nor any sign of a wound or tear in his garments. Perhaps he was but stunned. Reaching out to turn him, she gasped in shock. Her hands passed completely through him!

Chimes sounded in her head. "*You* were supposed to touch it. Not him!"

Mead closed her eyes and "saw" glaring whiteness. Opening them again, she stared at Taeryelun's still form. "What have you done to him?"

"Saved him from the consequences of your foolishness. He needn't have sacrificed himself. How do you expect to become a wizard if you won't use the tools I furnish you?"

Mead clenched her fists but schooled her thoughts. "I do not want to become a wizard!"

"I'm not entirely certain myself of your worthiness. Especially when you keep breaking things. Prove to me that you are not fit to be a wizard, and I will release you from my apprenticeship."

"Done, then." Mead could not believe she had heard aright. "Release the elf."

"No, he will be an earnest of your behavior." His "voice" hardened. "Do not attempt to lose deliberately. I will know if you do and you will forfeit…him." The chimes and his "voice" lightened again. "Try your best and if you then fail, then both you and I will know you are not fit."

Something about that condition seemed amiss. "The question is not of fitness but of desire. I do not wish to become a wizard."

"Few know what they truly desire. Are we agreed?"

Mead sighed. "What must I do?"

A soft chuckle echoed in her mind. "Find me."

The chimes faded. Mead quickly closed her eyes to find that the whiteness was gone. Opening them again, she gasped as the form of Taeryelun wavered and faded into the empty air. She sprang to her feet. "Find you? Only that? You must want me to fail, old one, with the directions you have supplied!"

She heard a soft whine and looked into the wolf's blue eyes. "He is alive, Pack Mother." Her fists clenched again. "The wizard took him. Now I must find them both." Her hands opened. How was she to do that?

The wolf glanced at the ground and Mead followed her gaze. At her feet was a long white belt. It appeared to be woven out of fine white hair or spiderweb. The buckle was a flat, featureless square of a curiously multihued metal. The colors seemed to flow across its surface as she watched, constantly changing, with never the same pattern.

Mead sighed. She dared not leave it where it was. "I will take it with me, but I refuse to wear it. Do you hear me, wizard?"

Wary of any contact with the material, she used her dagger to push the belt into a pouch, which she then fastened tightly. By the time she had finished, another wolf had appeared to join the Pack Mother. His fur was clean and damp with water, which he playfully attempted to shake over them.

Mead found her sleeve caught in the Pack Mother's sharp teeth. The wolf tugged gently, and Mead obediently rose to her feet and followed the wolves.

The young male led them to the top of a small incline. He sniffed excitedly about one spot, then sat and waited for Mead.

Mead crouched to examine the ground. There was a strange print in the dry soil, an old spoor which had weathered into something completely unrecognizable.

She looked up at the expectant wolves. "Forgive me, honored ones, but I know not this print."

The Pack Mother leaned forward and all but touched Mead's feathered wristlet with her nose.

For a moment Mead did not fully understand. Then she rose and looked about her. On the opposite side from their approach, the ground dropped away in a gentle slope. The small incline was actually a high hill. She looked up at the sky, getting her bearings. The stars were not visible yet, but she knew where a particular grouping would be.

"'A hill against the stars,'" she recited. "'Before that figure hangs Lunemysee's Necklace'…he was here! He was physically *here*—and that is *his* print!" She looked down the slope. The implications were dizzying. She could track this wizard, assuming he did not magically erase all signs of his presence as he must have done when he planted his latest toy.

Returning to the wolves, she dropped to one knee before them and bowed her head. "Thank you, honored ones. You have given me a chance to save my friend, and for that I am most grateful."

The Pack Mother rose to her feet and gently touched noses with Mead. The trader blinked as a blue-green aura sprang into being about the wolf, then vanished.

The young male rose and padded down the hill. He stopped and looked back at Mead.

Mead was grateful for the support of her staff. She looked back into the wise blue eyes before her. "Oh, Pack Mother, the honor you do me is great, but I cannot."

The wolf sat down, watching her.

"Honored Mother, I would truly welcome his company, and his aid would be most invaluable, but I cannot accept this gift. The wizard I seek to find is swift to anger. He seriously harmed the Seer who told me of this hill, and you yourself saw what befell the elf who only thought to save me. Mother of the most brave, most clever hunters, I dare not risk another life."

The wolf studied her. Then she slowly and deliberately licked a long line down her side. Mead stared, then looked toward the young male. "You mean, *he* is the one the Lady healed?" The wolf watched her. Mead mentally groaned. *I shall have to stop helping people.* "Please, Pack Mother, he found this print. That settles the debt."

* * *

And I thought elves *were stubborn.* Mead looked down at the wolf padding by her side and mentally shook her head. At least he wouldn't be with her long. He had come more as escort and as protection against members of the pack still hunting kingsmen. Or so she had gathered after the one time he had strayed out of her sight. Neither of them had yet fully recovered from that encounter.

She stopped and leaned on her staff, her fingers avoiding the new tooth scars in the wood. "I need to rest," she sighed.

The wolf prowled over the area as she settled herself against a tree. He bounded up to her, sat down a moment, then sprang up and bounded away again.

She stared absently before her, feeling a weariness not born of physical exhaustion creeping into her thoughts. She had tried so hard to keep to her word. None of the elves should have become involved in this; the wizard was *her* problem. Yet she could not deny the relief she had felt when Taeryelun had appeared.

Her fists clenched. Taeryelun. The elf was alive at least, thanks to her wizard. At the back of her mind was the thought that the elf might not have been in danger without the wizard's "aid", that the kingsmen had had nothing to do with his collapse. She shook her head. What happened was past. Taeryelun had come to help her; his efforts deserved better thanks than captivity.

Her fingers brushed the feathers of her wristlet as she remembered Taeryelun's concern, then stopped at a sudden realization. She had sensed no other's emotions since the elf's apparent death. Had the wizard withdrawn that "gift"? She tugged at the feathered band, but it was still tightly fastened about her wrist.

Sighing, she leaned back against the tree trunk. The young wolf padded up and laid the body of a short-eared hopper beside her. He sat and waited, watching her.

* * *

Mead glanced up at the stars as she drew her cloak about herself. A short distance away, the young wolf laid his head upon his forepaws, his eyes glittering in the starlight. She smiled at the star patterns, amused by the coincidence. The wizard was taking almost the same route she had originally intended to follow to the Tradegather. She wondered what along this path would interest a wizard.

The white wolf's ears perked, and he raised his head. Mead waited, listening, and faintly to her ears came the howl of a wolf.

The young male sprang to his feet and padded over to nose her face. "Yes, I heard," she said softly. "So you will leave me now?"

He whined anxiously.

"I shall be fine. My thanks, brave and sharp-eyed hunter, for your most valuable help and protection. Please convey my gratitude to the Pack Mother. I am truly in your debt."

The wolf licked his side, then gently nosed her face. Blue eyes studied her for a moment before the wolf turned and disappeared into the night.

She waited, listening, and soon heard two wolves call and respond in the distance.

Glancing about her sleeping place, she momentarily debated whether to move up into a tree. Yet with the abundance of wolf spoor in the vicinity, most creatures would keep away. She pulled her cloak tighter about herself and closed her eyes.

Chimes rang softly about her as she dreamed, and from somewhere in the thick surrounding fog the wizard repeated, "Few know what they truly desire."

"Do you enjoy the life of a trader?" Taeryelun's voice asked. He came forward out of the fog, attired in the formal robes he had worn when Drwseren had welcomed the Lady.

In her dream, she did not answer as she had then. Instead, she heard her voice saying, "I had as much choice as the wizard has given me. While my father was alive, I followed his ways, the scholar's way. When he died, I took up Mist's path—but I am a better fighter than trader. Haggling holds no joy for me."

Taeryelun's face and form blurred as she spoke, becoming that of a dark-eyed scholar dressed in a trader's attire. "But what do *you* wish to be, daughter?" he asked a small girl-child. "Trading may be in your blood, but not your spirit. And the life of a scholar is much too calm and placid for my adventurous child."

"Father?" Mead said, awakening. She looked up at the dawn-streaked sky and wiped tears from her face with a sudden anger. *Curse you, wizard! Leave my memories be*!

Throwing aside the cloak, she rose to her feet, then glanced downward when she realized a small weight was gone from her side. The pouch into which she had put the belt was empty, and an opening just large enough for the belt's width had been forced through the fastening. The belt was not on the ground, and there was only one other place it could be. She sighed, looked down at her waist, and sighed again.

The belt, like the wristlet, proved impossible to remove. She fingered the odd texture of the woven material and wondered what properties this "tool" possessed. Knowing the deviousness of her wizard, she did not doubt that she would soon learn. She only hoped she and Taeryelun would survive the experience.

Aspects of the dream continued to worry at her as she gathered up her weapons and prepared to resume the search. What she had said to Taeryelun in the dream had been her exact thoughts when she had spoken to the elf during the ceremony. How had the wizard known that?

She tugged at the belt again. *I see your ploy, wizard, but such tactics shall avail you naught. I shall not stay a trader all my life; my mother and I both knew that. But neither shall I become a wizard*!

She had once thought to become a scholar, though not the kingdoms' idea of such. Her father had been one of a city's shield of savants until, desirous of learning what the kingdoms choose to ignore, he had left the city and the kingdom to wander. It was at Drwseren that he had met the band of Free Traders who later saved his life when he had been robbed by bandits. Mead smiled sadly. Mist had tried to teach him to fight, but that had been one subject he had never mastered. She had thought her own love of knowledge had been killed by the sword that took his life, but her travels with the Lady had shown her that there was still much she desired to know.

Mead shook her head. Her plans for the future must wait until she had won free of this wizard by failing his test.

She paused to study another mark of the wizard's passage, uneasy that such prints were still so evident. Hadn't the wizard realized that she was tracking him? Unless his purpose was to make this test difficult for her to fail.

A short time later she waited with arrow nocked and drawn for a small animal to emerge from the concealing brush. She had departed from Drwseren with very little in the way of supplies; now was the first opportunity she had had to replenish them.

The snuffling sounds increased, and the long, flexible snout of a spiketail emerged from cover.

Mead waited. *Come on*, she thought. *A little more.*

More of the spiketail emerged.

Her fingers poised, but Mead did not shoot. All was not right with the spiketail's movements. The fear she was suddenly able to sense from it did not match its behavior. A faint suspicion formed. *Come closer.*

She stared as the spiketail moved closer to her position. The creature walked as though it was being drawn against its will.

Keeping the bowstring taut, she slowly emerged from hiding. The spiketail could plainly see her, but all it did was stare at her and quiver.

She lowered her bow. *Go.*

The spiketail vanished.

Mead briefly closed her eyes. So that was the power of the belt. Command. Subjugation of an animal's will. And more, perhaps? She put the arrow back into her quiver, fitting what the wizard had said with what she now knew. Had she been wearing the belt when she had encountered the kingsmen, could she have controlled them as she had the small spiketail? She shivered. She did not desire that type of power, but now, willingly or not, she had it. She must needs be wary of what she said and thought. She glanced toward where the spiketail had vanished. Very wary indeed.

* * *

Chimes rang distantly in her ears as she woke, and Mead quickly searched her memory. She could recall nothing about her dreams save that they disturbed her. Somewhere in the midst of one the wizard had remarked, "All knowledge is power. I but teach. Only you can decide what you will do with the lessons."

She stared up at the fading stars. The wizard was still on a heading towards the Tradegather. Somehow that no longer seemed like a coincidence.

*   *   *

Mead puzzled over the print before her boot. The occasional marks of the wizard's passage were fresher but she still could make nothing of them other than an unrecognizable smudge.

The breeze suddenly freshened, bringing with it a strong and unmistakable musk reek that caused Mead to straighten in alarm. Wulverin! Fortunate for her that she appeared to be downwind of the creature, for, though it was the size of the lesser wolves, it would attack beings many times larger than itself. However, the scent seemed to be coming from exactly where she wished to go.

Wishing for loras leaves to deaden her own scent, she cautiously edged forward, scanning the tree branches overhead. Wulverin, despite their size, were excellent climbers, and had been known to spring upon their prey from above. Soon she could hear the grumbling cough of the bad-tempered beast. The wizard's trail led directly towards the source of the sound.

Mead cautiously and quietly moved away, watchful that the breeze did not suddenly shift and bring her scent to the wulverin. She would give the creature a wide berth. Since the wizard's heading toward the Tradegather had not varied, she could find it once again when she was safely away from the wulverin. The temptation arose to test the belt of web against the wulverin's will, but she quickly put that aside. Taeryelun's life depended on her; she had no time for foolhardy games with a power she did not intend to keep.

When she again found the wizard's trail, she had by then also found an ample supply of loras leaves, which she liberally smeared over herself. She quickened her pace, anxious to make up the time lost detouring around the wulverin's path. The wizard was not that far ahead of her. She had to confront him before he reached the Tradegather, which was perhaps two days travel from her present position.

She had not journeyed much farther that day when a fouler stench than the wulverin's forced her pace to slow. Ogres or goblins. She nocked an arrow as she advanced.

From hiding, she observed a single goblin poking the butt of its spear against a print on the ground. She waited. There had to be more, especially since this could be the group that had wounded the young white wolf. A single goblin would not have survived long within the wolves' range, even with a trag-coated spear. She wrinkled her nose and tried to ignore the stench.

Soon her patience was rewarded by the appearance of another of the boney purple-skinned creatures. Certain that there were still more, she continued to wait. She could not bypass them until she knew all of their positions.

While she was waiting, certain suspicions began to come together. Surely it could be no coincidence that both these creatures and the wulverin had appeared to delay her pursuit of the wizard. Was this more of the old one's doings? Perhaps to force her to use the power of the web belt? Mead smiled grimly. The old one would be disappointed that pleasure then, if such were the case. She would need only the loras leaves and her arrows to safely pass this obstacle.

A grumbling cough behind her wiped her mind clear of that simple plan. Noticing that the goblins had begun arguing as if they had not heard the sound, Mead slowly turned.

The wulverin snarled at her from a distance twice her length away, the teeth in the bearlike head shining sharp and deadly.

Thoughts bounded through her mind like dropped beads as Mead drew back her arrow. The wulverin could have followed the wizard's trail. It could have followed her own—the loras leaves would have covered her scent but its eyesight was as keen as a wolf's. Its speed was such that she would have time for only one shot, but close upon the heels of that thought was the realization that she had never heard of anyone killing a wulverin with one arrow.

She could sense nothing from its mind—and then suddenly she could, as if the mere thought had opened her awareness to the anger and bloodlust of the beast.

The wulverin dashed toward her, and faster than the creature, came the realization that no arrow or command could stop this charge. The instant before the wulverin sprang, she ordered, *Leap over*! and threw herself down.

Mead lay still, half-expecting to feel the slice of the claws in those oversize paws. Instead, shrill goblin cries penetrated her hearing, along with rasping growls.

She sprang to her feet and bolted, leaving wulverin and goblins to settle their differences as they would.

Mead wasted as little time as she dared in returning to the wizard's trail, ever conscious of his growing lead, and determined to prevent his arrival at the Tradegather His trail had become easier to follow, with the smudged prints appearing more and more frequently, and her unease grew.

The trader came at last to a wide river. The prints led upstream along its bank, but she hesitated, walking instead to the edge of the bank. Her tracking sense tingled. The wizard had crossed *here*!

She studied the opposite bank, clean of any marks, and then turned her gaze to follow the line of prints upstream. There were hills in that direction, affording numerous and varied places in which to hide. Had she been attempting to elude a pursuer, that was the direction she would have chosen. Almost was she tempted to believe the evidence of her eyes.

Mead turned back to the river with a shake of her head, trusting more in the sense that had once enabled her to find Acorn Willowdaughter in an ogre-infested wood. No, the trail led across the river *here*!

She studied her newest obstacle. The current was swift, and, thrusting the end of her staff into the river's edge, she found the water to be deep as well. Hurriedly wrapping most of her possessions into her cloak and bundling it atop her shoulders, she eased into the waist-deep waters.

For ten slow steps she struggled against the pull of the current, using her staff as additional support. Upon the next step, however, the water abruptly disappeared from around her.

Mead turned in surprise. Behind her was a small stream, its murmuring waters barely ankle deep. Her own clothing, however, was damp from the waist down.

Muttering to herself at the deviousness of wizards, she redistributed her gear and continued on.

Her tracking sense had lead her to a small clearing, when a voice hailed her. Turning, she saw a man robed in white atop a nearby hill. "Not that way shall you find me, apprentice!" he called.

She stared at the distant figure in dismay. So the prints had run true!

Mead returned her attention to the clearing, suddenly aware that she was not alone. Despair overrode her earlier reluctance, and she used the belt to command. "Come forth!" she ordered.

Instead of the monster she had expected, what stepped forth was a shining vision from brightest legend. A unicorn. But this was not the ordinary woodland denizen, not with its thick shaggy coat that almost covered its hooves, the long beard and longer flowing mane and tail. What faced her was the shyest of the breed: the mountain unicorn.

The instructions she had received from the Glen of Ancient Voices returned, and, with a sinking heart, she realized what a Snow Peak's Child was. "Stay," she ordered in a stricken voice.

Distaste at what she must do filled her as she reached for her pouch-ladened belt. Rope would serve better to find the being as the Voices had ordered, but she had none.

Or had she? What fell into her searching hands was rope of shining white web. The unicorn tossed its head, fighting the spell of her command.

Suddenly recalling the other properties of the wizard's "toys," Mead tossed a length of the rope towards the unicorn, directing all the strength of her thoughts to one new need.

A net closed about the being, completely imprisoning it in close-woven folds. The unicorn thrashed wildly, but the length of rope remaining in Mead's hand held the net tightly closed.

Mead waited as the unicorn's struggles slowly quieted, and hoped that the being would not injure itself. The Voices had not said for how long the Snow Peak's Child should be bound, and for her own peace of mind she hoped the purpose of this imprisonment would soon become clear.

She blinked as the unicorn suddenly blurred in shape and slowly reformed. The body became more like unto one of the Great Cats, and the neck formed into a torso, still catlike, but possessing two arms with paws only a little dis-similar from the four which supported the body. The head was surrounded by a large white mane, and the face was also catlike, with slitted orange eyes and whiskers about the tiny nose.

Mead glanced up at the hilltop. The white-robed man had disappeared, but now she was certain that that had been but an illusion to deceive her. What she held in her net was, despite its odd appearance, her wizard.

The pawlike hands gripped the net strands. "So you found me, apprentice. My congratulations."

"And mine as well."

Mead turned her head to locate the new speaker. Slowly out of the concealing brush to her right stepped a brightly beautiful being. It stood much taller than she, its features concealed by a multicolored mask, its thin form draped with layer upon layer of light, gauzy fabric sparkling with color. At its back were wings like those of a moth, their patterns mirrored in the gauzy draperies and mask. She tried to detect its emotions but, like those of the wizard, they were hidden from her.

"You have captured a most vile and dangerous creature," the masked one said. "Long have I pursued him, following his trail of destruction across our land until he entered this world to escape me."

Mead glanced at the being securely wrapped in the very tool he had given her. This description did not match what little assumptions she had gathered about her wizard. "What has he done?"

"What has he not? Theft, murder, the acquisition of power for mere pleasure. Those who thwarted him did so to their grief. Kingdoms have been destroyed for the sake of a whim."

The furred one snorted. "I never heard such nonsense."

"And apprentices?" Mead asked, a heavy weight closing about her heart.

Delicate wings fluttered. "What?"

"How many people have died in his games?" Mead turned to the old one, not waiting for an answer. "Has he spoken truth?"

The ensnared being struggled against his bonds.

"Hold tight to that line," the winged one ordered, "lest he cast a spell."

Mead concentrated on her thin connection to the net. "Answer me."

The wizard's mouth slowly opened. "Some," he panted.

The laughter coming from behind the mask grated on Mead's ears. "Out of his own mouth he convicts himself!"

Mead looked away from the orange eyes. "What would you do with him?"

"He must return to our land. But first, command him to reveal where he has hidden the treasures he has collected."

Her thoughts on Taeryelun's whereabouts, Mead did not at first understand. "Treasures?"

"Gems. Gold. Wealth, Trader!"

Mead looked from the captive wizard to the beautiful winged being. The aura about the one was that of Wild Magic—unpredictable, chaotic, and nonaligned. About the other—was nothing. Suddenly she tossed the line away from her.

The yellow eyes in the brightly patterned mask narrowed. "You fool! That gave you the power of command over him. He would have had no choice but to obey. Retrieve it!"

The trader glanced at the furred wizard carefully disentangling himself from the folds of the net, then turned back to the wizard with no aura. "My quarrel with him cannot be settled in that way."

"That spell only responds to you. Obey me!"

She merely looked at the being as the old one shook off the net entirely.

"Mead," the masked one said in a strangely compelling tone. The wings fluttered slowly. "Mead Mistdaughter."

Suddenly she seemed to be locked back in a corner of her mind. She could not move, could not even think. All she could do was watch and hear, without any knowledge or comprehension of what she saw and heard.

"Pick up that rope," the being commanded.

Her body moved to obey, then awaited further instructions.

A talon-like finger pointed at the old one. "Wrap it about him."

White-furred ears laid back as the being bared sharp teeth. "You would have her bind me?"

"Unless you wish her harmed, you will allow this to be."

The white-furred wizard watched as she walked near. Orange eyes looked deep into hers, and a soft sigh came to her ears. "Ah, apprentice, you have much to learn."

He clapped his pawlike hands together. "Enough, simulacrum. You have served the purpose for which you were created. Shoo."

Mead abruptly returned to herself. She whirled, but the winged being was gone. She turned back to the wizard, restraining her anger by a great effort of will. "You have used me once again!"

"Ah, so you retained awareness of what occurred? Excellent. Most would not. That, apprentice, was a name spell—and one of the simplest."

"So I failed?" Somehow the thought did not fill Mead with the relief she had expected.

"Of course, if you must bandy your true name about so casually, you must learn to expect name spells. And know how to protect yourself against them."

"So I failed."

"I gave the simulacrum independence so that it could still act if you used the belt on me—as you did, though not in the way I had expected. The simulacrum's function was to test your motives and to demonstrate the workings of command." His whiskers twitched. "You hardly used the command spell. Even on me, when you had ample opportunity."

Suddenly aware that she still held the white rope, Mead dropped it. "If domination of will is your requirement for an apprentice, then I am glad I failed to prove worthy."

"Did I say you failed? You had but to find me, and you did." The slitted eyes half-closed. "What, no protests of your lack of desire for wizardry?"

Mead shook her head. "I no longer know what I want."

"Excellent. But you still have much to learn before you can begin to learn from me." Chimes rang softly, and the wizard's form began to fade. "When you are ready," his voice continued in her head, "you will find me."

"Find you? But I already found you!"

"In the form that I once wore. You must find me as I am now."

"Wizard! Wait!" She ran toward the wizard as his outline shimmered and faded, and tripped over a large object that suddenly appeared in her path. Picking herself off the ground, she stared into the bewildered gaze of Taeryelun, who was securely wrapped in the folds of the net.

* * *

"You have yet to tell me what became of you," Wilobe said as they walked across the open field to the Tradegather.

"There is not much to tell." Taeryelun could not mislay his feelings of guilt. He was to have protected her and instead, for his sake, Wilobe had become more deeply entangled in the wizard's games. He knew that she had not related all that had occurred, and the omissions disturbed him. Yet Wilobe seemed more at peace with herself than she had been when she had left Drwseren. "A moment after you left me there was a brightness—and then naught. Until I found myself ensnared."

"The fault for your capture is mine," the trader said swiftly. "Yet the wizard was only trying to protect you. Had I accepted this"—she patted a pouch by her side—"neither of us would have been in danger. My stubbornness could have cost you your life." She looked at him, and Taeryelun could almost catch sight of a terrible memory in her eyes.

She turned toward the east, from whence another caravan was approaching, and shaded her eyes. "Mist is in that caravan. Shall we go to meet them?"

* * *

Taeryelun watched as the laden wagons passed by where they stood. He had not recalled seeing so many when they had last encountered the caravan.

Wilobe stiffened as a wagon decked with chimes and bells neared. She looked swiftly at the driver, an old man mumbling to himself, then stared deep into the orange eyes of his white-and-brown weosun. The elf studied the wagon, but could see naught amiss. "Do you know him, Dark-Eyed Lady?"

"No. Yes," she corrected herself, "a little. But I have much to learn."

SOMEONE IS WATCHING

The feeling was back again. He glanced over his shoulder and jumped at a slight movement, then sagged against the door jamb. His own reflection in the hall mirror. What was *wrong* with him? All the doors were locked, there was no one inside but himself, and still he felt as if he were being watched.

He mopped his forehead. He must be going insane. First he kept hearing voices when no one was speaking, and now this. He reached for the communicator. He had scheduled a board meeting for first thing in the morning, but after the meeting he had to see a med tech.

He grasped the receiver, then whirled. Someone was here; he could feel it! Fear drew icy fingers along his spine as he stared at the empty room. He *was* losing his mind.

A high-pitched cry wavered at the very edge of his hearing, and he backed a step, the receiver falling from nerveless fingers. The sound had come from the very center of the room!

It came again, louder than before, and, with a moan, he turned and ran for the front door.

Frantically he fumbled at the newly-installed locks. The sound seemed to be coming closer. He undid the last one, flung the door open, and suddenly staggered as something struck his back.

Turning, he stared at the empty hall, then carefully felt his back. His jacket had three long rips that had cut through the underlying shirt as well.

The cry came again, this time from the very doorway.

He plunged down the steps and across the open space to his

neighbor's darkened dwelling. He was wheezing by the time he reached the door. He raised his fist to knock—and a bright flash of light momentarily blinded him.

When he could see again, he was staring at the tattered remains of his sleeve. Blood dripped from three long slashes across his arm.

With a wild scream, he turned and fled into the night.

* * *

"'A simple training exercise,'" Janice muttered to herself, "'just to see how well you can maintain your shield and disguise in a low-level culture newly developing esper powers.' Simple, hah! When I get my hands on that glob of green mist...'you won't need any weapons'—and I'll bet he knew all along about the nasty that's moved in here!"

She shook out the newspages and bent over them again, impatiently pushing her long red hair out of her vision. The seventh mysterious death in as many days had made page one, but that was the only difference in the report of this death from the six previous ones in this city. "And they call themselves 'newsbringers!'" she muttered. "They could take a few lessons from Earth reporters! Not a single gory detail!"

She slid off the bed and strode over to stare out the hotel window at the alien city below. As cities went, it wasn't very large. The tallest building was ten stories high and built more on a cylinder basis than the square, blockish structures she was accustomed to. Hard to believe that this was the second largest city on this planet.

"They're not used to this," she said softly, picturing in her mind the headlines deaths like this would have earned back on Earth. She shook her head. The newspages had yet to learn that the actual total of deaths was now closer to thirty. They also had yet to hear of the flashing lights in the sky outside a tiny town thirty deaths ago. She had pieced together a trail of unexplained killings from there to this city, and she still didn't have the slightest idea of the reasons behind them.

"No wreckage of any type of ship, but the killer has to be an offworlder. These people aren't geared for murders like this!"

She looked down at the gentle beings in the streets below. Her charges for the time span of this exercise, and she was failing them. "Dammit, Apson, couldn't you have allowed me *some* equipment?"

She could almost hear her absent teacher now. *Dependence on devices of technology leads to neglect of the most important tool of all—your wits, my dear Earthling.*

"I'd like to see *him* go against something that can slice a grown being into chopped liver with only his wits," she grumbled. She tried to picture it, then shook her head. Trouble was, Apson would be in no danger at all. Not much could harm his mist body.

Janice sighed loudly. "Well, griping is getting me nowhere. Time to use my low-level, mediocre brain.

"First, we have an offworlder, if strange lights in the sky are any indication. Why is it killing people? Old, young, male, female—there's no link to any of the murders. Their possessions are untouched, the bodies themselves…well, they aren't *eaten*. Just slashed.

"Dammit!" She turned away from the window and leaned back against the wall, her arms folded. "Five lousy minutes last night and I might have at least *seen* whatever it was!" She closed her eyes, trying to erase the memory of the last victim's face. "Poor little man," she sighed. "I wonder what he saw to die with such a look of fear?" At least he had tried to escape. None of the previous victims had even gotten outside the room of their attack. Most of the mutilated bodies had been found backed into a corner.

"Lucky for me that this world is beginning to develop psi powers. The way the newspages are reporting this, I would never had learned about it at all if I hadn't heard their death screams. I wonder how many died without me hearing? Thirty screams…" She shivered, but the chill she felt was not due to the room's temperature.

"I have no weapons, no way to call for outside help, and when I get my hands on that offworlder, I'm going to shake it until its teeth rattle!" She grimaced. "I had to mention teeth. I wonder how long they are?"

Shaking her head at the thought, she walked over to the mirror. Maybe this was some idle galactic's idea of sport. She had seen enough case reports to know that that wasn't altogether impossible. But usually such misfits preferred to set themselves up as kings or gods. Simple butchery like this should have palled long ago.

She looked at her reflection in the mirror. "And I suppose if I use a telepathic disguise today, my shield will act up again and another little kid will announce he can see me physically but not psychically. Can't do anything right lately, can you?"

Making a face at herself, she decided to forgo the telepathic disguise in favor of make-up. A pill darkened her skin to a more acceptable tint, a mousy brown wig covered her un-native red hair, and contacts changed her green eyes to hazel. Her facial structure was thin enough to pass within the native norm, and a few touches with a pencil changed the slant of her eyebrows. She grinned at the results. "Doubt if even my twin would recognize me."

* * *

Someone was following her. Gasping for breath, Hillith flattened herself against the curve of the wall and watched the empty street behind her. She couldn't see anyone, but she had the eerie sensation that whomever it was was drawing closer and closer…

"Mother," she whimpered in a small voice. She turned and began to run again. There was a flowerspace not much farther ahead. There would be adults there, someone to help— Blinded with fear, she collided squarely with someone directly in her path.

"Easy, now." The stranger steadied her as Hillith tried vainly to catch her breath. "I hope you're not hurt?"

Hillith focused on the athletic-looking young woman supporting her and dimly realized that here was help. "There's….someone…following me," she gasped. "Back there."

Her rescuer looked grimly over Hillith's head. "There is, huh? I'll have to see about that. You stay here."

She pushed Hillith gently but firmly against a nearby wall and waited a moment, studying her closely. Hillith gaped at her and suddenly decided she was *not* going to cry.

The stranger nodded. "Stay here, now. You'll be safe." She turned and ran lightly down the street.

Hillith watched her departing back and abruptly realized that she was alone again. "Wait! Don't leave me!"

Janice moved cautiously down the street, checking each possible hiding place with as much care as if she were in an enemy's target sights. Which she probably was. She grinned wryly. By choosing a psi again, the killer had led her straight to it. Its mistake. The kid had broadcast fear like a neon sign.

She scowled. *Ten years old, at most.* She glanced down an intersecting path, then continued. They weren't too far from where it had left its victim the night before and now the killer wasn't even waiting for nightfall to strike again. *Careless of it*, Janice thought. *Almost as if it* wanted *to be caught. Well, I'm willing to oblige it.* But where was her elusive offworlder? It couldn't have vanished *this*—

She froze, suddenly conscious that she was being watched. Moving quickly, she flattened herself against a wall. She looked swiftly about but saw no signs of the offworlder. Yet it *had* to be near. "I know you're here," she said softly in Galactic.

No answer.

She edged away from the wall, unconsciously falling into a fighting stance. The sense of a presence seemed to loom closer, but still she saw no one.

I know you're here, she repeated silently.

She flinched slightly as something howled in her mind and fought to keep her outer shield from slamming up in response. *Stop that*, she ordered. *I'm not afraid of you.*

Again there was no response, but someone nearby was radiating hesitation and strong puzzlement. But where was it? Janice backed a step toward the wall, trying to watch everywhere at once.

The presence seemed to come closer, and her nerve endings suddenly tingled as if she were in an electrical field. Then, just as suddenly, the presence faded away.

Light sandals slapped the pavement behind her, and she whirled to see the native girl she had rescued running toward her. "Stay back!" Janice ordered.

The agent ran, trying to follow the fleeting awareness of the killer. But, much to her surprise, it petered out before she had gone more than a few steps. She stopped and looked with both physical and psychic eyes.

Nothing. Where could it have gone so quickly? Even when shielded, a psi emitted a faint mental "light" that could be sensed. *Assuming it* is *a psi*, Janice added to herself. *It didn't have to be an esper to have "heard" me.*

She frowned. The impression she had received hadn't felt like a shield snapping up. Something slower. More like…smoke fading away. She shook her head. Even a transporter beam would have cut the thought patterns quicker. And she *knew* that no ship orbited this planet. So how had it vanished?

The young girl came up behind her. "He ran away? From us?"

"I'm having a hard time believing it myself." Janice tried to divide her attention between the girl and the street. "Did you get a clear look at him? What did he look like?"

The girl shook her head, thrusting her hands deep into the pockets of her long orange tunic. Deep yellow shorts peeked below its hem. "I never saw anyone."

Turning, Janice stared deep into her eyes. "Think hard! Nothing unusual? A shadow, a strange sort of animal, anything?"

"No, nothing. I saw nothing," the girl said blankly.

"Damn!" Janice scanned the street once again, then suddenly

noticed that the native was still staring sightlessly ahead of her. She sighed and snapped her fingers. "Sorry, Hillith. You'll be all right now."

The girl blinked dazedly. "How did you know my—"

"I'm good with names." Hillith looked at her strangely and Janice swallowed a grin. The kid was recovering rather well from her fright. "Tell me," the agent said swiftly, "if you didn't see anything, why did you run?"

"I—I don't know. There was something there, I could feel it! And then I heard a—a cry. I don't know. There *was* someone there, wasn't there?"

"There was something, all right." *And I wish I knew* what, Janice added to herself.

Hillith shivered. "Do you think he will come back?"

"Oh, I'm sure of it." Janice turned to her. "Which is why you are going straight to your dwelling and not walk through this area alone again until you hear that this killer is gone. Do you understand, Hillith?"

Hillith's eyes widened as she stared blankly into the agent's gaze. "I...understand," she said dazedly.

"Good." Janice straightened and snapped her fingers. "Go home, Hillith." She watched as the girl obeyed, and tried to stifle her conscience's yips of protest. *Okay, so I'm not supposed to go about hypnotizing people right and left. But after saving her once, I'm not going to let that offworlder have a second chance at her. There's little enough I can do to protect her.*

The bright splash of orange disappeared around a corner, and the agent turned away. *Stop feeling so guilty*, she scolded herself. *You're responsible for the entire planet, not just one individual.*

She looked both ways down the street and took a deep breath. *Right. Now to wait for it to choose its next victim. Hope whoever it is is psychic again.*

She leaned against the curved wall and frowned thoughtfully at the pavement. "I just might be overlooking something," she said slowly. Both Hillith and the victim of the night before had been psis—developing psis, true, but— Her eyebrows lifted. "I've been around Apson too long! Espers aren't all that common here!"

Yet the other reported victims in this city had also been psis. She bit her lip, angry at herself. She had assumed that because the newspages had missed murders that she had known of, she had missed others as well. But what if she hadn't? What if the thirty she knew of were the only murders thus far? True, it had taken her some time, using this planet's modes of transportation, to come from the other side of the planet and pick up the trail of the killer. Time enough for thirty murders or more. But what if there hadn't been more?

"It's hunting espers," she said softly. "Why?"

She shook her head, mentally erasing that question. Time enough for that once she caught her offworlder. The major question at the moment was "how?" and that wasn't much of a question at all. *Only two ways to locate an esper: natural and artificial. Artificial is next to useless with developing espers like these, so I can rule that out. Natural...if it can sense espers, then it must have some psi ability itself. And I should have been able to sense* it*! But I didn't. And only the most highly trained of espers can shield so completely that you never know that they're there.*

Behind her innermost shield, Janice suddenly shivered. *I'm in big trouble. The only thing I've learned on that level of training was the shield, and that's not my most reliable one.*

She gave herself a mental shake. *Stop that. You know enough tricks to handle most espers and at least put up a good fight with the rest. All you can do now is wait and try to appear like a perfect victim.* She glanced skyward in the general direction a particular star would be at night. *I seem to be getting a lot of experience in that.*

She mentally scanned the area again, her mind sifting through several plans. The subtle auras of nonespers reassured her slightly. *Only psi in the area is Hillith, and she's rapidly moving out of range. Either my friend is still hidden or it's long gone—and judging from its past behavior, I think it's hiding somewhere nearby.* She frowned, remembering her perception of its disappearance. *I'd swear that whatever it used wasn't a shield. Didn't feel right. Even if I'm wrong and it's using a shield, it will have to lower it to follow me—or its next victim. One and the same, I hope* She grinned twistedly. A shield of the type she knew was good only when the physical self was already hidden. When one had to move about, it was best to use something else. Even low level espers could be disturbed confronting someone who was there in the physical sense and yet "not there" in the psychic. The few times she had unwittingly snapped the wrong shield up had earned her puzzled looks from the more perceptive natives of this world. Undercover in a fully telepathic society a slip like that could mean her death.

Janice pushed herself away from the wall and turned back the way she had come. *If I dawdle here any longer, someone else might walk into range. Have to draw it into the open, and I think I remember passing a warehouse that had all the makings of a trap—with me as bait.*

She strode briskly down the street, confident that the killer would follow. If it was a Galactic, it knew that she stood between it and freedom. If it wasn't, her own mental "glow"—thanks to her own shielding since landing on this planet—resembled that of a developing psi, its favorite target.

It would follow.

The street soon opened into a flowerspace filled with people, but Janice did not hesitate. Her psychic eyes filled with the delicate auras of the natives, she slowed her pace to skirt groups of children running from one stretch of flowers to the other. Tall bushes with clusters of deep indigo blossoms stirred in the light breeze, adding their sweet fragrance to the pleasantly heady mixture that made breathing a delight.

She was almost at the edge of the flowerspace when she suddenly felt that she was being watched. The agent did not restrain the impulse to turn and look, rationalizing that that was what any normal person—esper or not—would have done. She studied the natives relaxing amid the bright stretches of flowers and felt a slight twinge of disappointment. Every native in sight had a matching aura. No blankness of psyche to physical body anywhere.

She turned and continued walking. *Still hiding, huh? At least you're following me.*

She wove her way among the natives in the busy avenues leading from the flowerspace, always with the awareness of her pursuer coming closer and closer upon her heels A low cry, like a distant hunting howl, echoed faintly in her mind. She found herself hurrying and, with an effort, forced herself to slow. A prickling sensation began between her shoulderblades, and her feet itched to run. She glanced over her shoulder, half-expecting to see the offworlder there, reaching for her.

She was almost running by the time she reached the warehouse. She stopped and leaned against the wall, scanning the interior for native minds and trying to catch her breath. The scent of burned wood filled her nostrils as, finding no one inside, she edged toward the entrance. She waited until the street was clear, then picked the lock.

Once inside, out of sight of any watching eyes, she sighed gustily and checked that her wig was still in place. "My friend is full of surprises," she muttered *sotto voce*. "A fear generator, no less. Glad I had my shield down far enough to detect it. Don't want to scare the poor thing off by not acting like the perfect victim."

Her eyes adapting to the mottled shadows, she surveyed her choice of trap. A fire had gutted this building not too long ago; the smell of burned and damp wood was still strong. The roof was open to the sky in several places, but there had been some attempt at clearing the blackened wreckage, enough so that paths existed between the piles of ruined goods and fallen roofing. All in all, a nice spot for an ambush.

She turned to leave the door ajar, then hesitated, remembering that several of the bodies had been found within rooms locked from the inside. Locks wouldn't deter the offworlder, then, but any inquisitive native would be kept out and safe. "Stay in character," she reminded herself and locked the door.

The agent moved back within the wreckage, finding a good spot from which to watch the door. She could sense the killer coming closer and tensed, waiting for the door to open. Suddenly the hairs on the back of her neck rose, and at the same time a low howl came clearly to her ears. It was inside with her!

She turned, glancing at the gaping holes in the roof, and tried to determine from which direction the sound had come.

A small piece of wreckage tumbled down the side of a pile, the tiny clatter loud in the silence. Well aware that psychokinetics could have been used to give her a false location, Janice still edged to a new position, keeping part of her attention on the suspect mound of goods.

Sunlight dappling the floor suddenly flared brighter, and a crumbled box midway between the mound and herself slid a short distance toward her, then stopped. Janice shied a fragment of roofing over the box, but her toss met no resistance. A strangely amused sound—a cross between a purr and a chuckle—came from the empty air above the box.

Janice concentrated, willing to see something there. A distort cloak, when stared at directly, could be seen as a waver in the air, especially when the wearer stood in direct sunlight. But she could see nothing.

The purring chuckle came again, and she fired another piece of roofing at the source of the sound. The tile shot straight through the exact spot and continued on to shatter against the precarious support of several large mounds of black. The support collapsed and the resultant crash—as she had hoped—raised a cloud of dust and ash.

The agent sneezed but continued to watch, straining to see any figure revealed by the billowing dust. But there was nothing. Only that throaty chuckle, which abruptly deepened into a low howl.

Janice let the fear the howl generated brush past her like a light breeze, her attention elsewhere. Gradually she had noticed that the closer the being came, the more she was able to pick up its emotions.

Whatever it's using to hide behind is no shield. I couldn't pick up its thoughts before because it's not thinking—just reacting. Like an animal. Right now it's puzzled a little—probably at me—excited, and hungry. Her analysis stopped at that. The being was very hungry. *I'm lunch*!

She suddenly realized that she had let the killer come too close. Her nerve endings were tingling as they had in the street, and the eagerness in the being's mind was close to a fever pitch.

She dove out of the way just as light flashed before her and heard a crash and clatter of wreckage as she rolled on the cluttered floor. Regaining her feet, she saw that her previous position was now buried and sensed that the offworlder was coming toward her. It was radiating pleasure and excitement.

So it likes cat-and-mouse games, huh? Let's see how it likes having the mouse fight back. She braced herself and stared intently at the empty air where the offworlder had to be. *Wide-angle shot, for a start.*

Reaching deep into her mind, she released a bolt of pure energy and fired it at the being. But her bolt encountered no resistance, no opposing mind. Recovering, she scanned her awareness of the being. *Like trying to hit a ghost. It's there, and yet...it's not.*

But her bolt had had some effect. The killer's excitement was now blunted by wariness. *Maybe now it will listen to rea—*

The tingling sensation suddenly returned in a rush, and the once-distant howl was now all too close. She threw up her arm as light blasted her eyes and staggered back as something heavy struck her arm. The light shut off as if by a switch, and Janice looked wonderingly at the remains of her ash-smeared sleeve. Blood welled from three small cuts across her arm.

The howl came from behind her this time, ending in a purring chuckle.

Turning to face it, Janice backed a step. *It wants me to run. It likes the hunt.*

She backed another step, and then another. The sensation of presence that was her only guide to the killer's location seemed to sweep closer, and she turned and ran. The offworlder's howl followed her like a shadow.

The agent sprinted to a long twisted bar of metal she had spotted atop a nearby pile of wreckage. She pulled the bar free, noting that the edge near one end was jagged and sharp. Holding the bar in both hands like a staff, she waited as the tingling sensation returned. Light flashed before her, and, squinting, Janice swung her make-shift weapon in a wide arc. Her blow connected solidly when something in the brightness, and a wild howl of pain filled her mind. “Gotcha!” she muttered.

The dazzling glare vanished, then abruptly re-appeared to her right. A blur of green-gray struck the bar, already raised to block any retaliatory blow, and rebounded. The agent quickly swung the bar down and sideways just before the light popped out again. The answering mental howl was tinged with anger as well as pain. A faint sheen glistened on the jagged edge of metal.

Janice pivoted slowly behind her weapon. The tingling sensation was still very strong; the killer had not given up on her yet.

As if to remind her of that, a howl so loud that it would have been deafening had it been audible began ringing in her mind. Trying to ignore the headache, Janice waited for the being to strike. Its usual victim would surely have been vulnerable with that mental din. The howl began to slip over into the audible range as well.

Brightness blazed behind her. The agent had only begun to turn when something grabbed the top of her raised weapon and something else slashed across her back.

Abandoning her weapon to whatever held it, Janice fell, then shoulder-rolled out of reach, her back objecting strongly to that maneuver. She climbed to her feet again, staring in disbelief at the sight before her.

The tall circle of glowing light was far too bright to see into, but emerging from the dazzle at a point five feet off the ground was a green-gray tentacle about as wide as her arm. This tentacle was wrapped about the top of the twisted bar, holding it upright. Below that one, a thicker tentacle waved aimlessly back and forth, the three long, sharp spikes a short distance from its tip clicking against the bar of metal on each swing.

A tiny trickle of blood ran down her back. Janice looked for something to use as a weapon, wincing as the offworlder’s howls ran up and down the scale. *At least it’s shut off the mental howl. Now I can only go deaf.*

The upper tentacle released the bar and the lower one stopped swinging to and fro just long enough for her former weapon to fall to the ground. More of the upper tentacle emerged from the brightness until the tip was questing slowly over the cluttered floor.

Now what's it up to? Janice wondered. *It's acting almost as if it's lost me. And I can't sense anything about it that would— Wait a minute, I can't "hear" anything! I can't even pick up its emotions!* She suddenly realized the reason for the being's mental silence. *My outer shield. It must have snapped up when the offworlder hit me. Old Tentacles here can't see me psychically and, from the way it's searching, it must not be able to see the physical world. Well, well.*

A puzzled note crept into the audible howls, and the upper tentacle began to retreat back into the brightness. Janice tossed a fragment of tile into the light and nodded thoughtfully when she heard it rattle against the clutter behind the circle. *Oh well, I'm the one who always said I hated an easy job.*

The agent picked up a larger fragment and pitched it at the lower tentacle. The killer shrieked loudly but, instead of returning, the upper tentacle vanished into the brightness. The lower one began to withdraw as well.

Coward.

Janice concentrated. *Don't know why this shield is always harder to lower than raise.* She caught a flicker of the being's surprise as she succeeded, then the lower tentacle vanished as had the upper and the light winked out.

The agent let her shield snap back into place and dashed across the open space to regain her weapon. Just as her fingers touched the bar, light blazed where she had been standing only seconds before. The spiked tentacle was a blur of green-gray swinging back and forth.

Janice lowered her shield again and the light popped out. Raising her shield, she shifted to a new position and waited, her weapon raised.

The killer did not disappoint her. Light flared exactly where she had expected, and Janice swung, connecting squarely on the emerging tentacle.

The offworlder squealed, and the agent sprang back as two of the thinner tentacles shot out towards her. Missing her by inches, the two tentacles groped over the clutter.

The agent moved back a few feet, then lowered her shield briefly. The tentacles shot toward her again, continuing on in the same direction even after she raised her shield.

How long are these things? Janice caught herself just before backing into a pile of wreckage. Glancing from the pile behind her to the tentacles before, she thoughtfully turned her weapon to its blunt side and carefully squashed the tip of the closest searcher.

The offworlder squalled and growled at the same time. The second tentacle swung towards its injured neighbor, and a third tentacle shot out of the circle of light and smashed directly into the mound of fallen roofing and blackened timbers. Janice, watching from beside the pile, only grinned and waited.

The killer squalled again as its third tentacle was buried under disturbed wreckage. The width of the circle suddenly expanded, and jointed legs—like those of a crab or an ant—abruptly emerged from within the dazzle. Part of the body appeared as well, and Janice was intrigued to see that the tentacles were jointed appendages close to the body, losing their hard outer shell after the second joint. Two of the spiked tentacles also appeared, and she began reconsidering part of her plan.

Not too weird-looking for an arthropod. I've got friends who look scarier. She used the twisted bar to push more debris atop the buried tentacle.

The being tried to retract the tentacle, but that one was pinned. The second tentacle swung over to help free it, followed more slowly by the one Janice had squashed.

The agent stepped before a mound a bit beyond and to the side of the one the being was occupied with and lowered her shield. Mental growls and whimpers filled her mind, then abruptly ceased as the creature "sighted" her. Janice waited, marveling at the fact that she still could not "see" the being on the psychic level even though it was right in front of her.

Suddenly the killer snarled and reached for her with its two free tentacles. Janice quickly raised her shield and darted out of the way, then realized that she needn't have bothered. The tentacles weren't long enough to reach her. *Finally*!

The killer strained to reach her previous position. Two of the jointed legs moved, and more of the body emerged from the brightness. The tentacles still were not long enough, but Janice was no longer watching their approach. Her attention was focused instead on a small round segment of body that had suddenly emerged with another spiked tentacle. This segment had a narrow slit lined with quivering tendrils.

That has to be its head. Hope the brain is inside.

Glancing at the straining tentacles, she braced herself and reached deep into her mind. Her shield lowered with a new-found ease, and the agent fired as massive a bolt of pure energy as she could muster directly at that segment.

The being's wild scream was abruptly cut short. The tentacles fell limply to the ground and the jointed legs buckled and collapsed.

Janice's knees felt as if they wanted to do the same. She leaned on the twisted bar, trying to clear her brain of the aftereffects of the bolt, and dazedly studied the fallen being. *Wonder if it's just stunned or—*

The tingling sensation abruptly grew stronger and Janice straightened worriedly. The circle of light closed down about the being until only a shimmering glow enveloped the whole of the visible creature. The body began to disintegrate, crumbling into dust, and soon only the glow remained. That, too, quickly faded, along with the tingling sensation.

Janice blinked. "I did it," she said softly.

* * *

The agent leaned back in her chair and watched the planet recede in the ship's viewscreen. "And so I headed back to my hotel—after first stopping to locate Hillith and give her the good news—and collapsed until you guys finally arrived." She glanced up at the hovering globe filled with green and white mists. "A whole month later!"

She shook her head. "I know you long-lived races have an oddly distorted sense of time, but really, Apson! If that was supposed to be a short training exercise, I'd hate to see what you call a long one!"

The mists above her head chuckled. *My awareness of time passage is considerably more accurate than your own, but in this case you have the right of it.*

"That's ok. Crislben told me why you were delayed." She shivered and sank deeper into the chair. "I thought one was bad, but a whole swarm? How do they travel through space? I couldn't find a ship."

The Devameners have no need of ships. They simply drift through space in their immaterial form until they reach a planet with a suitable food supply.

"Developing espers." Janice remembered Hillith and the death screams of thirty others, and her voice hardened. "Why didn't you people destroy these psi vampires long ago?"

We try. Every three hundred years they swarm and we obliterate all we can find, but a few will escape us.

"Like my little nasty."

Like your little nasty, Apson agreed. *"Psi vampire" is an apt description. They feed off intense emotional radiation. Fear is best.*

"So what I did, in effect, was overload its system." She chuckled and closed her eyes. "It died of an upset stomach."

You could put it that way.

"I just did." She opened her eyes and stared deep into the green and white mists. *Apson, when do I get my own ship?*

Perhaps after your next training exercise. It's a simple one. You won't even need any weapons.

"Someone is Watching" previously appeared in Shadowstar *#10, May 1983.*

HEARTSIGHT

Seiian stood on the gentle slope of the hillside and wiggled his toes in the mud. The watery sunlight, shining feebly through the mists, did little to improve the view: rock, clay, and scattered clumps of sickly growth. Somehow he had thought the lands beyond his parent grove would be more hospitable. Several days of traveling had proven him wrong.

He shrugged philosophically. After all, he had not planned to start looking for an ideal location immediately after his heartstone had dropped from his mother tree. Movement was an enjoyable sensation, and he intended to fully experience all the aspects of that before settling down.

He turned away from the barren land he had traveled and continued up the slope. Once he had reached the top, he could not restrain a small dance of joy. Green life stretched before him!

It was not the large expanse of life he was familiar with from his parent grove, but still it was green and healthy. There were trees and bushes and scattered patches of grass and wildflowers, all speaking eloquently of a fierce determination to turn the sad wasteland back toward life.

He heard a slither and rattle of stones as he bounced atop the hill and suddenly the edge fell away, carrying him down towards the cultivated greenness.

He landed face down in a quagmire of mud.

"Now mudslides!" There came a weary chuckle from above. "I suppose I should have expected something like that after all the rain."

Seiian levered himself out of the clinging mud and clawed dirt out of his eyes. Standing before him was a being so mud-covered that his species was all but indeterminable. Seiian inhaled sharply, forgetting the mud, and almost choked. A human!

The human was more interested in a round puddle at his feet than in Seiian. "Not that I don't appreciate a little help now and then, but there are easier ways of filling up a hole than bringing an entire hillside down. Hey ho."

Seiian froze in fear as the human reached downward, but the being merely unearthed a digging implement from the mound of mud before Seiian and went back to dig in the puddle. Seiian stared in surprise. Perhaps the human didn't know what he was. He absently brushed his muddy fingers on his kirtle, then slowly looked down to see that the front of his new leaf-green kirtle was wholly coated in mud. With a sigh, he began to pull himself out of the grasping mud, thankful that his mother tree couldn't see him now. What a scolding he'd have received, especially for allowing his heartstone to come into contact with—

His fingers brushed the pouch in which he had carried his heartstone and found it open and empty. "Oh no." Panicking, he searched the clods of dirt clinging to his kirtle, then scanned the ground before him. "Oh no!" He fell to his knees and started digging. Not here! He tried to summon the stone back. Not *here*!

"What's wrong?" the human asked. "Lose something?"

Any help, even human help, was preferable to the alternative. "My heartstone," Seiian moaned. "I must find it!" The hole before him widened as he frantically clawed at the mud.

"A stone, huh?" The human walked slowly toward him. "Several stones came down with you. One almost hit me."

"This is no ordinary stone." Seiian forced himself to calm. Panic would not help him locate the stone.

"I gathered that." Using the digging tool, the human carefully turned over several layers of mud from the mound before Seiian. "The one I saw came down just about…here." He proffered a bladeful of soil. "This it?"

Seiian almost did not see the mud-colored lump held before him. "My heartstone!" Snatching it from the blade, he held it against his chest, belatedly feeling he should guard it from the human's sight.

"Good." The human turned away and went back to digging. "I won't have people moaning near where a tree will be planted. Makes a tree feel unwanted."

Seiian gaped at the human, shutting his mouth only when he caught sight of a curious two-wheeled cart a short distance beyond the being. Small trees, their roots well-wrapped, rested within. So here was the being responsible for this garden in the wasteland. Seiian felt slightly ashamed of his behavior. Perhaps the human would accept his trust as thanks.

Opening his hand, he held out his most prized possession. "It's my heartstone. Don't you think it's a lovely color?"

The human stopped and glanced at it. "Very nice shade of gray."

Gray? Seiian looked at his heartstone and was embarrassed to see that it was still coated with mud. Finding a clean patch on his kirtle, he wiped until the green reappeared. Contact with the ground had caused facets to erupt out of the once-smooth ovoid. Seiian shivered at the change, but then decided that the sparkles twinkling in its green depths made it more beautiful than before.

He held the stone out to the human again. "Look at it now."

This time the human only paused between bladefuls. "Oh yes, a very lovely gray stone."

Seiian looked from the green stone in his hand to the human digging in the mud and generously decided that the human had been digging too long. He would find some other way to repay the human for finding his heartstone. Tucking the stone securely back into its pouch, he strode cautiously over to where the tall being was working. "I'm—"

"No names," the human said quickly. "In a land like this, elementary precautions are wisest. You won't live too long, little one, if you give your name to anyone in exchange for a kindness." He put down his digging implement and strode over to the cart.

Seiian followed, thankful that his flush at the well-deserved rebuke was concealed by dirt. "I only wanted to say—"

The human wrestled a young tree off the cart and staggered unsteadily back towards the hole. Backing hastily out of the way, Seiian slipped and went down into the mud again. He sat there a moment, watching the human work the tree into place, then decided to move to the drier ground by the cart.

The wood of the cart felt odd under his hands: peaceful and contented, with none of the agony he had expected to sense from a human-built device. The small trees inside dreamed of the giants they would become, and he climbed into the cart to better share their dream. He was about to introduce himself when the trees in the garden shrilled a warning. Danger!

He dropped below the edge of the cart side, then cautiously peeked out amid tree branches to see if the human had sensed the alert. The human casually thrust his digging implement into the ground, then straightened and turned to face the undamaged portion of the hillside. A being taller than the human stood there, its form and features encased in armor which glittered like mica.

Seiian shivered, thankful for the concealing armor. One of *them*!

"Human." The voice was deep and cold. "A trespasser has crossed my land."

"Oh?" The human hooked his thumbs into his mud-coated belt. "Tell me, neighbor, have you come to accuse me or warn me of some approaching danger?"

"A young pren, by the signs," the voice continued as if the human had not spoken. "Have you seen the creature?"

"A pren, a pren." The human scratched his head. "I don't think I'm familiar with that word. What does a pren look like?"

"Not too dis-similar from yourself, but with green skin."

"Green skin," the human repeated. Seiian held his breath, wishing he could still hide inside his heartstone. The human had no choice but to turn him over. But the human instead shook his head. "Turn your hunt elsewhere, neighbor. I have seen no greenskins."

Seiian stared in shock. The human had lied to one of *them*! The need to stay hidden battled with the desire to deflect in some way the terrible fate that must fall upon his protector.

Frost chilled the air as the armored being stood motionless. Finally its head turned toward the fallen portion of the hill. "You will allow me to cross your land."

The human laughed. "And kill all my work by your presence? No, the bindings of my father's father's father still stands. This patch of ground is forbidden to you."

"Only for so long as descendants of your ancestor live to hold it. Your work will die with you. You are the last."

"And you have made certain of that, haven't you. Unfortunate for you that the shedding of that much blood tightened the bindings."

"Since that will last only during the course of your short life, it is but a minor inconvenience."

The face of the helmet began to turn in the cart's direction, and Seiian quickly lowered his head. It seemed to him that he could feel its icy gaze through the side of the cart, and, with a shiver, he tried to make himself as small as possible. After a short while, the chill went away, and he slowly looked out to find the armored being gone and the human working once again on the newly transplanted tree.

Seiian sat down once again and tried to think while the small trees dreamed around him. The human was in great danger, and he had possibly made the situation worse. As much as the idea frightened him, there was only one thing he could think of to do to help.

Slipping quietly out of the cart, he glanced at the human, then moved on into the garden. A little farther on was an ideal location, with wildflowers nearby and two established trees within talking distance. He knelt and scooped out a shallow hole. Then he took his heartstone from its pouch. He gazed wistfully at it a moment, watching the sparkle and glitter of its facets. Steeling himself, he held it in both hands and concentrated. Slowly he raised the stone.

His wrists were caught and held in a tight grasp. "You may think me rude, but I don't care much for having someone's heart buried in my land."

Seiian stared dazedly up at the human. "I…want to help. You're all alone—"

"And you thought you could stay here and keep me company?" The human shook his head. "Little one, I appreciate the gesture, but I can't allow you to sacrifice yourself for a mistake my ancestor made. Now, if I release you, will you promise to put your heartstone away and listen?"

Seiian looked down and nodded. The human's grasp loosened, and he lowered his heartstone, slowly pulling his full awareness back from its depths. The open hole before him tugged at his gaze, and it was a struggle to return the stone to the pouch.

The human sighed above him as Seiian closed the pouch. The being brushed dirt back into the hole with his foot, then dropped to a crouch before Seiian. "Now, youngster, what you were about to do was very brave and very generous, but ultimately very foolish. You've seen my neighbor, haven't you?"

In spite of himself, Seiian shivered. "One of *them*."

"Exactly. One of those who hates all life. This one managed to get itself bound to one patch of ground, but its influence is still great."

"It caused the wasteland?" Seiian asked.

The human nodded. "It did. I have no great powers. I can protect my trees, but I wouldn't be able to protect you if you rooted here, any more than I can protect those flowers. I plant the flowers only because I wish to see some other color besides gray. But I won't have you stay just to ease my loneliness."

"But—" Seiian started.

"I know, you are not a flower. You have some powers of your own, I would guess. But you would take many years to reach your full growth and be able to withstand all the terrors that my neighbor would delight to send against you. I may not have that many years."

"But who will care for this when you die?"

The human glanced fondly at the trees around them. "I have made plans for my death. I may be the last of my family, but, believe me, my neighbor will not be able to do as it pleases with my garden. Come with me."

Seiian followed the human to the closest tree. "Touch it," the human directed. "See its innermost self."

Obeying, Seiian could not believe what his senses told him. "It says it's human!"

The being beside him nodded. "Yes. Each tree is bound to my life. When I die, they shall have my lifeforce, my "heart", as you would say. In this way, I will continue to hold the land and keep my neighbor bound."

Seiian struggled to understand. "But each tree you plant shortens your life!"

The human grinned. "Yes. That will please my neighbor. I gather my great-uncle sorely taxed its patience for living as long as he did. Yes, my neighbor will be pleased, until it realizes exactly what I have done." He patted the trunk of the tree. "A short life is a small price to pay to keep one of *them* captive."

He smiled down at Seiian. "Now, if you wish to leave after hearing all that, that direction would be best. If you still wish to help, just for a short time, I have a small tree that can't decide where she'd like to be planted. Or maybe it's a he. I can't tell at that age."

Seiian smiled back, finding it impossible to be sad when the human was so cheerful. "I will gladly help, although I feel I should do more after you lied to your neighbor to protect me."

"Lied? A lie to that one would be fatal. No, I told it the truth, little one."

"But I have green skin!"

"You do?" The human shrugged, but there was a broad grin on his mud-streaked face. "I wouldn't know. I can't see green. Never have."

———

"Heartsight" previously appeared in Twilight Times, *Spring 1999. Reprinted from* Minnesota Fantasy Review, *October 1988.*

HORSEFEATHERS

Clouds of incense, with overtones of fouler scents, billowed out the doorway of the grimy little shop as Smoke stealthily approached. The circled eye on the sign above the door seem to stare straight through her, but Smoke was determined not to be put off by that omen. She straightened her vest to hide her small pouch of coppers, and vainly tried to finger-comb her recently cropped brown hair into some order. Glancing at the sign again, she took a deep breath and strode up to the open door.

Inside, a man in long black robes peered myopically into a cauldron streaked with various dried substances, seemingly oblivious to the dirty brown clouds engulfing him. Smoke stood in the doorway and studied him with a sinking heart. This was the only wizard she could find in the whole city. He would have to do, although he suited his shop perfectly—from his thin beard and black-lined hands to the stains dotting his robes.

Smoke took another deep breath—and almost choked on the incense. "Are you the wizard?" she asked hoarsely.

The man did not even look up. "The sign reads 'magician,' doesn't it?"

"'Milburr, the magician,'" Smoke agreed. "I want to become your apprentice," she said quickly.

The magician looked at her, then slowly straightened as he saw that she was no ragged urchin. "What do your parents say?"

"They're dead." Smoke swallowed. "Goblins, in Rocktooth Pass. Two ten-days ago."

"In Rocktooth Pass?" The cauldron abruptly boiled over, and the magician swatted at the new stains on his robes. "Then how did you get here?"

"Free Traders found me and brought me to this city." Smoke backed away from the spitting cauldron and glanced at a pile of parchment atop a nearby table. A small mouse nibbled busily at another stack. "But I don't want to become a Free Trader. I want to be a wizard."

The magician peered at her face, then noticed the mouse and swung at it. The mouse scurried away. "Bah. You're only a child. Can't be more than eight."

"I'm eleven," Smoke replied, lifting her chin.

"A child," Milburr repeated. "What can you know of magic?"

"I can learn. I can read." The magician hurriedly pulled the parchment stack away. "And—" Smoke hesitated, reluctant to reveal her secret.

"And?" the magician prodded. "Well, out with it! I haven't all day." When she didn't answer, he turned away and stared back into the cauldron. "You have to do more than read to be a wizard."

Smoke straightened. "I can do magic already."

"Of course you can. Now go away and close the door on your way out."

"I can so do magic! I can call animals to me."

Milburr looked askance at her, his expression disbelieving. "Call one, then." He flapped his hand at the table. "Call that mouse."

"All right." Smoke stared at the spot where she had seen the mouse disappear and felt her forehead furrow in concentration. *Come*, she called. Soon she was rewarded by the sight of whiskers peeking around a pot on the table. *Come on*.

The mouse crept slowly out of hiding, his black beadlike eyes staring directly at her. "Ah ha!" Milburr cried.

Go! Smoke said.

The magician pounced, but the mouse had already scurried away. Milburr yelped as he missed, and the pot rolled slowly across the table, dripping a trail of red liquid.

The magician straightened and rubbed his elbow. He stared at the table and a strange gleam appeared in his eyes. "Well, boy, you certainly have Talent. Consider yourself my apprentice. By fire and earth and water I affirm it. Now grab that broom and start cleaning up this place."

"I'm not a boy," Smoke said.

Milburr retrieved the pot and drained it. "Well, you're not a young man yet," he said, wiping his mouth with his sleeve.

"But I'm not a boy," Smoke repeated. "I'm a girl."

"A girl!" The pot shattered at the magician's feet. "I can't have— You can't be a magician if you're a girl!"

"Why not?" Smoke asked curiously.

"Why— It just isn't done, that's why not!"

"I have to learn magic," she said stubbornly.

"Girls can't learn magic," Milburr insisted. "They haven't any talent for it."

"*You* said that I had Talent. And there have been women wizards."

"Not in the Kingdoms. And not in this city! Now get out of my shop!"

"But I'm your apprentice. You swore it. By fire and earth and water."

A sudden *pop* came from the mixture on the fire, and the magician started. He uneasily eyed the flames now crawling up the sides of the cauldron and backed a step away from both the cauldron and Smoke. "So I did. So I definitely did." He glanced wildly around the room and his gaze fell upon the stack of parchment beside him. "Oh yes, an oath is an oath."

Milburr looked back at her with a sudden gleam of interest. "I have a very important project for you, apprentice. One that only you, with your magic, could complete."

"Then I am your apprentice?" Smoke asked.

"Yes, of course! Didn't I swear to it? I was fortunate indeed that you came to help me, er—what is your name?"

"The Free Traders called me Smoke."

"Smoke, yes. Ah, I am fortunate indeed! Many years have I tried to complete this spell, tried and failed because I am lacking one important ingredient—one that only you, with your magic, could obtain. So, apprentice, I want you to seek out and bring to me the feather of a horse."

Smoke looked at him. "There're no such things as horses. That's just a legend."

Milburr lifted a sheet of parchment off the table. "But that is what the spell requires. You can read it for yourself."

Smoke reached for the sheet, and Milburr turned and gestured, parchment in hand, at the small jars scattered about the room. "You call these only legends? Each one obtained for this particular spell and now I will never complete it because my apprentice doubts me and is afraid to seek out—"

"I'm not afraid," Smoke interrupted.

"Then you will seek out a horse? And bring a feather to me?"

Smoke gave up trying to read the moving parchment. "I'm still your apprentice?"

The magician looked hurt. "I affirmed it by fire and earth and water. Only you can break it."

"Then I'll go."

"Good!" Milburr hurried her toward the door. "Go quickly. Have a safe trip. I must finish the mixture I am preparing now, otherwise it will be ruined, so I won't give you unnecessary instructions." The cauldron burped. "Hurry back with the feather!"

Smoke found herself out on the street. "But where do I go?" She turned back to the shop. "I'll need supplies, and—" The door slammed shut, and Smoke heard the bar sliding into place behind it. "Milburr?"

She tried to peer through the small grimy front window. "Milburr!"

She heard the muffled sound of an explosion inside the shop, and the inside of the window was suddenly streaked with liquid. "My mixture!" Milburr's voice wailed from inside.

Smoke backed away from the window and decided to start on her search.

Seeking out the market, Smoke spent a few of her coppers on food for the journey. She had her father's dagger to protect herself outside the city, and the memories of her family's travels to guide her on this new search. But where would she find a horse? There were four-footed beings similar to horses that ran wild on the wide stretches of plains between the Eight Human Kingdoms, but they resembled the horses of legend as much as a weosun of the Free Traders resembled the dull-brained aurochs the kingdom dwellers used as beasts of burden. Still, it was a place to begin.

Ducking into hiding each time she saw a Free Trader, Smoke cautiously made her way to the city gates. She was almost out the gate when she spotted one of the Free Traders who had rescued her coming toward the gate from outside. He was deep in conversation with his companion, and Smoke darted behind a cart before he could see her.

"I tell you, Witan, I did see them! A whole herd of Taisee! Flying above the Silvergreen Hills!"

"Are you certain they weren't birds?"

"Birds that resemble the four-footed plains Runners? With big white wings that stretch the height of two grown men? Or longer?"

"The tongue of a Trader. Taisee! You almost make me believe it."

"Ah, Witan, my friend. Don't be so shop-minded."

Smoke peeked over the edge of the cart as the two walked away. Spying no other Free Traders about, she ran out of the city gates and kept running until she was far outside.

When she thought she was far enough from the city to be safe from well-meaning adults, she slowed to a walk and thought over the Trader's words. She had never heard of Taisee, but if they resembled Runners and had wings, maybe they were what she was looking for. Smoke didn't know if Runners had feathers, but she reasoned that anything with wings should have.

She glanced up at the sun, then set off in the proper direction. She knew the way to the Silvergreen Hills. Rocktooth Pass was among those hills.

* * *

A few days later Smoke lay flat in the silver-edged grass that gave the Silvergreen Hills their name and studied the blue-white being grazing not far from her. A Taisee. The creature was so beautiful that Smoke could not believe she was actually seeing it. The body resembled the small and fragile horses of legend she had seen in her father's book, with a long flowing mane and tail that reminded her somehow of clouds. The wings were long, even longer than the Trader had described, with feathers that shone in the gathering dusk.

Smoke suddenly hated herself for what she was about to do. But, she reasoned, the Taisee could probably spare one feather, and she *had* to become a wizard.

Slowly she rose to her feet. The Taisee lifted his head, gazing at her with eyes that were a surprising light blue. *Stay*, she ordered. The Taisee's ears pricked forward, then, still watching her, he lowered his head and continued grazing.

Smoke could not believe her good fortune. She walked forward slowly and calmly, repeating her command over and over. The Taisee stayed.

Closer and closer Smoke advanced. Then, suddenly, she couldn't move another step. A curious lassitude invaded her mind, along with an acute reluctance to continue any farther.

Smoke backed up and looked at the winged being. The Taisee tossed his head and nickered cheerfully at her. Smoke advanced once again, determined to reach him this time.

But this time the reluctance was stronger. Smoke gritted her teeth and tried again. And again.

Finally she settled herself onto the long sweet-smelling grass and studied the Taisee. There was nothing she could see which prevented her from walking right up to the being, yet she couldn't get closer than twenty paces to him. The Taisee was looking very amused.

Smoke smiled ruefully. "I must have looked very foolish," she said to the Taisee. "There's a protective spell about you, isn't there?"

The Taisee's mane rippled blue-silver as he nodded his head.

Smoke sat up straight. "You aren't a captive, are you?"

The Taisee shook his head.

"Then why a spell?"

Feathers rustled as the Taisee started to raise his wings, and Smoke saw the answer to her question. The left wing hung limp and useless.

"Oh, you poor thing!" she exclaimed. "I could help. I broke my arm once and Father had to splint it. I'll go get some sticks and—"

The Taisee shook his head and whickered softly. He stamped one hoof firmly on the ground and looked encouragingly at her.

"Stay here?" Smoke asked.

The Taisee nodded. He swung his head toward his chest and then stamped his hoof again.

"You're supposed to stay here? Oh, I understand. Someone will be back to help you, and that someone put the spell around you to protect you until he returns?"

The Taisee nodded, and his mane swung down to cover one eye. Smoke, admiring the sheer beauty of the being, sighed softly. "I wish we could talk together, rather than just me doing all the talking." She rummaged in her depleted carrypouch. "I found some tartapples a while ago. Would you like one?"

The Taisee's front hooves danced a bit, and Smoke took that to mean assent. She started to climb to her feet, and the being backed up. Smoke sat down again. "Oh, that's right. I almost forgot." She looked from the apple in her hand to the Taisee, then gave up and rolled it toward the being. The apple rolled unhindered almost to his hooves, and the Taisee gobbled it greedily. He looked wistfully at the one Smoke was slowly munching, and Smoke laughed and rolled the last one in her pouch towards him. The Taisee wasn't satisfied until he had the core of her apple as well.

By then it had become so dark that Smoke could see only the

Taisee's shining wings. She laid back in the grass and studied the winged being against the twinkling stars, responding to his whickers with questions and comments of her own. But deep in her mind was the growing question of her apprenticeship to the magician.

* * *

A dream woke Smoke a short time later, a dream that was part memory and part warning. She awoke from the midst of the goblin attack on her family and knew before her eyes were fully open that goblins were nearby.

For a moment she did not know where she was. Then she saw the faint gleam of the Taisee's wings not far away and remembered. She stayed still, trying to locate by scent where the goblins were. She could hear low murmurs in the goblins' coarse tongue and tried to count the speakers. There seemed to be only two, and they were between her and the dozing Taisee.

Smoke slowly drew her father's dagger out of its sheath, thankful that the goblins' night vision was as poor as her own. Only that had saved her from discovery so far. The Taisee would be safe enough from the goblins within his protective spell. For a moment, she thought it might be fun to watch the goblins' reaction to it.

One goblin rose to its full height. There was something long in its hand, and as it raised the object to its shoulder, Smoke's heart froze. They had spears!

Smoke gathered herself to run, but knew she could never cross the distance to the goblin in time to throw off its aim. "Taisee, look out!" she yelled.

The Taisee started awake just as the goblin threw its spear. The weapon buried itself harmlessly in the earth as the Taisee dodged, then charged forward with a scream of anger. The goblin's answering exclamations sounded frightened.

Crouching low as she ran, Smoke searched for the goblin with the second spear. From the goblin cries, the Taisee's vision was superior to her own. Where was that second goblin?

Someone fell over her, knocking her dagger from her hand, and a heavy object banged into her leg. Grabbing the object, Smoke found herself in sole possession of a spear. Hearing mumbled complaints nearby, she swung the heavy end of the spear as if it was a quarterstaff and felt it connect with something.

Smoke stood, listening, trying to locate the goblin in the darkness. Something crashed into her from behind, knocking her to the ground.

Landing on the spear, Smoke stubbornly held onto the weapon and tried to throw the goblin off.

Suddenly the weight was gone from her back, and sweet apple-scented breath warmed her face. Smoke sat up and stared at the Taisee standing protectively over her. In the shine of the Taisee's wings, she could dimly see the two goblins gesturing angrily just outside the field of the protective spell.

Suddenly both goblins froze in midmotion. The Taisee nudged her shoulder, and Smoke turned to see a bobbing torch coming towards them. As the torch drew closer, a wave of calmness seemed to spread outward from it, and Smoke studied the woman carrying the torch with a wondering interest.

She was tall, robed and hooded in the green of new leaves, and peeking out from under the hood were heavy braids of a brownish-red. Her features were human, and Smoke's interest intensified. A woman wizard?

The woman stopped beside the two goblins. She seemed to study them for a moment, then passed her hand slowly above their heads. The boney, purple-skinned creatures abruptly came to life and instantly recoiled from her in terror. She stared at them, and the goblins turned and fled into the night.

Smoke stared in wonderment. The woman had not even said anything!

The woman turned toward them. She passed her hand before her and stepped forward, the shielding spell dissolved.

The Taisee bowed low as the woman neared them. "I apologize, Cloudstrider. Had I realized that goblins were abroad, I would have used a different spell. I am rested enough to aid you now, so you will no longer be in danger."

"Are you a wizard?" Smoke asked.

The woman smiled at her. "No, child. I am a Sensitive—a healer, if you like."

"But the way you controlled those goblins..."

"All part of the powers of a Sensitive. But what are you doing out here alone?"

Smoke straightened her vest. "I am an apprentice to a magician," she started. Something in the woman's gaze made her tell more than she planned. "He didn't want to take me on, not when he found out I was a girl. But I have to become a wizard, so he sent me to find the feather of a horse." She stopped suddenly, feeling confused. Why had she said so much?

The woman looked thoughtful. "The feather of a horse. Anyone who would send a child out into danger to find a nonexistent—" She caught herself up short and looked at the Taisee. "I may ask for a return favor sooner than you thought, Cloudstrider." The winged being nodded.

Smoke, meanwhile, had seen something shining in the long grass. Bending, she found herself looking at a feather the length of her palm, which gleamed whitely in the torchlight. She held it up to the Taisee. "You lost a feather. May I have it to bring to my magician?"

The Taisee looked toward the woman. She reached out and closed Smoke's hand about the feather. "Yes, of course you may. But do you truly wish to go back to him?"

"He swore the oath of apprenticeship," Smoke began hesitantly. "But he said I could break it. But I want to become a wizard! I can call animals to me!"

The woman raised her eyebrows. "A strong Talent, indeed. I am called Lifetrust, and I find that I am in need of an apprentice. I am not a wizard, true, but I can teach you how to talk to animals and how to sense them from far away. I know many wizards, and when you feel you have learned all you can from me, I am certain we can find one—who would definitely be far more powerful than a mere magician—to train you. Would you like that?"

Smoke nodded wordlessly. "I am called Smoke," she said finally.

Lifetrust nodded approvingly. "Not your true name, which is wise for one wishing to become a wizard. I must heal Cloudstrider's wing, and then we shall go back to my cottage and discuss how best to deal with your magician."

* * *

Milburr the magician was staring myopically into his cauldron when he heard a familiar voice.

"I'm back," Smoke said.

Milburr jumped, then turned and eyed her. "Gave up, did you?"

"Oh no, I found the feather."

"You found the feather of a horse? Impossible."

Smoke extended her hand and allowed him to see the feather. "Here it is."

Milburr studied it bemusedly, then slowly reached out to take it.

Smoke closed her fist about it and backed away. "I have the horse it's from right outside."

The magician stared at her as if in shock. "You have the horse it's from outside?" He shook himself, and Smoke retreated toward the door with a smile as Milburr stepped forward. "You fool, girl! Do you know how valuable a horse could be? Someone could steal—" He reached the open doorway and stared speechlessly, instantly falling under the spell Lifetrust had cast about the being which waited there.

Cloudstrider looked amusedly at the magician as Smoke climbed onto the Taisee's back and settled herself with a firm grip on his long mane. Smoke glanced once at the people who had come into the street and now were unable to do anything to the Taisee but stand and stare, and then turned back to Milburr.

"You affirmed me as your apprentice by fire and earth and water," she said solemnly. "By air, I say that I am no longer your apprentice." Cloudstrider opened his wings and launched himself into the sky. "Fare well, Milburr."

The magician stared after them for a long time.

"Horsefeathers" previously appeared in Twilight Times, *Spring 1999. Reprinted from* Dragonlore *#5, May 1984.*

CURSES, FOILED AGAIN

He watched as the sorcerer sprang his trap on the travelers. Hidden from view of his enemy, he edged closer through the brush, checking constantly for other predators as he moved. He moaned softly in sympathy as the sorcerer transformed the first of the travelers.

The shapechange into beast didn't diminish the first man's anger. Instead of a man struggling against the restraining ropes, a deer now tossed his antlered head. However, the bonds around arms and legs had fallen from the narrower deer limbs. Only the rope about his neck still held him.

Intent on that lone restraint, the watcher crept closer. Perhaps he could help with that.

The sorcerer turned to the second traveler, but the watcher paid no attention to the loud protests and cries which followed. He reached the rope's anchor and started working. Before too long the last strand snapped.

The sorcerer had almost completed the transformation on the second traveler when the freed deer charged. The sorcerer had time only to raise his hands before he was impaled on the vicious points of antler.

The watcher sat and waited, satisfaction and relief filling him as the sorcerer died. He waited for the curse to end, for him to return to human form. He waited.

It was only when the carrion crows began to descend that he realized he would have to find another way. He hopped away, following the trail of the last two victims.

* * *

Smoke moved cautiously forward, her right hand away from her dagger, parting the concealing brush, and her left reaching into her carrypouch. "Do you understand? I'm not going to hurt you; I just need to see how badly you're injured." In the back of her mind she could almost hear her mentor, Lifetrust, reminding her that her ability to talk to animals was not all-encompassing. *If they're frightened enough, or angry enough, they can shut you out of their minds. Don't trust your life on it.* And then Lifetrust had sent her out into the forests of the Silvergreen Hills to see what she could locate. *I found a* big *one, Lifetrust.*

The fingertips of her left hand brushed the packets of herbs and salves amid the clutter inside her carrypouch. Reassured, Smoke told herself to calm and to project those calm thoughts outward. "All right, bear, I'm just going to look at that nasty slice—"

The black-furred bear backed a step, big head swinging from side to side. He growled, but his muzzle didn't lift to show his teeth. **Not…bear.**

Smoke froze. "Not bear? You're not a bear?"

The bear seemed equally stunned. **You…understand me?**

"Of course I understand you. I've always been able to understand animals. What do you mean, 'not bear?'"

The bear peered at her short-sightedly. **You…a child.**

Smoke sighed and straightened. "Yes, I'm 12 years old and a girl and I'm going to apprentice to a wizard once my mentor is through training me to heal. Now, do you want me to heal that slice—what caused it, sword or spear?—or are you one of those who don't think a girl can learn healing magic?" *Bad enough Kingdom-dwellers don't think girls can be wizards*, she thought. *Now I have to put up with picky bears—or not-bears, whatever that is.*

The bear's ears flattened, and he sat with a thud. **Sorry. Not used to this. No one has heard me in so long—I couldn't find anyone who would help.**

"With that wound? I'll help. Just stay still." Smoke crouched down and cautiously examined the blood-matted fur.

No. With this. The bear waved a paw, and Smoke ducked just in time. **Everyone is afraid of me. I couldn't get anyone to listen, not even—** The bear's head lowered, and he whined softly. **That's how I was stabbed. No one would listen; they thought I was a wild animal.**

"And you're not." Smoke waited a moment to make sure he wasn't going to make any more wide, paw-swinging gestures, but he just sat there making odd whimpering noises. She reached again towards the wound, and the being deliberately turned that side slightly away from her. She ran a hand through her short-cropped brown hair and readied herself to jump in case her next question was wrong. "So, what are you?"

The not-bear looked at her. **Can't you tell?**

"I'm not a wizard yet." Smoke waited a moment. The big black-furred not-bear watched her with pleading in his brown eyes, and she began to feel that one of them was missing something. "You...*can't* tell me, can you. Is that it?" The not-bear's ears lifted. "All right, that leaves out *were.*" Everyone knew the legend of the werefrog Prince and the tales of the werewolf baron. Smoke was relieved she wouldn't have to hunt down werebears.

The ears lowered halfway.

"Oh, so that doesn't leave out *were* entirely." She thought furiously. If it wasn't a willing or a natural shapechange— "A curse, then?"

The round ears lifted. "A curse. Right." Smoke ransacked her memory for everything Lifetrust had told her about curses. "Is it something you fell into or did someone put it on you?"

The not-bear whimpered.

"Oops, sorry." *Slow down*, she reminded herself. *Curses are very sneaky— "layered," that was the word Lifetrust had used. If he can't mention it even when no one can understand him, there might be a trigger for something else as well.* "Did someone put this on you?" The ears lifted.

Smoke knew now that this was far beyond her ability to help. "I wish Lifetrust was here; she'd be able to call in a wizard to help you." *Not to mention healing that wound in a few minutes*. She wanted to take care of that injury, but she could understand why he felt the curse was more important at the moment. *He feels trapped, and that's bothering him worse than the pain. Still...* "Do you feel strong enough to travel? I can take you to her." *And I'll bet Lifetrust could break this curse without having to ask all these questions.*

The not-bear's head lowered. **Wizard can't help.**

"Did a wizard put this on you?" The large head shook from side to side. "A sorcerer?" The ears lifted. "Oh dear, this isn't one of those that has to be lifted by the same person who cast the curse, is it?"

Sharp teeth showed. **Sorcerer dead.**

"And the curse is still working? Ooo, this is a strong one. Who killed the sorcerer? You?"

The big head shook. **My spouse. While the sorcerer was casting the curse.**

Smoke stared at him a moment. "This…is going to be a problem."

He whimpered, and she saw that he was shivering slightly. *Shock—either from loss of blood or my stupid remark.* "Look, could I do something about that wound? I can't think about curses while you're bleeding in front of me—it goes against everything I've been taught."

The being looked downward at the wound and Smoke wondered what he was. *Not an elf, he's much too noisy. I'd never have heard even a transformed elf in the brush. Anyway, an elf would have gone into a healing trance with this wound. Probably a human—I can't think of anything else that would get into this kind of trouble with a sorcerer.* And where was he from? The nearby Kingdom she had grown up in didn't use his phrasing. And "spouse" wasn't a Free Traders' term—they tended to use "lifemate" or "lifepartner."

Then…you think it's hopeless.

"Me? I'm an apprentice to a Sensitive, not a wizard. All I know about curses is that sometimes it takes a kiss from your true love to break a curse—".

He stabbed me, the not-bear whimpered.

"Who? The sorcerer?"

My spouse. He broke into hiccupping sobs and clamped both paws over his muzzle.

"Oh," Smoke said slowly. *How do you get your true love to kiss you after she—he—just tried to kill you?* She shook her head. First she had to figure out the type of curse.

She waited until the sobs died down. "Sorry. Uh, so can you tell me what happened? Before"—she gestured—"this." She gritted her teeth as he whimpered. *I know he's in pain, but if he doesn't stop that, I'm going to douse him with sleep dust and close that wound*!

Sorcerer wanted…heirloom. Linden didn't understand what he meant, didn't know I had it.

"Heirloom?"

My family. A pendant. I had just had the chain fixed; I was going to give it to Linden. I had it in my pouch… His right paw scrabbled absently into the fur at his side before he seemingly realized the pouch was no longer there. **Wouldn't have done the sorcerer any good. The legend says it can't be stolen or bought, only given freely.**

"It can't be stolen?"

Or misfortune will befall all involved.

"Ah. And the sorcerer stole it from you." Smoke wondered if the sorcerer had known about that legend. Maybe he had thought the pendant worth the risk. "Why would a sorcerer want it? What does it do?"

Nothing, as far as I know. It's pretty, but— The big head lifted, his attention caught by something behind Smoke. **There he is. I've followed him for days. Don't frighten him.**

"Who?" Turning slowly, Smoke peered into the dappled shadows. Expecting a human, she almost overlooked the patch of brown until the horned head swung upwards to scent the air nervously. *A hart. Not something I'd expect to see here.* She noticed something dangling from the upper branches of the antlers, something that sparkled in the sunlight. Some of the sharp, forward-pointing tines on the lower rack seemed to be dyed an odd reddish-brown color. Smoke's eyes narrowed. Was that blood? "He was changed too?"

Behind her came a faint whimper, and the hart tensed, gathering itself to spring.

No! Stop him!

"Wait! Stop!" Smoke slowly rose to her feet, letting the brush swing back into place and blocking the hart's view of the not-bear. *Hope the wind doesn't change.* "Stay still," she ordered both beings.

The hart studied her curiously as Smoke straightened. Other than the pendant tangled in his antlers, he seemed perfectly ordinary.

What did you do? the not-bear complained. **I can't move!**

"I have some power over animals," Smoke said quickly. "Now be quiet."

She slowly moved toward the hart. "I want to help you. Do you remember what the sorcerer did?"

Human. Should fear, but not. Food?

He's completely changed, Smoke worried, not detecting anything other than "hart" in the voice. She looked again at the blood-stained antlers and realized what the not-bear had been trying to say, but couldn't, because of the curse.

Smoke scanned the plants around her. *What do I have that can distract him*? She rummaged in her carrypouch and pulled out several herb packets.

The hart's nostrils twitched and he slowly started towards her. "Ah, the rose petals, huh? Yes, you can have them." She backed towards the concealing bush, the hart following. She let him have two petals, then scattered the rest over the bush. "Wait for the right moment, then kiss him."

What?

"Kiss him!"

The hart, contentedly chewing on petals and leaves, reached for another mouthful, and a black muzzle darted out of the bush to meet him. At the impact, a glow surrounded both beings.

Smoke watched as antlers shrank back into the head, hooves grew into hands and bootshod feet, and the hart reared back and sat down as a human. He sputtered, spitting out leaves, the pendant askew over one ear, tangled amid his reddish-brown curls.

"Linden!" A black-haired man crashed through the bush to stand staring down at him. Smoke saw that the man's brocaded tunic was unmarked. *Maybe the change back to human form healed his wound as well.*

Linden pulled a leaf from his mouth and waved it at his companion. "Your idea, I suppose?"

"Uh, no," Smoke interrupted, "mine. Sorry."

"And who are you? Where are we?" The former hart noticed the chain sliding down his forehead and reached upward.

"Don't touch it!" Smoke and the former bear burst out simultaneously.

Linden sighed and closed his eyes. "Garfife, what happened? Slowly."

Garfife glanced at Smoke. "It's your heirloom," Smoke said.

The black-haired man removed the pendant, looked from it to his spouse, and then poured the chain into a pouch. He thrust the pouch at her. "It's yours. I give it to you freely."

"What?" Smoke almost dropped the pouch in surprise. "I can't—"

"I don't want it. You saved us. Please, take it."

"Garfife, what happened?"

"You killed the sorcerer, Linden. Don't you remember?"

"Last thing I remember was that scruffy man demanding our valuables—I *told* you you were too overdressed for travelling."

"He might not remember anything that happened while he was changed," Smoke whispered. "Some curses are that way."

"Oh." Garfife looked confused.

"How's your wound?"

Garfife looked downward in surprise. "I don't feel it." He patted his side. "I don't understand."

"Neither do I." Smoke shrugged. "You might have known you were 'not bear' because the spell was incomplete or because the sorcerer wanted you to remember. Or because of your pendant." She glanced down at the pouch in her hand and back at Garfife.

"It's yours, now," he repeated.

She added the pouch to her belt and nodded to Linden. "I'll be on my way, then." Retrieving the packets she had dropped, she left Garfife to his explanations.

"He changed you into a deer, Linden, and said he'd leave you that way unless I gave him that necklace."

"And then what?"

"Then he changed me into a bear."

She was soon out of earshot, but she hadn't gone much farther when a rabbit dashed out into her path.

Fear was reflected in its eyes and the ears flattened against its head, but it planted itself directly before her, rose up onto its haunches, and waved both front paws at her. **Not rabbit.**

* * *

"Lifetrust!"

At the shout from outside, the red-haired woman gave a final stir to the stew. Her student had been due to return hours ago. It wasn't like Smoke to travel so slowly. It was also unlike Smoke not to burst through the cottage door with news of whatever she had found.

The Sensitive opened her door to find a deer and a goat directly outside. Just past them, Smoke struggled to hold both a squirming rabbit and a turtle. A squirrel was perched atop the girl's head, and several small birds jostled for position on her shoulders while cats and a ferret wound about her feet.

"Do you have a cart?" the young girl demanded. "Some sorcerer was robbing people and turning them into animals. I found most of the couples that had traveled together, but, unless any of your wizard friends can break a 'true love' curse, we might have to do some traveling."

Lifetrust eyed the rabbit in Smoke's arms. He wiggled his nose hopefully at her.

Smoke noticed and added apologetically, "Uh, and there's also the slight problem of those who haven't found their true loves yet."

THE WINDKIN

Sweeprunners reported one of the Folk entering Windgard from the northwest. The Windrunner tossed his mane and waited atop his hillpost, ears pricked for any further report. The relay of the sweeprunner's identification soon came: the clear whinny code for a wizard.

The Windrunner snorted. Probably Salanoa returning to her small cottage in the Gray Hills. He glanced down at the herd, most dozing still in the cool of the early dawn, and stifled a sigh as young Elin charged up to him.

Skidding to a halt, the gray and white spotted colt dropped a hasty bow. "Permission to escort the wizard, sir," he said eagerly. At his Elder's assent, he made an even sketchier head bob and raced away.

He runs well, the Windrunner thought as Elin quickly disappeared over the horizon. *A proper Son of the Wind* He shook his head, amused at the twist his thoughts had taken. That one? A proper Son of the Wind? When he wasted every possible moment chatting with wizards, elves, and even those mischievous fairies rather than assuming those adult responsibilities as befitted his age? When he continually perturbed the oldsters by demanding to know the whys and wherefores of what-had-always-been?

Something would have to be done about young Elin. Even his own age-herd was beginning to murmur against him.

The black stallion sighed and hoped that the youngling would not badger the wizard too much with his questions.

* * *

Elin felt as if he could soar with delight. Excitement and anticipation lent wings to his hooves and he fairly flew across the long grass.

Salanoa was coming! Was here in Windgard at last!

Of all the wizards in the Free Lands, Salanoa was his favorite. What cared he that the oldsters whispered that she had been a human—one of the ancient and now-vanished enemies of the People of the Wind—before becoming a wizard? She was less abrupt than the silver-garbed wanderer Graylod and did not speak in riddles as did the flame-haired Guardian. Best of all, she lived not far from Windgard and did not mind his numerous visits.

The reddish sun was directly overhead before he caught sight of a slowly moving brown dot on the horizon. Soon he was close enough to whinny a greeting.

"Ah, Elin! Rightly the elves named your people the Fleogende, the Winged Ones!" She prodded his gently heaving side. "Where was the herd today? The southern border by the Low Peaks? You took all morning to reach me!"

Elin snorted in answer to her teasings, ruffling her hair with his breath. He studied the wizard, wondering as always how humans could ever have been such a threat to the People. She was tall, yes, taller than the Highland elves, but he, Elin, was taller still. Her long brown hair framed her face, highlighting her grass-green eyes. Only the gold of her pendant with its magical brown stone relieved the brown of her garb.

He nuzzled her backpack. "I can carry that," he offered.

Salanoa smiled, starting off again with her easy stride. "Not this time, my young friend. Kelan would have my stone if I let his precious scrolls out of my care."

"Scrolls? What are those?" Following, he sniffed carefully at the pack. It smelled magical, with the nose-tickling scent of age and the dry tang of parchment. "Smells like that 'book' you had, filled with those black markings like sparklewing tracks." He snorted and tossed his mane at the memory. "My eyes kept crossing."

The wizard laughed. "Few of the Folk have your people's total recall."

"Not even you?" Elin was surprised. Salanoa's memory went back several ages, and she was one of the youngest of the wizards.

She smiled. "Even Kelan, our Lore-Master, forgets occasionally. That is why he has so many records and books of lore in his castle." She adjusted her pack. "Even I must consult the Lore-Master when my memory fails. Or when my knowledge is incomplete. I should teach you to read someday," she mused, "and turn you loose in Kelan's castle. Stored there are answers to questions you have yet to ask." She laughed. "If that is possible. What new questions have you saved to ask me, my curious friend?"

* * *

They walked across the plains and through the scattered forests of Windgard, heading southeasterly toward the Gray Hills. The journey took five times as long as it would have taken Elin to run it, but he did not mind keeping to the wizard's pace. Salanoa was an excellent traveling companion. She told him stories of the past ages when he ran out of questions and drilled him in the elvish and dwarvish tongues. He had once been surprised to learn that there were languages other than the Common Tongue that all the Free Folk used. Salanoa still teased him about his thick Windkin accent. "Practically another language," was her usual comment.

Elin's ears twitched at memories of his first attempts to talk with travelers. "How many languages do you know, Salanoa?"

The wizard touched the brown stone of her pendant with a distant look in her young-old eyes. "More than are used today."

* * *

A few days later, after escorting Salanoa to her home, Elin trotted slowly back to the herd. He was in no hurry to return. Herd life seemed more boring than usual after Salanoa's tales, and her comments always required quiet reflection to be fully understood. This time was no exception. Why had she compared Windgard with the long-dead Last Kingdom?

"Elin! ELIN!" A blue-black colt that could only be his best friend Hahle thundered towards him. "Thank the Winds I found you!" Hahle gasped as he pulled up sharply. "You have to get back to the herd!"

Reflex was such that they were galloping before Elin thought to ask, "Why?"

"Why? *Why*? You know how much Fedrar and Hurdon grumbled the last time you ducked out to 'escort' Salanoa. Now they've gotten the oldsters stirred up. And you should hear the wind those old bags of bones are spinning. 'Escort duty,'" he mimicked in a quavering voice, "'is to be done at a distance, keeping out of sight of the intruder. Not strolling along *with* them!'" He snorted. "Not that I see why you'd want to talk with elves and wizards, but what's the fuss? And the way they go on about the last time the Lore-Master was here! We were only foals then! You'd think it was a crime to talk to a wizard! I mean, magic *is* indecent, but if you ignore a wizard, they're liable to take offense and turn you into something unnatural."

"The wizards aren't that sensitive to insult," Elin disagreed.

"Insult? Where's the insult? We leave them alone and they should leave us alone. And most of the Folk do. I've only seen a few elves and just the three wizards—"

"We've isolated ourselves from the Free Lands and you think that's good?"

Hahle swerved aside, shaking his head. "Save your arguments for the herd, huh? No need to twist my tail. You could learn to fly for all I care; it's *them* you have to convince."

"Sorry."

A sparklewing sprang up from the long grass beside them, its wing feathers shimmering like the dwarf jewels its ancestor had stolen in the elfin tale. Elin wondered if the oldsters could prevent him from hearing any more such tales. Let them try! Only the Windrunner could enforce such a restriction, and the Windrunner would not become involved in mere petty jealousy.

* * *

The night wind was drawing darkness across the sky as they neared the herd. A black stallion waited as they approached, the herd silent behind their Elder.

Hahle gulped. "I didn't think they were *that* riled!"

"Stay here, Hahle," Elin said. "I don't want their anger turned against you as well."

"Windspin!" Hahle snorted. "You think I'm afraid of those—Ow!"

"Stay here!" Elin repeated.

Hahle licked the sore spot on his side. "All right! No need to nip a fellow!"

Elin approached the herd and bowed his head to the ground before the Windrunner.

"Elin." The acknowledgment betrayed nothing, yet Elin felt his heart sink. "I have heard distressing reports concerning you."

Elin looked up to meet the Windrunner's neutral gaze. "I—"

"He has neglected his duty to the herd and brings ridicule upon the People!" an oldster snapped. "He—"

The Windrunner looked calmly in the speaker's direction and the oldster lapsed into silence. "Few younglings volunteer for escort duty as often as does Elin. He does not neglect his duty to the herd." The stallion turned back to Elin. "He does, perhaps, take longer than some to return from escort, but his familiarity with Windgard will serve him well when he reaches the age for sweeprunning."

"Escort duty is to be done at a distance," the oldster persisted, "staying—"

"—out of sight of the traveler," the Windrunner concluded. "But when the traveler is a close neighbor, what harm does it cause?"

"Salanoa isn't the only one he talks with." Fedrar pushed through the herd to confront Elin.

The Windrunner eyed the chestnut colt. "You are out of your place, youngling."

"But I've seen him! I've seen how he talks to elves and dwarves!"

"The Winds have informed me of his indiscretions." The ice in the Windrunner's voice chilled Elin and cowed Fedrar. The chestnut colt quickly bowed, backing into the herd.

"What say you, Elin? How do you explain your behavior?"

"I—" Elin stammered. He looked at his hostile audience and despair closed over him like a stormy night. He felt his head droop, and with a flash of anger forced himself to look up. He had done nothing shameful! He met the Windrunner's eyes and spoke directly to his Elder, ignoring all others.

"I think we are wrong to isolate ourselves from the rest of the Free Lands. We treat our neighbors and those who could be our friends as mistrusted enemies. For what reason? None of the Memory-Keepers can recall and none of the Teaching Chants mention any betrayal by the Folk."

He turned proudly to Fedrar. "Yes, I speak with elves and dwarves and wizards. They are not monsters or Evil Ones in disguise, but people like us. They share the same faults and virtues as we do. And they, too"—he turned back to the Windrunner—"wonder at our treatment of them."

"Magic-users!" old Vyton rumbled as if the word was a curse. "They wonder why we will not allow their foul spells to taint us?"

"We are discussing Elin's speech with them," a bay mare interrupted impatiently, "not their spells."

"Not even those spells Elin teaches the younglings?" Fedrar retorted heatedly.

Before anyone could say or do anything, Hahle charged into Fedrar, knocking the colt off balance. "You take that back," Hahle said through bared teeth. "I was there, too, Fedrar. Elin didn't teach any spells. Take it back or I'll—"

"Hahle."

The blue-black colt looked back at the Windrunner. "But, sir, he's lying!"

"I am not!" Fedrar denied.

"Elin, what were you telling the younglings?"

"The tale of Helundar and Taerye," Elin said, feeling sick at heart. Helundar was of the People, but Taerye was his elf friend, who had used a great deal of magic to get the two out of their numerous difficulties.

A Memory-Keeper raised her head in astoundment, and the Windrunner nodded to her. He said nothing, but Elin sensed his disappointment.

Hahle glared at Fedrar. "My grandsire told me that one."

Elin groaned inwardly at the lie. He himself had only heard it from Salanoa. "Hahle—"

"I don't remember that tale," an oldster wondered.

The Windrunner stamped a hoof. "Enough. I have decided."

The herd's murmurs stilled and Hahle moved to stand beside Elin.

"Elin, you are but a youngling, so I will only warn you this time. If you wish to remain a member of the herd, you must follow our ways. The herd has few dealings with magic. You will abide by that."

Elin opened his mouth to protest, but the Windrunner repeated, "As a herd member, you will abide by that tradition, Elin."

Elin's ears lowered and he bowed his head.

"Hahle, you and Elin will begin sweeprun training. At last star you will start for the Highland borders. Sehsron and Renw will be alerted to watch for you."

The herd murmured at that, and the Windrunner raked them with an icy glance. "That is my decision."

The herd began to disperse, foals tripping sleepy-eyed by their dams, stallions and mares leaving to relieve others on sweepruns. Elin stayed where he was, head bowed. He heard the oldsters mumbling as they ambled toward the stream, felt the breeze accompanying the Windrunner drift away.

Hahle nickered excitedly. "Sweeprun training!" He dashed around Elin, rushed away and then returned to nudge his gray-spotted friend. "We get to learn under Renw!" He tossed his mane proudly. "I'll show him who's still a foal!"

He whirled suddenly and his ears half-lowered. "Well, Fedrar." He bowed mockingly. "Coming to gloat? Or is the punishment too severe for you, Wise One?"

Fedrar snorted in disgust. "Don't walk air. The Windrunner just wants to be rid of you two."

Elin raised his head to meet the colt's angry eyes. "I don't see why you're so envious of me, Fedrar. Everyone knows you avoid escort duty as a troll would sunlight. You could have—"

Fedrar's ears laid back in anger. "Don't talk filthy to me, wizard friend!"

Hahle bristled.

"Fedrar."

The chestnut colt looked startled at the Windrunner's call. "Sir?"

"You will be on escort duty until I say otherwise."

Hahle chortled gleefully, but subsided at Elin's swift look.

"But-but, sir!" Fedrar gulped at the Windrunner's stern glance.

The black stallion studied the night stars. "Restel is escorting a dwarf to the Low Peaks. Go take over from her, Fedrar."

"Y-yes, sir." The colt bowed low and dashed away.

Hahle's ears twitched with suppressed mirth as the Windrunner walked toward the stream. Once the Elder was out of earshot, Hahle squealed with laughter and raced in a wide circle. "That settles the insult!" He stopped and nudged Elin. "Aw, cheer up. You haven't lost your real friends. You can't run a race with an elf. Or a dwarf." His ears perked. "Somebody's coming."

A red roan hurtled out of the night and jerked to a stop before them. "Hahle!" Renw gasped, breathing hard. "Elin! Sehsron said one of you was in trouble. What happened?"

"Sweeprunning," Hahle crowed. "Elin and I get to sweeprun with you."

Renw snorted. "You foals are sweeprunning? Then why does Elin look as if—" He broke off, spotting the whispering cluster of oldsters glancing their way. "Oh. Oh, Elin. Did they finally decide to stop you?"

He tugged at Elin's mane. "You're too friendly for your own good, youngling. But don't worry, a few sweepruns and you'll find a new interest."

Elin lifted his head in surprise. How could Renw think that? How could they both think that he could forget his outsider friends so easily? He had thought Renw, of all his friends, would understand. Or did he? His hide twitched at a sudden breeze as he followed Renw's gaze to see the Windrunner watching them.

"Quit calling us younglings," Hahle grumbled. "You're only a few seasons older."

"Old enough to run you into the dust, foal."

Hahle danced a few steps. "I can outrun you any day, oldster."

Elin ignored his friends. He looked at the herd, saw their eyes furtively flicking toward him and away. Did they expect him to change shape? He remembered the murmurs, could hear them even now. "*Magic-user. Elf-friend. He speaks with that wizard constantly. Not even the Winds know what they are plotting.*"

"I hear she's going to change him, turn him into an elf."

"Corrupting the young, he is, with all his talk about magic. And he was such a fine foal until that Lore-Master came around."

Elin shook his head angrily. "I'm leaving for the border now," he announced.

Hahle looked baffled. "Now? Why? We have until last star. And Renw just got here."

Elin reared. "I'm leaving now!" He dashed off into the night, heading north for the Highlands.

Hahle and Renw exchanged glances. "Off again," Renw groaned. "Let him run alone for a bit, Hahle. He'll calm down. You know Elin never stays angry long."

* * *

Elin raced faster and faster, letting the wind of his passage sweep his mind clear of hurt and anger. But questions raced on swifter hooves. Why did the People dislike outsiders? Why? What was the harm in talking?And sweeprunning—why was Windgard so protected? Why was Windgard so protected? What did they fear?

Tradition, the oldsters said. Elin snorted in disgust. The be-all and end-all of everything. Tradition. Memory mocked him. *"If you wish to remain a member of the herd, you will follow our traditions."* Well, he didn't have to be a herd member. He could always leave the herd.

His pace faltered at the rebellious thought. Leave the herd? Leave Windgard? Where would he go? He couldn't go to Salanoa. Her cottage would be the first place any searcher would look, and he didn't want to cause trouble for the wizard But he couldn't give up his ways! Herd life was so limited. He sighed. There were so many things he didn't know, so much he wanted to learn that he never would in Windgard. And if he stayed, he would be restricted from meeting any outsiders. Even Salanoa!

Somehow that decided him. He glanced back at Renw and Hahle

and stopped, waiting for them to catch up. Let the herd believe he followed their narrow-minded traditions and watched their border against nonexistent enemies. He was no foal to be frightened by tales of evil magic-users lurking beyond the borders. He couldn't seek sanctuary with Salanoa, but, thanks to her, he knew of the lands outside. Far north of the Highlands, through which none of the Free Folk ventured, was Dewin Heights and the castle of the Lore-Master. There he might find the answers he sought.

He glanced up at the winking stars. Tomorrow, he vowed, they would guide him even farther north than Windgard's borders.

* * *

The black stallion watched as the three younglings raced northward. "Watch over him, O Winds," he whispered, "and guide him to his destiny."

A light breeze whispered about the Windrunner and swirled up into the sky.

"The Windkin" previously appeared in Twilight Times, *April 2000. Reworked from the version in* Shadowstar *#21-22, Spring 1986.*

SRIKE WATCH

Leereho knelt in the long grass by the small stream and drank gratefully of the cool water. He splashed his dusty face with more water, dampening his white-blond hair with the welcome moisture. Feeling cooler, he glanced up at the sun overhead.

A long, weary run. His legs ached at the memory. But if he was to bring the ill tidings swiftly to the Elder, he must continue to run, through the heat of the day and on again into the night before he could stop to rest again.

Leereho thought longingly of the waybread in his pouch, but knew he dared not risk the time. If the Highlanders found an elf of the Great Woods here within their borders, their anger would be great. And, he supposed, justified. It would have been wiser to have gone through Windgard, even if it had meant a long detour. Being followed by the watchful Fleogende, however irritating, was not the same as being followed by the Highland elves, kin though they were to him.

He carefully stretched his stiffening leg muscles and prepared to depart. A faint sound came to his ears and he froze, listening. Voices, approaching so swiftly that he would be seen if he tried to run. He found a tangle of long grass and scraggly bushes and hid himself within, trusting his gray and green travel garb to complete the camouflage. He pulled the hood of his gray cloak over his revealing blond hair as the voices drew closer.

"Hahle, there's no sense in following Elin," said one voice in a thick accent. "If he feels that his outsider friends are more important to him than the herd, then that's that. You heard the Windrunner last night. Elin has made his choice."

The second speaker snorted. "Well, he can just *un*-choose."

Peering out cautiously from among the bushes, Leereho caught sight of the speakers. His eyebrows rose in surprise. Fleogende. Distant kin to the unicorns and the swiftest runners in the Free Lands. Elf-friends, they had been in ages past. Seldom now did they stray from their homeland Windgard. What was this pair of colts doing in the Highlands?

Leereho shifted position slightly to keep the pair in sight. The black colt trotted up to the stream and drank noisily. His roan companion watched the surrounding area with a trained eye. Leereho held his breath as the roan's gaze swept over his hiding place.

A light breeze swirled about them, and the roan came fully alert, ears perked, listening for the slightest sound. "Hahle, be still," he ordered softly. "I smell magic. There may be elves about."

The black colt raised his dripping muzzle. "So?"

"So, be silent! We aren't in Windgard."

Hahle shook his mane and pawed the ground. The roan glared at him, then returned to his study of their surroundings. Leereho waited, his unease growing as precious moments slipped by.

The breeze shifted again. Leereho could see the roan's nostrils flare as the big head swung about. "Come," he ordered his younger companion. "Swiftly."

Leereho emerged from hiding as the two galloped away. He looked after the swift Fleogende curiously, wondering briefly why they were heading north towards Dewin Heights. That they were even outside Windgard was most unusual. He shrugged. Then, not sure whether the roan had sensed his presence or that of approaching Highlanders, he struck off westward, resuming his journey to the Great Woods.

He had not gone far before he realized that he was being followed. His pursuers stayed out of his sight, but he knew they were there. Only an elf could hear another elf.

The scout let his hood fall back, hoping the Highlanders would mistake him for one of them with his blond hair. The ploy seemed to work. The sense of presence behind him lessened as the day went on. Leereho sternly told himself to stay out of the Highlands next time. There would come a day when his blond hair would fail to reassure the Highlanders.

He had to slacken his pace as the ground slope grew treacherous. Soon he could see the blue waters of the Ea sparkling on the floodplain far below. He made his way carefully downward, leaving the loose dirt and scree undisturbed under his light step.

A mothbird cried out in alarm from the trees ahead, and Leereho froze on the slope, his hands reaching for the bow on his back. He glanced up at the sky through the thinning trees and felt the flame of anger leap up within him. They dared!

Across the blue-green sky a rhagandras drifted lazily. About the size of a raven, the creature was a bizarre mockery of a bird, from its tooth-lined beak to the sharp talons on its wing-joints. No feathers muted the harsh red-violet of its naked skin. Wings that were flaps of skin enabled the rhagandras to glide easily on the winds, its beady eyes surveying the lands below.

Leereho's anger grew. The Shadows dared send their spies so far into the Free Lands? Slinging his bow once more onto his back, he climbed up the hill a short way until he reached an outcropping clear of sheltering trees. He nocked an arrow to his bowstring.

The rhagandras saw him. It shrieked its blood-freezing cry and swooped toward him, beak and claws extended.

Leereho's arrow was swifter. The rhagandras crumbled and plummeted to the ground. Leereho watched with satisfaction, marking where it fell, then slid down the hillside after it. He had to retrieve the arrow. Its unfamiliar markings would betray him to the Highlanders. But a dead rhagandras, on the very borders of their land, would be a warning he could leave them, more effective than any words, one that the Highlanders could not mistake.

The dying rhagandras hissed and snapped its toothy beak as he approached. He killed it swiftly with a stone and retrieved his arrow, heedless of scratches. Only in its bataog form were the creature's claws envenomed and a scratch deadly.

He gingerly moved the evil creature to a cleared spot where it would easily be found. Then he resumed his journey.

The elf increased his pace as the faint notes of a horn echoed in the hills behind him. The call seemed distant, but if the Highlanders were on the move, he had best not remain.

Moments later, he slid to a halt at the top of a cliff. The floodplain stretched invitingly far below. He glanced about as the horn sounded once again. Too far to jump, and no time to find another way down. At least there were many easy hand-and-foot holds on the cliff face.

Leereho sat on the edge and checked to make sure his sword and bow were securely fastened on his back. Then he carefully lowered himself downward.

He had climbed about a third of the way down when he heard a sound more chilling than any of the Highlanders' horns. Clinging to the rock face, he turned his head as echoes of the shrill cry died away. A second rhagandras! How could he have forgotten that the creatures always traveled in pairs!

The red-violet body swooped toward him, talons extended to rend and tear. Leereho ducked his head and let his cloak take the brunt of the strike. The rhagandras circled for a second attack, and Leereho wasted a moment looking downward for some place with room to stand and fight before he began climbing back the way he had come. He was not down far enough to jump without injury, but he was a vulnerable target here on the cliff face.

The shriek of the approaching creature almost deafened him. He stopped where he was and drew his dagger left-handed, clinging to the rocks with his right. The rhagandras struck again, managing to scratch the elf's face with one wing talon.

The pain quenched his anger like a dash of cold water. He had been warned often enough about his temper. Hatred and anger were the Shadows' tools; Leereho had no use for them. Not here.

Leereho glanced at his dagger as the rhagandras flew away, and smiled grimly at a faint line of purplish ichor. Placing the blade between his teeth, he climbed upwards a short distance more.

He listened uneasily to the rattle of falling rock and carefully reached for his next handhold. The ledge beneath his feet abruptly fell away, and his reaching fingers clamped onto a small hold. Below the shriek of the attacking rhagandras came the soft hiss of shifting earth.

The creature struck and Leereho lost his grip on one handhold. Placing the tips of his soft boots against the rock wall to brace himself, he pulled his dagger from between his teeth. The rhagandras glided just out of his reach, taunting him.

Leereho lost his temper. He threw his dagger at the creature—and his last handhold abruptly gave way.

He twisted as he fell, trying to protect himself, as well as striving to catch at some outcropping of rock. He did not succeed.

He landed all wrong, too hard, and on his left arm rather than his side. He felt a bone snap and then his head hit something hard.

* * *

The red sun had not moved far across the sky when Leereho regained consciousness. He sat up cautiously, wincing at a sharpness in his side. His left arm was broken and he possibly had cracked a rib, but the elf was more concerned at the throbbing in his head and the whirling nausea if he moved too quickly. If it was a concussion, he hoped it was slight. He still had far to travel today.

He climbed carefully to his feet, trying to ignore the warning aches of bruises, and, when he tried to stand, discovered one sharp pain that did not go away when ignored. "By the Green, not my ankle, too!" he muttered aloud, easing back onto the ground.

He glanced worriedly up at the sky. The rhagandras was nowhere to be seen. Was it already on its way back to the Shadows? He might have managed to wound it. The knife toss had felt right when the blade had left his fingers, but he had not seen the creature after he fell. Leereho had no choice but to continue on.

If he could.

The abuse his body had suffered had triggered reflexive survival responses that did not obey his conscious mind. If this had been an ordinary journey, he would have found a safe, sheltered place for a two or three days' trance-induced healing. But this was no ordinary journey.

He had no time for a healing trance, no time to rest and allow his body to repair the damage. The Elder had to be warned now! The Watch Tower *must* resume its duties once again!

But, despite his desire to remain conscious, his body resisted his will. The world slowly seemed to retreat from him. He no longer felt any pain, no longer felt the rocks against his side.

He fought the trance as he went under, struggling to wake when every instinct said to rest. He surfaced once and saw the Moon overhead in the starry night sky. He groaned in frustration as the trance closed over him again. He had no time for this. The Elder must be warned!

Sunlight glared into his eyes when he surfaced again. He struggled to hold onto the thin thread of consciousness. His abused body resisted, sending the dream creatures from his strife-torn trance to haunt him. He painfully reached out and closed his good hand about a sharp rock, rejoicing in the warning pricks against his palm. This was real! He *would* remain conscious, no matter how much his body wished to rest.

He blinked and tried to focus as two dream creatures stubbornly remained, watching him. He grimaced as he recognized them. The two Fleogende from the Highlands. Why did he have to dream of them? Useless to believe that they would have come this way. They had been heading for Dewin Heights when he had last seen them.

"Say, I remember him now," the roan said suddenly. "He comes through Windgard often. Runs rather fast, too. For an elf," he added hastily.

The black snorted.

Leereho felt like echoing him. All he needed was talking dream creatures to distract him. "You will not fool me," he said thickly. "I know you are dreams. Real Fleogende avoid all contact with outsiders."

The two Fleogende exchanged glances. "He must not have met Elin," the black said sourly. "Too bad he can't understand us."

The roan's ears twitched. "You sure about that, youngling?"

"Highlanders never can. That's what Vyton says."

The roan studied Leereho. "This one is no Highlander," he decided. "And, herd ways or no herd ways, he needs help. Our help."

"Hah!" the black snorted.

Leereho was surprised. Dream figures offering help? He was worse off than he had thought. He struggled to rise to a sitting position, gritting his teeth against the pain. "I must warn the Elder," he muttered aloud. "Even if I have to crawl."

The roan eyed him. "He could always ride," he said to the black colt.

"Ride? Don't talk dirty, Renw." Renw turned toward him and the black stepped back. "You're serious! That's—that's indecent!"

"Windspin. Never bothered Helundar."

Leereho jarred his broken arm and gasped at the pain. He glanced up at the figures above him, surprised that they hadn't vanished. He could still hear them. *Were* they real?

"It will bother the oldsters!"

Renw looked at the black mildly. "Who's going to tell them, Hahle? The Windrunner will know, though—can't stop the Winds."

"Yes, the Windrunner will know," Hahle said triumphantly. "Remember what he did to Elin for just talking to outsiders. This...*riding*," he said with revulsion, "goes against all traditions. Renw, you can't do this!"

Renw appeared not to have heard as he studied the elf. "Here, just help me get him to his feet. Then you can run along home. Sehsron will be looking for you by now."

"I'm not leaving you, too!"

"No sense in both of us getting into trouble, is there?"

The roan lowered his head. Leereho felt warm breath against his face and shakily reached out to touch the soft muzzle. They were real!

He wasn't dreaming!

"Where are your people, elf?" the roan said slowly, speaking each word as clearly as he could. He had to repeat the question before Leereho recovered from his astonishment enough to speak.

"No good, Renw. He doesn't understand you," Hahle began when Leereho interrupted.

"No, I understand. I thought…I had dreamed you two." He shook his head, trying to organize his thoughts. He looked up at the roan. "Please, carry a message for me to the Elder of my people. To the Watch Tower in the Great Woods."

Renw snorted softly. "I'll have to take you, elf, along with your message. I don't know where your Watch Tower is. And I think your people would do better at healing your hurts than mine. How badly are you injured? Can you stand?"

The detachment of the healing trance began to seep into his mind again, and Leereho struggled to shake it off, to focus his mind on the Fleogen's questions. "My…ankle is broken. I…"

"This one?" The soft nose carefully hovered above the injured foot, then swung back towards the elf's chest. "And this arm, too, I'd say. Too bad they're both on the same side." The roan sniffed at the scratch on the elf's face. "You didn't get this in your fall. What attacked you?"

Leereho closed his eyes in despair. Precious time had already been lost. Had the second rhagandras already returned to its Shadow masters? The isolated Fleogende would probably dismiss his warning as merely a fever dream.

"Renw, over here," Hahle called in a strange voice. "There's something…it's…it smells *wrong*!"

Leereho opened his eyes as the roan turned away. He levered himself up on his good elbow. Had they found the second rhagandras?

"I've never seen anything like this before," the black colt said nervously as Renw joined him. "Looks like something out of one of Elin's tales."

Renw looked, then backed a step in horror. "Blessed Winds. A srike!" He shook his head, then returned to examine the creature. "It's from one of Elin's tales, all right, Hahle, and from the Memory-Keepers', too. This is why sweeprunning patrols were begun long ago."

"To guard against that little thing?"

"Don't be deceived by appearances, Hahle. That 'little thing' is a shapechanger. And it has larger kin." Renw glanced worriedly at the sky. "The Windrunner must be warned." He looked again at the fallen creature and shuddered before turning away. "Come help me with the elf, Hahle. We have little time."

Before long Leereho found himself balancing unsteadily on his good leg and hanging onto the black colt for support. The roan knelt down beside his injured foot and waited.

"Renw, he's yanking my mane out!" Hahle muttered.

"Quit griping and stand still. Easy now, elf. Lift that foot a little higher. Steady now, don't slide off me."

Leereho settled himself into place on the roan's back. He carefully slid his broken arm under the belt holding his sword to his back and made a rough sling with the belt ties. Paler now, he clutched the roan's mane with his good hand.

Renw looked back at him. "Secure? Hold on tight, then. I'm going to stand up."

Leereho gripped the Fleogen's sides tightly with his knees and calf muscles as the roan rose to his feet. Hahle snorted when the elf remained on.

Renw tossed his tail. "You have been carried by People of the Wind before, elf."

Leereho relaxed his grip on the silky mane. "Yes, in my younger days. In an age long past, when the Fleogende and elves were friends."

Hahle snorted. "That's the thanks we get," he muttered.

The roan pawed the ground. "Stay out of the Highlands on your way back, Hahle. No need to stir up our neighbors more."

"I'm coming along," Hahle said mutinously.

Renw glanced at him. "No, Hahle. You must run swiftly to the Windrunner. Tell only him that srikes have been seen and that they have attacked the Folk. Can you remember that?"

"Of course. But, Renw—"

"Don't argue. Warn the Windrunner. Srikes are the Eyes of the Shadows. Their presence might mean nothing, or everything."

He began walking, giving the elf time to accustom himself to his stride. Hahle followed. "The Windrunner probably already knows. The Winds tell him everything."

"We can't leave this message for the Winds to carry. You have to bring it, Hahle. Go."

"I'm going, I'm going." Hahle trotted away a few steps. "May the Winds guide you, Renw."

"Run with the Wind, sweeprunner."

Hahle's head lifted with pride. He turned and sped away.

Renw walked on. "Hahle's a little young for this," he said, as if in apology.

Leereho let his eyes close. "So am I."

"You can speak of ages past and still call yourself young?" The Fleogen snorted softly. "I have heard it said that knowledge, not years, ages a wizard. You elves must age the same."

Leereho's eyes snapped open. Where had he ever gotten the idea that the Fleogende were closed-minded, magic-hating beings? Either he had severely misjudged the Fleogende or this was no ordinary one.

"Comfortable up there, elf? Brace yourself. We had best hurry. You want to warn your people, and I want to get back to mine as soon as possible. Hahle gets into so much trouble on his own that he might not be believed this time. And srikes don't go away when ignored."

"'When the rhagandras fly, the Shadows are near,'" Leereho quoted.

"Right." The roan broke smoothly into a canter. "Are you staying on back there?"

Leereho closed his mind to the throbbing in his ankle and arm. "Yes. You can go faster if you like."

"I do like." The roan surged forward, and Leereho held on tightly, discovering with pleasure that his body had not forgotten its old riding skill. He looked at the nearing horizon and allowed himself a small measure of relief. At this Fleogen's pace, his warning would reach the Elder's ears by nightfall. His birthstar must have smiled upon his mission. The death of the second rhagandras had bought the Lands a small measure of time, and the Fleogende's aid would turn that time to the Land's advantage. There was still a chance that his warning would be in time.

"Rhagandras," the roan beneath him mused. "'Andras' means evil, doesn't it?"

Leereho almost fell off. "You speak Elvish?"

"I understand a little of it. One or two phrases. One of the younglings of the herd tried teaching me before I began sweeprunning. He's very fluent in Elvish and some of the dwarf tongues."

"Fluent," Leereho repeated numbly. Even back in the days when they were elf-friends, the Fleogende only spoke the Common Tongue in their dealings with the Folk. Even the legendary Helundar. Someday he would have to meet this youngling.

The roan's ears twitched. "You still awake back there?"

Leereho suddenly realized he had missed a question. "Sorry.

Memories. What did you ask?"

"Was that the message you wanted delivered to your people? Srikes? Or something else?"

"Something else. Something for which the rhag—er, srikes—are only the first warning. There are signs of magic massing on the border between the Lands and the Shadowlands."

"I thought I smelled mountains on you. You've come from the border? Do you sweeprun for your people?"

"I'm a scout, yes. You, too? Wait—you said you've seen me before. I don't remember seeing you when I've crossed Windgard."

The roan chuckled. "Good. You weren't supposed to. A good sweeprunner stays out of sight of the person being escorted."

"Then I am honored to be in the company of an excellent sweeprunner," Leereho said formally. "But why do your people guard themselves against the rest of the Folk?"

The roan tossed his head. "Because…that is how it is. The Memory-Keepers might know the beginning of it. Why do the Highlanders do the same? The herd is no worse in their behavior towards outsiders than the Highlanders, elf."

Leereho sighed softly. The roan spoke truth. Who was he to criticize the Fleogende when his own kin behaved no better? "I ask your forgiveness. I am called Leereho. I offer you my friendship."

The roan's ears twitched, and Leereho wondered why the Fleogen seemed amused. "No apologies necessary. I'm Renw. Now, my friend, let's see if we can find your Watch Tower before the Shadows send any more srikes spying."

—

"Srike Watch" reworked from the version in Shadowstar *#25, October 1987.*

THE LORE-MASTER'S APPRENTICE

"Long ago—long before elves or humans had entered the Lands yet long after the Shadows had been exiled to their place of imprisonment—there roamed the plains of the Lands tall, thin, four-legged beings acknowledged by the unicorns as distant cousins. The fairies name them Windlords... Their coats were silver, their hooves white, and their eyes opal. Swifter than the winds, they were beings of great wisdom, yet they were mute.

"When the Gates into the Lands opened and the elves entered with their white horses, the Windlords freed the—"

The watching brown wizard choked on a spurt of laughter, and the black-robed Lore-Master interrupted. "Let us not attempt to rewrite the Records just yet, Elin. Read the lore as it is written."

Elin lowered his ears and his long tail twitched. "Yes, sir." He shook his long mane out of his eyes and continued. "When the Gates into the Lands opened and the elves entered with their white horses, the Windlords called the horses to them, and the elves never saw their animals again, save within the Windlord herds. Later the humans entered through the Gates with their many breeds of horses, and again the Windlords called. No horse ever stayed long in any being's ownership upon entering the Lands, and any attempt to regain possession of a horse was thwarted by the Windlords. The elves soon discovered that a few Windlords had gained possession of a Gate and were calling more horses and horselike beings to them. This is how the sky-running—"

"Taisee," the brown wizard prompted softly.

"—Taisee and others entered the Lands. The High Council then sealed that gate for all time.

"After an age, it was discovered that the mixture of horse and Windlord had produced a new being, now with the speed and intelligence of a Windlord, yet capable of speech. Horses and Windlords no longer existing, the new beings have been given many names—'Windkin' by the wizards and 'Fleogende' by the elves, to name but a few—yet the fairies still call them 'Windlords.' In their own tongue they call themselves 'the People of the Wind.'"

"Well done, Elin," Salanoa said as he finished. "Until your addition, I thought you recited from memory. Kelan, I salute you. I had feared his forward vision might not be able to focus enough for reading. And the possibility that he could be taught to read so quickly—!"

The Lore-Master nodded in acknowledgment of her praise and smoothed his small black mustache. "His own retentive memory greatly aided that. He needs only be shown a word once to remember it."

Salanoa laughed. "Or hear it once. You will find—"

The eyes of the two Wise met and they continued their discussion on another level.

The birds of these hills are terrible gossips, Kelan. I could not help but hear reports of Elin's progress. Was it truly so bad?

The reading, no. What was difficult was finding the means for him to hold the scrolls open or turn pages while reading. He was most insistent that I not use a spell.

It is too soon to ask him to throw aside his people's ingrained distrust of magic. His love of knowledge brought him this far. He may yet accept another training.

Which reminds me, Salanoa. Could you not have warned me he would come?

Me? When I did not know myself? I but told him where the largest source of lore existed; the herd's behavior made him seek it out. Besides, you yourself foresaw that someday you would again have an apprentice. What use is precognition when it tells you an apprentice would come but not in what shape?

The veil of the future draws aside but slightly. Still, you are right, I should have been prepared. There are no humans now in the Free Lands, and the elves and dwarves care little for matters beyond their own affairs. Still—

It is hardly Elin's fault that your castle is so crammed with records that no one of his bulk could turn easily. He is not *clumsy*!

No, he isn't.

Their conversation taking hardly the space of a breath, the brown wizard finished her spoken sentence. "—your apprentice has a great love of lore. Why, what's wrong, Elin? Aren't you pleased to discover that what you used to call sparklewing tracks actually mean something?"

Elin stared thoughtfully at the bound volume open before him. "But it's all wrong," he said, stamping a hoof.

The brown wizard and black exchanged glances, then looked again at the gray-and-white spotted Windkin.

"The Children of the Wind existed long before unicorns," Elin said heatedly. "Why, they fought with the Green to help imprison the Shadows! And, according to the Memory-Keepers of the herd..."

Kelan looked speechlessly at his new apprentice, now beginning to recite a tale. The wizard caught up a quill and looked frantically for a clean piece of parchment. Salanoa laid a hand on his shoulder. "Steady, my friend. Elin will be here for a time." She grinned mischievously. "You could always teach him how to—"

Kelan glanced at his apprentice's four hooves, then closed his eyes and raised a hand to stop her. "No. Oh no. I refuse to teach him to write!"

"The Lore-Master's Apprentice" previously appeared in Shadowstar *#16, December 1984.*

THE TWIN BOND

The ship plunged headlong through the outer layer of atmosphere, shuddering as the excessive heat of its passage damaged systems normally protected by hull. Within the stricken ship, its sole passenger groggily scanned the starfield for the attacking ship's return. One bright spot seemed to be growing larger.

"Closing in for the kill, huh?" the agent muttered softly. "Have I got a surprise for you!"

Despite the urgency of the passing seconds, she seemed almost to be moving in slow motion. Her fingers felt oddly clumsy as she activated the self-destruct and fumbled almost perilously while she programmed the over-riding coordinates. But there was no time for questions. With a last glance at the closing ship, Janice turned and stumbled toward the lifepod.

A mournful hooting began as the lifepod's hatch opened. Janice paused, one hand on the edge of the hatch, and looked back into the control room of the small ship. "Sorry, Ship." She mentally shook her head. *When Apson learns I can't even keep a loaner intact for more than a month, I'll* never *get one of my own.*

It took almost all her will to remember where she was and to force herself to turn Her body was strangely reluctant to obey. She started to duck her head to enter the lifepod when the ship shuddered violently, and an explosion from behind flung her in through the hatchway.

Precious seconds ticked by until the ship's computer, acting on preset programming regarding the presence of animate but nonresponsive beings within lifepods, sealed the hatch and released the pod toward the planet below. To deflect attention from the escaping pod, the targeting computer activated every weapons system to fire upon its attacker in the remaining seconds before self-destruct.

The ship's death lit the sky like a display of fireworks. Its attacker, which had prudently withdrawn when fired upon, returned to find nothing of the agent's ship but small fragments that would burn up as they fell through the atmosphere.

* * *

Jennie woke from an uneasy sleep with the vague feeling that she had left the gas on. She padded sleepily out to the kitchen and stood bemusedly eyeing her new electric stove. Her head began to ache and she felt very sleepy, but she did not want to return to her bed just yet. Something was wrong. Something was very wrong. She checked the heat registers twice and even returned to the stove before finally retiring with a very throbbing head.

She stared up into the darkness. She felt she should take something for this headache, but getting up again seemed beyond her. She was *so* sleepy.

The headache abruptly exploded into pinwheels of colors behind her eyes and vanished as suddenly as it had appeared. Jennie clutched the covers. "Janice!"

* * *

Awareness returned slowly, sense by sense. A rhythmic *tick-tick* from somewhere nearby. Softness under one side of the head and fresh air—a curious mixture of woodsmoke and mint—blowing upon the other. An overall feeling of lightness.

Opening her eyes, she looked about in mounting confusion, not recognizing anything. She seemed to be enclosed in a small sphere—barely large enough for her to stretch out fully or stand completely upright—with padded walls, floor, and ceiling. A small nonpadded band of metal ran completely around the middle of the wall, its gleaming surface interrupted by lighting panels and tiny air ducts. The ticking came from a small panel of brightly flashing multicolored lights not far above her head.

She levered herself up to a sitting position, wincing as her head strongly protested the movement. Raising a cautious hand to her head, she found a bleeding cut on her forehead and a large lump on the back of her head. She looked again at her surroundings and realized that the red patches on floor and wall were her own blood.

She looked again at the patch by her knee, a memory stirring dimly.

Scarlet blood. Very bright scarlet blood. That was important. That meant something from the days before...before...

Before what? She frowned at the gap in her memory. The throbbing in her head intensified, and she decided to drop the question. The memory would return, along with the reason for her being here. Although, judging from the lump on her head, she hadn't entered willingly.

She turned out the pockets of her short jacket and trousers and found neither money nor identification. A pocket in her left sleeve held a pen and a penlight, the two on the sides of her lightweight jacket held a palm-sized metallic square covered on all sides with geometric designs and something that resembled a collapsible screwdriver, and an inside pocket held what appeared to be a fancier penlight. The trousers pockets held only an extra elastic band for her hair. She was wearing a short-sleeved turquoise shirt, a light brown jacket and matching trousers and short brown boots. She was also wearing an odd necklace of a lightweight yellow metal. The chain held two curved rectangular plates which fit over her collarbones and a small square which rested in the hollow of her throat.

"All of which tells me absolutely nothing," she sighed. "What am I doing here?"

Blood ran down into her eyebrow, and she brushed at it absently, her eyes searching for the way out of this padded cell. There were fewer specks of blood on the ceiling than the rest of the sphere. It was possible that the hatch was concealed there, but she could see no seams.

A loud *tick* came from the multicolored panel, and two blue lights went dark. She slid over to kneel before the panel. Almost all of the lights were dark, save for three yellow and one red. She tried pressing the flashing lights with no result, then saw three small circles etched into the metal at the end of the panel. The first one she pressed turned off all illumination within the sphere. The next controlled the air, switching from the minty mixture to an unscented cooler flow. The third circle was larger than the first two and did not depress at a touch as they had. She puzzled over that for a moment, then noticed several rectangular shapes etched into the metal band between lighting panels. She idly traced one shape with her fingertip, and, with a faint whir, a short drawer popped out.

Inside was a quantity of wrapped brown wafers. She thoughtfully rewrapped and replaced a wafer, wondering how long she was expected to stay within this sphere.

The next drawer held what seemed to be medical supplies. Mopping blood out of her eyebrow again, she reached into the drawer for the gauzelike substance at the very back. There was a hissing sound and coolness against the back of her hand. She snatched her hand out as if bitten and peered into the drawer. She did not see anything, and the skin on the back of her hand was unbroken, but she was still uneasy. The sudden lessening of her headache did not help matters. She finally used an instrument from the front of the drawer to drag out the gauze, then firmly closed the drawer.

Then, her cut cared for, she turned back to the largest of the three circles. She lightly traced the outline of the circle, and a loud *click* came from overhead. Thus heartened, she continued to trace the circle, which slowly began to come out from the metal band as the ceiling seemed to draw farther and farther away. By the sixth tracing, the hatch was open and padding had withdrawn to reveal hand-and-foot holds in the side of the sphere.

She cautiously peeked out of the open hatch, but what she saw drew her out of the sphere entirely. "I don't think I'm in Illinois anymore," she said slowly.

* * *

Sleep refused to return. Jennie sighed, tired of staring at her darkened ceiling, and glanced at the alarm. Fifteen minutes before it was due to go off. Jennie sighed again, giving up sleep as a lost cause, and climbed out of bed.

She pulled a book off the shelf and removed from it a folded letter. She turned on a light to read it again, although she knew the words by heart. "Dear Jennie, Burn this after you've read it."

She bit her lip and let the well-creased letter refold itself. "Oh, Janice, something's wrong—I know it! Where *are* you?"

* * *

"Where am I?" she asked slowly, staring in awe at the forest about her.

The trees were enormous. Thick shaggy trunks stretched upwards towards the sky. The very light seemed a greenish-yellow, shining down through masses of foliage. She looked bemusedly at one of the shorter trees—a mere fifty-footer—unable to believe that any fern could grow so large. The undergrowth of small ferns and long silky grasses stood higher than her knees. The air smelled—and tasted!—of mint.

"I'm either dreaming, or—" She reached down to finger the lacy fronds of a fern by her knee. "I'm not dreaming. This is real." She turned back toward the sphere. "And so is that."

Viewed from the outside, the sphere resembled more a globe on a pedestal. She crouched in the long grass to study its base. "The grass is singed slightly near those round legs. Those look like rocket thrusters…it's a spacecraft! Now what was I doing in a tiny spaceship?" She touched the back of her head, wincing as her fingers explored the tender lump. She concentrated, trying to remember, then finally shook her head. Rising, she placed her hands on her hips and turned to survey the forest. "Well, who's for a bit of exploring?"

She climbed back into the sphere for a pocketful of brown wafers, turned out the lights as she left, and, after a bit of experimentation with etchings on the outside of the sphere, closed the hatch. She had had a small worry that closing the hatch might activate the craft's liftoff procedures, leaving her stranded, but the tiny craft stayed resolutely put. Thus assured, she strode off to explore this new world.

The forest was a riot of color and life. Each step brought a new discovery: black and white striped climbing animals with fluffy tails like squirrels and the voices of frogs, a tiny flying thing with iridescent scales, and an even tinier something that looked like a sideways walking feather.

Only once did she feel the lack of a weapon, when a huge furred creature burst from the undergrowth and ambled toward her on all fours—only to continue past her to gnaw on the thick trunk of a tree. She stared thoughtfully at the creature, noting the swirling of brown and gray and black in its coat. For just a moment, something about its fur sparked a bit of a memory, an image of— She shook her head and continued onward.

The trail of the tree-gnawer was easy to follow. She found several stumps, all varying in freshness, but no logs. She followed the drag marks on the ground until she began to sink on the edge of a bog. The drag marks continued out across the marsh.

She looked back the way she had come. "Beaver?" she asked aloud. "*Big* beaver," she answered herself.

A small cloud of gnatlike creatures began to swarm about her, and she suddenly realized she must reek of blood. That was not right. That was dangerous. Obeying the urgings of her inner alarm, she followed the bog edge until she found a small pool to wash the blood from her face.

She stared thoughtfully at the face in the pool. Although she knew she was seeing her reflection, she was seeing someone else as well. Someone with the same long red hair and green eyes as herself. She reached out to touch the mirrored face, and it vanished in the spreading ripples.

* * *

Jennie returned home from work full of plans. She had wangled a leave of absence from the lab—"family troubles," she had told Doctor Hospersen—and was going to drive up to the cabin where this business with Janice had begun and wait there for Janice to reappear. However long it took!

She tossed her keys on the kitchen table and continued on into the bedroom to pack a suitcase. A short time later she emerged, suitcase in hand, and surveyed the rest of the apartment for whatever else she would need. "Let's see, I called Grandmother earlier, so she knows I'll be gone. I should cancel the paper—no, Grandfather will want it; he'll probably keep an eye on the place anyhow. I'll just throw this in the car and—" Reaching for her keys as she spoke, she froze in midmotion.

Resting on the kitchen table only inches from her keys was a small globe with what seemed to be green and white mists swirling beneath its transparent surface. Jennie blinked. She had read and re-read Janice's letter often enough to recognize her twin's strange "paperweight" when she finally saw it.

She opened her mouth, shut it, then tried again. "Janice?" she said in a hoarse whisper. Swallowing, she backed a step and looked wildly about the apartment. "Janice, are you here?"

Her mirror image did not appear. Anxiety making her reckless, she turned to the globe and demanded, "Where is she?" before remembering what she was speaking to.

She seemed to hear a soft sigh inside her head. *I had hoped to find her here with you.*

Jennie stared at the globe. Surely this wasn't happening to her. "You *do* sound like Grandfather," she said bemusedly.

That you should sound like Janice is a greater wonderment, since you both speak in the same manner—verbally—unlike myself and your ancestor, who I must meet someday.

"I have to be dreaming. Things like this just don't happen to me." Jennie took a deep breath. "What happened to Janice? Why did you expect to find her here? And how did you find *me*, I should like to know?"

I am not at all certain as yet that anything has *happened to her.*

"Well, I *am*! Something is wrong; something is *very* wrong!" She sat down as other questions reared their ugly heads. "Why would Janice come here? Not World War III?!"

No. No, the problem is not anything on *your planet. Rather, the matter is more because of your planet. But I explain myself badly. Suffice it to say that Janice is greatly overdue for a most important meeting, and her ship was last seen heading toward this region.*

"Her…ship…? Jan can pilot a spaceship?" Jennie shook her head in disbelief. Images of her twin's driving ability on the expressway somehow did not transfer well to outer space. "Maybe she changed her mind. There aren't any 'no exit' or 'one way' roads out there."

The possibility exists. Perhaps Crislben will bring news of her when it arrives with the ship. I will make certain you are informed.

"Could I come along?" Jennie surprised herself by asking. "Just to meet the ship and see if there's any word?" she added hurriedly. "She *is* my twin." A sudden thought struck her, and she glanced out the window, half-expecting to see a spacecraft descending out of the sky onto the parking lot of the complex. "Uh, where *is* your ship going to land?"

Crislben has the coordinates of where we first met Janice. I could try to contact it, however, and—

"No, no. That's fine." Jen breathed a mental sigh of relief. It was entirely possible that, with O'Hare airport traffic, one spaceship might be overlooked landing in Evanston, but why risk it?

She eyed her suitcase, then decided to bring it along. No telling how long this ship might take to arrive. "My car is out in the lot." She scooped up her keys, then hesitated, wondering if she was supposed to carry the tiny alien. The small globe levitated off the table and hung silently in midair.

Jennie kept calm. "Right. If you'll just follow me—" Mentally she was thinking that it was going to be a very interesting two hour drive up to the Wisconsin cabin.

* * *

The small sphere gleamed faintly in the light of the setting sun as she returned, weary but vaguely triumphant. Her memory was returning in bits and pieces, and each small fragment of information was savored. "My name is Janice, I have a twin, Jennifer, I'm a chemical lab technician, and what I am doing out of Illinois I haven't the faintest clue. Oh well." She leaned against a huge tree. "I remember meteorites…" She shook her head cautiously. "But that probably has as much importance as the last meal I remember eating in Evanston, or the last lab test I was running." She yawned widely. "Maybe I'll remember more tomorrow."

The grass and ferns were so comfortable, she was almost tempted to bed down outside, but only almost. This *was* an alien planet. She would be much safer inside the sphere. She smiled fondly at the tiny spacecraft. Its image had greatly changed from the prison she had first thought it to be. Now it was comfort and security and possible rescue. She had decided that, judging from its small size and relatively simple controls, it had to be something along the line of a lifeboat. And lifeboats usually contained food, water, medical supplies, and some means of calling for help. She hoped that by the time she found a communicator, she would remember how to use it.

She yawned again and decided to turn in. She had wanted to see if the star pattern stirred any memory, but she was so exhausted now that if she sat down to wait she *would* be sleeping outdoors tonight. She peered at the etchings on the outside of the lifeboat and pressed the hatch release. The hatch slowly swung open, the soft interior illumination lighting the shadows.

Janice looked thoughtfully at the glow. She distinctly remembered turning out the lights. She glanced down at the ground, but the bent grasses could have been due to her own tramping about earlier. She carefully swung up to the edge of the hatch and peeked inside. A slow grin spread across her face. "'Look, look!' said Baby Bear."

* * *

Jennie carefully controlled her expression as she pulled up to the last toll booth on I-94. She hoped her small alien passenger—Apson? What kind of a name was "Apson" for an alien?—was behaving itself this time. One could hardly explain to toll booth attendants about a paperweight that moved by itself. Especially when it hopped between the back and front seats. At least she had had enough change for the previous tolls.

She risked a glance at the passenger side as the car directly before her stopped at the booth and saw no sign of the alien. Slightly relieved, she pulled forward and handed the attendant her dollar. As he handed her her change, however, his eyes widened suddenly and his hand shook. Jennie was almost afraid to look.

There was a small globe on the dashboard directly before the steering wheel, where no globe had been seconds before.

Jennie pulled away from the booth as quickly as she dared. "I thought you wanted to remain inconspicuous," she said between her teeth.

I misjudged the coordinates.

"Terrific. You certainly have a strange idea of secrecy."

It is difficult to judge coordinates with a moving vehicle.

Jennie blinked. Somehow this did not sound like the alien was merely moving between the front and back seats. "What have you been doing, Apson?"

Attempting to locate Janice. The mists swirled gently. *She is not on this planet.*

Jennie frowned. "You know that for a fact, or are you just guessing?"

I have been unable to touch her mind anywhere on this planet. Therefore she is not here.

"Then whoever said she was coming here was mistaken."

It appears so.

"What will you do now? Go back to where she was last?"

And try from there to pick up her trail? Yes, that sounds wise. But that will have to wait.

"Why? Janice could need help!"

The meeting with Councilor Nicpan should not be postponed any longer.

"What's so important about this meeting that you'd risk Janice's life?"

Because each delay risks your planet's life. The Councilor wished to interview Janice as a native of this planet in regard to certain...decisions. In her absence, someone must represent your people. And that someone will have to be me, as the next knowledgeable authority.

Jennie studied the road. Apson was leaving a great deal unsaid. But somehow she had the impression that, as much as she would like to know whatever it was, she was better off not knowing.

"Janice wouldn't have deliberately missing something that important."

I know. She had been at base for some time awaiting the Councilor's summons.

"Then why—"

—did the Councilor not see her earlier? Unknown. Why did Janice leave base? Also unknown. The message I received from her was cryptic—as usual. Something had come up and she would be back as

quickly as she could. I had assumed that, as she is responsible for a number of planets, something had happened on one of them. But when she did not return, I found that she had received no messages prior to departure.

"So you started checking her planets?"

I had time to check only one. In view of the information and the circumstances, Earth seemed the likeliest.

"But—" Jennie stopped and bit her lip, watching the road ahead for the Fort Atkinson exit.

The alien mists seemed to glow in the deepening dusk. *I am very sorry. This must be hard for you. I, too, am concerned for her.*

Jennie looked thoughtfully at the small globe. Not only did Apson sound like Grandfather, but he—it also *felt* like him. Which might make her plan a little easier.

*   *   *

"Now I know how the Three Bears felt."

Janice grinned ruefully as she perched on the edge of the open hatch and surveyed the chaos below. Every drawer—more than she had thought possible in the limited space—hung wide open, and the contents were scattered over the floor in an astonishing array. In the midst of a circle of wafers in various stages of unwrapping was a huddle of gray and white fur, a black-and-white ringed tail tucked neatly around the outside. Judging from the slow and even breathing, the creature was blissfully asleep.

"Nosy little fellow. Must be pretty smart to have figured everything out. Wonder if he locked himself in and couldn't get out or..." her eyebrows rose "...hadn't wanted out yet?"

She studied the huddle, trying to figure out how large the being actually was. Nowhere near as big as that huge tree-gnawer, which would have easily towered over her if it had stood upright, and maybe shorter than that brown striped tree-climber—also larger than herself—she had seen high among the branches on her way back to the sphere. Although the being was curled up so tightly that she couldn't even see its head, she thought her furry intruder might be more her size.

She blinked as an image hit her mind. Something...furry, with... The image wavered in and out of her memory. "Hang on to it," she muttered, clutching the hatch edge. "Fur. What color fur? C'mon, don't lose it. What's in the background?"

The image retreated back into the depths of her lost memory and stubbornly refused to come out. Janice banged her fist against her leg in frustration, then sighed and rubbed her forehead.

A soft "*chirrup*?" came from below, and Janice looked down to meet large yellow eyes set in a black-furred mask. Fluffy white fur ran from the short snout down throat and belly and the underside of the being's upper limbs. The pointed mobile ears had long delicate featherings of gray on their tips.

"Hello," Janice said in a calm and even voice. She carefully moved back from the edge enough so that the being wouldn't feel trapped and gestured at the wafers. "Do you really like that stuff?"

The being's head turned to follow her gesture, then swung back toward her. Whiskers about the small black nose twitched as the being sniffed the air. It suddenly squeaked and reared back, and one five-digited paw darted toward the extended hatch control.

"Hey!" Janice protested.

Squarely hit, the hatch control retracted and the hatch swung shut in her face.

"Why, that little—" Janice stared at the closed hatch a moment, then scrambled down the side of the lifeboat. Her fingers ran over the etchings, locating the proper one by touch in the darkness.

The hatch slowly swung open, and Janice was at its edge before it had cleared 45 degrees.

"What's the big—" she started. She looked inside and blinked.

The being had done a swift job of partial sphere-cleaning in the short time the hatch had been closed. All the wafers were now in a big pile directly in the center of the sphere's floor. The intruder itself sat at the base of the ladder. It chittered softly as her eyes met its yellow ones and offered up a wrapped wafer on the palm of its handlike paw.

"Well, you *are* clever," Janice said unsteadily.

The creature cocked its head and chirped as if in answer. It dropped the wafer and ran on all fours over to an open drawer. It patted the drawer, trying to push it back into place.

"You don't feel like intelligence class, but you're no dumb animal either."

Janice did a doubletake, recognizing the voice that spoke as her own. "What am I saying? Why do I expect to be able to sense something about you?"

The being abandoned its efforts and turned toward her, its ears perked.

Her hand went to the cut on her head. "For a moment, I felt like I was trying to…read your mind. But that's crazy." She shook her head.

"I must be more tired than I thought. You wouldn't happen to know where I am and how I'm supposed to get back to Earth, would you?"

The creature sat down and watched her. Janice smiled. Between the black-ringed tail and the mask, the being's resemblance to a very large raccoon was hard to ignore. "I guess not." She studied the chaos, hoping to spot something that vaguely resembled her expectation of a communicator. "Well, since you've taken up residence, if anyone calls, I'll be outside."

The being darted forward as she backed away from the edge and chittered urgently. It snatched a wafer from the pile and offered it.

"No, thanks. They're not exactly my idea of food. Why am I expecting you to understand me?" She pulled a wafer from her pocket and waved it at the being. "See, I've got some. Okay?"

The being chattered excitedly and bounced up and down.

"Obviously it's not okay." She looked over her shoulder at the deep night shadows. The night sounds, now that she was listening for them, were many and varied, ranging from deep mumbles to shrill trumpetings.

Something was moving slowly through the brush not far distant, something large by the sound of it. She found herself reaching out with her mind, straining to—

She started violently as clawed fingers touched her hand.

Chittering undeterred, the being poked its nose out of the sphere and patted her other hand.

Janice tried to move out of reach of the claws now plucking at her sleeve. "Look, kiddo, believe me, I'm not your type." She looked back over her shoulder. The heavy something sounded closer, but nothing moved in the shadows Her inner alarm suddenly roused again. She was silhouetted against the light from the open hatch.

Reflexes she had forgotten she possessed took over. "All right, move aside, I'm coming in." The creature scampered down the ladder as she entered, then began chattering when she remained perched on the hand-and-foot holds, watching the darkness. The main controls were within reach of her foot. She doused the lights and waited, drawing the penlight from her sleeve pocket. The creature's complaints had died with the light, but something kept brushing against the back of her legs.

"Just a minute more," she said absently.

There, something had moved within her vision, a blob of darkness detaching itself from deeper shadows. She took a deep breath and aimed the penlight in its direction.

One glance at the fanged horror revealed in the small beam of light, and she had hit the hatch release with her foot and was down the ladder before she had even formed the thought to move. "Lots of big, sharp, nasty teeth!" She shuddered, then frowned thoughtfully at a twinge of memory.

"Chirrup?" came from the darkness.

"Sorry." Janice turned on the lights and surveyed her cellmate. It still looked edgy, sniffing at the air, and when Janice copied the action, she knew why. A whiff of carrion and blood—the scent of that hunter outside—was being delivered by the air vents. She hit the switch that changed the air supply and watched the being calm in the unscented flow. "I can breathe your air, so I hope mine is ok for you." The creature watched her, ears perked, then delicately chose a wafer and began to unwrap it.

Clearing a space on the floor with her foot, she sat down and leaned back against the padded wall. She had known the sphere was not large, but with two beings of approximately the same height and size—not even taking the big fluffy tail into account—occupying it, it had even less space in which to move about.

Her cellmate finished the wafer, then began to run its clawed fingers through its tail fur, chuckling contentedly.

"I hope you don't snore," Janice commented. She yawned and let her eyes drift closed. *I'll bet Kirk never got caught in a situation like this.*

* * *

What was that curious expression you used when we entered the transport beam?

Jennie looked around the small, dimly-lit room they had arrived in and decided that reality was definitely stranger than TV. The only sign of her point of entry into the ship that had suddenly appeared out of the night to hover over the meadow near the cabin was the glowing square beneath her feet. No matter transporter, no console—it was almost a letdown. "Huh? Oh, it's just a…a joke."

The words "Beam me up," if I have translated them correctly, seem appropriate, I suppose, and the rest appears to be a name. Correct?

"Cor— Look, it's just a joke."

Janice has been reluctant to explain it, also, the mists complained. The globe dropped a short distance, then looped in midair and swung back to hover over her shoulder.

Bright light blinded her momentarily as a door slid open before her. Something rustled within the brightness, followed by a slithering sound.

Put this on.

"Wha—" Jennie turned toward the globe and found a yellow necklace hanging in midair before her nose. She uncrossed her eyes and glared reproachfully at the sphere. "Apson—"

On, quickly!

"All right!" She hesitantly reached out with both hands and the necklace practically attached itself about her neck. "Don't rush me!" Fingering the thin chain, she wished she could see if it looked as odd about her neck as it felt. Two narrow rectangular plates rested atop her collar bones and a smaller square fit in the hollow of her throat. "What *is* this, Apson?"

Her only answer was a slithering sound from the doorway. Turning, she found herself confronting what appeared to be a short bush. Jennie blinked and looked again. The "bush" stood only a little higher than her waist and had large, fleshy leaves of turquoise. The leaves rustled.

"Sprout," said a voice in English practically in her ear. "Apson, I knew you would find her."

Jennie's hand flew to the necklace she wore, suddenly understanding its purpose. She wasn't certain how, but in some way this was translating for her.

The bush slithered toward her on its flexible roots, revealing glimpses of a single thick trunk through the curtain of its leaves. "I don't mind telling you, Sprout, it nearly curled my leaves when the death knell on your ship went off—"

What? Apson interrupted.

"—but I'm glad to see you're safe. So, what happened this time? You're lucky Apson went hunting you. Not much call of late to swing out this far."

Crislben, when did the alarm sound?

The plant-being waved a few leaves at the globe. "Last sleep cycle, I think. What does it matter? She's safe."

"No," Jennie said, suddenly rousing from her stunned silence, "she's not safe. I'm sorry. I'm not Janice; I'm her twin, Jennie."

The bush seemed to sink on its mobile roots. "Not Sprout?"

"Apson, we've got to find her! If her ship is destroyed—"

"She's dead, then," Crislben said softly.

"No, she's not! I'd know!"

The globe darted out through the doorway.

"Apson!" Jennie ran after the tiny alien and soon found herself in what had to be the control room. She stared in awe at the vast expanse of stars in the wall-sized viewscreen. "We're moving?"

No. The image on the screen flickered and was replaced by darkness. It flickered again and bluish outlines appeared around the tiny shapes that were the cabin, her car, the road, trees, and distant farmhouses.

Time is short. I will send you back.

"No." Jennie almost did not recognize her own voice. "No, I'm coming with, to find Janice. You may not have the time—or maybe you just don't care!—but that's my twin out there and I'm going to find her!"

The globe settled onto a depression on a console. *How*?

"How? I don't know. Maybe I'll go to those planets of hers and —"

I repeat, how? You have no ship; this one is returning directly to base in an attempt to save your world. We cannot divert to search for an agent who is most likely dead.

"She's not dead!"

"Her ship has been totally destroyed," Crislben said. Jennie turned as the plant-being slowly entered the room. "The alarm is only triggered then."

"Look, I'm her twin. I'd *know* if she was dead."

How?

Jennie looked from one alien to the other and sighed. This was hard enough to explain to a human. "Some identical twins share a…bond—a twin bond, researchers call it. I'm not entirely certain how to explain it…odd similarities, usually between identical twins raised apart from each other. Jan and I never really noticed it in ourselves until we went to different colleges."

She looked at her audience, then thrust her hands into her pockets and looked at the floor. "We do things alike. I don't mean just dressing alike, or sounding alike, but other things—like choosing the same major in college for a time, having friends with the same first names. Sometimes things that happen to one of us also happens to the other. We even both sprained the same ankle on the same day—several hundred miles apart!"

She raised her eyes and looked at the mist-filled globe. "So don't tell me she's dead. I know she's alive and I know she's in trouble."

The globe rolled along the top of the console. *You experienced this phenomenon while both of you were on the same planet.*

"And last night," Jennie added.

Last night?

"Yes, something woke me, something that was happening to Janice. That's why I was all packed to leave when you arrived."

You knew I was coming? The alien sounded disturbed.

"All I knew was that she needed help. You're the one who said that she's not on this planet."

"Caught you by the root tip there." The turquoise leaves stirred about Crislben's midsection. "Let her come."

She will only be in the way. She is naive.

"She'll be in the way as much as Sprout usually is." The words came to Jennie in clear, unaccented English, but from the way the bush was rustling, the being was not as calm as the translation sounded. "The Great Gallblister doesn't want to see me; I'll pilot her wherever she wishes to travel."

You will take this ship back to base and stay there until my business with Councilor Nicpan is finished.

The topmost leaves stood straight up. "Are you giving me orders, you unstable weather anomaly?"

The sphere lifted off the console and hovered before Jennie, the green and white mists inside swirling gently. *You may come with us on one condition: that you take Janice's place at this meeting with Councilor Nicpan. After the meeting, we three will search for your twin.*

"After? But Janice could need—"

Janice is one of my most capable agents. I am confident in her ability to survive until we reach her. Which is more important: your twin, or your planet? The alien paused only a second. *I know which Janice would choose.*

"I know which, also." Jennie closed her eyes briefly at a remembered stab of pain. Janice had chosen when she had left Earth. "All right, I'll take Janice's place."

No one must know that you are not Janice. Can you do this?

Curiosity about Apson's insistence twinged, but relief was stronger. At least the alien wasn't asking her to do anything difficult. "Yes."

"Of course she can do it. I thought she was Sprout until she said differently."

If mere physical resemblance was required, any Tele-Two or above agent could have substituted for Janice, Apson said softly, drifting back to the console.

Jennie glanced at the globe, curious as to how that could have been done. What was a Tele-Two? Lights on the console blinked as the sphere settled atop it. "Uh, I'll need my suitcase," she said, eyeing the screen and the overhead view of the cabin. "It's still in the trunk of my car."

Crislben moved after Apson. "You would have dared risk a substitution for Janice at base?"

In view of what has happened, yes.

Crislben's topmost leaves stirred. "You should have tried that sooner. You know what some were saying about Sprout when I left? That she vanished because she was afraid. Afraid. Sprout." All the leaves on the upper half of the bush were swaying now. "A few blamed this meeting, said the responsibility was too much for her." A root snaked out across the floor, then drew back. "But I knew what they meant. And I told them, too. Any agent who faced down a Devamener on her very first assignment wouldn't run just because someone at base tries to kill her."

Jennie removed her fascinated attention from the swaying bush. "What? Someone tried to kill Janice?"

"Twice. Apson didn't tell you?"

I will retrieve your suitcase. The globe vanished so quickly that Jennie barely had a chance to open her mouth.

Jennie looked at the door, then turned back to Crislben, who was now before a console. Long bluish filaments had appeared from between the leaves and were gently tapping controls.

"Who's trying to kill Jan?"

"If we knew that, Janice probably would not have vanished."

"You think she ran, too."

The filaments froze. "I think that whoever tried before tried again."

Jennie took a deep breath. "So, my turning up as Janice should surprise somebody."

The filaments resumed their tapping. "Quite probably."

Jennie slowly counted to ten. "That devious little alien. He wanted me to come along all the time."

The view on the screen swung away from the planet and up towards the stars.

"Do you wish to return, knowing what you do now?"

Jennie frowned. "I'm tempted, but only just. This is the only way I'll find Jan." She glanced at the door. "I should help Apson get my suitcase."

"The item is already in your quarters."

"What? How—"

The stars suddenly seemed to move on the screen. Jennie watched, excitement and fear rising within her. The full realization that she had left Earth was numbing. *Is this how Janice felt*? she wondered.

Crislben retracted its filaments and slithered over towards her. "Now, pay attention. What I'm about to tell you is the same thing I've told Janice and all new recruits. Always keep in mind that you are among aliens now. No matter how closely in word or gesture we may seem to those of your planet, we are not. Our cultures are different, and so are our mannerisms, behavior, and—most importantly—motivations. Assume nothing until you have enough knowledge to base your assumptions on, and you shall do well. Take Apson, for example. Will you now accept everything it says, unquestioningly?"

"Well, I—"

"Don't. It's impossible for you telepaths to lie when speaking mind-to-mind, but there are ways around that. Apson's way—and I haven't even told Sprout this—is to simply not tell you everything."

Jennie shook her head. "Wait a minute. I'm no telepath."

The leaves around Crislben's midsection rustled. "Oh? From the way Apson left, I thought—" Its leaves stilled.

"Why are you telling me if you haven't told Janice?"

The leaves around the being's midsection began to rustle again. "I think she already knows." Crislben slithered toward another console. "You should learn to speak Galactic."

Jennie touched her necklace. "But doesn't this—"

"Oh, that's well enough for beings who don't use your manner of speaking—like me, for instance. But some of Janice's friends might become suspicious. Then, too, the band has limits: you have to be within range of a translator and you can only use those words the translator already has in your language. Anything else comes through as noise."

A yawn caught Jennie by surprise. "Who programmed the translator for English? Janice?"

Crislben's midsection rustled. "Not at first. She made numerous additions, however. She said the accent was wrong."

Jennie muzzily wondered how unaccented English could have an accent, then was suddenly aware of how very tired she was. Somehow learning a new language was not very appealing at the moment, as helpful as it might be to find Janice. "Well, Galactic might be a good idea, but—"

Why should she need to learn Galactic? Apson interrupted. The globe drifted slowly over to the console top. *I shall be with her at all times; I will translate for her.*

Crislben waved a leaf at her, but Jennie didn't need the hint. *Uh huh,* she thought to herself, *and what happens when there's something you don't want me to know*? "When can I start learning this Galactic?" she asked quickly, trying to stifle another yawn.

Crislben's midsection rustled again, and Jennie decided that that had to be the being's form of laughter. "Whenever you wish to root yourself in for the night cycle. I'm about to do that myself; I can show you how to hook in with the ship's teacher."

"Root myself in—oh, you mean sleep? Now would be fine."

Crislben slithered toward the doorway. "I hope you don't mind waiting to see the rest of the ship. I need my rest and nourishment." The shorter roots at its base stretched and curled. "Unless you'd like Apson to show you the ship."

"No, no, I'm rather tired myself. Good night, Apson," she called back as she left the control room in Crislben's wake.

The plant-being could actually move rather swiftly down the corridor, although Jennie had to watch not to step on any of its roots. "Do you mean you actually, uh…" she suddenly wondered if it was polite to ask about the being's sleeping and eating habits and decided to change the subject "…use sleep-learning? It's not considered very effective on Earth."

"As Janice explained it to me, the method used on your planet requires auditory stimulation while the brain is in a state of relaxation. Ours also needs the mind to be relaxed, but the teacher links telepathically into the brain."

"Uh—" Jennie started.

"It is quite painless, although you may feel disoriented when you uproot."

"Uh—"

A door slid open before the alien to reveal her suitcase sitting forlornly in the center of a small room. Lights sprang on as Crislben entered, illuminating a bunk jutting out of one wall and a wide shelf with a normal chair before it at the other. Two narrow doors were at the opposite end of the room.

Crislben slithered over to the bunk. A tendril came from between the leaves to lift a silvery shining band from a recess in the wall near the head of the bunk. "Put this around your trunk—no, your people have their brains in their heads—around your head when you are ready to begin. To activate, tell the ship in a clear thought what you wish to learn. The lesson will begin when you are sufficiently relaxed."

The shorter roots at its base were curling and stretching as Crislben replaced the band and started backing towards the door. "Pleasant night cycle."

"Uh—"

"Oh, and the loo is through there." A left waved towards one of the two small doors.

"The what?" Jennie asked, but the door had slid shut behind the alien. She shook her head and went over to open the door Crislben had indicated. "Oh, the bathroom." She shook her head again. "Now I know what Jan meant about accents."

A short time later she was seated on the bunk examining the band. Although it shone like metal, it felt more like plastic. It was a plain, unadorned, nearly complete ellipse, with no wires, nothing that seemed to link it to the ship. Taking a deep breath, she carefully placed it on her head. She felt a momentary coolness across her brow, but there was no other sensation.

She stretched out on the bunk and tried to settle herself comfortably, half-expecting that the band would make that difficult. Instead, she discovered that, no matter how she placed her head, she was not aware of the band at all. She had to reach up with her fingers to make certain the ellipse was still in place.

She finally lay quietly and waited for something to happen. A second later, the lights in the cabin went out.

Jennie controlled her start of surprise. "Nice. Automatic lighting. Wonder what other surprises this ship has." She closed her eyes and concentrated on holding a clear thought. *I wish to learn Galactic.*

Nothing happened. Jennie told herself firmly to relax and began to repeat the instruction to the ship over and over within her mind. By the twenty-third repetition, she was sound asleep. Her dreams were filled with voices droning on and on.

* * *

Her dreams were filled with monsters. All kinds. Large, fanged *things* and large, delicate, reed-thin things. Monsters with fur, monsters with leaves, monsters that snapped large beaks and ruffled their feathers at her. They kept advancing on her, trying to attract her attention, and her only way of escape was blocked by a furry curtain.

She wasn't frightened. She wanted to turn and try to talk to the monsters, but, as if possessed, her hand slowly reached out to the curtain of black and brown and gray.

Janice opened her eyes to see another monster looking down at her. She blinked.

The yellow-eyed monster vanished, but bright sunlight was streaming down from above her.

She sat up and glanced around the sphere. The pile of wafers had almost been replaced by a pile of wrappings, but there was still more than enough left for her. She made a face. *Unfortunate, but at least I have some food that's supposedly safe. No telling how long I'll be here.*

She climbed up to check outside the sphere for her raccoon friend. She could see two trails trampled through the underbrush: one very large, and the other more the size of her roommate.

She perched on the edge of the hatch, surveying the forest around her and delighting in the ever-present smell of mint. It was a lovely morning; she couldn't see clouds, but there was sunlight, and a nice light breeze. Three songsters were battling with a medley of notes overhead, and there was no sign—or smell—of the fanged horror of the night before. "Perfect day for exploring," she decided.

Janice climbed back inside and combed through the debris, looking for either a communicator or something to use to carry supplies. Much as she would like to plan to return to the relative comfort and security of the lifeboat, she didn't want to tether herself to it. She had a nagging feeling that she was supposed to *do* something, and the longer she sat around not doing that something, the worse the feeling would grow. "At least I remember that I'm *supposed* to be here…I think." She shrugged. "It's better than feeling I was just dumped here."

She found a small bag with a carrystrap underneath a few things she recognized from the medical supplies drawer. "I wonder if he got jabbed, too," she said with a grin. She began filling the bag with wafers. "Hello, what's this?"

She held up a long strip of clear plastic, divided into compartments filled with a colorless liquid. Opening one, she tested it with a fingertip, then tasted. "Water, finally!" She emptied one compartment, licking her lips when she had finished. "Wish I had found that last night." She found a few more water packets, added those to her bag of supplies, and sorted through a few more items the raccoon had dumped out of the drawers.

Finally she stood and slung the carrystrap over her shoulder. "No communicator, no weapons, not even any rope to help me climb those over-sized trees if Old Toothy finds me. Could be worse, though." She doused the lights and climbed out of the sphere.

She measured the width of a large clawed footprint near the base of the lifeboat and shook her head. "Uh huh! Sure, Janice."

The big predator's trail pointed toward the beaver bog. Sealing the hatch, Janice strode off in the opposite direction.

*   *   *

She opened her eyes to darkness. She turned her head to glance at the time and discovered that there was no alarm clock.

Surprised, Jennie sat up—and the lights sprang on, revealing the small quarters on the spaceship. "Yesterday was no dream, then."

She sprang off the bunk and hurriedly got dressed, only remembering the band when she started to comb her hair. She studied the ellipse in her hand thoughtfully, wondering if it had worked, then realized she'd find out soon enough. Replacing the band in its wall recess, she finished combing her hair and started off in search of the two aliens.

After a few wrong turns, and several nonresponsive doors, she finally found her way back to the control room. Apson was in the same spot atop a console. She looked at the stars on the screen and stood a moment, admiring the view. "Hello, Apson. Any news on Janice?"

No. Nor will there be, now that her ship is known to be destroyed.

"Everybody knows?"

Since I was not there to suppress the news, it is very probable.

"Grapevines are always more efficient than most people would like them to be."

Councilor Nicpan is still on base.

"Well, I guess that's good news. So you told him—it—that I—or, rather, Janice—was coming?"

No, only that I would be arriving soon. I deemed the value of surprise more important in this instance.

"At least I won't get shot the second I step off the ship. But won't anybody be going out to investigate the wreckage of her ship?"

If we knew where the wreckage was. An operative's movements are not that closely monitored. A search of her sector would be made, however, were it not for the fact that those few agents not currently on assignment were at base when both attempts were made on Janice, including the agent whose sector is closest to Janice's.

"You suspect her fellow agents?"

Before now, I would have believed an agent's training and psychological testings would have made any betrayal of the Bureau impossible. However, since both attempts took place on base, I no longer know whom to trust.

Jennie suddenly felt more forgiving of the trick Apson had played on her. "But, surely, there are other people besides agents at your base? After all, anyone who tries twice to kill Jan and fails both times can't be much of an agent."

The mists chuckled softly. *You underestimate your twin.*

"And what's the motive? The meeting?" Jennie eyed the small sphere. "Did Janice know what would happen at this meeting?"

Most of it, yes. The main reason for this decision was due to a recent report of hers.

"Which is?"

The mists gently swirled within the sphere.

"C'mon, Apson. You'll have to tell me sometime if I'm going to pretend to *be* Janice."

Sometime, perhaps. But not now.

Jennie thrust her hands into the pockets of her jeans. "All right, forget the decision. The report still exists, right? And you would fill in for her if she wasn't there—at least that's what would be thought, right? So where's the motive?" She shook her head. "I don't think this meeting could be the reason behind the attempts. Was Janice investigating anything recently?"

I have not given her any assignments.

Jennie briefly wondered what Apson's position was in this Bureau. "Why did she leave base, then?"

The tiny alien did not answer. Jennie turned away from the globe and walked closer to the speckles of stars on the screen. "Apson, Janice trusted you—otherwise she would never have left Earth in the first place. I'd like to be able to trust you, too, but I can't—not while you keep withholding information from me." She turned around to face the mist-being. "I'm not Janice. I'm not pledged to uphold the honor of this Bureau or die trying. I'm here to help my planet and to find Jan, and I refuse to get killed just because you won't tell me what I need to know to do both!"

Apson seemed to sigh. *I do not know why Janice left the base. I sorrow if this causes you mistrust, but I must withhold information from you that Janice knows because, as you have said, you are not Janice.*

Janice can shield her mind. You cannot.

"Telepathy, again? Won't everybody be able to see in my mind, then, that I'm not Janice?"

I will be with you constantly. My presence will shield you.

"Then—"

—but the more you know, the more the possibility exists that knowledge may be plucked from your unprotected mind. I cannot allow the risk.

Jennie sighed. "Can't you teach me to shield my mind?"

You exhibit more telepathic ability than did Janice when I first met her, but there is not time enough to learn.

"How soon will we reach your base?"

Within the limits of the Councilor's patience.

Jennie frowned. "Another secret? Don't your people know where their base is?"

The location of Earth is what must be protected.

"Oh."

Jennie glanced at the screen, then scanned the various consoles, wishing she understood their operation. "Who's the head of this Bureau? Councilor Nicpan?"

A rustling sound came from the doorway. "The head of the Bureau of Closed and Restricted Planets has been the same being since its founding several hundred of your years ago. Apson."

Jennie turned to look at the globe. "You? But…you recruited Janice… You go off looking for missing agents… Why?"

I like to keep involved.

"To interfere, I say," Crislben inserted, slithering toward the nearest console. "How is your sensory center this cycle, little sprout?"

"Uh…I feel fine, Crislben, thank you. Apson, how is Councilor Nicpan involved, then?"

The Council of which it is a member once held major responsibilities in areas that the Bureau now controls. The Bureau is yet new enough that the Council still has final say on some decisions.

"'Say,' is right," Crislben commented. "The Council debates forever when something should have been decided rotations ago. Planets left unprotected while that—"

Crislben, Apson warned.

"—*rustle* Nicpan tours base, attends dinners—it hasn't even looked at any reports. All Janice had to do was make one appearance at one interview but it never had time to see her. Sprout's been tied to base so long, it's no wonder she left."

"Governments," Jennie said in disgust. "How you can allow yourselves to remain under control of a petty bureaucratic tyrant—" She stopped at a sudden stillness. Crislben's topmost leaves were standing straight up. She sighed, familiar with the response if not the expressions. "Let me guess. You already had this conversation with Janice."

In almost the exact words. It is uncanny how alike you are.

"Only when we're apart. When we're together we're as un-alike as possible." Jennie glanced closer at a console top. The little squiggles oddly seemed to make sense. "Is this written in Galactic?"

The rustle of leaves sounded as if a violent windstorm had hit. "No, you can't."

"Can't what?"

"Can't fly my ship. I'll introduce you to Janice's ship—"

Crislben!

"—when we dock; it should be ready to flight-test by now. But I won't let you fly my ship."

"But— Hey, my driving is much better than Janice's any day! She—" Jennie stopped as the full import sunk in. "I thought you said Janice's ship was destroyed."

"The one Sprout's been using is—was—an ordinary Bureau ship, like this one but smaller. Her ship, her operative ship, was having its personality traces installed while she was on base to link with it, the next-to-final stages before commissioning."

"Personality—?" Jennie murmured.

We will be far too busy at base to see it, Apson warned.

Crislben rustled at the little alien.

* * *

Leaves rustled behind her when she stopped to study an odd patch of color in the underbrush not far ahead. Janice glanced back over her shoulder but saw only the now shoulder-high ferns and grasses. The sound was not repeated, so she cautiously advanced onward, trying to spot the odd color again.

Leaves rustled again—this time to her right. She stood on tiptoes and saw a trail of grasses swaying parallel to her own path. Before she was entirely conscious of what she did and why, she reached out with her mind. The sudden flow of thoughts within her mind that were not her own surprised her momentarily.

...good food (contentment)...danger (anxiety)...play (happiness)...

She took a step to the right, then froze, her eyes on the nearly invisible tripwire a few feet before her.

Something chittered from the brush just past the tripwire, and a whiskered, black-masked face popped into sight. The yellow eyes widened as the being spotted her, and suddenly it was bounding toward her like an over-sized puppy.

"No," she said helplessly, "don't—"

The gray-and-white creature stumbled as it encountered the wire.

Darkness flashed up about them, met over their heads with a metallic crash.

Janice pulled out her penlight and flicked the beam about the tall grass until it illuminated the furry gray huddle entangled in the tripwire.

"Terrific. You, I don't need to have around."

...play? (confusion)...

She flicked the light up and around their prison. Two large slabs of metal met at a slant overhead, and two more sealed either end like a small A-frame. The space enclosed could easily accommodate one of the beaverlike creatures. She moved through the grass, ignoring the scolding chitters behind her, and examined each side.

At the base of one of the slanted pieces she found the slot the tripwire end had fitted into, surrounded by a rectangular bulge. She patted her pockets and located the collapsible screwdriver.

There didn't appear to be any screws or bolts on the bulge, but there was a thin line between the bulge and the base of the wall.

She shifted her grip on the penlight and felt what seemed to be additional settings. Hoping for a brighter light, she tried each setting, finding a red beam, a blue beam, and a dark setting that raised a glowing red spot on the wall and a brief impression of heat. "A laser!"

"Chirp?" came from somewhere near her elbow.

"Hang on," Janice said, switching the beam back to white light. She fit the end of the screwdriver between the bulge and the wall and tried to pry the cover off. "We should be—c'mon, you!—out of this—nugh!—soon."

A faint hissing sound came to her notice, and she turned the beam about to see jets of a bluish smoke spouting up from the ground.

"Gas!"

She redoubled her efforts, managing to widen the line between bulge and wall.

The creature chirped behind her. *...play?...*

Danger! Janice sent back.

The being barked sharply and paced back and forth behind her. It nosed her, following her arm down to the bulge, then sat down beside her and inserted its claws into the widening line. One quick heave, and the cover flipped off, revealing a mini-microchip nightmare.

"Oh, damn!" she coughed. "I haven't time!" She pushed the raccoon back, set the penlight to laser and played the beam back and forth, hoping to hit something vital.

A line of sparks flared and died. Coughing, her eyes streaming, Janice did not at first realize that the hiss of jets had faltered and stopped until a whirring hum suddenly started. She flicked the beam back to white light and flashed it about their prison. The bluish smoke was rapidly thinning out. Pleased, she shone the light on the panel and was faintly surprised at how much damage she had done.

She coughed, wiping her eyes, and bent closer to the panel. "Not bad, huh? Now let's see if I can get us out of here, assuming I haven't melted that circuit already."

She suddenly realized that she was missing a nose prodding her elbow and flashed the beam about, illuminating a mound of gray fur nearby. "Oh no!"

Bending over the being, she was relieved to detect signs of breathing. "I take it back. You, I need around." She patted the soft fur and went back to the panel.

She crouched before the seared microchips and then the optimistic confidence died. Janice stared from the jumble before her to the screwdriver in her hands and wondered just what she expected to be able to do. "You're a chemical lab technician, not an electrician!" she muttered.

Her hands weren't about to believe her. A fingertip traced the tripwire slot, and she went back among the tall grass to find the wire. Cutting the arrowhead-shaped end off the tripwire, she brought it back to the panel and inserted it like a key into its keyhole. When nothing happened, she tried turning it, first one way and then the other. The slot clicked.

Sunlight appeared in a rush about them as the metallic walls retracted and vanished. A snuffling chitter came from behind her and she looked back to see the being shaking its head as if it were a human disbelieving its own eyesight.

"I know how you feel." Janice replaced the cover to hide the damage. "It's an awfully elaborate trap. I would have thought anyone trying to kill me would attempt something simpler."

She shook her head. “Lab technician. I don’t know what I am now, but I’m certainly not that anymore. The things I’ve been doing, this telepathy—when did I learn to mindread?—and now someone’s trying to kill me.” She lifted a hand to her head. “I remember that much. Someone was trying to kill me.” She bit her lip. “Wish I could remember more.”

She switched the penlight to laser and fused the key into its lock. “I came here for a reason, and someone was trying to kill me. Hope those two aren’t connected.” She scowled. “What a cheerful thought!”

The raccoon groggily attempted to climb to its feet, then sat down with a thump. It looked bleary-eyed at her and gave a weak bark.

Safe! Janice sent. “You’re ok; just inhaled too much smoke. Give me half a second and then we’ll see about leaving.” She stepped over the panel to outside the trap and looked carefully along the camouflaged line of metal. “Ah, here’s the matching keyhole. One minor question answered.”

She stepped back within the confines of the trap and over to the furry being, then pondered a moment. How did one go about carrying a raccoon as large as oneself?

* * *

Jennie took another sip of water and was relieved to feel her sudden coughing fit coming under control. All she needed was to have Apson decide she had some weird disease. Not that she thought he would send her back to Earth at this stage, anyway.

Leaving the loo, she smoothed the short jacket she had donned, and surveyed her new outfit in the mirror behind the closet door. She was certain the clothes she had found within were Janice’s, just as her quarters had to be her twin’s. She met the green eyes in the mirror. “Your clothing sense has improved, Jan.”

She closed the closet door and headed for the control room, wondering how much change the star pattern had undergone this time. The starfield on the viewscreen always seemed to move and change very slowly while she was in the control room, but each time she left and re-entered, the stars were vastly different. “Don’t know why they’re so worried,” she muttered. “I have enough trouble finding the Little Dipper at home.”

Turning a corner, she almost bumped her head against a hovering globe.

Our plans must be accelerated. The green and white mists seemed agitated. *Follow me.* Apson darted away. *Quickly.*

"Accelerated? What do you mean? Why? Apson? Apson, slow down!" Jennie broke into a run to keep up with the globe. "What happened?"

Someone attempted to learn the locations of closed worlds in this sector, Apson replied curtly.

"This sector? Janice's sector?" A sudden thought hit her. "Earth is a closed world, isn't it."

Earth was one of those planets whose location was sought.

"Was the someone caught?"

There was a soft sigh within her mind. *Entry was not fully gained into the records, which would have activated the safeguards. Apparently the spy panicked.*

"Pity. At least you know there was an attempt. Why are the locations such a secret? How many people know them—or know where to find the information?"

The locations are kept secret to protect the worlds. If a closed world is near a traffic path, then it is listed as "Closed" and ships are warned away. Closed worlds outside the fringes of Galactic commerce are known only to myself, the roving agent of that sector, and any resident agents assigned to that closed world.

"So someone was attempting to tap into your records?" Jennie felt she was beginning to get the hang of talking to Apson. Anything the tiny alien seemed to back away from was the best thing to ask about.

A door slid open before the globe, and it darted inside. Jennie followed to find herself in a familiar tiny room. A small square on the floor began to glow as Apson hovered over it.

Bureau ships are among the swiftest in the Galaxy, but it will yet take a few more cycles to reach base. You and I shall go on ahead.

Jennie stepped cautiously onto the square, then frowned. "Hey, I thought you said the range of Galactic matter transporters was very short, say from an orbiting ship to the planet below. And that this isn't a matter transporter."

Correct on both accounts. Hold out your hand.

Against her better judgment, Jennie obeyed. The globe dropped onto her palm, and she quickly brought up her other hand to help cradle the sphere. "Apson, what—"

A faint rustling came to her ears. "Stay out of trouble, Jen-sprout, until I'm there to pull you out of it."

"I'll try, Crislben." She started to look for the plant-being, then realized she had been distracted. "Apson, how—"

She felt a tingle in her palms, and the dimly lit room about her suddenly became very brightly lit and much larger.

"Wha—" Jennie swallowed and stared at the examples of extraterrestrial sculpture—or was it furniture?—about her. "Apson, where are we?"

The green and white mists had stilled within the globe's transparent surface. *At base.*

"Just like that. What *was* that machine, if it wasn't a matter transporter?" The tiny alien was silent, and Jennie sighed. "Another secret?"

Another secret.

She shook her head. "I don't know how you manage to keep track of what all everyone is supposed to know or not know. Okay, I'll mind my own business—*this* time. But we'd better start looking for Janice soon."

Very soon. Please remember, though, that from now until we leave base you *are Janice. A mistake could be fatal for your twin.*

"And a superb performance could be the same for me as well. What do we do now that we're here?"

We seek out Councilor Nicpan and settle the matter of this much delayed meeting.

"Good! Are you finally going to tell me what it's about?"

Take the door to your right, turn left, and then turn right again once we reach the main corridor.

Jennie counted to ten again. Obviously, getting information out of Apson was going to be harder than she had thought. She started forward, then stopped and looked at the globe in her hands. "Apson, are you all right? I know you said you'd stay with me, but I didn't expect you to stay this close."

There was a sluggish eddy of movement in the mists. *You are correct. Janice would go alone to see Councilor Nicpan.*

"Now wait a minute, I didn't say that. I merely asked if you—"

A narrow slot opened in the wall and a small rectangular shape drifted out to hover before her. *Clip this onto your belt or conceal it about your person in some way. When pressed, it activates a low-energy force shield. This is only minimally effective against high-energy weapons, so you must still be wary.*

Jennie uneasily shifted the globe to one hand and pocketed the small box with the other, wishing she could pocket the globe instead. "But what about my 'unprotected mind?' Apson, you can't—"

I will be close by at all times. I will maintain a mind shield for you, although you appear to be creating one of your own.

"I what? How—"

Have I permission to tap into your surface thoughts whenever you need instructions?

"Apson, I'm going to need all the help I can get. I don't know this place! What am I supposed to say to this Nicpan, assuming it's even willing to see me right now?"

Be *Janice. You have been kept waiting by a rather important individual who must decide on a matter vital to your planet.*

"In other words, politely angry. But what *is* this matter about?"

The Councilor will ask the questions. You need only answer as honestly as you are able, without betraying your true identity.

"How can I answer honestly about something I know nothing about? You can't expect me to ad lib on something important to Earth!"

Take the door to your right, turn left—

"And then right again when I reach the main corridor. Apson, I'm beginning not to trust you again."

I will give you further directions when necessary.

"Thanks a bunch."

* * *

"Yes, thank you, I do know what I'm doing," Janice muttered in answer to a questioning chirp. "I think." The white-furred snout moved from her elbow to her hands. "Hey, c'mon, who's the lockpick here?"

Nose to screwdriver probe, the inquisitive creature chittered at the keyhole. *Play?*

Janice sighed wearily, wishing her furry friend wasn't so insistent on tagging along with her. One did not involve natives in… She shook her head as the thought petered out. *In what? I wish I had my memory back. I'm getting awfully tired of wondering when and where I learned to do things.*

Her furry friend turned and clucked at her, then sat back on its haunches and stared up at the outside of the metallic A-frame before them.

"Thank you." Janice bent over the keyhole again. She hadn't expected to find another of the strange structures in the area, and certainly not one already sealed. She winced as the creature idly dragged its claws down the metallic slope. Why plant big traps all over the landscape? The technology involved didn't seem to fit with what she had already seen of this planet. Of course, for all she knew, the civilization centers of this world were on the other side of the planet.

Her friend's gray-tipped ears suddenly perked up, and its large eyes looked skyward.

"Then again," Janice said as a high-pitched hum came to her ears, "I could be wrong about that."

* * *

Stop staring at the aliens, Jennie, she told herself as she walked briskly down the busy corridor. *Remember, this isn't strange to you; it's all perfectly normal. And besides, if one of them is Janice's*—your *friend, it might take your staring as an invitation to talk.* Her gaze fell upon one four-legged entity that looked as if it were constructed of sticks. *Wouldn't you like to engage in idle chit-chat with that?*

The being's six stalked eyes swiveled to follow her as she passed, and Jennie found her hand hovering near the shield control again. *You're getting as paranoid as Apson*, she scolded herself. *Of course they keep staring at you as if they've seen a ghost. Jan*—your *ship was destroyed. The grapevine probably has you listed as dead.*

She counted the doors as she had been instructed and stopped at the thirteenth from the last corridor. *This one, Apson*? When no answer came, she peered closely at the sign beside it. The third line appeared to be in Galactic, and it matched the directions Apson had given her. She mentally crossed her fingers and pressed the admittance panel.

The door slid open to reveal a tall pillar of bright green flesh. Two long-fringed green eyes opened wide. "Yes?"

Jennie took a deep breath. "Sector Operative Janice. The Councilor has been expecting me."

She blinked as the eyes vanished, then reappeared lower on the pillar, apparently studying something on the wall beside the door. "Confirmed. Scanning."

Sparkling light engulfed her, then vanished. "Confirmed Sector Operative Janice. Enter."

The pillar shrank into a ball, which bounced back as she entered. "Follow."

Mentally shaking her head, Jennie obeyed.

The ball bounced up to an interior door, then stretched upward to form a pillar. The long-fringed eyes blinked at her. "Wait." the door slid open, and the pillar slowly inched its way through the opening.

Jennie blinked. *Wait?* I'*d wait. But would Janice?* Be her, *remember?*

She entered the room a split second after the pillar and nodded familiarly to the being behind the desk. "Sector Operative Janice, Councilor."

The large brown puppy eyes in the seal-like face opened wide, and the being seemed to recoil. *Oh dear,* Jennie thought, *you thought I was dead, too*. It grasped the edge of the desk with webbed flat digits. "You, you—"

"Yes, I'm late. Sorry about the delay, Councilor Nicpan, but my ship had a slight accident. Of course, you probably already knew that." The Councilor gaped at her like a stranded fish, and Jennie decided to press on while the being was still off balance.

"Now, I'm sure you're as eager to get this meeting over with as I am, so"—she eyed a squat something resembling a hassock, then reconsidered and seated herself on the edge of the desk—"what would you like to know?"

* * *

"I'd like to know how that thing manages to maneuver around these trees," Janice muttered as a large floating platform slowly descended beside the metallic A-frame. Beside her in concealment, the raccoon squirmed excitedly. *Play?*

Stay!

Janice looked for the operator of the air sled, then noticed a pyramid of three slightly flattened cannonballs hovering in the bow. A tiny scanner protruding from the top cannonball rotated back and forth, finally locking onto the metallic structure.

I'm in luck, a service robot! She frowned as she watched the landing. *Question is, is that thing directed or programmed*?

The robot drifted off the grounded sled and over towards the keyhole. There was a wild rustle of grasses beside Janice, and she turned to find her furry friend gone. She turned back towards the robot and groaned.

The native was carefully stalking the robot, which was still drifting towards the structure. It caught up with the robot and cautiously batted it with one paw. The robot staggered, but continued toward the structure. The creature batted one of the bottom cannonballs again, sending the robot spinning in a circle. The mechanical drone recovered and continued on its path.

Chittering happily, the raccoon bounded ahead and planted itself squarely in the robot's way.

No, Janice sent. *Danger*!

The native's ears perked. It started to move, and the robot daintily lifted itself over the obstruction and continued on.

Janice smothered a laugh at the raccoon's puzzled chirps. *Definitely programmed.* She began to edge toward the platform, keeping one eye on the robot.

The drone hovered before the keyhole. A compartment opened in the top cannonball, and a key attached to a tendril snaked down and inserted itself into the lock. The metal walls vanished, revealing the still form of one of the brown tree-climbers, the white stripe down each side pale in the light. Janice stared at the creature, looking for signs of life, when she heard a soft growl.

The raccoon's nose wrinkled, and its ears flattened. It growled again, its fur bristling, and took a step toward the robot. *No!* Janice sent. *Danger*!

The robot drifted inside the trap, heading for the still creature, and the raccoon dashed after it. A swipe from one paw sent the robot careening away for several yards before it recovered and halted its wild flight. Returning, it was knocked away again as the snarling native kept between the robot and the fallen tree-climber.

Janice saw a red light wink on atop the scanner eye, and she crouched down out of sight. The scanner rotated, studying the area, and finally focused on the raccoon.

Suddenly the top cannonball seemed to sprout a wig of wildly waving snakes, as every available extensible and tool shot out of storage. It advanced on the raccoon, waving its equipment. The raccoon backed a step, and an alarm siren cut in as well. Barking, the native turned tail and ran.

Extensibles and tools stilled and snapped back into storage, but the robot continued the siren's blare for a few seconds longer. The scanner rotated, studying its surroundings, then the alarm shut off and the red light blinked out. The scanner rotated again, and finally locked onto the tree-climber.

Janice glanced in the direction of her departed friend, both sorry for it and relieved that it was out of danger. *Unless it trips over another wire,* she reminded herself. *Interesting reaction, though. You wouldn't expect an animal to defend a member of another species. Must tie into that food-offering behavior somehow.*

An electronic hum caught her attention, and she turned to see the robot hovering over the tree-climber. An answering whir came from the platform, and one side slowly unfolded into a large crane.

The crane arm swung out and over to the waiting robot. Grips gently closed about the tree-climber, and the platform shifted slightly as the crane began to lift the creature's weight.

Janice glanced at the robot. It was hovering over the crushed grasses where the creature had rested. A white light glowed from one of the bottom cannonballs, and within seconds new grass stood straight and healthy.

The crane gently deposited the motionless creature on the air sled and folded itself back into part of the platform. Janice scrambled aboard as the robot began to reset the trap and hid against the side of the creature, out of sight from the controls. The platform shifted and slowly lifted into the air, hovering in one spot until the robot drifted on board. Then it rose higher and began to move carefully among the trees.

Janice smoothed the soft fur before her, suddenly conscious that she could detect nothing of the creature's presence. *Poor thing. Sorry I came too late to help.* The memory of the raccoon's groggy behavior earlier came sharp and clear. *A few more seconds in that gas and we would have been dead, too. The robot's owners would have been surprised. Wonder if they've found my improvements yet*? She patted the still body, her expression grim. *Just wait and see what I do for an encore.*

* * *

"Wait?" Jennie repeated. "I've waited far too long already. There isn't all that much more you'll need to know. You've seen my report; the decision is standard procedure."

And several worlds on a lower level have two already, Apson prompted.

"Several worlds on a lower level already have two," Jennie repeated obediently. *Two what, Apson?*

The Councilor's nostril flaps snapped closed. "I do not explain myself to a mere operative. I said you will wait until I can see you, and you shall wait."

Jennie's angry retort died on her lips as Apson prompted her once again. "Very well," she replied slowly, "but I feel it only fair to warn you that I intend to file a complaint with the Council on your continual delays. I shall also remind the Council that, until recently, planets could be and were gutted while that body deliberated on whether or not those same worlds were to be protected. Policy and procedures have been changed before; they can change again." She raised an eyebrow as she stared into the being's liquid eyes. "Now, are you certain you want me to wait?"

A few moments later she stood outside the door to the Councilor's quarters. *I blew it, didn't I, Apson*?

On the contrary, the responses you evoked were most enlightening.

How so?

One of the flaws of mechanical shielding is its inability to compensate for strong emotions.

'Strong emotions' is right. If Nicpan is like the usual bureaucrat, I've gotten you and Janice in a lot of trouble.

Agents are known to be quick-tempered and impulsive. Anything short of physical violence could be excused. A touch of exasperation entered Apson's "voice." *In this case, I think I could even find an excuse for physical violence.*

Thanks, but I think I can control my temper. You knew it wouldn't want to talk to me, didn't you?

I knew.

But you deliberately sent me in anyhow. She scowled at the closed door. *What was so enlightening?*

Do you remember the way back to my office?

Apson, I'm staying right here until you tell me what was so enlightening.

A faint sigh came to her mind. *Among other things, its fear when it first saw you.*

It's afraid of me?

Of Janice, Apson corrected her. *I couldn't catch why. You had best stop glaring at the door and retrace your steps before you give the Councilor further reason for mistrust.*

It suspects I'm not Janice?

"Janice! *Tweewo*! Janice!"

Belatedly remembering her role, Jennie turned. Among the few beings in the corridor, she recognized the distinctive stick creature departing, but closer to her stood an entity resembling a giant furry parrot with arms instead of wings. Its face near the big parrot beak was peach-colored, the rest of its head and body was turquoise with gold patches on its shoulders, and its short stubby tail was fire-engine red. Waving at her with one flawed hand, it minced toward her on four-toed clawed feet as if walking on an invisible branch.

That is Sinhgiki, Apson informed her, *the agent whose sector is closest to Janice's.*

Friend or foe? Jennie asked.

Sinhgiki stopped a few feet away and began bobbing up and down. "Janice! My nest was filled with glad music to learn you were alive. You had us all so worried! Apson brought you back, didn't he. I knew it! Only his ship could have brought you back so quickly! When is he going to let us lowly operatives have his secret drive, experimental or not? Surely you asked him?"

Caught up in the melodic notes of the being's speech, Jennie suddenly stumbled across the question in the translated speech. "Uh, he didn't say."

Sinhgiki clicked its beak. "I thought I interrupted something. Apson sending orders already? You barely got back." It scanned the ceiling with one eye. "Let her at least catch her breath, Apson!" Its other eye closed in a wink at Jennie. "There, that's settled. We girls have to stick together. Have you been to see your ship yet?"

"My ship? Uh—"

"How did I know about it? Apson may have gone off branch on security lately with that Councilor about, but, as it turns out, mine's only a few berths down. I've seen you going in to talk to yours but you were being so secretive I thought I'd follow your tune. I agree, continual imprinting is good for a ship, even if the techs frown on it. The techs should be finished with mine fairly soon, too. Mostly body damage. I know, you keep telling me not to wait until they're coming through my viewscreen to fire, but why waste a shot? Only warns them what to expect."

The large parrot began walking her down the corridor in the opposite direction as she spoke, and Jennie asked, *Apson?*

Go. I will be close by.

Jennie mentally shook her head. Apson was definitely paranoid. *I didn't ask because I was afraid of her,* she thought clearly. This friendly, if wordy, alien would be the last creature she'd be suspicious of. She found it hard to believe she was an operative.

"Apson's ship must be the fastest in the entire Galaxy," Sinhgiki was saying. She whistled a series of notes. "And don't remind me of drone ships. They don't count right now. It always frustrates me to know that there are all those marvelous super-super warp speeds for drone ships, but because we have animate life on board, our ships have to plod along like an old btweni on its last three legs. Safety regulations!"

* * *

Janice struggled to keep her eyes open. She was beginning to think that, with the cautious speed of this air sled, she could have made better time walking. She yawned, watching as they carefully weaved around the numerous trees. *I'd hate to be stuck behind this robot on Lake Shore Drive. And it doesn't even have the excuse of looking at the scenery!*

* * *

Jennie struggled not to gawk at all the varied ships hovering in the enormous repair dock. Some of them were so huge that the service robots working on them looked like gnats. And there were so many different types!

Sinhgiki whistled at a distant alien. "That reminds me. Did Survey ever find Mqinlk?"

"Who?"

"That scout Survey lost. I thought you two were friends, especially after the way you reacted when he was reported missing." One clawed hand combed the feathery fur about her beak. "It wasn't long after that that you left base."

Jennie waited, but Apson was silent. "No. No, I don't think he's been found yet."

Sinhgiki whistled a mournful note. "It's only the lucky ones like you that can survive the destruction of your ship. He was a good scout, one of the best, I heard. Wasn't he the one that found your Earth?"

Apson remained silent, and Jennie began to worry. *Why couldn't they have impressed some details in my mind along with the Galactic lesson?* She glanced up at the ship they were nearing and gasped at the numerous slashes and gaping holes in the brightly colored surface. "Sinhgiki! Oh, that poor ship!"

Orange appeared around the outside of Sinhgiki's eyes. "You hadn't seen her?" She cocked her head, one eye focused on Jennie and the other on her ship hovering above them. "She doesn't mind too much. Just so long as I bring her in every now and then for resurfacing." The large brown eye closest to the human closed in a wink. "She likes to make every shot count, too."

Jennie glanced at nearby ships, noting similar—though not as extensive—damage on most of them. But one ship three berths down seemed unmarked. Hovering only inches above the floor, the sleek gray vessel seemed almost as large as Sinhgiki's ship, despite their different forms.

Sinhgiki chortled deep in her throat. "Yes, your ship is lovely. You should have it painted with colors, though, not that dull gray."

Jennie stared at the ship with growing excitement. Jan's ship. She had to see it closer. "I like gray," she said defensively. "I'll talk to you later, Sinhgiki."

Mqinlk's area included the fringes of Janice's sector, Apson said as she left Sinhgiki's berth.

Welcome back, Jennie replied. *Where were you when I needed you?*

Survey reports that nothing exists at the sector coordinates near where his ship was destroyed.

Nothing?

Nothing. To be precise, a void. However, sector coordinates are assigned only to habitable worlds; navigational hazards are given Galactic coordinates. I have told Crislben to divert to those coordinates.

Not until I'm aboard, Jennie said firmly.

You are needed here.

Either Crislben comes for me or I will tell Sinhgiki what your "space drive" actually is.

Apson sounded amused. *You think you know?*

Do you want to risk it?

The amount of time needed for Crislben to come in for you and then start out again may be the deciding factor between life or death for Janice. Do you want to risk that? There was a pause, and Apson sighed. *I appear to be out-voted. Crislben informs me that it will go nowhere without you.*

Jennie mentally blessed the plant-being. She had almost reached the berth of Janice's ship. Compared to some of the ships around it, it looked almost dainty, although it was much larger than she would have expected for a one-person ship.

Retrace your steps back to my office and we will await Crislben there.

In a minute. I want to see Jan's ship.

Must I remind you that you may be in danger in the open?

Jennie grasped the shield control and turned to briefly scan the repair dock. *I think you just want to distract me from Jan's ship. I'll only take a minute. Besides, that machine of yours can send us to Crislben's ship in practically no time at all, right?*

She entered the berth and stared at the ship before her.

* * *

She stared at the ship as the air sled slowly came in to land on the opposite side of the camp. *Emergency class one-being planet hopper.*

Wouldn't trust that thing to even reach orbit. She looked around for a second ship, but none was visible. *All this equipment couldn't have been brought in by that hopper; it would take a good-sized freighter, or—* She blinked as a fuzzy image came to her of a merchanter firing weapons no trade ship would have. The memory faded as quickly as it had come, and, with a mental shake, she looked about for the robot.

The scanner was not pointed in her direction. She slipped cautiously over the side of the platform and into concealment by several tall stacks of crates. She paused there a moment, getting her bearings. Behind her, the platform was slowly unfolding into a crane; ahead, behind several stacks of equipment and a second air sled were two medium-sized pre-fab buildings. Off towards her left seemed to be the power plant, and to her right— She watched as the crane lifted the body in that direction and decided to follow.

Stacks of empty containers provided excellent cover as she moved, but afforded her very little view of anything past the next cluster of containers. Then a stench of blood hit her nostrils, and she briefly debated with her stomach as to whether or not to continue.

The next stack gave her a clear view of an odd collection of machines. She glanced around the corner of the stack and froze. She stared at a rack of large drying pelts. She *remembered.*

She stood before a curtain of furs, a collage of solid grays, swirled browns and blacks and white-striped brown. Behind her came the slap of sandals against the stone floor and the sweet rich aroma of aqras. *She turned as the resident agent came through the doorway.*

"Offworld, correct?" Bithe set her tray onto the communications console and shook out the sleeves of her caftan. "Had but to see it to know to call you."

Janice made a noncommittal sound as she turned back to the curtain. One look had convinced her that this was the same type of fur that had been turning up elsewhere in this sector. Still, for it to have appeared on this *planet and in such a large quantity— She caught up a mug from the tray and took a large gulp of* aqras, *almost burning her mouth on the hot drink.*

"Such exotic colors." Bithe nervously smoothed the bluish fuzz on the back of one hand, and Janice smothered a smile. The same short coat of fur covered all the natives of Mirn from the top of their seemingly bald heads to their toes, and ranged in color from pale to dark blue on females, and pink to deep red on males.

Bithe caught the direction of her gaze and wrinkled her nose at the agent. "What do we?"

Janice gestured at the curtain. "Where did Yiy say he found this?"

"Girso, the fur seller. Wouldn't have expected him to trade in oddities. Usually stocks only the highest quality furs."

Janice glanced at the samples of his usual stock—the long stretches of purple fur covering the walls and dotting the floors of the polar base—and took a careful sip of her drink. "You didn't sight any ship?"

Bithe gestured ignorance. "Out for some time. Yiy says not, and recorder recently malfunctioned." She glanced at the doorway. "Like not, Janice. If offworlders have arrived, may need help and his *help—"*

"—is worse than useless. I know, Bithe. I don't know who ever decided he was agent material—"

Bithe gestured. "Ship-size mistake!"

Janice nodded. "But you'll have to call me when you need help. I can't stay right now. I'm wanted back at base. Survey recently lost a scout out this way; otherwise I would still be back there. Councilor Nicpan will probably be furious that I've been gone this long."

"Council!" Bithe gestured again. "Council chose Yiy!"

Recalled to her surroundings by a nearby electronic hum, Janice withdrew around the corner as a robot drifted by. More memories came flooding back.

"Yiy!"

The second resident agent of Mirn turned as she entered the cavern, his pinkish fuzz pale against the deep red uniform he wore. His habitual sneer was more pronounced than usual. "See ship scratched," he said, gesturing at the Bureau ship behind him.

"Not my doing." Janice hesitated a moment, studying the agent. She had tried to uncover the reason behind his dislike of her—even going so far as to think her own red hair might be a factor—with little success. The friction between the two resident agents was no help either. Janice had wondered why the previous operative of this sector had chosen resident agents from two opposing city-states. Somehow it fit that it had been the Council's decision.

"No? Thought pilot always responsible for ship." He tipped his head toward the interior door. "Bithe now claiming Yiy in league with offworlders?"

Janice smiled, although she was surprised by his defensiveness. "No. You did well to find that curtain. Was that the only oddity you found?"

"Flitter thinks sitter blind?"

Janice paused at his use of the nicknames for sector operatives and resident agents. Had she ever thoughtlessly used those? "Far from it! I was only wondering if you'd come across any strange-colored gemstones or new metals as well as the furs."

"Gemstones?" Yiy looked thoughtful. "New swordsmith starting up. Will check shop." He smiled suddenly. "Enjoy journey to your homeworld Earth."

Janice shook her head, disturbed anew by that memory. Because of the time factor, she had planned to simply swing by Earth rather than resume the course from which Bithe had called her to see the curtain.

But once out in space she had reconsidered. Councilor Nicpan could wait. Mqinlk had gone out on his ill-fated trip to help her. She had asked the fragile insectoid's aid in this fur smuggling matter since, while she was unable to identify the furs' planet of origin, Mqinlk had discovered many planets, some of which were now her responsibility. Soon after that request, she had received an indignant message from him about careless records-clerks, just as his ship left base. Without a ship or coordinates, there was no way to follow him even if she hadn't had to wait for Councilor Nicpan. It was only after his ship had been reported destroyed that she was able to learn about a navigational hazard with sector coordinates and *then* only after reminding Survey (who monitored every scout's location as if black holes would suddenly wink into existence just to swallow them all) just who was the operative of the sector concerned.

Janice remembered changing course, but her memory from that moment up until waking inside the lifepod consisted still of hazy incidents amid gaping blanks. The clearest memory was of the merchanter.

She glanced up at the sky. *I've got until that merchanter comes back to shut this place down—starting with those traps. Time to start trying doors.*

* * *

Jennie sighed, resisting the urge to pound on the ship's unresponsive door. She heard the click of claws against the flooring and turned, one hand activating the shield control.

Sinhgiki came out from behind a tool rack in the next berth, one clawed hand close by her orange belt. "I knew you would be unable to enter," she said, the song absent from her voice as she spoke in Galactic. "You're not Janice. Who are you?"

Jennie was careful to reply in the same language. "But I am. I—"

"No, don't deny it. You are very good, but you didn't react to this—" she winked one eye. "Janice only explained that custom to Pswigtg and myself shortly before the knell of Mqinlk's ship sounded."

Jennie tried again. "Oh, that! I forgot, Sinhgiki, that's all." *Apson!* she called.

Sinhgiki chortled deep in her throat. "Perhaps. But Janice never could resist slaughtering my language whenever possible. You never whistled once."

Jennie knew better than to try. *Apson, I'm in trouble!* "Some friends," she said lightly. "Go away on a short trip and they won't even recognize you when you return. Do you think I could have passed Nicpan's security check if I wasn't Janice?"

The parrot-like alien hesitated. "No."

"Fine, then." Jennie hated herself for trying to deceive the friendly alien, but she had promised. "You tell *me* who I am. If I'm not Janice, but I can pass a security scan, then who am I?"

Sinhgiki stared closely at her. "Your mental shielding is very good. I can't tell from your mind who you are. Physically, you are Janice. *Twee*! I have it. If you are Janice, then you should be able to enter your own ship."

Jennie mentally sighed. She had been afraid the alien would think of that. "Allow me a fair opportunity, Sinhgiki!" she said, struggling with the Galactic translation. "Someone's been trying to kill me, I've had one ship destroyed, Nicpan refuses to see me—"

And your ship is deactivated and you've misplaced the control activator, Apson chimed in. The small globe drifted into sight behind Sinhgiki. *Again. Did you* have *to take it with you when you left base*?

Sinhgiki cocked one eye at her superior. "She *is* Janice?"

She may be acting oddly, but so might you be in her situation.

"Who else would I be?" Jennie asked.

One brown eye closed in a wink. "The sister-duplicate for whom Janice was hatching a surprise?"

I've just received a surprise of my own, Apson commented. *Councilor Nicpan has left base.*

"Without seeing Janice?" Sinhgiki squawked indignantly.

"Why?" Jennie hoped it wasn't due to something she had said.

The small globe drifted over to her. *The official excuse was that the Councilor had a prior commitment elsewhere. I have filed your complaint with the Council and my own should be reaching them shortly. Until then, we can but—* The globe seemed to hesitate in midflight, then floated up and down before her. *Sinhgiki, do you always frighten your friends into activating force shields against you? Switch it off, my dear paranoid Earthling, and come with—*

A rasping buzz suddenly echoed in Jennie's head, and the globe abruptly dropped to the floor. Sinhgiki clapped her hands to her head, hunching over as if in pain. A piercing whistle escaped her and she crumbled to the floor.

Jennie backed a step, staring from the still globe to the birdlike alien. The buzz grew louder.

* * *

Janice raised a hand to her head. Psi attack! She snapped up her shield, but the buzz painfully remained. She tried again, wondering if the injury that had temporarily taken her memory had also affected her psi talents. Something *twisted* in her mind, and the buzz vanished.

Shaken, she pulled a metallic square out of her jacket pocket and pressed geometric patterns in a specific sequence. "Time to call for reinforcements."

* * *

The buzz was gone from her mind. Jennie lowered her hands from her head and looked cautiously around. Aliens in nearby berths appeared to be either still in pain or unconscious. Neither Apson nor Sinhgiki stirred. She backed up against the ship's hull, feeling extremely helpless, and watched for any sign of movement. Not that she knew what to do if she did see anything. She had no weapon, her only defense was a low-energy force shield, and her protector was either out cold or dead.

Her gaze fell upon the tool rack. Somehow she'd feel much better if she had something in her hand.

She edged cautiously across the open space, trying to watch everywhere at once. The repair dock had plenty of hiding places for a sniper. She was beginning to wish she had listened to Apson.

She carefully lifted a likely-looking tool from its place. An alarm began hooting overhead, almost startling her into dropping the tool. She froze, afraid she had made a betraying sound.

An oddly shaped weapon appeared at one end of the rack. Jennie waited until the hand holding it emerged, then she swung down with the tool with all her might. There was a hissing shriek of pain, and the weapon flew out of the assassin's grip.

Dashing after the weapon, Jennie picked it up only to have a yellow light strike her like a blow. She gasped in pain and shock. The weapon was a smoking ruin at her feet and she felt bruised and sore. *But alive. Thank you, low-energy shield!*

She looked up at the second weapon in the assassin's other hand. "At least tell me why!" she demanded.

The bulging eyes placed where ears should be on the creature's head widened, then narrowed. A finger flipped a switch on the weapon, then tightened on the trigger.

Blue light stabbed down from above, engulfing the being, and Jennie, amazed, saw that it came from Sinhgiki's ship. The light shut off, and the assassin folded bonelessly to the floor. A red beam of light flashed out from the ship, and there was a sudden explosion a few berths down.

A door slid open in the ship behind her. "Come inside, Janice," said a vaguely familiar voice. Jennie hesitated, suddenly realizing that the voice, not the translator necklace, spoke English. "Hurry, there may be another." Jennie hurried.

* * *

Janice completed her set of instructions and pocketed the control activator. *Hope Purdey doesn't run into any techs. Otherwise the cavalry will never arrive.*

She pulled the stunner from her inside jacket pocket, wishing she had something more powerful, and continued toward the power planet. The use of a psi disrupter had to mean that the smugglers suspected her presence, since she hadn't noticed any creature so far on this planet with psi powers enough to warrant use of that weapon. With the surprise factor gone, she was going to have to hit them very hard and very fast.

She paused outside the power plant and decided to risk the pain of the disrupter in order to see if anyone was inside the building. She opened her shield a crack, then lowered it completely. The disrupter was not operating at all. Neither of the two minds she could detect were on edge—the one inside the building was even asleep! She snapped her shield back up. *Probably a third around somewhere, completely shielded,* she decided. *I'll have to watch out for that one.*

Alert for any passing robot, she edged up to the door and slipped inside. The interior was dimly lit, and Janice understood why when she saw the being dozing before the flickering scanner screens. Bright light was painful to a nocturnal's eyes. She glanced over the controls, keeping one eye on the smuggler, and realized that she had come to the right place. Everything was here and all nicely labeled: robot controls, communicator, trap indicators— She found the power switches for the traps and switched those off, then continued reading, flipping power off as she went. She hesitated over a switch marked "force fence." *Probably to keep out any carnivores attracted by the stench.* That switch went off as well.

She turned, stunner in hand, at a slight sound. The nocturnal yawned and rose to its feet to stretch. It peered closely at one screen, then, blinking several enormous eyes, turned toward her.

Dark-adapted eyes opened wide as it stared at her. Three arms shot into the air, and with a shriek, the being collapsed in a heap of quivering limbs.

You big scary alien, Janice scolded herself. *You frightened the poor thing!*

She kept the stunner directed at the nocturnal. "Answer my questions truthfully and do as you're told and I won't hurt you." Thoughts of the near-intelligent creatures this being had trapped for their fur prompted her to add, "Much."

* * *

Jennie entered the control room cautiously, feeling as if she had stepped into a trap. She had not seen the owner of the voice, nor had she heard it again since entering. Somehow the way the door had closed behind her hadn't helped her suspicions, either. Especially after the way it had stayed shut so stubbornly when she had wanted to enter earlier.

Glancing at the darkened viewscreen, she looked over the console until she found the right control. *Might as well see what's happening in the repair dock.* But what appeared on the screen was a vast expanse of stars. "The ship's in space! How did we get out here? What's the big idea?"

'Those were your orders, Janice."

Jennie turned completely around, searching for the voice's owner. "Where are you? Who are you?"

"Janice, are you all right?"

"That's Ja—*my* voice! With a British accent!"

"I *am* your ship. Whose voice should I have?" The voice seemed to hesitate. "Perhaps you should visit the sick bay, Janice. A psi disrupter can do serious damage to an unprepared mind."

"That other weapon wasn't too much fun either, even with a force shield." Remembering it, she switched the device off. "Wait a minute. You said, 'my orders.' When did I give you those orders?"

"Before you entered. I had not expected to see you in the repair dock, since the signal point you wish me to go to is off-planet. Do warn me next time. I might have left you behind."

"Might have left me," Jennie repeated bemusedly. Relief washed through her. Janice was all right! She looked up at the viewscreen and saw a small but familiar ship's outline growing larger. "That's Crislben's ship!" She looked for some form of communicator. "How can I talk to it?"

"I can open communications." The voice seemed to hesitate again. "Are you certain you wish to speak to Crislben? It has been demanding I return."

"It will stop once I tell it the news. Go on, open hailing frequencies."

The stars on the viewscreen vanished as the image of the plant-being took their place. The leaves on its top half were swaying angrily. "I repeat, turn back immediately."

Jennie put her hands in her pockets. "Sorry, Crislben, no can do."

The leaves of the image stilled. "Jen-sprout! What are you doing there?"

"I think I've been kidnapped. Crislben, Janice is all right! She's called her ship to her!"

"That answers the question of how you're flying that ship. Tell it to turn back. Apson's been raging like a thunderstorm once it recovered to find you gone without a trace. It thought you were dead when it couldn't sense your mind."

"Couldn't sense my mind? Why not?"

"Your mind shield might have something to do with that," the ship inserted.

"What mind shield?"

Crislben's midsection began to rustle. "And you said you weren't a telepath. Takes a rather high psi level to produce that shield."

"Crislben, I don't know what has happened but I assure you that—"

"Come back to base and we'll settle your mind shield there. Apson's trying to resolve these attempted murders and it will need your help. We'll go out after Sprout in my ship."

"Crislben, I don't think this ship wants to do that."

"That ship will obey everything you say. Simply tell it to—" The image wavered and vanished.

Jennie stared at the stars on the viewscreen. Crislben's ship seemed to be falling behind. "What happened?"

"You ordered me to proceed to the signal point. Why do you wish to change your mind?"

Jennie didn't want to return to base, either, but this ship's single-mindedness was beginning to unnerve her. "I'm not changing my mind. Janice ordered you, not me." *Oh, great*, she told herself, *why not really confuse the poor thing. It's only obeying orders.* "Look, I want to proceed to the signal point, too. But Crislben might get upset and try to stop you."

"No Bureau ship is as fast as an operative ship." There was a definite note of smugness in the voice that was so like, yet unlike, her own.

Jennie smiled and seated herself before the console. "Good! I was getting very tired of Apson's evasiveness. How long will it take us to reach the signal point?"

"Not long."

Jennie sighed. "Must be contagious." She yawned. "I'll go take a nap until then."

"The chair is comfortable. You should stay where you are."

"Why?" Jennie asked. She suddenly felt too tired to even go looking for Janice's cabin. "What's wrong?"

The voice sounded faintly apologetic. "Sleepy dust. You are obviously unwell. Dealing with that killer has made you believe you are someone else. You need rest."

Jennie could barely keep her eyes open. "You can't do this!"

"I am programmed to consider what is good for you."

Jennie's last thought as she drifted into sleep was that Janice would have to do something about her ship's programming.

* * *

Janice finished programming the robots to dismantle the traps, and decided to warn Purdey to be on the look-out for the merchanter. Pulling the square activator out of her pocket, she tapped out her instructions regarding the merchanter and actions Purdey might take if she found it while on her own. The ship's acknowledgment seemed slow in arriving, but Janice dismissed that impression. *It's her first time in action*, she told herself. *Things are bound to be a bit confusing to her. But once we get through a few missions, she'll be just as good as her namesake, if not better.*

Returning to her preparations for the merchanter's eventual return, she kept one eye on the screens of the two robots she had patrolling the camp for the second smuggler. She would have to capture it eventually, but first she had to make certain that it wouldn't redo what she was undoing here. So far she was content to wait until it came to investigate the robots' new commands.

Checking the screens again, she noticed that several of the large predators had found the processing unit. She was strongly tempted to let the predators do her hunting for her, but the nocturnal hadn't known anything about the smuggling operation but its own part in it. It hadn't even known about the psi disrupter. Janice hoped the second smuggler might know more.

With a sigh, she lowered her shield to check on the being's whereabouts, then smiled and turned to face the door, her stunner out and ready.

Much to her surprise, however, the smuggler *backed* through the doorway, its weapon directed at something behind it. Taking no chances, she stunned the smuggler and went to investigate. Two large paws sent her sprawling.

* * *

Jennie slowly grew conscious of something pressing against her upper arms. She felt a soft prick like a kitten's claw in her right arm, and the last of her drowsiness vanished. Jennie opened her eyes—and stayed very, very still.

Hovering directly before her face was a metallic lump covered with sensor eyes of every size and shape. A long flexible cable connected that to the top of a larger, bulge-covered lump hovering before her chair. The pressure on her upper arms vanished, and two new bulges appeared on the main lump. The eyed "head" retracted to its proper place and the odd, lumpy device drifted back a short distance.

"Your physical injuries were very minor, Janice," remarked a familiar voice with a British accent. "Some surface bruising from a sonic weapon, a slight loss of blood from two small puncture wounds—"

"Mosquito bites," Jennie corrected, eyeing the lumpish robot.

"Thank you," the ship answered. "The psi disrupter left you physically unharmed. However, there still could be mental side-effects. If you would lower your shield, I could—"

"I don't have any mental shield," Jennie said firmly.

"Janice, a shield protecting your mind from any psi influences or detection is definitely present."

Jennie briefly debated with herself whether to tell this ship that she was not Janice, then decided against it. She'd probably just get knocked out again "for her own good." "Look, as far as I know, I don't have any mental shield. And if I did, I wouldn't know how to lower it. End of discussion, ok? Now, how soon will we reach the signal point?"

She glanced at the stars on the viewscreen as the ship remained silent. "Well? We *are* still going to the signal point, aren't we?"

"Resident Agent Bithe has reported the close approach of an unidentified merchanter to the closed world of Mirn. As per your recent orders, we have diverted to Mirn."

"What?"

"Janice," the ship continued, sounding very confused, "how can you be asleep here and yet send instructions from the signal point?"

"Easy. I'm not Janice. I'm Jennifer." She took a deep breath. "Did she ever tell you about me?"

The ship hesitated. "You're supposed to be on Earth."

"I was. Apson and Crislben brought me to base."

"Does that mean you know about the surprise?"

"What surprise?"

"Coming up on Mirn. Scanning for merchanter."

Jennie stared at the viewscreen. A dot of light rapidly grew larger. "Won't the merchanter be able to spot us?"

"An operative ship's cloaking screens render it invisible to normal detection devices."

"Don't count on them having only normal equipment. If Mirn is a closed planet, this other ship shouldn't have been able to find it without help."

The dot of light became a brown and green planet, half-masked with clouds. Jennie glanced over the console, trying to locate the scanners.

"You're very perceptive, Jennifer."

"Jennie."

"Jennie. I am called Purdey."

Jennie grinned and shook her head. Considering the British accent and the line of work, somehow that fit her twin's notion of rightness. "Just don't let Jan call you *Avenger*, ok?"

"All right. Merchanter located."

The screen seemed to focus in on the south polar cap, sweeping across fields of whiteness before a long dark shadow appeared.

"Are you sure it's the right ship?" Jennie asked.

"Since this planet's main weapon is a sword and that is the only starship, yes."

"What do we do?"

"I have my instructions."

Jennie watched the screen, but nothing seemed to change. "Well?" she demanded.

"The ship's crew is absent. I have sent down drones to secure the ship and hunt for the crew."

Jennie studied the ice fields. "Why would they land there?"

The viewscreen's focus shifted to the left of the grounded ship. "That cave is one of the entrances to the resident agents' base."

"What? Have you spoken to them? Are they under attack?"

"An operative ship may speak only to its operative."

Jennie groaned and drummed her fingers on the console. Apson's little secrets... "Could *I* speak to them then?"

"Yes. I shall open communications."

"Good. Hey, how come you're speaking to me?"

"According to my sensors, you are Janice. Ready to open communications. The female is Bithe, the male Yiy. Channel open."

Jennie took a deep breath. Which one had called about the merchanter? "Hello, Bithe. This is Janice. Are you all right down there? Come in, please." She waited a moment, then began again. "Hello, can you hear me? Are you all right? Please respond."

The viewscreen suddenly shimmered and reformed into a pink-furred being wearing a deep red uniform. "Janice! Need help. Offworlders attack. Please come."

"I'm right above you, uh—" Jennie hesitated. Was this the male or the female? "Help's on the way."

"Please! Come down and help. Bithe hurt. Need help, Janice. Asking for you."

"I'll be down as soon as I can. Out." She stared at the image of the merchanter. What to do? "Can I get down there, Purdey?"

"There is no need for you to go. The drones will handle the attack."

"They're expecting Janice. If you send the drones down alone, they might think they're from those offworlders. Besides, you heard him. One of them is hurt, no telling how seriously, and asking for Janice. Look, I've got the low-energy shield, I'll go down with the drones, and bring the big lump over there along to take care of Bithe. Okay?"

"Should be safe enough. What weapons do you have?"

"Uh, actually, I don't."

"My fault. That quick departure from base. I'll set a selection out from the armory."

"Uh, thanks." Jennie wondered what the ship thought she was. One part of her mind wondered what *she* thought she was. *You're carrying the masquerade just a bit too far.*

A short time later they materialized within a cavern large enough to house one or two ships Purdey's size. Jennie glanced at the glittering swarm of robots about her and wished two particular producers could see the strange variety of forms.

The swarm drifted off towards an interior door, and Jennie followed, one hand fingering her strange weapon and the other grasping the shield control. *I hope Purdey keeps her word and lets Apson and Crislben know where we are.* She glanced back at the floating lump behind her. The ship had seemed almost offended at the request until Jennie had reassured it that she didn't doubt its ability to handle one ship.

She could hear distant blaster fire as she followed the robots into a fur-lined control room. The red-uniformed being she had seen on the ship's viewscreen was flipping a switch back and forth on one console with a very visible air of frustration.

He looked up, and Jennie wished she could interpret his expression. "Janice!"

The main body of the swarm suddenly sped off towards the sounds of blaster fire. The lumpy medical robot hovered a moment between Jennie and the resident agent, then slowly drifted out another door. Yiy silently looked after the departing swarm, then shook himself and beckoned her over to the console.

Jennie looked around the room. "Where's Bithe?"

"See her in moment." Yiy flipped the switch again. "Help needed. Relay damaged when Bithe locked and armed entrances. Now cannot control blasters."

Jennie started forward, then stopped and looked around the undamaged room again. "How was she hurt?"

"What?" Yiy did not look up from the balky switch.

"If she locked and armed the entrances from here, how was she hurt?"

Yiy turned. *Me and my big mouth,* Jennie thought as she saw the weapon pointed in her direction. She carefully kept her hand away from her own. "Where's Bithe?" she asked.

His mouth twisted. "Dying. As brave, meddling flitter should have died. Before left Mirn last, enough canisters put aboard to flood entire ship with poison gas."

"Gas!" Jennie remembered the impressions from Janice that had awakened her.

"Flitter thought to deceive Yiy by returning and pretending not to know."

Jennie backed a step as Yiy jerked up his weapon. "Yes! I was wrong." Remembering the hospital classes on handling psychotics, she waited as the Mirnian lowered his weapon again. "Why do you want to kill me?" she asked, keeping her voice calm and steady.

"Said I would be next operative. Promised! Instead Bureau chose simpleton. Plan changed. Yiy must wait." He raised the stubby weapon again. "Tired of waiting."

"Who promised?"

Yiy's brow furrowed. "Council."

"Surely not the entire Council. Who promised you, Yiy? Who gave you lies for your help?"

"Not lies!" Yiy gripped the weapon with both hands. "Yiy's messages not answered long time, yes. But, then, gifts arrive. Other promises. Other would take care of flitter. Yiy must wait. Yiy tired of waiting!"

"Yiy!"

Yiy turned to where a blue-furred Mirnian leaned weakly against a doorway. The weapon swung stiffly towards the unarmed intruder.

Mentally crossing her fingers, Jennie drew and fired. Blue light enveloped Yiy, and the being collapsed without a sound.

Jennie stared at her shaking hands, then noticed that Bithe was beginning to slide down the side of the doorway. Pausing only long enough to pull the weapon from Yiy's limp fingers, she reached the second resident agent just as a lumpy drone drifted up. A bulge detached itself and snaked down on cable-end to hand before the Mirnian's nose.

Bithe batted it weakly away. "What *is* that thing?"

"Help. Strange-looking, I'll agree, but help. Just close your eyes and rest a moment."

Bithe glanced suspiciously at the eyed head swinging toward her, then closed her eyes. The bulge drifted over her nose again.

"How badly are you hurt?" Jennie asked.

"Not hurt. Was locked in room. Air smelled normal, but Yiy said poison gas."

"What kind?" Jennie glanced at the medical robot. A smaller bulge had popped off to attach itself to Bithe's shoulder. "How do you feel?

Drowsy? Head ache?"

"Did. Better now."

Jennie felt something gently bump her shoulder. She turned to see a hovering globe filled with green and white mists. "Apson!" She looked closer at the yellow band about the globe. "Apson, what is—"

"I once thought," said a voice from her necklace, "that nothing could get into as much trouble as one Earthling. I shall have to revise that opinion."

* * *

Jennie sighed as she watched the gray ship dart away and vanish among the stars. "I wish I was aboard."

"We will reach Janice not long after her ship does," Crislben commented. A small screen before it pulsed with the steady beat of Purdey's homing signal. "My ship is not as slow as some."

"I know." She watched as the viewscreen flickered to show the merchanter following behind them, towed by invisible tractor beams. "But she was so worried. She hasn't heard anything from Janice since the instructions about the merchanter. I wish I could have gone along with her."

"You know why Apson said you could not. Maintenance of a high level mind shield can be harmful to a developing telepath."

"Then why did Apson give it to me in the first place? And why hasn't he removed it yet?"

Crislben waved a bluish filament in her direction. "Apson did not raise the shield. It was unconscious at the time."

"Well, *I* certainly didn't!" She rubbed her forehead. "Sorry, Crislben. I didn't mean to snap at you. I guess waiting around while Apson interrogates the prisoners is beginning to get to me."

"You do want to know who was trying to kill Janice and why, don't you?"

"We know why: so Yiy could become sector operative."

"That may have been the motive in Yiy's eyes," Apson said as the yellow-banded globe entered the room, "but it was not the reason for the attempts at base. I suspect had Janice been an easily corrupted being, or a less perceptive one, Yiy would have had to wait a long time for his appointment."

"Then what was the reason?" Jennie asked.

Apson settled atop the console before Crislben. "It appears that, on her own, Janice may have uncovered something of the operation that I had been attempting to stop for a long time."

"The leak on the Council," Crislben inserted. "The drain on the Closed worlds."

"Exactly. You see, Jennie, the Bureau was originally set up when there were very few worlds needing to be closed off and allowed to develop in their own way apart from the Galactic Union. At that time the Council had full authority over the Bureau. But, over time, the structure changed as more and more inhabited and inhabitable worlds were found. The Council's time was so taken up with the open worlds that soon its only authority over the Bureau became the closing of a newly discovered planet and the appointments of resident agents and sector operatives. And, until recently, the Council has full access to all records on the planet concerned—including its coordinates—each time a decision had to be made. I changed that when the Bureau acquired Survey."

Crislben's top leaves swayed slightly. "The Council debated so long over whether some planets should be closed that the worlds were dead before the Bureau was allowed near them. Now an operative is assigned almost as soon as the planet is discovered."

"It appears now that not all the records were turned over to the Bureau, and not through Survey's fault, Crislben. Janice appears to have come upon that fact. I was attempting a different approach. I had long suspected that the leak might be very high up, but the one responsible has been very careful and I could not go against the Council without proof. Janice's report presented a perfect opportunity." The green-and-white mists swirled gently.

"And?" Jennie prodded.

"I admit that my plan did not quite go the way I had expected. I had thought someone would attempt to discover Earth's coordinates."

"And someone did attempt," Crislben inserted, waving a few leaves. "It had to be Nicpan, Apson. It was the only Councilor on base."

"I still need proof, Crislben. Every one of the prisoners we've taken, including Yiy and the assassin at base, has been mind-blocked on the identity of the Councilor involved. Someone could be trying to discredit Nicpan."

Crislben's answering rustle was definitely disrespectful.

The globe rolled toward Jennie. "I apologize for risking your life."

Jennie shrugged. "Well, at least we caught a few."

"Poor Sprout," Crislben remarked. "She would have liked to have caught at least one of those attempting to kill her."

* * *

The power plant door crashed open, only slightly disturbing the nocturnal dozing before the flickering screens. The being who entered gave a contemptuous glance at the two legs resting atop a console and let out a bellow that rattled the thin walls of the building. "Where is Nm'est? Is this its idea of efficiency? Why is the equipment shut down?"

The nocturnal stirred and blinked several sleepy eyes as the intruder continued its tirade. "Where is the ship? It was to have stopped at—"

The intruder started forward as the nocturnal's eyes began to close. "Wake up and tell me—"

It stared at the weapon that had appeared in the nocturnal's hand. "Are you crazed?" it bleated. "I am your leader!"

The nocturnal's form shimmered as a telepathic disguise dropped to reveal a very different entity. "Why, Councilor Nicpan!" Janice said brightly. "How nice of you to finally decide to see me!"

* * *

Janice waved at the landing ship. She sprinted over the field to greet Apson and Crislben as they emerged from the airlock. "I thought you two would turn up once Purdey took off. Don't blame the ship, Apson. That was the only communications equipment I had at the time and later I couldn't risk frightening off the smugglers."

She gestured at the stacks of material on the edge of the landing field. A gray-furred creature bounced around the working robots like an over-sized puppy. "If you think this mess is bad, you should have seen it before I found a ship to put some of it in—and believe me, the owner is not pleased about that at all. Personal yachts never have all that much room."

She stared as one more being stepped from the airlock. "Jen! What are you doing here?"

"Blame Apson. He came to Earth looking for you—"

"—and persuaded you to come in my place. Ah, Jen! Apson is *not* Grandfather, however much he sounds like him. He's got a devious little mind—"

"—and Grandfather's an old conniver, too, in case you've forgotten. Actually, I—"

"—thought you were persuading him, and that was probably his plan all along."

Janice, how could you think that of me?

"Easy. Jennie, remind me to tell you about a simple training exercise I had, where someone told me I wouldn't need any weapons." She turned suddenly on the globe. "How *dare* you risk her life like that! That would-be killer—"

"Look who's talking about life-risking! You never even thought about how your taking off would affect Grandmother and Grandfather, did you?"

"As much as I enjoy family reunions," Crislben interrupted, "there is no profit in wasting sap on wilted leaves. Janice, you look well for someone who has survived poison gas."

"Huh? How did you hear about the fur trap?"

Crislben is referring to what caused you to crash your ship.

Janice shook her head. "No, this time I didn't crash. My ship was attacked by the merchanter. I had to self-destruct it." She paused, remembering her slowness and flecks of red.

"Yes, that's right," Jennie agreed.

"What's right?"

"Bright scarlet blood. That's one of the symptoms of carbon monoxide poisoning."

"Uh, Jen, I didn't say anything. When did you—" She turned to the globe again. "Apson, it was bad enough when we used to finish each other's sentences. Did you have to teach her to mindread as well?"

Actually, Janice, I think you're to blame for this. As well as for a very difficult to lower high level mind shield.

Janice raised her eyebrows and glanced at Jennie. "You got the psi disrupter? No wonder I couldn't find it here." She sighed. "Only fair, I guess, considering what you—" Her green eyes widened. "Jen, have you been picking up any other—"

"Nothing as clearly as that gas attempt. But I think I know now why I've been taking some odd evening classes."

"Sorry, Jennie."

"Nothing you could do." She waved at the gray ship nearby, pleased that Purdey had remembered to keep her presence a secret from her twin. "Actually, it's been rather interesting. Even meeting Nicpan."

"You met—" Janice turned to glare at Apson. "And I suppose you spoiled the surprise, too."

Janice, if you had any idea of the trouble I've gone through to keep your surprise a secret—

"What surprise?" Jennie glanced from one being to another and had a sudden suspicion. "Janice, if you think I want to—"

Her twin grinned. "—become Earth's resident agent, the answer is—"

"—do I get a ship, too?"

"The Twin Bond" reworked from the version in Shadowstar *#19, October 1985.*

KATHRYN SULLIVAN

Kathryn Sullivan has been writing science fiction and fantasy since she was 14 years old. Some of the short stories in *Agents and Adepts* are those from the world set up in *The Crystal Throne* that had escaped into print zines and ezines.

Kathryn's stories have appeared in *Professor Bernice Summerfield and the Dead Men Diaries*, *Twilight Times*, *Anotherealm*, *Shadow Keep Zine*, *Fury*, and *Minnesota Fantasy Review*.

Kathryn is Distance Learning Librarian at Winona State University in Winona, MN, and coordinator of the library's webpages. She's owned by two confused birds—one small jenday convinced that he's a large guard dog and one large cockatoo who thinks she's a small lap dog with wings.

Her webpage can be found at: http://kathrynsullivan.com